Poet's Seat

Dedicated to Diane

Poet's Seat is a work of fiction. Names, characters, businesses, organizations, places, events and incidents either are the product of the author's imagination or are used fictitiously. Any resemblance to actual persons, living or dead, events, locales or institutions is entirely coincidental. The author disclaims any responsibility for despicable thoughts you may have or loathsome acts you may commit as an imagined result of reading this novel.

Cover Image © 2011 by Jane Coltrane Jones

© 2012 Wilson Roberts

Wilder Publications, Inc.
PO Box 632
Floyd VA 24091

ISBN 10: 1-61720-894-9
ISBN 13: 978-1-61720-894-2

First Edition
10 9 8 7 6 5 4 3 2 1

Poet's Seat

by Wilson Roberts

Prologue

Baku, Azerbaijan – December 2001

Nathan watched dancing laughing children encircle the Director on the wide pavement in the boulevard park beside the Caspian Sea. Boys and girls chattered, taunted, begged for American dollars. Tall, lean and tan, his hair a white mane, he stood smiling inside their circle. The oil slick water reflected the gray sky and the morning air was cool and damp.

A car horn distracted him for a moment. Turning, he looked toward Nathan at the water's edge. He waved, holding his forefinger in the air, nodding his recognition, indicating that he'd join him in a minute or two. In the background, oil pumps moved up and down in the Caspian like huge mechanical dunking birds. Old and rusted from lack of maintenance, they leaked into the water. Waves, heavy with dark gobs of crude oil, broke against the shore, covering the sand and rocks with thick, sticky gunk. There was good reason that Forbes Magazine had described Baku as the world's dirtiest city earlier that year.

Leaning toward the tallest of the children, the Director spoke to him in Azerbaijani, handing him several bills of paper money. The boy grabbed them and spoke to the others who scampered off laughing and pointing back at him. Seconds later they reformed their circle around a woman who had come from a tourist hotel across the boulevard, an American, Nathan could tell from her clothing and bearing. At first frightened by the children, she forced a smile. The Director walked toward her.

"It's only a game," he told her. "Quite harmless. A traditional thing. Tell them your name, they'll say theirs, and sooner or later, they'll let you go. Sooner, if you give them a few dollars. American money is a good thing to have circulating here, you know. They don't much care for us, but they rather like our currency."

Looking at Nathan, he pointed to a bench overlooking the Caspian. The woman in the midst of the children had already taken money from her purse and was holding it toward them. The same tall boy took it, yelled his name at her, and ran off in search of another mark. The others followed, yelling their names over their shoulders.

On the adjacent boulevard three tanks rumbled past clusters of Azerbaijani soldiers and police. Pacing, their faces tense, eyes darting everywhere, watching the children, tourists, everyday passers-by, they held AK-47s and Uzis loose at their sides, ready to fire should trouble erupt. They smoked and talked among themselves in loud voices, made passes at women and spoke gruffly to anyone else who came close to them, waving them off with their free arms.

"Pity about the water," the Director said when they were seated, pointing at the Caspian. Barges filled with oil moved across the slick sea. They could hear the rumbling of the nearest derricks.

"Makes our pollution in the States seem pretty insignificant," Nathan said. The Director shrugged. "Just because someone else has a bigger tumor on their face doesn't mean you should ignore yours."

"Lovely analogy."

"Nothing lovely about pollution." The response was brisk, clipped, not an invitation to further conversation. He rested his arms on the back of the bench and looked up at the sky. "So, Nathan, why did you contact me?" There it was. *Why did you contact me?* Nathan had seen him twice before in the eighteen years he'd worked for the agency. The day he had recruited him and the day he sent him into the field after fifteen months of training. Now they were meeting for the third time and he was already all business. Just as before, when they met in another park, that time in early October at the Audubon Park in New Orleans, the smells of food and the sounds of music coming from the annual Cajun Festival.

"You'll know only what you need to know, Nathan."

"That's fine with me, sir."

"You'll be totally loyal, following orders that may seem vague or incomprehensible, or even stupid."

"I understand."

"Then go. I'll contact you whenever necessary. There should be no need for you to contact me, although you will know how to do so at all times."

It seemed a lifetime ago. He had followed orders, done what he believed was needed, questioned things only in the privacy of his mind, something he had been doing more often over the previous three or four years as he came to realize he had sacrificed a personal life and gained nothing in return. He had abandoned his education and foregone lasting relationships with women. He had no children. He hadn't been in touch with his parents in over ten years, when he called his father who had succeeded in tracking him down in China in the early 90s, leaving an urgent plea at the embassy for Nathan to call home.

The bastard hadn't had a clue what he was doing there, but he had pulled strings with his Senator who had contacted a friend at the State Department.

After going through many channels, a letter from his father had reached Nathan, telling him how distraught his mother was over his disappearance. Perhaps if the old man had apologized for regularly beating the shit out of him when he was a kid, Nathan's response might have been kinder. Saturday in the Hunt household was Judgment Day. His father would ask him what he had done wrong during the week. Nathan would either confess or say nothing. It didn't matter. Jared Hunt would whip him with a paddle for the sins he had committed or the ones he had denied. Nathan wrote back and told him never to contact him again, then had his control at the agency shut down whatever pipelines had enabled his father to contact him.

He was alone. He had chosen to be alone. His relationships with people were utilitarian. They served his ends or were ignored, discarded or killed. And Nathan's ends were not personal; they were the agency's. He had no time and had never developed the emotional capacity for the personal. Both had brought him to this moment. He had been in Azerbaijan for eight months, working with Armenian dissidents, escorting American civilians and their political supporters as they sought to make deals to take advantage of the former Soviet Republic's vast oil reserves and smuggling western operatives across the border into Iran.

When he heard the Director was in Baku, Nathan contacted him. It was time to make a break with his past, to make peace with himself. He took a deep breath, knowing it could be one of his last. The agency did not let its people go gently. The Director walked over to the bench and indicated for Nathan to take a seat.

"I'm through," he said as he sat, clasping his hands to hide their shaking. The Director did not respond. He sat on the bench, looking at the smooth dark surface of the Caspian, cluttered with oil derricks and barges. Trucks and tanks rumbled along the boulevard behind them. Overhead, MIG 25r Foxbat fighters sped south, their mission to keep tabs on the Iran/Azerbaijan border. It was useless. The Iranians weren't invading Azerbaijan, but their ideas had. The ancient Soviet promises of collective temporal paradise had not been able to compete with the Ayatollah's eternal realm of individual luxury in heaven. Once the Iron Curtain had flaked into piles of rust, the influence of Shi'a Islam exploded in Azerbaijan, and was greeted by a rise in Salafism, an ultra-orthodox form of the Sunni branch of Islam.

The jets passed, the sound of their engines a distant and fading roar. The Director turned, staring in silence at Nathan who ground his left thumb into his right hand.

"I can't do it any longer," he said after a long moment The Director sighed. "Do what, Nathan?"

"Any of it."

"And just what is *it*?"

"Manipulate, spy, kill, kiss the asses of all the bastards who want oil and power and will screw over anyone they can to get it. The whole pile of shit you trained me to do." He felt the sharp tang of anger in his words.

"Can't do it any longer, or won't?"

"Can't, won't, there's no difference."

"There's a huge difference."

"President Aliyev and his cronies are as corrupt and ruthless as the Communists ever were. For crissakes he was First Secretary of the *Azerbaijan Communist Party* and he's never presided over a clean election. Two years ago his police beat the crap out of opposition party supporters in Baku who were demonstrating over fraud in the parliamentary elections. Journalists covering the events were assaulted and leading opposition figures were jailed, beaten and starved."

"It's not a perfect situation. That's one reason we're here."

"Oil, Azerbaijan's proximity to Iran and Islamic terrorism are why we're here."

The Director shrugged.

Nathan rolled his eyes. "Look what they did to Vajif Hadjibeyli."

"A chairman of the Peasants Party isn't much of an improvement over a Communist."

"Bullshit. He was arrested by the local cops who beat him so badly in the street that he had a concussion. Then they took him police station suffering from a concussion and refused him medical attention. He wasn't allowed to see his lawyer or telephone his family for ten days. Aliyev and his government cronies are thugs, crooks and untrustworthy bastards, yet George Bush praises him and talks about inviting him to visit the White House next year. What kind of message does that send?"

The Director shrugged. "That Bush appreciates well executed political corruption? Look at the way our 2000 election was decided."

"Not funny."

"Developing moral scruples, Nathan?"

"We're talking about a President who uses the press and television news to broadcast images of death and destruction resulting from protests and skirmishes. That flat out tells the public the bad guys control the elections and anybody who objects to the way they run the government will end up in prison with no rights to a fair trial; a President who's running the show by manipulating people with fear."

"Which president are you speaking of?" the Director asked. "Don't expect politics to be fair or politicians to be clean. There's not a one of them who applies a moral code to national and international affairs. They simply can't, no matter what they say as candidates. We're seeking expediency, Nathan, not moral purity, and the only expediency that matters is what's best for us, for the country, especially after what happened on September eleventh."

"Our country and our country alone?" Nathan sighed, running his fingers through his hair and shaking his head.

"What is a country other than a place where the people we love live? They're the ones to whom we're morally obligated, even if morality has nothing to do with how we execute those obligations."

Nathan sighed and rubbed his face with his open palms. "I'm not making a moral point and I'm not making a political one. My point is that I'm burned out. I can't see anything before us but chaos with no hope of order."

"Burned out. It's such a pathetic term, Nathan. Weakness does not become you."

He understood the manipulation, felt his face redden, his stomach tighten. "I'm burned out, but I am not weak. Don't confuse the two."

"What do you propose doing?" the Director asked, ignoring Nathan's reaction.

"I don't know. Get a job. Something that'll keep me from thinking. Let me empty my head."

"That sounds foolish, Nathan, sophomoric. Empty your head, indeed."

"Maybe I'll finish my degree and teach."

"Your head can't get empty enough," the Director said, ignoring Nathan's last comment. "And you have too many dangerous things in it, dangerous to us, dangerous to you."

"I don't want them anymore."

The Director smiled. When he replied his voice was soft, his tone patient. "But you have them. How will you empty your head of them?"

"Repression, suppression, denial. I can do it." He shook his head. "No. You can't."

"I can't what? Put this all behind me? Bury it? Or do you mean I can't leave the agency?"

"People don't leave the agency because they're troubled by the things they've seen and done. You can't put things behind you. They'll always be there, in your mind, in your dreams, too close to the tip of your tongue to allow me to ever feel secure once you're no longer under my control." He exhaled in a loud slow stream and turned on the bench to face Nathan. Their eyes locked. "I have a simple proposal for you. It's the only one I will make.

I'm sure you understand the alternative. Stay. Or..." Keeping his elbows at his sides, he spread his arms, palms up, leaving the rest unspoken.

Nathan understood. Raising his eyebrows, he motioned him to continue. "Take a leave of absence. It will give you time to restore yourself and think things through."

"I don't want a leave of absence. I want out."

The Director scowled, his voice thick with sarcasm. "I suppose you want to live somewhere quiet, pursue ideas, live a simple free life. Become the philosopher you never were."

"Something like that." Nathan looked at him, held his eyes.

Waving his hands in the air, the Director exhaled in disgust, this time speaking what he had left unspoken moments before. "It's a leave of absence or termination," he said. "Termination from the agency is quite permanent." He stood, walked over to the water's edge. Leaning down, he scraped his finger through a large glob of oil residue. Off in the distance three sharp pops echoed from the parapets of the city. He turned, smiling.

"Probably backfires," he said. "Although someone could have been terminated. The Azerbaijani police are quite accomplished at dealing with their dissidents in that way."

"A leave of absence could work," Nathan said.

The Director nodded. "A leave of absence could be for an indeterminate time, you understand."

"What does indeterminate mean?"

His smile was vague as he wiped the oil from his finger in Nathan's hair. He let the message sink in before responding. "It means until we need you. This is a very special offer, you understand. I don't let my people go. They either stay, or they are terminated."

"Why would you need me?"

"You're a bright man, one of the brightest we have, one of the most promising. You're a brilliant asset to the agency and could well have been my successor, had you put yourself in the right circumstances and made the appropriate choices. Think about what's going on in Baku today. This country could easily become another middle-eastern Muslim theocratic state filled with people who hate the west, using their oil to blackmail us, using the money we pay for that oil against us." He looked off at the oil slick on the Caspian.

"And?"

The Director narrowed his eyes and stared directly at Nathan. "We're looking at a clash of civilizations at least as fraught with danger to the United States and the rest of the west as the cold war was. We're living in an era in which theocratic absolutist ideas are clashing with the liberal democratic ones. One side will be concerned with eternity and attaining Paradise, the other with the pursuit of wealth and happiness in the world."

Nathan pressed him. "Why do you want to keep me? What do you think I could do for the agency?"

"If you take this leave it will mean I misjudged you, that you're weaker than I had thought. However, I want the opportunity to use you if I need to and need to ensure your loyalty." He walked back to the bench and sat. "Your leave of absence could be a very long one, years. It could last forever. I can't see the future. So tend your garden. Mind your roses. Plant yourself like a vegetable somewhere and live the good life. Go to films. Read books. Vote for Democrats who promise more butter than guns. You'll probably finish that philosophy degree and join the Civil Liberties Union and live in the comfortable liberal coma that people like me maintain for people like you seem to want to become."

"What's wrong with that?" Nathan looked away. A small boat moved between the oil rigs, breaking the slick surface as it plied the sea.

The Director sucked his lips over his teeth, playing with them long moments before replying. "Nothing. It's a way of being I envy. That's why we exist, Nathan, why the agency exists. It's why we have diplomats and armies and all the other agencies. In order for the liberal state to exist, there must be a conservative force to preserve it. We are professionals, and our job is to manage violence. In our case, the client is the liberal state, the underpinnings of which we inherited from the Brits and established in our Revolution."

"I don't think I'd call the United States a liberal state," he said. "Bush stealing the 2000 election wasn't a liberal victory."

The Director smiled, a professor correcting a dense student. "But it is a liberal state, in the broad sense, the classical sense. Just as in the broad, classical sense, the agency is a conservative force."

Nathan shook his head, not wanting to go where he was being taken. The Director ignored him. "I was visiting with my daughter and her family last week. She and her husband have two children, a boy and a girl, a year apart in age. They are raising them very carefully, in a community that started out as a hippie commune in Vermont. They're schooling them at home. They have no television. The books they have for the children are screened for any indication of violence. When I drove up, my granddaughter, Victoria, was playing alone in the front yard. Her father was splitting firewood and keeping an eye on her. She ran to me, and you know what the first thing she said was?"

"I don't have a clue."

"'Tommy was mean to me, Grampy. He's in his room.'" My son-in-law put down the axe and came over. 'I don't know where he gets it,' he said. 'Tommy says terrible things to her, about hitting, killing, what he'd like to do to her. Julia says he experiments with words, putting them together until he finds phrases that express what he's feeling. But I don't understand how he can feel those things. He certainly doesn't learn them here.'"

The Director smiled at Nathan. "The natural inclination of human critters is to paint ourselves blue and beat each other to death, to rape, pillage and gain ascendancy over everyone else, all in order to spread our own seed, and exclude the seeds of those we defeat. If Julia and Matthew want Victoria and Tommy to have equal opportunities, they must create a structure that inhibits Tommy from pummeling Victoria and allows them each to flourish. The challenge is to create a balance between the conservative structure and the liberal freedoms allowed within that structure."

Nathan shook his head. He'd read Samuel Huntington's works during his training period. It had provided interesting grist for discussion of theory, but theory had been of little value as he worked in the field. "So the agency, the military, the CIA, NSA and all the other alphabet organizations are the equivalent of parents enforcing time out on a kid who's ready to pound the daylights out of his little sister?"

"It's an imperfect metaphor, but it works."

"Horseshit. It's an intellectual and organizational way of pounding the shit out of other countries to get oil and whatever other goodies they have that we need or want."

The Director shrugged. "Of course. The west is addicted to oil. Addictions lead to crime, local and personal, with narcotics, global and national with oil. Your point?"

"That I can't do it anymore."

"It's a little late in the game for you to be making moral judgments, Nathan."

"I'm making a personal judgment not a moral one."

"You could have fooled me."

There was another series of popping sounds in the distance. The children had released an American couple from another circle and were chasing one another in an elaborate game of tag.

An elderly man sat on a wall at the Caspian's shore, casting his fishing line into the water. Whatever he caught, boots, tires, oil-drenched seaweed, even a fish if he were lucky, would be inedible. Still, he kept at it, pulling in his line, casting it over and again, like his father and grandfathers and great grandfathers had done. The children, at their game, ignored him.

"It's an observation, not a judgment," Nathan said. "Maybe that's what we have to do, pound others, take what they've got to assure peace and prosperity for ourselves."

The Director nodded, laughing. "Perhaps. Or perhaps it's all a game. We do it because it's exciting, because it's fun."

Impatient, Nathan cut the discussion short. "I'll take the offer for a leave."

"An indefinite, unpaid leave of absence," the Director said. "You understand what that means. No more salary. No more federal health insurance. No more exotic weapons. No more globetrotting. No more bargains at military commissaries. No government pension."

"I understand."

"It's quite interesting, don't you think, Nathan, that to combat Socialism, we created the ideal socialist state for our military people and those who work with them. Hospitals, department stores, travel, pensions, all free or at little cost."

"I hadn't thought about it."

"You should. You'll be giving it all up." Nathan shrugged.

The Director made a humming sound in his throat. "Where will you go?"

"I don't know yet. Some where in New England. Somewhere rural. Quiet."

The Director stood, offering his hand. Nathan clasped it. The older man's grip was strong, warm.

"You still haven't answered my question," Nathan said. He looked him in the eye again. "Which one?"

"Why do you want to keep me?"

Still holding his hand, the Director looked at the fisherman, then back at Nathan. When he spoke, the tone was vague, non-committal. "Who knows? Perhaps I have too much invested in you, personally, to see you terminated. Your work has been extraordinary, you know. Perhaps something will come up where I need you. I want to know you'll be available if that happens." Nathan bristled, but said nothing.

The Director saw his discomfort and smiled. "I won't be here forever, but there will continue to be problems that must be dealt with. Perhaps that's why I need you, so that I know the agency will be in good hands once I'm gone. Then again, perhaps I'm just a sadistic son-of-a-bitch who wants to think of you spending your life squirming, wondering when the phone will ring and you'll pick it up and find me there, on the other end, calling you back into service. Perhaps all of the above."

He dropped Nathan's and hand walked off. Twenty feet away, he stopped and turned, the sun full on him. It was a posture and movement that looked rehearsed, the choreographed manner of his turn, his stance, the sun lighting him for the most dramatic effect.

"Nathan." His voice was soft. "Good luck. Be careful. Don't call me unless the situation is dire."

He walked to the side of the boulevard. A dark green Mercedes limousine glided to a stop beside him. The door opened from inside. He got in and the car sped off. Nathan walked back to his hotel and made arrangements to fly home to the States, paying with a personal credit card.

Book One
Graham, Massachusetts 2010

Chapter One

Tiger said to me, "We've got no chance of getting out of here without a few major bruises and cuts." We were sitting in Ducky's Bar on Route 2, a few miles west of Graham, Massachusetts.

I sipped my beer. "You had to tell those huge farm kids that the U-Mass football team could improve their game by taking their helmets off and sticking their heads up their asses."

"Who knew the big one's brother was the quarterback? Besides, you're the one who wanted to stop here for a beer."

"I wouldn't have to drive you home from work if you hadn't lost your driver's license going eighty on the Mass Pike. For crissakes, the cop's writing you up and you give him the finger."

"I was pissed. People were passing me and I'm the one that gets stopped. Then he starts scolding me like I was some punk kid while he's writing the damn ticket."

"And you had to ask him if he pounded his meat after every stop?"

"Like I said, I was pissed."

"So here I am, driving you home to Yardley Falls because you were pissed and then pissed off the cop."

She grinned at me. "Hey, it gives us quality time to hang out, and I'm getting my license back in three days."

"Right and this is real quality time we're looking at with those assholes you've stirred up."

She grinned again, rubbing her right fist into her open left hand. "Could be kinda fun though."

Tiger, Catherine Ann Kelly to her mother, and I are janitors at the community college in Graham, Maintainers II, in the politically correct terminology of the Commonwealth of Massachusetts. Most people would regard our jobs as scut work. For me, making sure things are tidy keeps many demons at bay.

Next to Cloyce Peck, she's the strongest, biggest member of our crew. She's also my best friend. How can anyone not love a six foot one, two hundred and fifty pound lesbian who weight trains, bench presses two hundred and ten pounds, and is forever grouching about how unfair it is that men, even wooses like Peter Entman, the psychologist who lives next door to her, can press more? On top of all that she plays guitar like Doc Watson and has a voice like

Emmylou Harris, which she does everything possible to rough up, sounding as much like Tom Waits as she can.

I was taking her home after work. It was supposed to be simple. I'd drive her to the Falls, drop her off at her house, then head back to my place at Barton Rooms in Graham, a warren of single rooms and hallways above a block of stores and offices on Main Street. I'd go to bed and dream about sweeping cigarette butts off the college's enclosed patios and cleaning urine off the men's rooms floors. Your idea of a college education is different from that of most people when you're the one cleaning up its buildings. Scrubbing *Dean Brosky Sux* from toilet stalls and washing references to Kierkegaard's leap of faith from blackboards puts a unique spin on keeping an intelligent perspective on the vagaries of the human condition.

Of course that's not all I dream of. I often drop off to sleep thinking about Shelley Randall, who teaches freshman English in room S-212 Tuesday and Thursday nights. She's been a part-timer, adjunct faculty in the p.c. jargon of the day, at Graham Community College for several years. No doubt she will have to keep on teaching part time, given the way public colleges in Massachusetts aren't hiring many full time Profs anymore. At least, I hope she keeps on teaching there. One of these days I might manage to break through my torpor and talk to her. Maybe I'll even ask her to dinner. Some day I will have to come out of hiding.

Life can be difficult for part-timers at the college. The Commonwealth pays them lousy salaries no benefits, and the union allows their classes to be larger than those taught by full-time faculty. Still, the part-timers keep coming back, hoping things will change, that they'll get full time jobs with benefits and be able to stop running the highways between colleges in Holyoke, Springfield and Westfield to the south and as far east as Gardner and Fitchburg.

So far, Shelley seems to be hanging in there, but there's not much hope. The towns have no money; Graham lost its entire tap and die industry in the Seventies, has the highest tax rate in the state and some of the most underfunded services. The state has no money, and the Feds are pouring the country's treasure into the empty pits of Iraq and Afghanistan. George Carlin described us as circling the drain and I'm afraid he was right.

The kid across the circular bar from us stared at Tiger. "Hey bitch, you wanna repeat what you said about the U-Mass team?"

He was big, six-five, six-six, with hands that seemed to wrap around his beer bottle one and a half times. His sandy hair was cut in a grotesque mullet, a crew cut on top and bleach-streaked hair hanging from two inches above his ears and resting on his shoulders. With a drooping mustache and a small goatee, a tattooed snake running up his left arm and disappearing under the rolled up sleeve of his tee shirt, he looked tough, and the muscles bursting from the tee's sleeves said, very tough.

I nudged Tiger to be quiet, but things weren't going to be as simple as I had hoped.

She leaned forward, baring her teeth at him. They glistened in the light from a Coors sign over the bar. "You mean what I said about them playing better ball with their heads up their asses? That what you mean?"

I shrugged. She was on a roll and nothing would stop her. I love Tiger. She's my best friend, but she does get me into bucket loads of shit. Not that I can't get into it all by myself, but with Tiger it's a calling, the result of something approaching divine inspiration. With me jumping into the bucket results from stupidity, and perhaps something more, something left over from years before, a need for punishment as atonement.

"Yeah, that's what I mean," the kid said.

She waved her hand. "Aw, I take that back."

I relaxed a bit. Then she leaned forward with a sneer I knew she'd been practicing in the mirror on slow nights as she was cleaning the women's rooms at GCC.

"Hell, they were playing with their heads up their asses. Probably loved the stink. And the jerks still lost. What I meant to say was they'd play better with their heads up their asses sitting on the bench and letting the debate team take the field."

She turned to me. "Come on, Sanders, let's get out of here. The intelligence level here is thirty degrees lower than the remedial classes at the county jail."

"House of Correction," I said as she headed for the parking lot. "We're Maintainers and the jail is a House of Correction."

The kids raced us for the door. We got out first. They were close on our butts.

"You smart ass bitch," the quarterback's brother said, reaching for her shirt.

"Sonny, that's the nicest thing anybody's said to me all day." Tiger pushed his hands away, kneeing him in the crotch. When he bent over she twisted his ears and kneed him on the chin. Blood and teeth spurted from his mouth as he went down on the ground, his face up against the right front tire of my '05 Toyota pickup. As I glanced at him, I noticed the tire was bald. I'd have to hit the used tire store soon.

I grabbed the second one as he came for me and turned his right arm behind his back. There was a loud crack and he was down in the gravel next to his buddy. The third one stepped back, raising his hands, palms outward. I felt a rush of the old rage. His face was an indistinguishable blur.

For an instant I was in a dozen other places, facing enemies long buried, forced into a realm of semi-forgotten sins. His voice broke the moment. It was fearful, almost childlike. He was as big as the other two, but there was something different in his eyes. The quarterback's brother and his pal on the ground had mean eyes and nasty sneering curls tot heir lips when they spoke. This one was the kid who tailed after them, wanting to be in on the action, the one who has to yell, *hey guys, wait up for me* and then runs after them because they won't wait and laugh at his eagerness to be one of the guys, the one who always has to sit in the back seat and buy the last case of beer when the other two are out of money.

"They were acting like assholes," he said. "I don't want any trouble. Jesus, I don't want any trouble." He was talking to me, looking down at his buddies lying on the parking lot, groaning. Blood poured from the nose of the one by my front tire.

Tiger took a step toward him, pointing to the quarterback's brother lying in the gravel a few feet from the other one. "You were an asshole too, laughing and urging shit-for-brains here on."

He shook his head. "No. No I wasn't. I can see how you might think so, but I wasn't. Honest."

"Were too." She took another step forward. "You're an asshole. They're assholes." She pointed at the two on the ground. They had crawled around a bit. Both their heads were now by my truck tire. One was trying to push himself into a sitting position. Her voice was soft, almost soothing, as she spoke to the kid with his palms up. Licking his lips, he flicked his eyes from her to me. I moved into the background, watching.

"Just admit that you're an asshole," she told him.

The kid looked at her, took two steps backward and gulped. He was big, not as big as the quarterback's brother, but big. Bigger than Tiger.

She took two steps forward. "Were you saying something or was that a whimper of raw fear?"

"Yes," he said.

"Yes what? Raw fear or were you in some inept way trying to speak?"

"I guess so."

"You guess what? Fear or speech?" She was matching him, step for step forward to each of his steps backward.

"Speech." His voice was low. He looked down at his friends for support. They both had managed to sit up. They rested their heads against the side of the truck, their eyes shut tight, probably wishing they were still at the bar, drinking the beers they had left sitting there to follow us outside, confident they'd dispense with us and be back inside before the foam settled in their mugs.

She smiled at him the way the asp must have smiled at Cleopatra. "And what were you trying to say, sonny?"

"I'm an asshole." He mumbled it.

"I couldn't hear that. I'll bet you couldn't either. I know my friend Sanders didn't hear it. Right Eddie?"

I shook my head. "Did you fart and want us to think you said something?" I asked him. I wasn't about to let Tiger have all the fun, but as soon as I said it I felt lousy, diminished.

"No. I said it." The kid's eyes were wide as he looked back and forth from his buddies to Tiger and me. I regretted goading him.

"Said what?" Tiger asked.

"What you wanted me to say."

"And what was that?"

His faced turned red and he looked again at his buddies, their eyes still shut tight. If it wouldn't have cost them their last ounce of cool, they would have stuck their fingers in their ears. They should have covered their mouths back at the bar.

"What, precisely, did I ask you to say?" That snaky smile still slithered across her face.

"That I'm an asshole."

"Are you?"

"What?"

"An asshole?" He nodded.

"I can't hear a nod," she said. He was backed up against a red Chevy. She was breathing in his face. "Say it."

His face reddened. He looked at his feet and mustering a kind of courage, raised his eyes to meet Tiger's. I liked him for it. His voice strengthened. "I'm an asshole."

"And your buddies are assholes."

"And they," he pointed at the two on the gravel, "they're assholes too. Major assholes." What resembled the beginnings of a grin flashed across his face.

"There's hope for him," she said to me as she patted him on the cheek and gave him her sweetest smile. "Work on it, dear. You might get over it. You'd like that. Right?"

He nodded again.

"What say?" she asked.

"I'd much rather be a hay pounder back on the farm than be an asshole, ma'am."

She patted his cheek again, a little harder than before. "Drop the ma'am, sonny." She pointed to the quarterback's brother, who was trying to get up. "I actually preferred his smart ass bitch comment."

He opened his mouth to say something. I signaled him with a hand gesture to shut up. He did.

"You boys better get back on into bar and finish your beers before they get warm," I said. The two on the ground scurried up and the three of them went back into Ducky's.

Tiger and I climbed into the pickup. After a couple of tries it started. I pulled out onto Route 2, headed west for Yardley Falls, the windows rolled down, the air, blowing across us, warm for a late October night. A couple miles down the road a cruiser passed us headed east, going fast, lights flashing, siren screaming.

"Must be a fight somewhere," I said.

"Probably a bunch of jerks in a bar getting into it."

"No doubt." Tiger rolled down her window and lit a cigarette. "No smoking in my car. You know that."

"This is a truck."

"Still no smoking."

"Those dickheads at Ducky's aren't the only assholes out here tonight." She sighed, tossing the cigarette out the window.

"You could start a fire like that."

"Too damp. All the rain we've been having. Not much chance of a fire. "I'm an on-call fireman, and I say you could start a fire, tossing a butt out along the road."

"Firefighter. You're an on-call firefighter. We're Maintainer IIs and the members of the Yardley Board of Selectmen are now members of the Yardley Selectboard. Times have changed, Sanders. You gotta get with the new terminology."

"Doesn't change what a smoldering cigarette can do along the side of the road."

"Sometime you are such an asshole."

I reached over and squeezed her shoulder. "Yeah, aren't we all?"

§§§

It was one o'clock when I stopped in front of her house in Yardley Falls. She and her partner Dawn own a small hundred and ten year-old Victorian on Oak Street, which they have been renovating since the day they passed papers on it. No sooner had I killed the engine than Dawn came out on the porch, smelling of a subtle perfume, her lipstick understated, wearing a thin nightgown designed to drive men and women to sexual distraction.

"Jesus, she's a babe," I said. "And she's my babe, toots."

"Where have you been?" Dawn asked, face wrinkled with anger and concern, arms crossed over her breasts, her right foot tapping on the porch floor. "I've been worried sick. You should have been home by ten-thirty."

Tiger jerked a finger at me. "Dickhead here wanted to stop at Ducky's for a beer, the U-Mass game was on the tube and we had a disagreement about its outcome with a few farm boys at the bar."

Dawn shook her head in mock dismay. "Chad and I have been pacing. I was ready to call the police." She looked at me, winking. "I suppose you've been leading this poor soul astray again."

Tiger nudged me to be quiet. "You might as well have called the cops. Everybody else has. Must be our night."

Chad grinned. "Big night, Tigermom?"

Chad was Dawn's son, a senior at West County Regional. Handsome, smart, he was a multi-talented athlete, a star student. Dawn and Tiger doted on him, planning his future as a doctor, or nuclear physicist, or astronaut, whatever struck either of them at any given moment as the most challenging and prestigious thing the boy could end up doing. He was the product of Dawn's late teen-age marriage to a lawyer in the Falls. They'd had a fling after he did her parents' divorce. They married when she told him she was pregnant and split up a few months after Chad was born. Tiger adored the kid and he regarded her as his second mother. She never missed one of his games. Dawn never saw one of them. Too violent, she claimed. She'd been a cheerleader in high school and seen enough football and football players to last her forever.

Tiger snorted. "Whatever you do, don't call the cops when I'm late. Who knows, they could be looking for me anyway."

"Are they?" Dawn's eyes widened. Chad came out on the porch and put an arm around his mother's shoulder.

Tiger grinned at me. "Could be. Let's wait until we see what *The Graham Enterprise* has to say in the morning."

"You coming to our Halloween party next week?" Chad asked me. "Wouldn't miss it."

"Cool," he said. "It's a costume thing, you know. Bring a date." I had to laugh. "I haven't had a date in years, but I've been known to be pretty good with costumes. You won't know me."

"Terrific," Tiger said. "Want a cup of coffee, Eddie?"

I looked at Dawn. She shook her head and rolled her eyes. I got the message.

"I'm tired, and who knows, there may be a good fire and they'll have to call me out tonight."

§§§

Route 2 from Yardley descends a steep hill into Graham. From halfway down there is a fine view of the town and Poets Seat Tower sitting on top of the five hundred foot high ridge that separates Graham from the Connecticut River.

The tower was built before the First World War, in honor of a minor poet named Henry Lewis Thompson who, according to local folklore, used to climb to the site for poetic inspiration. Local lore also says Emerson admired him, although I doubt that these days anyone outside of Graham has heard of him, with the exception of doctoral candidates combing the Internet, desperate for dissertation material. The tower is far more impressive than the poet. An open stone structure, it rises three stories above the ridge. Climb the interior staircase and from the top there's a fine view of the river valley and the surrounding hill towns.

Lit by spotlights, the tower dominated the view from the highway as I drove into town. You've got to hand it to a town that has as its most prominent landmark a monument to a poet, even a forgotten one. All Thompson's obscure verse is worth it for the presence of the tower and the park the town has created around it.

I was home before one thirty, if you can call a single room in Barton Rooms home, one with little more than a bed, a hot plate and a shared bathroom down the hall. After setting water to boil for instant coffee, I put my *Tosca* CD in the player, the volume low since the walls were paper thin. A friend named Billy Melnick had given me the latest posthumous collection of Charles Bukowski's poetry and reading through it I wondered if Buke had written it or if Black Sparrow Press had hired a drunken horse playing horny old man to grind out the worst of Bukowski-like verse without any of the brilliant lyricism the man had been capable of while he was alive and writing his own stuff.

One of the worst things that can happen to a writer is to die. It brings out all the family members and editors who claim to have truck loads of unpublished works, most of which they've cobbled together themselves. The best of them come from notes the dead writers leave behind. The worst, and the bulk of them, come from the febrile and feeble imaginations of those trying to cash in on the writer's marketable remains.

Still, most writers have piles of junk they never publish, just keep around hoping they can salvage a line or an image here and there. I wondered if any of the English Profs at GCC had ever read Bukowski, or if they were too hung up on Archibald McLeish and Robert Bly and the erudite stuff academic poets write for one another to read. Black Sparrow published all of Bukowski's stuff while he was alive, good and bad. If all they had left were the piles of shit, they'd publish that. Who wouldn't? Shit or not, it sells.

Saddened by the poems, I put them down and picked up Karen Armstrong's biography of Mohammed. Reading it, I forgot how long I had been alone. Between lines I caught memories of Shelley Randall walking the halls of the college, lovely, cool and distant looking. Fantasy is a safe way to conduct an affair.

I fell asleep in my chair long before Tosca died.

Chapter Two

The next night, during our break at work, Tiger and I sat in the cafeteria drinking coffee from our thermoses. I was eating a meatball grinder I'd picked up at Village Pizza before coming in. The college doesn't bother to keep the café open for those of us who work at night, but there is a microwave just outside the door. I used it to heat the grinder and the roll was soggy, the meatballs so hot they burned my tongue. I flushed my mouth with cold water as Tiger told me about an open mike Thursday at the Graham Town Common Pub and Microbrewery, the Townie to most of its patrons.

"The acoustics suck with that tin ceiling they've got, but it's a great place, and it's the only spot between Northampton and Brattleboro for someone like me to play for an audience. And Northampton and Brattleboro drive me up the wall. Noho's too politically correct and Bratt's got too many coupon clipping offspring of the rich for my blood. I wish there were more places to play here in town."

I was about to comment that Graham, like all economically struggling towns, was full of people too cheap or too poor to pay the cover charge so open mike performers could get five bucks for playing, or a free beer if they preferred. I didn't get a chance. My fantasy English Prof, Shelley Randall, came rushing into the café, eyes so wide she looked like she'd just seen bears in the parking lot. Not as far fetched as it sounds. It's not unusual to find bear and moose in the lot. They've never hurt anyone, but they do hang around scaring people.

"Tiger, where's Security?" Shelley asked.

Tiger looked at her watch. "Doing rounds in the north end. Why?" I tried not to look at Shelley with too much longing, but she was talking to Tiger, her eyes intense, her voice trembling, so I stared at her.

Shelley either didn't notice or didn't care. For good reasons, it turned out. "A kid in my class is having some kind of fit, rolling around on the floor, throwing up, screaming about snakes trying to get out through her eyes." Before Shelley had finished Tiger was calling Security on her mobile unit. "I'm a trained E.M.T.," I said, already headed for the door. Shelley followed me.

When we got to S-212 a group of students stood in a circle. I broke through. A small girl lay still on the floor, eyes open, skin gray, a pool of vomit around her, covering her face and hair. She wasn't breathing.

Whipping a dust rag from my back pocket I wiped as much of the puke from her face as I could and began mouth to mouth, gagging as I did.

"Gross," a boy behind me said.

Tiger came in, still speaking into her mobile unit, telling Security to call an ambulance. "Move it. Now," she said to the kid, pushing students from the room.

"Class dismissed," Shelley said, her voice shaky. We'll pick up with Flannery O'Connor's ideas about the grotesque in fiction next class. Read *Good Country People* and *Greenleaf*."

I kept up the mouth to mouth until the last of the students were gone. It was just for the show. The girl was dead. Not even an E.R. doc and paddles could bring her back. As soon as the room was empty I sat back on my haunches and shook my head.

"Shit," Tiger said.

"My God, can't you do anything?" Shelley's voice was a whisper. "Not for her," I said. "Who was she?"

"Andrea Lane."

"Henrietta Lane's kid?" I asked. Shelley nodded.

Even a janitor would know this was bad news. I was sure of it. Henrietta Lane owned Willey and McClannan, one of Graham's largest Real Estate and Insurance firms, and a good bit of the town's commercial property. She was also a prominent member of the Graham Community College Foundation, an organization set up to augment the Commonwealth's inadequate funding of the college.

She and her husband Arnold and their daughter had come to town ten years before, bought out Virgil Willey and Bob McClannan's agency, picked up other properties on the cheap, an easy thing to do in a mill town without any mills. They bought Smith's View, the town's most ostentatious house, sitting among several acres of trees bordering Mountain Park, and changed its name to Llanarch. Zip. Instant aristocracy. Two years later Arnold died of a heart attack leaving Henrietta to run the businesses. Willey and McClannan flourished. She fixed up the commercial buildings, kept the storefronts full, their office spaces as well occupied as any in town. People don't have much good to say about her business style or personal life, but they coddle up to her money and the social position it has bought her.

Nobody knew where the Lanes came from, but they were loaded when they hit town. I'd heard all kinds of wild rumors about where and how they got their money, but I chalked it up to the small town sourness that often develops when people with money move in and set themselves up in visible and lucrative ways. It wasn't important to me and I wouldn't have bothered to check it out through the old channels even if I could.

"What's the Lane kid doing at a community college?" I asked Shelley. "Kind of money she comes from, how come she's not at Wellesley, Smith, Harvard, Williams, some place like that."

She replied in a monotone. "She flunked out of Wellesley in her freshman year and started taking courses here to rehabilitate herself academically. Wellesley said they'd take her back if she kept a decent grade point average for a couple semesters. We do give pretty substantive courses here, you know." At the end, her voice sounded defensive.

She was right though. I'd taken a few courses at GCC myself. Hell, they were free to employees and their families, so why not? The good ones were as good as any I'd taken during my years at the University of Pennsylvania ages before. The bad ones were bad, but then so were the bad ones at Penn.

Security came in with the ambulance guys.

"No hurry, Steve," I said to one of them, waving my hand at the dead girl. "She's gone."

Still, he zapped her several times with the paddles, intubated her, did everything by the book. It didn't matter. She stayed dead and they hauled her off to the morgue at County Medical Center on the other side of town.

By the time it was finished, the ambulance gone, the room cleaned up, it was quitting time. I went to my Maintainer II closet, threw on a jacket and my Red Sox hat. Tiger was standing at the foot of the third floor staircase. Chad was with her. Except for the three of us, the building was empty. Our voices echoed in the hall.

"I thought I'd pick up Tigermom," he said. "Actually, Ma made me. She was afraid you guys might get into another bar ruckus tonight." He grinned at Tiger and cuffed me on the shoulder. The kid had all the makings of a politician or businessman.

They walked off toward visitors parking area at the front of the building. I started down the hall, headed for the door to the employee's lot. The lights in S-212 were on. I had turned them off before going to my closet. I looked in. Shelley was sitting on the top of the desk, staring at the spot on the floor where Andrea Lane had died. She looked up as I stood in the doorway.

"What happened?"

I shook my head and shrugged. I shrug a lot. It saves me from making stupid comments, sometimes.

"One minute I was talking about O'Connor's *A Good Man Is Hard to Find*, the next Andy started thrashing in her seat. Then she fell on the floor and

I came to the café for help." She looked up at me. "When we got back she was dead. It happened so fast."

I looked at the spot on the floor, shaking my head. "That sums it up."

"So what happened?" I shrugged again. It was an inadequate response and I tried to answer. "Drugs, maybe. An overdose. Some bad shit. Or maybe she was an epileptic and choked on her tongue, or a diabetic and went into insulin shock. Hell, I don't know. I'm just a Maintainer II. I'm pretty good with rest rooms and blackboards, but I don't know shit about life and death."

That got her. She almost laughed. She did smile. It looked good on her. "At least you've got a full time job. I'm an adjunct instructor in English with a beat up Chevy, a cheap apartment in Eagle Falls, no medical insurance or pension and an extensive knowledge of life and death in literature."

I gave her my widest, most winning smile. Tiger calls it my broken babe magnet. It hasn't attracted much of late. "With that one sentence I've learned more about you than I did in all the time I've worked here."

"Seven. I've been here seven years, and you'd have learned more earlier if you'd ever bothered to talk with me." She got up from behind the desk. Her hair was black with a few streaks of gray, pulled back in a ponytail. She loosened it, shook her head, letting it fall around her shoulders. Her body was firm and well shaped. She was less than an inch shorter than me.

"You work out?" I said.

"I swim at the Y, run a couple days a week and do some exercises on the weight machines." She reached for her books. Her hands shook. There were no rings on them.

"You look like you need a drink," I said. I wanted to tell her she looked like she needed a good long session of lovemaking with me. That would not only be uncool, it could get me fired in the Commonwealth of Massachusetts.

"Several."

"I'll buy. Maintainer IIs make more money than adjunct professors."

"By a long shot, unless you calculate it by the hour."

"Don't. You do that and we'll start figuring out what the full time faculty gets per hour. That'll depress us both."

She looked back down at the floor. The carpeting was still damp where I had cleaned up after Andrea. The smile faded. "I'm already depressed. I'm about as depressed as I can get. She was a good kid, in spite of her mother, and I thought she was getting her act together."

I gave her my best crooked, sarcastic grin. "How can you speak that way about Henrietta Lane? She's a pillar of Grahamfeldian society."

She smiled again. "Henrietta Lane is a real bitch. Grahamfeld*ian*. I like that, Eddie. It's so Brit. You make it up?"

I nodded. "I didn't know you knew my name. How is she a bitch?"

"Edward Sanders. Sure I know your name. You live in Barton Rooms. You're an on-call firefighter dreaming of a full time gig on the big red trucks and you were staring at my tits when I was asking Tiger where Security was. Henrietta's an evil bitch because she manipulates people any way she can, sex, money, information. She steals security deposits with trumped up damages. The houses she built in the meadows have substandard lumber and cheap concrete in their foundations and she gives the building inspector head. You're staring at my breasts right now, you know. I'm giving you the scoop in Henrietta Lane and you're staring at my breasts."

I felt my face redden and brazened it out. "What's not to stare at? They look great. I hope this doesn't get me fired. How do you know all this?" She stared in my direction but she wasn't looking at me. She was looking inside, thinking, drifting. Her expression changed, a decision reached. She smiled and pointed at me. "Maybe after a few drinks I'll give you a better look at them and I promise not to get you fired unless you turn out to be a lousy lover. I know all about Henrietta because I lived with the building inspector for three years and she owns my apartment in Eagle Falls. I know all about you because I asked Cloyce Peck a couple of years ago, after you left that fake paper on Hemingway and the death of God on my desk."

"You knew it was me?"

"I saw you put it there."

"You never said anything. And yet you just criticized me for not bothering to talk with you."

"I'm shy. I'm a slow mover. What's your excuse? Putting that paper there was a first step at a come on, but you never followed up."

I laughed. "You got me. I'm a slow mover too." I left it at that. There wasn't any point in explaining that I'd never been able to have long term relationships and that short ones had ceased being worth the effort. It could be a dangerous conversation, leading into discussions of why I was a loner. That was something I never talked about with anyone. Instead, I deflected her by asking why she had gone to all the trouble of finding out about me and never acted.

"I had just broken up with the building inspector," she said, fiddling with a piece of chalk. "And I wasn't ready for any kind of involvement. I'm not sure I am yet. What can I say?"

"You're not a slow mover tonight, threatening to get me fired if I'm not a good lay."

She looked me in the eye, pointing to the floor. "One of my favorite students died right there tonight. Things like that can change a woman's perspective. At least temporarily."

"A man's too. The effect's gender neutral. I used to be a good lover but I've had damned little practice in the last few years. I hope you'll take that I'm out of sexual condition into account before you decide to report me to the Dean of Administration. And, let's drop the talk about Henrietta Lane."

"Sounds right to me. I want that drink, those drinks. Then I'll take you home and show you how I look without this blouse and bra on."

§§§

Most tables at the Town Common were empty. We forked out a two-dollar cover charge to pay a kid with a scraggly beard and a beat up acoustic Gibson playing Appalachian folk songs on a small raised stage at the rear of the room. Nobody seemed to be listening to him.

Billy Melnick, was a regular and sat at the bar several stools away from four other men, each alone, each with a beer. Billy, who always sat on the same stool, was writing in a notebook. It was he who had given me the Bukowski book that put me to sleep the night of the fight at Ducky's. In his forties, tall, with yellowish skin and thinner than any living man should be, his graying hair pulled back in a ponytail longer than Shelley's. He's a veteran of the first Gulf war, Green Beret, a sergeant he insists. He'd been a student at the college for some time several years ago. He fancies himself a poet and makes a living freelancing for small cross-country skiing magazines and doing small-scale maintenance projects for people. It was Billy who turned me on to Bukowski's poetry.

A man and woman were playing Scrabble at the table by the door. I could see the words *AN* and *IMAGE* on his tiles. A copy of *Waiting for Godot* was by his elbow. I leaned over him. "If you play Scrabble while you're reading Beckett does that mean you can get absurd?"

He gave me a glance and looked back at the board. "I'm not reading Beckett."

I was glad Tiger wasn't with me and that I was at the Townie. If she had been and we were at some joint like Ducky's or the Opry House up in South Guilford, and the Scrabble jerk was there I'd've wanted to pound on him. Tiger would have abetted me.

That's one of the reasons I'm a Maintainer II and not a professor, or even an adjunct professor of Philosophy. There were too many obstacles in the way of getting the papers I needed to prove I was educated. My first act after the Director granted my leave of absence was to go back to school. I hoped to finish the degree in the literature of philosophy I had left undone years before, when I took the opportunity presented to me by a professor at Penn. He had noticed my restlessness and appreciated my willingness to try anything and made me an offer to pursue a life I couldn't turn down. Through him I met the Director and as a result lived what for a long time seemed to be a fine and exciting life. Then a day came when I couldn't drag my ass out of bed, go into the bathroom to shave and face in the mirror the monster I had become.

Being back in school after life in the agency didn't work for me. There seemed to be more obstacles than ever before. Their numbers were overwhelming. I dropped out again and finished my education by reading wider and deeper than any dissertation advisor would have demanded.

Three of five regulars at the bar looked up from their drinks, waved, said something along the lines of howya doin' Eddie and turned their attention back to their beers. Shelley and I took a booth in the rear, near the kitchen.

"The usual, Eddie?" The waitress stood by the table, tapping her pencil against the back of her hand. "Missed you last night. Heard there was a little action up at Ducky's."

I looked up at her, straight faced. "That so?"

"You didn't hear?"

"Not a word, Cat. Tell me."

"I heard the Yardley cops are looking for you. Seems some farmer kid got messed up so bad that he's in the hospital on life support."

I felt a sick chill rush through my gut. "How bad is he?"

She laughed. "Tiger and her hunk stepson stopped in for a quickie. She told me to hose you a bit when you came in."

I exhaled, surprised by how relieved I was. "I've got great friends," I said to Shelley. Cat laughed again.

"Tiger said you wouldn't be alone." She looked at Shelley, raising her eyebrows. "Hi Professor Randall."

"Cat," Shelly said. "You doing all right?"

"Wonderful. I love U-Mass. What do you want?"

"A glass of Multipulciano."

"Tiger told you to hose me," I said to Cat.

"Yep," she said. "And I've got your blackened turkey burger coming right up."

"I thought the kitchen closed at ten."

"Tiger again. She ordered it for you and told me to keep it warm." I split the burger with Shelley. Every time she leaned across to take a bite her scoop neckline dipped. I had a fine view of the swell of her breasts.

"You're staring at my tits again," she said, wiping mayonnaise from her upper lip.

"You didn't have to lean so far over to eat the burgie," I told her. "You'd be disappointed if I didn't." I ordered another beer for me and another glass of wine for her. "So what happened at Ducky's?" she asked. I told her.

"Jesus. You're nothing like the building inspector and you're a different breed of dog from any of the academics I've gone out with. Finish that beer and let's go to my place."

§§§

Her apartment was on the ground floor of a brick triple-decker two blocks off Avenue A in Eagle Falls. A village in the town of Ashmont, across the Connecticut River from Graham, Eagle Falls was built as a mill town. The mills were long since gone and for years and downtown Eagle Falls consisted of crumbling factories and row houses, double and triple deckers, most of them red brick, cheap shelter for the young, desperate druggies and alcoholics who came in from the surrounding hill towns and cities to the south where life offered them even less hope than it did in Eagle Falls. Recently things have been improving for the downtown. There is an environmental Discovery Center, a vibrant theater and several fine restaurants, all part of what the locals refer to as the Eagle Renaissance.

Shelley went into the bathroom as soon as we got inside. I looked around the living room. There were several paintings, abstract blotches of color and design, none very pleasant to look at. A spinet piano sat against a wall, on it several photographs of men and women with happy, playful smiles. One showed a much younger Shelley in a bathing suit, tanned and laughing, standing behind the wheel of a sailboat, her hair tossed by the wind, a drink in her hand. The water was a startling turquoise color, the island in the background green and mountainous. Bookcases lined the other walls. As I was reaching for *Yeats, the Complete Poetical Works*, she came into the room naked. Her breasts were magnificent. The rest of her was magnificent too.

"Well," she said.

"It's been so long, I think I'm going to come just looking at you."

"Do that and I'll have a talk with the Dean of Administration."

"You sure I'm not taking advantage of you because you're vulnerable after what happened tonight?"

"Of course I'm vulnerable. I wouldn't be so forward if I weren't, but I'm an adult with a good mind and the ability to make it up on my own. Like I said, I've been thinking about this for a long time. Tonight was only the catalyst. Besides, I'm a feminist. I did my doctoral studies at the University of the

West Indies on images of women in post-colonial Caribbean literature. A feminist can get laid with anybody she wants, any time she wants."

"That's impressive," I said.

"It was a lot of work and the professors at UWI were tough, but I did it. Not that it's done me a hell of a lot of good in the academic marketplace." She spread her arms. "Here I am, an adjunct instructor of English, teaching freshman composition in the boonies of Massachusetts."

"That too," I said. "I was more impressed that a feminist can screw anybody, anytime. It's enough to make a feminist out of me."

Her laugh was quick and full. "Well almost any time. I wouldn't have wanted us to be kicked out of the Townie tonight, maybe banned from ever going back because I boffed you on the table."

"Indicated was the word you needed when you said you'd been thinking about this for a long time." I ran my index fingers around her nipples.

"Indicated?"

"Earlier. You indicated that you'd been thinking about this for a long time. You didn't say it. Surely an English Prof knows the difference between saying something and indicating something. And, we wouldn't have been kicked out or banned. It would have been a great show and a good excuse for them to raise the cover charge."

"You're a piece of work, Sanders. What are you indicating?' "I'm indexing. That's another arcane academic skill, Professor Randall.

"Oh shut up. We can talk later." She pulled me toward the bedroom. "Your condom or mine?"

I emptied my pockets. Except for two dollars and thirty cents there was nothing in them. "I haven't had any need for them for a long time."

"I guess it's mine." She unrolled a rubber, dangling it in the air as she moved backward to the bed. "What are you going to think about?"

"Getting laid with you."

"I mean to keep from coming too soon so I don't have to talk with the dean."

"The Red Sox."

She laughed. "The building inspector thought about code violations. I think they made him come sooner. The Red Sox?"

"Yeah. I replay that game in '86 when the ball went through Billy Buckner's legs in the bottom of the ninth of what should have been the last game of the Series. The Sox should have won the pennant that time. Thinking about it always slows me down."

"Don't want any errors between the legs?"

"None." I undressed and lay next to her. We kissed, our tongues darting over lips, hand exploring each other's bodies. She was as horny as I was, our movements quick and desperate. We made love fast. Then we made love slower.

"Now that was a nice fuck," she said when we finished. "My, how you talk for an English professor."

"Adjunct instructor and feminist scholar. I read too much D.H. Lawrence and Henry Miller in grad school. They corrupted my language in spite of their sexist rot."

"Can I assume you're not going to turn me into the Dean for sub-standard sex?"

"May. The correct word is may. *May I assume*, you should have said. I guess I'll have to turn you in for using bad grammar."

I ran my tongue over her left breast. "Well maybe I won't turn you in."

She ran her fingers through my hair and I licked her nipple again. "Don't neglect the other one," she said.

I didn't. After another round of love making, she flipped on her side, scrunched a pillow under her head and yawned. "You have to go now."

"Just like that?"

"Yep. I'm tired. It's time to sleep. I think I'll sleep very well, thanks to you."

"I can sleep too."

"At your place. Not here."

"I'm dismissed, like your class." There was a tinge of anger in my voice. If she heard it, she didn't react. Laughing she stroked my dick. "Nothing like my class. You'll like the homework assignment much better than they'll like theirs."

"Which is?"

"Find a nice place to take me for dinner tomorrow night after you get off work. Dutch, of course. Then we'll come back here for a repeat performance."

"But you want me to go now."

"I do. I'm used to waking up alone. I'm not ready to change that. I don't know if I'll ever be ready. Besides, you might snore.

"So might you."

"I might. I don't know."

"Aren't you curious?"

"Not enough to let you stay overnight. Yet."

She patted my cheek, just like Tiger had patted the cheek of the kid at Ducky's once he'd told her he was an asshole. I didn't know whether to be annoyed or not. Not, I decided.

Instead, I kissed her.

"That was nice," she said.

"It was all nice." I pulled on my trousers and shirt.

She looked sad. "Except for poor Andy Lane. It was a bad night for her." I pretended to be smoking a pipe. "The study of literature has much to teach us about the interplay between Eros and Thanatos."

"You're one hell of a janitor," she said. "Maintainer II."

"That too. You're one hell of a Maintainer II, Sanders." I leaned over and kissed her again. "Got to go start my homework."

"So far you've got an A. Keep it up."

"I intend to." I pulled the bedroom door shut behind me.

"Turn the latch on the front door so it locks behind you on your way out," she called.

Back in my Barton room, I stretched out on my bed too tired, too content to take off my clothes. No CDs. No book. I put my hands behind my head and slept until ten after nine the next morning.

Chapter Three

Tiger's voice came over my mobile unit as I was trying to scrub BEVERLEE ORMAND IS THE WORLD'S WURST FUCK from the wall above the urinal of the third floor faculty men's room wall. It had been written on the tile with an indelible red ink Sharpee pen the author had left lying on the sink. I was having trouble getting it to look faded, let alone removed. Beverlee Ormand was headed for a modicum of immortality.

"You got a phone call," she said. "Down at the main desk. Security said whoever it was told them you'd better get down there damned fast if you wanted to keep your job." She paused. I could hear the smile in her voice when she continued. "Said it was a woman."

Hoping it was Shelley wanting to know where we were going to have dinner so she could plan how to dress, I left Beverlee Ormand to history, at least for the moment, and took the stairs down to the main desk two at a time.

"Hi," I said into the phone, turning my back on Security, shielding my end of the conversation from prying ears.

"This Sanders?" The voice was a woman's. It wasn't Shelley and it wasn't at all warm. It was harsh and unfriendly.

"I'm Sanders. What's this about?"

"This is Henrietta Lane. We need to talk. Tonight. As soon as you get off work."

"I'm sorry about your daughter, Ms. Lane. I'll be glad to meet with you, but I have plans for tonight."

"You've got new ones. With me. And you'll get over to my place as soon as you put your last goddamn broom and dust rag away and wash your hands. You don't and you can kiss waxing floors and swabbing toilets goodbye. And Sanders, this is between myself and you, nobody else, understand?"

She hung up before I could say anything about the use of reflexive pronouns.

§§§

I called Shelley, told her something had come up and rescheduled for the next night. She sounded miffed, but agreed.

"Tomorrow might not have the same outcome as tonight would have," she said.

"I'll have to take that chance. I hope it does."

"We'll just have to wait and see. Tomorrow night, or I just might have to have that little chat with your dean."

"Laura Loblolly."

"Who's that?"

"The Dean of Administration at GCC. My boss. Dr. Laura. L. Loblolly, Junior, Ed.D., as she signs her name on memos."

"Dr. and Ed.D.? And Junior? I never met a woman who was a junior before. She's got to be insecure as hell."

"She's also into feminist fat, says fat is a political statement. Has to weigh in at close to two-eighty in soft pudge and she's chair of the Love Your Body Coalition. She tried to get Tiger involved, but that was like trying to get Mike Tyson to join the Eastern Star."

"From what I've seen of Eastern Star women, both of them have the right weight, but I just can't imagine Tiger in one of those frilly gauze gowns they wear."

"It's not a pretty picture," I said. "Tomorrow, for sure?"

"For sure." We said goodnight.

§§§

I rang Henrietta Lane's doorbell at ten-fifteen. A man in his late forties with a short beard and shaven head opened it. He was tall, heavy, very muscular, wearing a medium tee shirt when he would have been much more comfortable in an extra large. His sleeves were rolled up. He smelled of cigar and Brut cologne for men. It wasn't a pleasant combination.

"Sanders." It was a statement, not a question. I nodded. "You the butler?"

"I'll show you buttle right up your goddamn Yankee ass, you give me any shit." The accent was Texas. Real Texas, heavy on the ess sound along with the Deep South drawl. His style was World Wrestling Federation theatrical intimidation, too much too early, but said with enough inner anger to work.

I followed him inside. The back of his head had a number of creases too deep to shave. Tufts of close-cropped black hair grew from them. He led me into a mahogany hallway, the walls covered with embossed leather and hung with large paintings of the Hudson River School variety. An antique oriental runner covered the polished maple floor. Three wide doorways lined each side of the hall. Light and Shostakovich came from the second room. Texas shut the front door and pointed toward the light and music.

"In there," he ordered.

I walked into a huge room. It was at least forty feet by twenty, with fireplaces at each end, their faces black marble, their mantles supported by pilasters with intricate carvings. One large Oriental rug covered most of the floor. There were several couches, seven or eight armchairs, each with its own hassock, all soft polished leather. Silver boxes and candlesticks sat on end tables and coffee tables. Bookcases lining the walls on either side of the two fireplaces were filled with worn volumes, probably bought at auctions and used bookstores and put on the shelves unread to underscore what the room was supposed to say, and what it said quite well to a casual observer. Money. Lots of money. And taste. Which is something Henrietta Lane did not look as though she had. Perhaps it had been the long dead Arnold who had decorated and filled the house. More than likely, it had been done by an interior decorator who had been instructed to make the Lanes appear sophisticated and wealthy instead of just rich.

She sat in an armchair by a fireplace with a burning gas log. A cut glass cruet filled with red wine and two matching glasses sat on a table beside her. One was full, the second empty. The only light in the room came from the gas log and a Tiffany lamp next to her chair. It made her appear as though sitting in a soft spotlight. She glanced in my direction as I entered and quickly turned her attention to a Persian cat sprawled across her lap. She couldn't have been more than forty-five, but she looked ageless, her skin the whitish blue of skimmed milk, her hair pure white. Diamond earrings dangled from each ear and her fingers were heavy with gold and jeweled rings. She was deliberately and skeletally thin. A flowing salmon colored silk blouse covered the bones and blue white skin of her arms and upper body. Silk slacks with a muted leopard skin pattern completed the outfit. The butler's middle finger, which twitched every time he looked at me, was bigger than her wrist. She did not ask me to sit.

"You let my daughter die last night," she said, eyes on the cat. The voice was hard, strong, in sharp contrast to her wasted but expensively clothed appearance. Her words were measured and calculated. They were planned for the maximum effect."She was the only child my husband and myself ever had. He's dead. Now she's dead. And I am one very angry woman. You do not want my anger coming in your direction, Sanders."

She had ambushed me. I expected to be asked about the kid's death. Had she said anything? *Tell Mommy I love her. I see a long white tunnel with Daddy standing there.* Perhaps, I had thought, she'd even thank me for trying.

Texas had edged closer, the twitching middle fingers lost in his massive fist. I managed to speak. "She was dead when I got to the room."

"You gave her mouth to mouth."

"I knew it was too late for her. I did it until the room emptied out to keep the students from freaking."

"You got there too late. If you'd hustled your ass you might have saved her."

"I don't think so, Mrs. Lane. I know you've got to be pretty overcome with grief right now."

"Fuck off." The words exploded through her thin lips, cutting me off in mid-thought. "What do I know from grief? I'm angry. My kid's dead. You let her die. I don't like losing things. I've lost my kid and I am one very pissed off lady." She looked up from the cat for the first time since glancing at me as I entered the room. She had ice blue winter eyes, the brows above them thin cruel pencil lines. Her nose was straight, the nostrils thick. A hard nose to pick, I thought. Such thick nostril walls must make it hard to breathe. Maybe she couldn't get enough oxygen to her brain. Her lips were thin purple lines, her mouth turned downward, like someone had drawn an upside down U on her face.

I flushed, angry, but willing to cut her some slack. Her daughter was dead and I had been present at the time she died. It was enough to throw any parent off balance.

"I'm sorry, Mrs. Lane. Your daughter's death is a terrible thing, but I didn't kill her and I didn't let her die. She was dead when I got there and I got there as fast as possible. You must understand that there wasn't a thing I could do."

"I must understand, Sanders? I must? I don't have to understand anything. Especially from the likes of you."

There was a light clicking sound. I felt something hard against the base of my skull. I didn't need the smell of gun oil to know what it was.

"Don't give Mrs. Lane any shit, Sanders."

"You think it's my fault your daughter died so you're going to have your goon shoot me? Gives new meaning to 'the butler did it.'"

Texas ground the muzzle of his gun into my head. "Shut up janitor and don't even think about being a funny guy. I hate funny guys. Somebody gave me the chance and I'd cut the nuts off of Lettermen, Leno, all those late night jerks, even off of goddamn Johnny Carson if he hasn't been embalmed and stuck in a fifty thousand dollar casket somewhere. Maybe I'd do it anyway, if I could find the fucker and dig him up. I'd cut George Burns' nuts off if I could, and they's got to be shriveled and dry, old as he was and dead as he is. That's what I think of funny guys. They don't make me laugh."

"What does make you laugh, Texas?" I hadn't finished saying it when I knew I shouldn't have, but he was the kind of man who pushed all my buttons.

I had chided Tiger for inciting the kids in Ducky's and for shooting the Statie the bird, but I had a history that included equally hot-headed behavior. As a boy and a young man I had often gotten into trouble as a result of my explosive temper. The agency had taught me to tamp it down, a necessity in the work I did. I learned to harness it, using it as a tool rather than something that would fly out of control. After leaving I managed to keep it down. I was not about to risk my job at GCC by blowing my stack over the incompetency of the administrators I had to put up with. There's a Zen in concentrating on keeping waste cans empty, blackboards clean, bathrooms tidy and smelling good, floors shiny, in maintaining at least the appearance of order. It's what keeps me calm while I'm working so that I don't get in much trouble on my own. It has allowed me to bury some demons, although they are never buried deep enough.

Texas hit me hard with the gun and pushed me forward until I lost my footing and tripped over a hassock in front of a chair. I fell face down. "Let me show you what makes me laugh. Call me Texas, you piece of shit." Holding the gun in my face, he grabbed me by the back of my belt and turned me over until he had me lying on my back, spread-eagled over the hassock. Grinning, he kicked me hard in the balls. Then he laughed. It was a humorless sound, something an animal might make before leaping upon its prey.

"Randolph, that's enough." Henrietta's voice cut through his laughter. "I think Sanders and myself are ready to have a constructive conversation now." Stupid macho got the better of me. There I was, gasping for breath as a result of the kick in the nuts, my eyes filled with water, feeling like I was going to puke on Henrietta Lane's antique rug. And what do I do? I open my mouth. The same damned big mouth that gets me into bar fights, unless Tiger's mouth does it first. It also has loused up at least one relationship, and gotten me in jail on drunk and disorderly charges more than once since taking my leave of absence. I opened it and choked out what was intended to be a laugh of my own.

"Randolph. Not Randolph Scott for crissakes? That your name, Texas? Randolphfuckingscott?"

My mouth got me another swift one in the nuts.

I heard Henrietta's voice through the ringing in my ears, the rasping of breath in my throat and the sound of groans coming from my big macho mouth.

"That's enough. No more, Randolph. Go to your room. I will be fine. Myself and Sanders have things to discuss and I don't think he's in any shape to present a problem to me. Am I correct, Sanders?"

I managed to nod my head. I just wanted Randolph out of the room, as far away from my crotch as possible.

"You sure, Mrs. Lane?" he asked, the disappointed tone of his words making it clear that he wanted to play with me a bit more.

"Positive."

He gave her a diffident nod and left.

"Have a drink, Sanders," she said and poured wine from the cruet into the empty glass.

Still in pain, I sensed rather than saw her holding a full glass of wine out to me. Taking three deep breaths, I managed to sit up.

"Got any vodka?" I asked.

"The pure potato stuff from Poland. Arnold and myself always believed in going first class. I still do." Putting the wine down, she walked to a glass front liquor cabinet and took out a bottle of Luksusowa vodka. She poured a small tumbler full, handing it to me. I drank it in one gulp.

"The bottle, please." My voice sounded small, pained. She started to pour another tumbler. "No. The bottle."

She passed it to me with a loud *tsk* of disgust. "I might as well have given you a bottle of Popov if you're going to drink it like that."

I drank a long draught from the bottle, took three more deep breaths and then took another one.

"Randolph is quite loyal to myself. He can be far more brutal if I wish. Now, we are going to discuss how you can atone for my daughter's death."

"I told you, I didn't have anything to do with her death." I hoped I didn't sound as though I were whining. I think I did.

"She died. Your mouth to mouth failed."

"I explained that."

She raised a warning finger, cocked and waved it at me. It looked like a stiff white caterpillar. "I'm sure you want to keep this conversation between myself and you. There's no need for Randolph to mediate, is there?"

I shook my head.

"You can make up for your failure, Sanders."

I played her game. Later, I could go to the cops, swear out a complaint against her, assuming the cops would believe anything a Maintainer II at GCC might have to say against a leading citizen like Henrietta Lane. Probably they'd just have a good laugh and then Chief Grover would mention it to Henrietta. Henrietta would tell Randolph, make a few suggestions and I'd have prostrate surgery by foot.

I put my head between my knees, took one more deep breath and looked up, into those ice blue winter eyes. There was no emotion in them. It was like looking into a vast emptiness. "What do you want me to do to atone for your daughter's death?"

She gave me a slight smug nod. "That's better. I want you to nose around. Talk with students. Ask around in the low-life places people like you frequent. Find out who sold my daughter the bad drugs that killed her. Find out and you get to live and you might even keep your job."

"Why me? I'm just a janitor."

She gave me a knowing look. "Sometimes janitors can be useful for more than keeping things clean. People don't notice janitors. You're especially lacking in notability." For a moment I thought there was an undercurrent to what she said, as if she somehow knew more about me than she let on, but I discounted the feeling almost immediately.

"You know it was drugs? Did she have any kind of medical condition?" She sat back down, crossing her legs. The leopard slacks hung from them like drapings around a coffin. "Sure, she had a medical condition. She was a congenital loser." Her voice was thin and cold, as though she were speaking of an acquaintance she mildly disliked. "Flunked out of Wellesley. Flunked out of Elkins Academy before that. Got tossed out of The Reasoner School for offering to sell marijuana to a teacher. Out of Reasoner, for the love of God. Reasoner. That's kindergarten through ninth grade. She was in junior high school when she tried to sell dope to a teacher."

I wondered who Andy's role models were and decided not to broach the subject. Randolph was not that far away.

"Why don't you ask her friends?" It seemed like a simple solution.

Henrietta took a cigarette from one of the silver boxes, put it in an ivory holder and lit it, blowing smoke out her nose. I was surprised it didn't whistle as it came through those puffy slits of nostrils.

"She didn't have any friends. Like I said, she was a loner and a loser. But being a loner and a loser shouldn't kill you. We'd all be dead if death was the result of that."

"I'd be dead at least sixty times over," I said.

She took another deep drag, the cigarette holder cradled in the palm of her hand. "I know you would," she said, giving me a look that said I know more about you than you want people to know. A sudden chill stabbed me, but I kept my mouth shut, and it wasn't because of Randolph.

"We'd all be dead if death was the sure reward for screwing up. She wasn't a bad kid, Sanders. She just managed to louse things for herself more often than not. Then some son-of-a-bitch went and sold her some bad dope and now she's dead. I do not intend to accept such a loss without penalty. People do not get in my way or take what is mine without payment."

"I would guess that dealer's screw up could get him dead." Her smile was grim. "That's none of your affair. It's between myself and whoever sold it to her. You just find out who it was. Now get out of here. Call me by Saturday with a progress report." She wrote a cell phone number on her business card and handed it to me. "Use this number. Be discreet. Don't use my name. Don't use yours if you're smart. I don't much care if you use the dealer's or not."

I put the card in my pocket.

"Leave now, Sanders. We're finished for this evening. You go now." A minute later I was standing on the circular driveway leading up to and away from Llanarch. I looked back at the house. Randolph was standing at a second floor window glaring down at me.

I was baffled. Henrietta's eyes and voice had been cold when she spoke of her daughter, as if she were more angered by the loss of an asset than grieving over her death. I thought of my earlier sense of there being something beneath the surface of her pressing me to find those responsible for her daughter's death. Why she was tapping me for this job when Randolph was clearly comfortable doing her dirty work? What did she know about me, and how did she know it?

I was struck by a deep uneasiness. For nearly a decade I had worked hard at creating my own peace. Eddie Sanders was real, solid. Some might see my life as marginal, a janitor in a community college, living alone in a rented room, driving an aging pickup truck. I didn't give a rat's ass. It was my life, as Willie Nelson sang, and it worked for me, kept me safe.

If Henrietta knew about me others might also know. I got in the truck and sat staring through the windshield, seeing nothing but the clear glass within the sweep of the wipers and the dried carcasses of bugs on the perimeter, trying to convincing myself I was reading too much into her words.

By the time I got the key into the ignition lock, I decided she had put the onus of finding Andy's dealer on me for more practical reasons. I worked at the college where she believed I had enough access to students to nose around and find out who the local dealers were. I had been present when her daughter died, and she was projecting onto me the anger she felt over that death. I turned the key. Right. And I've been in the Valley too long and heard too many pop shrinks theorizing about why people do this and why they do that. Something else was going on. I didn't have a clue what it was, but I knew I would not be comfortable again until I knew. The problem was, once I knew I might be more uncomfortable.

As I drove off, the pickup belching smoke, it occurred to me that since the night before two women had threatened my job and kicked me out of their homes. I did not enjoy Henrietta Lane's use of the motif at all. She wasn't playing a game and she had upped the ante too much.

Chapter Four

Billy Melnick sat alone on his stool at the bar in the Townie, scribbling in his notebook, a mug of dark beer in front of him. It was eleven-thirty and the bartender was washing glasses, putting them away, tightening corks in wine bottles, wiping the bar with a damp cloth, doing all those chores that sent out the message that he wanted to close and get home before midnight. Two people sat in a booth near the rear and a man sat alone at a table by the front window working on a crossword puzzle, a half empty mug of beer next to the newspaper. The place was quiet, the street outside still. A Bela Fleck CD played from speakers scattered around the room. I once asked a friend of mine, a banjo picker into old time southern mountain string band music, what he thought of Fleck's music.

"Damn," he said. "I'd sure as hell like to play the banjo like that, then not do it."

"Writing poetry?" I asked, pointing at Billy's dog-eared notebook and sliding onto a stool next to him. His tall thin body was hunched over the bar, hair pulled back in his unvarying ponytail, his beard just on the respectable side of scraggy. Mark looked discouraged as I ordered pale ale, but smiled and went to the taps and drew me a mug.

"Dude," Billy said, extending his fist for me to poke with my own. "I see you're on your usual stool," I said.

"Damn straight, dude. This is my spot. Ain't nobody sitting in this poet's seat when I'm around. And damn straight I'm working on my poetry, and it's primo Bukelike stuff, man. Read this." He pushed the notebook toward me, almost knocking his beer over. The poem was hand printed in neat block letters, several words crossed out. It was pure Melnick, striving for all he's worth to sound like Bukowski and almost making it in the worst way possible. He read it in a beer inflected tone.

When she read her poetry on stage her clit hardened and she got so wet she was afraid she'd have a spot on the back of her dungarees when she stood to leave and everybody would know what poetry did for her was something no man would understand.

"I mean, it's a little rough man, you know. I can tighten it some more, but it's the real thing, muck around with the lines, you know. I've got six or seven notebooks with stuff like this and I'm getting ready to send the whole batch off to Black Sparrow Press. Now that the Buke's dead someone's got to write raw life stuff, you know, and I've been around, seen enough, done enough. So, what do you think of it?"

"It sounds like you, Billy."

He smiled. "Yeah. And the Buke too?"

"The Buke too." The poem was over the top, crude as only Billy could be crude. Bukowski could make something similar work, but Billy was a bar stool poet, lacking in grace and vision. Still, I was used to humoring him. When he'd been at GCC a few years earlier, he'd been my work-study student. While he worked for me, he turned me on to Bukowski, describing him as a poetry god.

I'm not one for reading poetry anymore. Give me a good novel, maybe a biography or history. Bukowski's work was fun, moving at times. I wasn't reverential like Billy, but the man's poetry did something with language and life that the academic poets dominating the literary journals and poetry readings these days couldn't begin to do. Billy didn't understand much beyond the sex and shit-stains in the poems, but he was a good worker. I gave him the worst toilets to clean. He never complained, and his stories about the Gulf War were amusing.

He was one of those vets who are compelled to talk about the war and will be compelled to talk about it their entire life. He'll be sitting in a corner of a nursing home some day, drooling in his wheelchair, trembling, looking out the window at people coming and going in the parking lot, and he'll be telling war stories, real, imagined, who knows? Who cares? The telling and the listening are what matters. What else are stories for?

"Emily Dickinun inspired the poem," he said. "Emily Dickinson?"

"Never had a dick in her, you know man. I got to thinking about her sitting down there in Amherst writing poems and getting all hot and twitchy in that little room of hers, tickling her clit with the feather on her quill."

"I think they'd stopped using quills by the time Emily Dickinson was writing," I told him.

He waved his hand in the air. "Yeah, so whatever she was tickling it with, and that got me to thinking about this woman I know who writes poetry but doesn't fuck."

"Not with you, you mean?"

"No man, she doesn't fuck, you know. She says she gets horny like everybody, and when it gets bad enough she writes a poem. She says a poem is better than an orgasm. I mean, is that some sick shit, or what?"

"Her poetry any good?"

He shrugged. "I don't know. It's all about her mother and birds and death and shit like that. She got an MFA in writing from U-Mass, if that means anything."

"I don't believe it does."

I hadn't sat next to Billy to talk about poetry. I was hoping that hanging out at the Townie almost every night he might have talked with enough young people to have some ideas about the local drug scene among kids Andy Lane's age and where she might have gotten any bad drugs. I asked him if he knew anything.

His laugh was a long snorting sound ending in a sardonic grin. "Shit, Eddie, you working undercover for the cops now? I thought you were hot for the fire company."

I shook my head. "Cops and I don't mix well. It's a favor. For a friend." I tried imagining Henrietta Lane and I as friends. It was a bit of a stretch, but Billy didn't need any details.

"Shit, man. Some of these kids around here are out of their minds. There's this one guy, twenty-three, four at the most, comes in here and sits at the bar to get shitfaced on beer every night, and he's telling me the other day that half of the kids he knows around here are packing and the cops here don't have a clue. Fifteen and sixteen year old kids wandering up and down the three blocks of downtown, and they've got pistols, knives, stashes of all kinds of dope. It's wiggy, man, what's going down here in this little burg. Makes me shit to think what the cities are like."

"So how do I find out more, like who's dealing bad stuff?" He was quiet for a moment longer than he should have been, his eyes wandering around the room. "I don't have a clue, man. I'm 43, not a hell of a lot younger than you are, just hipper, you know? But as far as those kids on the street are concerned, I'm just another geezer. If I come up to them on the street and ask them that kind of crap they're going to walk on me. I ask them if I can score a little dope and they're going to figure me for a cop." He gave me a knowing look. "Besides, I got better sources for smoke and shit than doing that. You? You're so straight they'd just as soon shoot you as talk, think they're doing you a favor, saving you from Alzheimer's or a heart attack, something like that."

"You're exaggerating."

He turned his palms up. "Little old Graham ain't what it used to be, man, you know. I hear things. I don't know squat, but I do hear some wiggy shit. Like I said, there's this guy that comes in here I was talking about, and maybe another couple kids in their twenties that hang out here sometimes, tell me things. Maybe they're blowing smoke. I don't know. They sound like they know what they're talking about. You need to talk to a kid, if you can find one dumb enough to talk to you. I'm out of the loop. Just another beer swilling poet at the Townie, you know?"

"Thanks," I said. "That tells me something."

He gave me a sad grin that faded into an expression of dejection. He reached over and grabbed my arm. "That's what I am, Eddy, a goddamn loser of a beer swilling poet."

His voice sounded desperate and his eyes were watering. He took a long swallow from his mug. "My life's come to shit, you know that? I mean, I got enough to eat and drink and I write some poems and I got some friends to hang with. Hell, I even got laid last year, but I got nothing, really. I look around at the drunks staggering out of Albie's and Jay's Café and I see guys like me." He grinned. "Albie's that's what those of us in the know call the Prince Albert Bar. Older boozers like them scare the hell out of me, shuffling down the street from bar to bar with faces that look like war zones of the soul. I can't end up like that, Eddie. You know the old fisherman, guy with a nicotine yellow mustache and beard, pants so big he's got to wear suspenders to keep them up, walks around with a pole and basket, goes fishing in the skating pond up in the park?"

I nodded. I had often seen the old man chewing on a cigar as he came back down from the park, no fish slung over his shoulder.

Billy continued. "I was walking up there one day when he was fishing on that little dock they got, and I sat down next to him, asked how it was going. You know what he said? Said he never caught a thing except for a kid's plastic dump truck."

He sighed. It was a wavery, frightened sound. "You know what else? The old guy told me he used to be an artist. Went to art school in New York, had a little studio there, and never sold enough stuff to make it worth shit for him. He started on the juice, now he lives in one of those houses for half crazy old men and spends his life fishing where there aren't any fish."

He signaled Mark for another beer and sat in silence for a full minute before sighing again and looking at me. "That's me. Him, I mean. He's me if I don't do something, find something that'll make me mean more than Billy Melnick, rummy bar guy, odd job guy and poet who's got to read his shit to people in bars because no one else wants to see it. No one else thinks it's worth shit."

He turned away, running his hand over his hair. He grabbed his ponytail, twisted it several times and stared into his beer, running his thumb and forefinger over the condensation on the mug, turning it as he wiped it clean, only to have the moisture reform before he reached his starting point. There was more he might tell me about the scene in town, but I'd spent enough time with Billy to know he was too far gone in self-pity to think beyond himself. It was time to bag it. He wouldn't tell me anything until he was ready, and ready might never come.

§§§

I called Tiger just as soon as I got back to Barton Rooms.

"Shit Eddie, I'm just getting ready to get down to a good session with Dawn. She'll kill me if I don't make it happen. What in the hell do you want? It's after midnight." There was a brief pause. She must have looked at the time. "It's one oh nine. Jesus, Eddie. One oh nine."

"I never noticed you had a digital watch."

"I don't. It's the alarm clock."

"You're in bed?"

"What'd I just say about me and Dawn? Damn straight I'm in bed. She's in bed. We're about to get down to some really serious nibbling. Now go get a life and I'll call you in the morning."

"Actually, I wanted to talk to Chad."

"He's cramming for a math test tomorrow."

"I won't take long. It's important, Tige."

There was a clunk as she set the phone on the night stand. She yelled for Chad to pick up. There was a click. "Yeah," he said.

"It's Eddie Sanders," I said.

"Don't keep him on long. It's a big test." Tiger hung up.

"Hi, Mr. Sanders." Chad was always very polite with me, formal. I think it was because Tiger and I worked together at the college. Like a lot of people, he thinks anyone who works at a college is doing some kind of elevated work. A professor or a Maintainer II, it doesn't matter. We all labor in the vineyards of higher education and are entitled to some respect. And who was I to argue. A guy who'd be called a janitor at the YMCA was a Maintainer at GCC. That may be a measure of some respect. At least it's intended to be.

People who understand the system know better. Public higher education in the Commonwealth of Massachusetts is a poor stepchild to the private colleges and universities, all of which manage to carry enough sway with the Legislature to ensure that public schools offer no real competition to them. The result is a two-tiered system of higher education. The privates have more money than God and can provide all kinds of benefits to their employees, all kinds of perks to their students. They've got state of the art computers and equipment, libraries packed with books and journals, rare scholarly collections, full-time faculty, great campuses and topnotch buildings with the budgets necessary to keep them in good shape.

Students in the publics get the dregs. Funding is mediocre in good budget years. Libraries have to cancel journal subscriptions in bad ones and they can't afford but the barest selections of new books. Then there are the problems brought on by deferred maintenance on everything from buildings to computer systems, leaky roofs, bricks falling out of walls, antiquated equipment and not enough money to keep it running. Harvard spends megamillions to design and build a complex of new buildings; Graham got barely enough funding to throw up an aluminum storage building for classrooms when it had to close down parts of its main building to clean out the asbestos that the Dean of Administration had long insisted wasn't there until it began to flake and he was four years dead from lung cancer. It's been hardscrabble for years, although recently the Commonwealth came up with money to redesign and rebuild the entire center of the main building as part of the asbestos abatement program. Now the college has to scramble to find a way to pay for its maintenance.

In addition, the publics, from the community colleges to the universities, are in danger of being turned into vocational technical institutes and job mills. Even the best intended members of the legislature argue for increased funding on the basis of their potential for training future workers. The privates talk about the importance of education for the individual. The publics are defended in terms of the improved workforce they help build and the income they generate for the communities where they are located.

Over sixty percent of their courses are taught by adjuncts and it's getting worse. There used to be five Maintainers doing the jobs Tiger and I do and we don't get work-study students anymore. Laura Loblolly's one gross and skanky woman, but I'd consider doing lewd things to her if it would get me another Billy Melnick on work study.

Anybody who wants a dramatic look at the difference between the privates and the publics should go up to the Berkshires and drive the five miles between North Adams and Williamstown. The contrast between the Massachusetts College of Liberal Arts and Williams College is infuriating. It's like going from Roxbury to Beacon Hill, the South Bronx to Park Avenue, Harvard to Bunker Hill Community College.

"Tough test coming up? " I asked him.

"Naw. It'll be a piece of cake. Math's easy for me, like breathing or something."

"Easy as football?"

I could hear his soft chuckle. "Yeah. I get to think the same way in both, seeing variables and calculating fast. Music's like that too. Wish I had it so simple in English and Government. But I still have to study for the test. What do you want, Mr. Sanders?"

"Andy Lane," I said. "I've got some questions."

"Pretty tough," he said. "Tigermom said there was something about snakes trying to get out through her eyes." I heard him shiver. "But I didn't know her. Doubt if I ever saw her. The Lanes and people like me travel in different circles. Besides, she's Graham and I'm Yardley Falls."

"From what Tiger said, does it sound to you like Andy got hold of some bad drugs?"

"Anyway," he said.

"So who's dealing around here?"

"Around here or around Graham?"

"Graham."

"You're not looking to score, are you Mr. Sanders?"

"Hardly. Vodka, beer and coffee are my drugs of choice."

"Coach'd banish me to study halls and detentions if he caught me with any booze. Coffee's as far as I go."

"But you're in the loop, right?"

"Kids talk. Why?"

"I was wondering about Andy Lane, what could have killed her, how she might have gotten it, and I don't know how to get that kind of information."

"There's dealers in Graham. Hell, there's dealers everywhere. Guy gets an itch for dope and he'll deal to scratch the itch. If I wanted, I could get just about anything by talking to the guys standing out in front of West County Regional, right there where the school busses come in and load and unload."

I was surprised. West County Regional is as rural as a school can get. It sits on the Highway in the boonies outside of Yardley Falls. There are half a dozen houses nearby and acres of rolling farmland and woods. Norman Rockwell would have creamed his jeans to have had such an idyllic setting in which to paint a New England school.

"Anything?"

"Sure. Smoke, acid, X, heroin, speed, crack and blow. There's always a connection."

"Graham must be rolling in the stuff then?"

"Rolling."

"Where would I start looking?"

There was a long silence on his end. "I don't know, Mr. Sanders, maybe the Walker brothers. What's left of them. Maybe Elmore."

"How do you know this?" I heard the suspicion in my voice. Chad is a good kid. I didn't like thinking of him knowing what I was asking him to tell me.

"Like I said. Kids talk. It's safer to pick stuff up in Graham than to buy it front of the school. Some of the farm boys don't mind scoring there since they don't like going to town anyway, but anyone thinking about the future, college, the military, a halfway decent job, stuff like that, isn't going to take a chance getting busted by the vice-principal for something as stupid as buying dope at school."

"The Walker brothers? You're sure?"

"I'm not sure. I've heard they deal. They can't be the only ones in town, but they'd be a start."

I thanked him. "Get on that math kiddo."

"I'll ace it, no sweat."

§§§

I took a forty-minute shower, the water pouring over me. I still ached from the kicks I'd taken from Henrietta Lane's thug. Shelley would have to give me some time to recover before following through on her threat to talk to Dean Loblolly. The hot water was soothing. I fell asleep for a moment, leaning against the side of the shower stall. I was sliding toward the drain when I caught myself, slapped my face a few times and got out. Last thing I needed was a fall and a concussion. Sore nuts were bad enough.

I dried off and once back in my room I stretched out on my bed, trying to piece something together that would help me make sense out of the day and the things I had learned. I stared at the ceiling, looking for patterns in the cracked plaster, trying not to think about what Henrietta Lane knew about me and how she knew it.

Chad's suggestion that I talk to the Walker brothers seemed like a good start. They were local scavengers and scumbags. Three of them, Percy, Archie and Jack, along with two cousins, Wilfred and Arthur Gagnon, abetted by their mother, Shirley Walker, locked up a local kid in their house. Donny Parker was handcuffed naked to a radiator in one of the bedrooms and they starved him, beat him, sodomized him, burned his testicles with bare electric wires, forced him eat feces and urinated on him, along with a number of other things the cops said were too disgusting to release to the public.

The kid, who died after weeks of torture, was described in the newspaper's daily reports on the crime as mildly retarded, the final indignity heaped on him. The Walkers and Gagnons buried the body in the Ashmont Plains, a flat sandy area across the river from Graham. A couple of dogs dug it up and one of their owners got curious about the bones her mutt was gnawing on the front porch and called the cops who eventually found the remains of Donny's body. The investigation revealed that some of the Walkers' friends and neighbors had taken part in the torture, some of them even spitting on

Donny to amuse and mollify Percy Walker. He'd take visitors up to the second floor and showing the kid off as if he was a new pet, give people a paddle of one-inch lumber and ask them to hit him or do whatever they felt like doing to him.

"Stuff a sock in his mouth first," he was reported as telling one woman who admitted she might have broken Donny's wrist with the paddle. He handed her a filthy sock and watched as she filled the kid's mouth with it, almost choking him to death.

The three Walkers and the Gagnons were convicted of various degrees of murder and manslaughter. Percy was the ringleader. He and his brother Archie got life in Cedar Junction. Shirley got a suspended sentence for her part. Elmore and two younger brothers, John and Jimbo, were never indicted. They lived in another part of town and no one would testify that either of them had been in the house where the Parker kid had been tortured and killed. Like their brothers and cousins they were known stoners, but on this count they were legally clean. The friends and neighbors who joined in on the fun got off by bearing witness against the Walkers and Gagnons.

I called Billy Melnick. He didn't answer and I left a message on his machine asking what he knew about Elmore and drugs.

§§§

I don't remember my dreams from that night, but from my weariness as I woke up, I knew there were many. I was furious. For years my life had been quiet. I cleaned in a college; I liked keeping corners free of the things that gather in them unattended, making sure the lights had bright bulbs, making floors shine each night, removing traces of the day from them. My working world consisted of rest rooms, hallways, classrooms and faculty offices. My contact with people was minimal. It was a manageable life.

Finding the job and keeping it the first few years had not been easy, but it was what I needed. It stopped the memories, suppressed the guilt. I was part of creating order in a place of some intellectual ferment. I wasn't the philosophy professor I once thought I would be, but I wasn't out on the edge. Life was contained. I was safe. I lived in a satisfactory room in a comfortable, adequate town. I didn't need my weapons and they were carefully stashed away. I had no complications beyond the ones I chose.

Now events were intruding on my hard won peace, my simple, ordered life. If I were someone less careful with my words, I'd say it made me want to kill.

Chapter Five

The canoe slipped through the dark waters of Turner's Cove on the Connecticut River. Tiger and I paddled upstream, the river calm, smooth, its surface broken only by our paddles and the occasional leaf floating by. I was in the stern. There was no breeze. In the early morning stillness I took deep breaths, as if I could inhale the deep blue October sky into my body. The small white clouds above seemed to be keeping pace with us. An eagle soared above its aerie, a tangle of twigs high in a pine tree on a small island. I was envious, watching it glide on thermals we couldn't feel. Out on the open river sunlight streamed through the red and gold trees along the banks, turning the dark water brilliant colors which eddied and broke in the wake of our paddles.

I had called her at seven and asked her to meet me at Crewitt's Doughnuts on State Street, one of a dying breed of locally owned and operated doughnuts shops with its own recipes, so much tastier and substantial than the stuff served up by the chains, to say nothing of the boxed things supermarkets sell and call doughnuts. Dawn brought Tiger in and dropped her off. We each bought two containers of coffee and several jelly doughnuts, then hopped in my pickup and headed for the river.

"I get my license back tomorrow," she said as we turned onto the Route 2 by-pass.

"That's a frightening thought."

She shot me the bird and grunted something unintelligible, stuffing a doughnut in her mouth as she did. Ten minutes later we unloaded the canoe and carried it to the river's edge.

I waited until we were in the river paddling toward the middle of the cove before filling her in on my meeting with Henrietta Lane.

"Shit," Tiger said.

"I was hoping for something a little more helpful from you. Definitely something more articulate."

She took a doughnut from the bag and passed it to me. I dipped it into the paper coffee cup I was gripping between my knees. "Henrietta says it's your job and maybe your life if you don't help her?"

"I'm not so worried about the job. She doesn't work for the college. Being on the Foundation gives her some credibility and clout, but not in the area of personnel management. We're State employees with a pretty good contract. The union will bail me out if someone like her goes after my job.

Hell, if the college can't get rid of that idiot secretary in the Registrar's office, they won't be able to can me on some charge trumped up by somebody on the outside."

"The one who's always bitching about being asked to type and take dictation? The one that hates students and refuses to take any orders from faculty? That one?"

"Yeah, Myra Hillborn. She's worthless and the contract keeps them from letting her go."

Tiger lit a cigarette, letting the first blue smoke drift over the water. "That's because Loblolly's too lazy to do the documentation on her."

I smiled and cocked my head. "Whatever. They're not going to fire me."

She clenched the cigarette between her lips as she paddled, smoke writhing around her head. "But her other threat?"

"That bugs the shit out of me. Randolph, her Texas zombie, looks like he's got a lot of kill miles on him."

"You can tell that by looking at someone?"

I nodded, my voice soft, serious. "Sometimes. With practice." She snorted a quick laugh. "And you've got that kind of practice?" I looked at the eagle, swooping, riding the thermals with inborn grace and a lifetime in the wind. I rested my paddle across the gunwales, the gentle rocking on the river soothing. From the other side of the Cove a truck engine echoed as it wound up a hill. A fish broke the surface and disappeared, circles of water spreading out, rippling the reflected autumn colors.

Tiger and I know each other well. She's my closest friend and I'm damned lucky. It just happened. I got a job at the college, she was there and that was it. I'd helped her nurse three broken hearts. Then she met Dawn and told me she was afraid to try again. I egged her on, pointing out that women like Dawn and kids like Chad came along, maybe once in a person's lifetime.

Her good sense and loyalty have bailed me out of trouble several times. She saved my job more than once in the early years when my mouth or ready fist was about to screw things up. But the me she knows is the me who's a Maintainer II at Graham Community College, Eddie Sanders. The me who's her buddy. The me she can count on to drive her back and forth to work when Dawn can't. The me who'll back her up when she's the one to get into a fight for mouthing off in a bar. The me who's there for her when life's cesspools overrun and she's up to her nostrils in it, just as she's there for me. Any other me we've never discussed. She doesn't ask and I've never offered any information.

I rotated the paddle as it lay across the gunwales. Water dripped from its flat end and hit the river. Like the fish, it sent out shimmering concentric circles of reflected reds, yellows and scattered greens. The echoing roar of the truck faded, the silence in the Cove broken only by the occasional white sound of car tires on Route 2. The river gurgled against the side of the canoe. The eagle soared above. Tiger waited for my answer.

I took a deep breath. "I have that kind of practice. Leave it at that."

"So, after all these years, you're a man of mystery." There was a tense, forced playfulness in her voice.

"Sounds like something from a cheap novel, doesn't it?" I licked the sugar coating from my fingers, keeping my voice light, shaping a grin designed to defuse any chance of serious discussion.

She turned, saw it and raised her eyebrows. She got it. "If I was on the beach reading such a trashy book, I'd start digging sand crabs for entertainment. What are we going to do?"

"Me. What am I going to do? This is my problem."

"Yeah, and the kids at Ducky's the other night were my problem. Like I said, asswipe, what are we going to do?"

"I'm nosing around, trying to see what I can find out. That's why I called Chad last night."

"He told me what you asked. I thought it sounded weird. Now I get it. What about you and the English professor?"

"He said maybe the Walkers would be a lead, but I doubt it. They're too marginal and they've been too visible lately."

She laughed, the sound echoing on the quiet river. "Nice shift away from the English Prof, Eddie. Shit, the Walkers are too dumb to know they're marginal and with the brothers and cousins in jail, they're already invisible again. People don't want to remember that they've got slime like those creeps living around them."

I took another bite from the doughnut. It was filled with a seedy raspberry jelly that crunched as I chewed. "I might talk to Elmore, but I'm not sure he can tell me anything useful. You think of any students who might?"

"There's a couple of Goths, some high school stoners, sad, kinda out of phase kids who hang around in the Art wing in the evenings working on some god-awful paintings. I'll sound them out. You'd scare them off. They're used to me. The Goths talk to me about their dances down in Northampton and how their parents don't understand them. They think it'd be cool to have a parent like me." There was a note of self-deprecation in the way she said it.

"Chad knows it's cool," I told her. We were paddling again.

She grunted, but from behind I could see her cheeks puff in a smile. "Elmore might be a help," she said. "He's as marginal as the others because he's a stoner asshole like them ,but he's not stupid. Ignorant, foul, depraved, but canny, you know. I remember him from grade school, confounding the teachers. He was a Walker, but there was something bright about him, something trying to get out."

"Did it?"

"Being a Walker was overwhelming. That's how people treated him, like just another Walker retard. Nobody gave whatever intelligence he had a chance to get out and he didn't know how to do it. It's there though and it could make him dangerous."

"From what I've heard, they're all dangerous."

She laughed. "The others are dangerous because they're stupid and perverted. Elmore's dangerous because he's as much a sicko pervert as they are, and because he's not stupid."

We pulled in on the far shore and tied the canoe to a sapling. A small ledge hung over the water twenty feet above us, the sun full on it. We climbed up. It had a fine view of the Cove and the river below and was sheltered from what little breeze had begun to stir. Except for one canoe on the far side, we had this part of the Connecticut to ourselves.

"Too bad you're not a woman, Eddie," Tiger said as she stretched out on the ledge. "We could have ourselves a fine time up here."

"Hey, you're a woman. I'm a man. That's the Opry House formula."

"Damn shame, hunh?" We were quiet for a while. The river lapped the shore. The eagle rode the thermals. Tiger dropped off to sleep. I watched the eagle playing tag with the clouds, flying free and easily, fearing I was about to be brought to ground. After all these years in Graham my life was threatened with change. I hated the idea. I'd worked too hard, too long to put the past in the past, something left years behind me that would not intrude upon my life. I couldn't bear the idea of letting my history slide in and disrupt it. Now because a street dealer sold the wrong kid dope that killed her, I was at risk of being sucked into the swirl of violence and death. It pissed me off.

I wasn't sure what Henrietta knew or how she knew it. I was sure she knew I was, or had been, more than what I had worked so hard at becoming and that meant she was something other than what she appeared to be. But what? The question ate at me, making impossible an easy rest, like the one Tiger was enjoying on the ledge in the sun.

With a sudden swiftness the eagle swooped and dove toward a tiny islet twenty feet off shore. It disappeared below the low bushes. In seconds I heard the screeching of a creature being torn apart by talons and beak, a frantic, hopeless, high-pitched sound. I shut my eyes, shivering. Minutes later, the eagle rose, flew to its aerie and settled down with its young for a quiet family meal.

Tiger slept through it, basking in the autumn sun, her chest rising and falling with the regularity of her breathing. I envied her. She loved and was loved. She worked hard, did what was expected of her, took care of her friends and was faithful to her beliefs. When her parents grow old and feeble, she'll take care of them as they had taken care of her. She slept as though untroubled.

I smiled. If someone had told me twenty years ago that I would be sitting on a rock ledge overlooking the Connecticut River envying the lifestyle of my best friend, a weight training lesbian, I would have told them they were nuts. I looked over at her, the shadows from the surrounding trees keeping the sun from her face. She looked comfortable. Safe. I loved her.

§§§

Once the canoe was bungeed in the pickup's bed and we were banging down the road toward the college and a long afternoon and evening of brooms, rags and urinals, Tiger said she was playing the open mike at the Townie that night.

"Doesn't start until nine," she told me as we pulled into the employee parking lot. At two o'clock half a dozen cars were still there. Community college students like to get their classes over with early in the day so they can get to jobs, fetch their kids from day-care, do all the daily life chores privileged students at the private colleges don't have to be concerned with. Traffic doesn't pick up again until shortly before evening classes begin at seven.

"We get off at ten and I can be at the Townie by ten-fifteen," she said. "That leaves me plenty of time to do a set. I told Georgie Preston to sign me up as soon as she gets there. That way, maybe I get to play before midnight when the room's almost empty. You want to come?"

"Wouldn't miss it."

Five minutes later I was punched in and headed for my storage closet in the south end of the building. Randolph sat on the hallway bench across from the closet, picking his fingernails with a long bladed knife. When he saw me coming, he sat back, crossed his legs and laid the knife on his upper thigh, his right hand stroking the handle.

I saw at once that it was a Gerber knife, a single edge mini Applegate-Fairbairn, a folding knife designed by Rex Applegate for close quarters combat. With a fourand a half inch double beveled blade, the Applegate has an opening stud on both sides, so right and left-handers can both use it. It's designed to be opened with one hand. A knife like that isn't cheap. The best discount price on it would be over a hundred and seventy bucks. It was built for one purpose. Randolph was serious about his weapons.

Walking past him the way I'd walk past something a dog left on the sidewalk, holding my breath and stepping around him, I unlocked the door and went into my Maintainer II office, a medium sized closet with shelves and cleaning supplies. A dust brush sat on the shelf just to my left. I picked it up by the brush end and turned. He was standing in the doorway, smiling, just as I knew he would be.

"Mrs. Lane don't think you're moving fast enough, janitor. She told me to get some action out of you."

"Smart of you to come to the school instead of ambushing me from an alley, or on a back road. That's more your style. Remind her that she gave me until Saturday."

"She don't need to be reminded of shit and you don't know shit about my style. Gonna teach you a bit about it now, though." He stepped inside, shutting the door behind him. The knife gleamed in the light as he waved it in front of me.

Before he could make a move I had the butt end of the dust brush tight against his windpipe. With my left hand I twisted his wrist. I heard it crack as the knife clattered to the floor by my foot. He wheezed and tried to recover as I kicked it to the rear of the closet. I kneed him in the groin, all the time increasing the pressure of the brush handle against his windpipe. Tears came to his eyes. His breath rasped as he struggled to pull air into his lungs.

"This is my style you useless piece of walking shit," I said, leaning into his face, ensuring that my spittle hit him in the mouth. "You tell Henrietta Lane that I'll do what I said I'd do. Tell her I'm not doing it for her. Maybe for her daughter. Sure as hell for other kids around here who might be in danger of getting their hands on the stuff that killed Andy. After you've told her that, get down on your knees and beg her to send you back to East Cowflop, Texas. Today. I see your ass anywhere near me, near where I work, near where I hang out, and they're going to find what few shreds of it are left floating below the Eagle Falls dam when I'm done with you."

I gave his wrist another twist. He choked back a groan, tried breaking free and got a second, harder knee in the nuts.

"You broke my wrist, asshole. You broke my goddamn wrist." He was whining.

"This is a pretty good time for you to leave my place of work, Randolph. Go dog go." I reached around him, opened the door and pushed him out. Tiger was standing in the hall, her eyes wide.

"Having a little sex in your office?" she asked. "I came to borrow some toilet bowl cleaner and it looks like I interrupted something important."

"Randolph did get screwed," I said. He was leaning against the wall, eyes still tearing, holding his wrist and gasping, half bent over from the pain in his nuts. I understood what he was feeling. I didn't have the slightest twinge of sympathy for him.

"Doesn't look like he got his rocks off," she said.

He forced himself upright. "This isn't over, you mother humping son-of-a-bitch. I'll see you in a fifty-five gallon drum filled with cement before it is. Give me my knife."

"You don't have one anymore," I told him.

He started toward me. I wagged my index finger in his face. He backed off, snarling as he sidled away. "I spit in your mother's milk."

"The man's a little pissed off," Tiger said.

"As am I,' I said, leaning toward Randolph. "East Cowflop, Texas, Randy. Go there with haste. I understand it's very good for your health." Sneering, he shot me the finger as he backed down the hall toward the double doors leading outside and burst through them. The doors slammed behind him.

"My my, such language," Tiger said. "And he's not even a student."

"No. They just talk to their teachers like that when they get anything lower than an A."

"Grade inflation," she said. "I hear it's a major problem at Harvard, too."

§§§

It was Thursday and I looked for Shelley. Her office was locked and her classroom was dark. A printed form from Student Services on the door said class had been canceled due to illness. During my break, I called her. After four rings, her answering machine picked up.

"Too bad," I said after the beep. "Tiger's playing at the Townie's open mike tonight, sometime after ten-thirty, and I thought you might enjoy hearing her. She's good. We could use the time to make plans about where to have dinner tomorrow night." I left her my number.

Counting Dawn, Chad and me, there were about fifteen people at the Townie when Tiger began to sing. Billy Melnick sat at the bar, writing in his notebook. Sam O'Bannion, a local lawyer who ran a fishing camp for kids out on the Green River in Dublin, was there, along with three other men. The rest of the crowd sat at tables surrounding the stage, all with instrument cases scattered on the floor around them. Like most open mikes, this one was performers singing for other performers and a handful of curious drinkers.

She came on the stage dressed in black, like Johnny Cash, her hair combed into a Nineteen Fifties duck's ass. Quickly tuning her Gibson J-200, she put a harp rack around her neck, put a Marine Band harmonic ain it and started to play. Her opening number was *Ring of Fire*. From that she moved into Towns Van Zandt's *Pancho and Lefty*, a long minor chord from the harmonica setting a melancholy mood leading into the first lines.

The line in the song, *now you wear your skin like iron*, always gets me. I poked my forearm as I listened. It didn't feel like the iron it had become years ago. I put my hand in front of my nose, breathed into it and smelled the result. There was no scent of kerosene, nothing a good mint wouldn't cover. Tiger played for at least half an hour, a couple of Emmylou songs, *Boulder to Birmingham* and *My Antonia*, a couple of blues, *St. James Infirmary* and *Troubled in Mind*. She did three of her own compositions, one with lyrics we had collaborated on, and ended with *A Boy Named Sue*. She was in fine voice, clear and lyrical when the song called for it, harsh and raspy if necessary, her preferred style.

Tiger is as fine a singer and instrumentalist as you'll hear anywhere. She could make a good living in folk clubs, bars, the college circuit, if she were willing to put up with the life, moving around, sometimes flying, staying in little no-tell motels and eating in fast food joints. She claimed to be satisfied with a few open mikes and playing after dinner at friends' houses.

When she finished, Sam yelled over and asked if she'd do a few more. There were four other people signed up to play. Not one objected. She did three more numbers to the enthusiastic applause of the other musicians waiting their turns on the stage. One of them, a heavy kid with acne and a banjo told me he'd die happy if he could perform as well as Tiger.

She came back to the table and a skinny blonde girl with Rasta locks took the stage, set an Appalachian dulcimer on her lap and began singing *Barbara Allen* in an off key voice. I know mountain music. She didn't.

Tiger was relishing the attention of the handful of other musicians and hangers on who were patting her on the back, thanking her for singing, encouraging her to do more with her talents.

"I think they liked me." She sat the table and downed half a pint without breathing. Dawn leaned over and kissed her hard.

"You were great, Tigermom," Chad said.

Mark the bartender came over, a pitcher of beer in one hand, gripping the handles of four mugs in the other. He set them down in front of us and looked at Tiger. "The bosses are thinking of making this a regular thing, well sort of regular anyway, you know, do an acoustic folk open mike one Saturday night a month. They've left it up to me to organize. You want to anchor it, sign people up, play the opening set and fill in if there aren't enough performers?"

She ran a hand over her cropped hair. "I don't know," she said. "She'll do it." Dawn, Chad and I spoke in unison.

"Shit, I'll do it," she said. "One Saturday night a month sounds good. Maybe I can find a featured performer for each one. Ed Vadas one month, Joe Lada another, maybe Julia Burrough. There are a lot of good people with bands, in bands, who'd love to do an acoustic solo thing. Plus, the woods are full of great musicians who never play except in front of their wood stoves."

"We can't pay much," Mark told her. "Free beer and food, five bucks for the performers from the cover if we got enough, the balance for you. That okay?"

"Dandy," she said.

I put my arm around her shoulder. "You've got a part time gig, Tige."

"Just like you, Eddie. Maintainers with a mission. Me with my music, you with the fire department. Cool, hunh?"

"Wicked cool," I said.

She looked at me, smiling at my idiom. "So tell me, why do you want to be a fireman?"

"We're fire-fighters these days," I said. "Remember?"

"Shit, like we're not janitors, right?"

"Maybe a little more politically correct than that. There are three women in the department here."

She shrugged. "So, why do you want to be a fire-fighter?"

"Like Vonnegut said, to save lives, to save things."

"Who?" she asked.

"Vonnegut, Kurt Vonnegut. He's a writer."

"He likes firemen, firefighters because?"

"Because they save people's lives."

She nodded again. There were a few long minutes of silence at the table. We drank the beer and listened to the skinny Rasta blonde butcher *Little Mathy Grove* and *Fair Margaret and Sweet William*.

Tiger drained her mug, poured some more from the pitcher and leaned toward me, speaking in a soft tone so Chad and Dawn couldn't hear.

"How about you, Sanders? You save people's lives?"

It sounded like a question. She may have meant it as one, but it wasn't. "Not lately," I said.

Chapter Six

The dream the telephone shattered was more vivid than usual. It was night, three, four a.m. I crept through thick jungle undergrowth, the air redolent with wet tropical earth and vegetation. Exotic birds started and fled as I moved through the bush, the flapping of their wings out of place in the deep blackness of the night.

I came to a village at the edge of a clearing. Studying at a map in the light of a small pocket flash, I located the village leader's home. I moved in stealth around the huts, slitting the throats of several sleeping dogs. When I came to the house, I slipped inside and found him asleep on a mat. I took a piano wire garrote from my pouch. No one heard me. He died without waking, small beads of blood on his neck where the wire cut in.

I was sweating when I picked up the phone. It was ten in the morning. "Dude." It was Billy Melnick. "I have some totally hot shit news for you. I mean stuff that'll knock your socks off, you know."

He asked me to meet him at the Riverside Café, a small breakfast and lunch place on Main Street, a few doors up from Barton Rooms and nowhere near any of the rivers running through Graham.

"What's it about?" I asked.

"You'll see, dude. It's excellent, I guarantee."

He sat in a booth, a cup of coffee and a plate of hot cakes golden brown with maple syrup in front of him. A small white paper bag with a McDonald's logo sat at the end of the table next to the sugar, salt and pepper. I ordered coffee, home fries, a slab of breakfast ham and an English muffin. The Riverside is one of the few remaining places where the home fries are stir-fried on the grill with onions, garlic and green peppers. Most places serve you small deep fried chunks of potatoes and call them home fries.

"Ready?" Billy asked when the waitress had gone.

"Tell me." I leaned forward, resting on my elbows. His eyes widened in excitement.

"Live in a town like Graham your whole life and you know things. Things you don't even know you know, you know. Then, like on top of that, you find out things that surprise the shit out of you. And sometimes you find out that the new things you found out are tied in with the old things you knew and didn't know you knew." He gulped deep breaths between his rapid fire words.

I reached over and patted the back of his hand. "Can you drop the mind twister and make it simple for me?"

He guzzled his coffee, choked, put the cup down and leaned across the booth. He spoke in a near whisper, looking around at people in the nearby booths and at the counter, making sure they didn't hear him. "This is heavy shit, man. Really heavy."

"I've dealt with heavy shit before, Billy." Images from the dream were itching scabs on the surface of my mind.

"Know a guy named Evans Cornell?" He rested his open hand over his upper lip, letting it drop over his mouth, as if people in the Riverside would be trying to read his lips.

I shook my head.

"Lives up on Chancellor Street, by the park, you know. Big white house with a porch, lots of trees, a babe wife who spends the whole day gardening around it in shorts and a tank top. They got a Lexus RX-350 and a Beemer M-6 convertible in the garage, a home on the Cape, another place somewhere in the Virgin Islands. The dude teaches English at Ralston College, goes back and forth to Europe a couple of times a year, mostly to see relatives in Italy. Good dude, you know. He's got five small rental cabins next to the Audubon preserve up on Parsons Hill in Yardley. Four, five years ago he had an ad in the paper looking for someone to help him do maintenance on them, shit like that. I answered it and him and me been working together up there ever since. Dude says working with his hands helps him forget about reading the shit students write."

He tilted his coffee cup back and forth, watching the coffee as it made small brown waves. Taking a deep breath, he looked back up at me.

"We've got pretty close, me and Evans, over the years. He's a down to earth cat, and the Ralston crowd gets pretty hoity-toity for him, you know. I mean, he's brilliant and all that, writes papers and gives lectures and belongs to all kinds of literary societies and stuff, but when he bangs his thumb with a hammer and says 'son-of-a-bitch, that fucking hurts,' it comes out natural, not like there's some stiff-assed prick in the back of his mind using that language just so he can show me he's one of the guys. You know the type I mean, right?"

I nodded. He went on.

"So we go up there to the cabins and work, do some beer, a little smoke. Once I see he's a regular dude, I tell him about my poetry, let him see some of it. Finally, he tells me how the people he works with bore the shit out of him. Not professionally, you know, but personally. He's big into all that academic crap they talk down there, but says he'd rather smoke dope with me, get drunk and work on the cabins or screw around with this old T-Bird he's rebuilding than go to faculty parties and deal with all the political and academic bullshit they all get so revved up about."

He leaned across the table toward me. "It's sad, you know. Dude's got no friends. Me, maybe. I don't mean we're asshole buddies, like we don't go places, do things together except work on his places up there, but we talk and tell jokes, and with the smoke and beer he gets so he trusts me. We got super stoned up there one night, the kind of zonked that you think your brains are leaking brilliance, and he starts talking about how he doesn't really know who in the hell he is."

"Tough place to be," I said.

He nodded. "Yeah, well we're up there listening to jazz, chilling. Dude's got a world-class jazz collection. Almost everything Louis Armstrong recorded, some Ornette Coleman stuff, like *Birds of America.* That's about as wiggy as sound can get. He's got jazz I'll bet not more than a couple of hundred hard-core jazz types know about. Anyway, we're up there stoned out of our gourds one night and I start telling him about Iraq and how a bunch of us were making money over there, dealing smoke and some major horse. There's never been better heroin. He was blown away by how I smuggled shitloads of it back into the States. I lived real good off the bucks I made from selling that shit. Still do. Made some cool investments. Bought Wal-Mart early on, IBM, a couple baby Bells. Not big time, you dig, but enough to keep me from having to finish school and get some kind of nine-to-five gig.

"Evans thinks I'm cool and he's super stoned and drunk on his ass, sure as hell not thinking real clear, and starts telling me all kinds of wild stuff. Says his real name's Edward Corelli, like in the Jersey mob Corellis. Evans Cornell's his cover. For the WASP crowd he hangs around with, them at Ralston College and the other hoity-toity schools around Amherst and Northampton, dudes and dudettes like that, you know. But in real life, he's Eddie Corelli and his old man runs the mob."

"Sounds pretty far-fetched to me," I said.

Billy shook his head. "I believe him. The old man cleaned him up, you know, sent him to private schools, Deerfield Academy, Princeton, Yale, all that shit. People do things like that, Eddie, make up false identities, live under cover, lead a couple of different lives. It's like a cheesy novel. Can you believe such shit really happens?"

"As I said, it sounds far-fetched, but if it's true, you're lucky you're still alive. A man tells you something like that and then starts thinking about it, he could conclude it might be a smart thing for him to have you gone." Billy shrugged. "I thought about that. Woke up the next day and said to myself, whoa, I know shit I'm not supposed to know. He gets to thinking about what he told me and how he shouldn't have, and next thing you know my ass could be real dead. I talked to him about it a couple of days later when we were straight. Dude laughed and said it was like talking to a shrink talking to me about it. Got it off his chest. Said he couldn't ever talk about it to anyone. His family didn't give a shit if he had conflicts, and the Ralston College crowd, hell, there's no way he could say anything to any of them. But me, I'm his buddy. And, besides, like I said, I've told him things about me that I haven't told anybody else, not even you. It's weird, you know, but it's like Evans and me need each other."

"Like priests confessing to each other."

"Exactly, because there's nobody else we can go to with that kind of shit. I don't suppose a straight dude like you can really dig that, right?"

"Probably not," I told him.

He put a wad of hotcakes in his mouth, his chewing loud and wet, maple syrup gumming his mustache. "Now, this is the big thing, Eddie. This is what counts. When Evans was a grad student at Yale he spent the summer of '93 in LA, and one night he went to a reading Bukowski was doing at some club. This was just six or seven months before the Buke died."

"Your poet god."

He leaned forward, his face excited. "And Evans had an old pocket tape recorder in his jacket and recorded the whole thing. It's the only recording of that reading. Bukowski. Can you believe it? An English professor at Ralston and he's into Bukowski? And he's got a recording of him, a recording of Buke reading live. Is that cool, or what?"

"This is big? How is it bigger than what this Evans Cornell has told you about himself?"

"Man, that's squat compared to these recordings, and what's big is that he's kept them all this time."

"There must be lots of recordings of Bukowski reading."

Billy shook his head, his eyes gleaming. "Not this reading, man. There were two sixty-minute recordings with stuff on them that's never been published, a version of "Love Is a Dog from Hell" really different from the one in the book, and some others like that too, well known poems in different versions. This was years after the book came out and Evans says the versions of the poems on the recordings represent a radical shift in the Buke's thinking. Christ, he's all excited about them. You know, it's that scholarly kind of shit English professors love to sit around and talk about."

"Interesting, if you go for that kind of stuff, but what's this got to do with me?"

He barked a nervous laugh, waving his hand sideways. "I'm getting to it, dude. Chill. See, Evans goes to some kind of academic gathering in Atlanta last month and he gets to drinking with this guy from Trenton State and slips up and mentions the recordings to him. Major fuck up, you know?"

"Major," I say, feigning interest in his story.

"Next thing you know, the word's all over down there in Dixie. A bunch of younger professors at the conference are buzzing about the recordings, asking him all kinds of questions. He said the Trenton State dude was salivating every time he saw him, begging Evans to let him hear them." He made that same nervous laugh again. "Shit, I didn't think professors from Ralston would lower themselves to talk to people from Trenton State. Anyway, night before last he's out to dinner with some honey junior English major from Smith and somebody tosses his house. Trashes the place. He said it was a total disaster when they got back there, broken dishes, drawers open and shit thrown all over."

"Cornell takes the junior English major back to his place?" The waitress had brought me my coffee and breakfast. I put a dollop of ketchup on my plate, forked some home fries and swiped them through it. They tasted fine.

Billy grinned. "Yeah. The babe wife's been down in the Virgin Islands sailing with friends. Then she spent a few weeks at their house on St. Whatever. Evans brings the Smithie chick home for a little of the old in/out action, which is nuts, I figure since the wife's due back day after tomorrow, but he lives on the edge, right? But women, dude, from what I know of them they can sniff a strange woman on their husband from a mile away."

"From what I've seen of your life, you don't know much about women." He gave me a quick mean look and shrugged. "Yeah, well anyway, at first he takes it to be a robbery. Looks around and nothing's missing. His wife's jewelry's all there, so's the Flastscreen, DVD, DVR, and the silver. Whoever tossed the place was looking for something specific."

"The recordings."

"Actually they're on CDs now. He transferred them over using his computer and made two copies. He says the tapes were in bad shape, broken in places, crumbling. It was hard making the transfers and the tapes were pretty fucked by the time he finished, but he stored what was left of them and one set of the CDs in a bank safety deposit box, says their only value is to establish provincial or something like that."

"Provenance," I tell him. "It means where something comes from." He shrugs. "Like I give a shit. Anyway, he figures it was the Bukowski recordings they were after, especially since his CD deck was left open and his CD collection was scattered all over the floor. Somebody wants them bad enough to go up against a Corelli, although they don't know he's a Corelli, but they sure as hell want those recordings." He nodded, looking satisfied. "Which they never found, by the way."

"What'd the cops say?"

"This is where it gets super interesting, man. Cornell never calls the cops." I had to smile. Billy was dragging it out, milking the telling for all the drama he could. "I'll bite. What not call the cops? Because of the junior English major? Afraid it'll crop up in the police report that Ms. So-and-so was there and was interviewed by the police and his wife will find out?"

"Jesus no, he sent the chick off in her daddy's Porsche as soon as he saw the inside of his house. He doesn't call the cops because of all the dope he's got stashed in the place, which, incidentally, the tosser never found."

"He's into drugs?"

"Big time. Evans Cornell aka Eddie Corelli, is a major player, laundered by his father's money through prep schools and the Ivy League, teaching at Ralston, living in the ritzy section of Graham, you know, like off the radar screen, and making sure dealers from New Haven to Burlington, Vermont get their supplies and pay their bills. He keeps enough of a stash around so he can use it when he needs it, so he can produce something fast to prove he's on line, if you know what I mean. For seed, shit like that. Cat never touches the stuff himself, except for the smoke, which he likes as much as I do. Plus you gotta do a little smoke if you teach at Ralston. It's part of the cover, you know.

"And he told you all this too?"

Billy nodded. "Like I said, we're each other's father confessors. I mean, besides me he's got nobody to talk to about his real life. Absolutely nobody, man. Can you imagine what that must be like? Talk about being isolated. The babe wife thinks he's Evans Cornell. She's never heard of the Corelli family, except maybe what she reads in the newspapers or sees on TV when one of them gets shot or sent to jail. Shit, she thinks the Graham Garden Club is a tough group. Everybody he works with assumes he's just another ditz-head scholar, which he is. The guy loves libraries and academic journals, research. Lives super schizy, you know, respectable professor, mob executive. Gotta be a trip living like that."

"There are ways of dealing with it," I said. "It's like acting, Billy. You put yourself in the minute, and that's all there is, just the minute. When your friend is Evans Cornell, that's all there is, just Evans Cornell. Eddie Corelli doesn't exist. When he's Eddie Corelli, there isn't any such person as Evans Cornell."

Billy laughed. "Like you know all that kind of shit, hunh?" I took a deep breath. "I read a lot."

"So, Evans knows that what he said is safe with me, that I'll keep it to myself, I mean. He just laughs and says I rat him, he'll rat me for the heroin dealing and all the other stuff I told him. And then he'll have me goat tied, he says."

"Goat tied?" I thought I knew all the permutations of torture and death. "The way he explains it, they lay you on your belly, pull your legs up behind you and tie a wire around your neck and ankles. You fight to keep your legs up, but sooner or later you get tired and got to relax them and when you do you start to choke and you pull them back up. You can't keep them up forever, though." He closed his eyes and shuddered. "He says it's an old Sicilian tradition."

"Lovely," I said.

"Right on, dude. So, you can see that with me, he's safe."

"You told me about him," I said.

"Yeah, but you're cool and besides, he doesn't know I told you, and I did have a good reason for telling you, right?"

"I don't know about that, but I do know how to keep secrets." He nodded, as if he understood. "Anyhow, the night his place gets tossed, he looks around, sees what's going on, figures it out, calls me and gives me the CDs. Tells me to keep them secure."

"You're sure there aren't other copies?"

"There's the broken and fucked up tapes in the safe deposit box, which he says are totally useless. He just kept them proof that he made the recording. Them and the two sets of CDs are it. The dude's a little paranoid and careful. He dumped the computer file, just in case, hides one set god knows where, doesn't even tell me, and wants me to have the other set if somebody finds where he's stashed other one, or if he gets killed."

"Why did he pick you? He's connected. He doesn't need some burned out Gulf War vet barfly from Hicksville, Massachusetts for back up. The Corelli's have heavy hitters."

He ignored the burned out vet bit. "But him and me, we're simpatico, you know. Remember, with his old background, the Corelli shit, I mean, he's never felt comfortable with the Ralston types, puffing their pipes, running out their politically correct bullshit, spending their old money and sipping cocktails in the faculty club. And with his new background, the Evans Cornell scam, Ph.D. from Yale and a house in the uplands here, he doesn't have shit in common with the guys he grew up with. He doesn't dig academic type people, but he loves academic bullshit. He doesn't dig mob type people, but he's tied in with them, depends on them for the money to keep the babe wife and the place in the islands. Plus, he's super-loyal to his old man. Loves the old dude. Jesus, he talks about him like he's some kind of saint." He put a forkful of pancakes in his mouth, his eating sounds louder and wetter than before. I waited for him to continue. He swallowed, took a long sip of coffee and grinned at me.

"Then he meets me. I'm not a gangster and I'm not a WASP, just a polak kid from the Connecticut River valley who's got some tastes like his own. So we bond. I do a little painting for him, some carpentry, plumbing, shit like that, you know, take care of whatever the rental places need. We lift a few, toke up every now and then, talk about poetry and whether or not to fix the roof on one of the cabins. Presto. The cat's got a buddy. Plus, what do mob types give a shit about recordings of poems by some dead drunk out in California?"

"He like your poetry?"

He hunched his shoulders. "A little, I think. I mean, how can you really know? He made some suggestions for revising it, says I got energy with the language, but when you come right down to it, at the bottom, when it comes to literary tastes, he's just another academic. They don't know much more about real poetry than the mobsters, what with all the artsy constipated shit they write for each other, you know?"

"Except that he likes Bukowski."

"Except for that. And I'll bet you he doesn't talk about that to them Ralston professors anymore than he talks about dealing drugs from New Haven to Burlington."

I studied him for a moment. He eyes glittered with excitement. He was still eyeballing the room. Nobody was paying us any attention, except for the waitress who watched our coffee mugs, ready to refill them if necessary. "And why did you want to see me this morning?"

"Two reasons, dude. One, see that paper bag on the table?" I nodded, looking at the torn, grease covered white paper bag with the McDonald's golden arches on it.

"When we leave here, I want you to take it with you. Just act like you'd set it there when you came in, pick it up and walk out with it."

"The CDs?"

"They tossed my place last night while I was at my office in the Townie, writing. I mean they wrecked the place. Broke the back of the toilet, pried up some floorboards, dumped my shit all over the place. Bastards would've turned me upside down and looked inside my asshole if I'da been there." He was smiling broadly, relishing being in on something far larger than what your average Graham drunk might happen upon in several lifetimes.

"Why give them to me?"

He gave me a pretty good imitation of Mickey Rourke doing Bukowski in the movie, *Barfly*. "Dude, it's obvious. You're the last person anyone would expect to have them. You got no connection to Evans Cornell and I'm just a guy you talk to at the Townie from time to time, but somebody out there knows me and Evans hang out up to his cabins and must've figured that I know something about the recordings, me writing poetry and all."

"What you really mean is that nobody's going to suspect that a janitor in a community college might have a Ralston College English professor's recordings of a poetry reading."

"Something like that."

"Just like that," I said. "Just," he said.

"What do you want me to do with them?"

"Hide them, man. I'm telling you, they're like money in the bank. There's already a shit-load of Buke fans around the country who'd orgate just listening to the stuff on those recordings."

"Orgate?"

"Come. Have an orgasm, you know." I laughed and shook my head.

"Anyway, now that Buke's dead, sooner or later the academics'll come out of the woodwork looking for stuff they can use to write dissertations and journal articles on him, a literary cosmetic and formaldehyde job by undertaker-scholars. Could be a gold mine for some poor fuck teaching freshman composition at Trenton State."

"There's a poem in that cosmetic and formaldehyde job," I told him. He sighed, grinning. "Yeah. This is all so cool."

"You love this, don't you, Billy?"

"Love it? Christ, man, it makes me understand that chick I was telling you about, the one that says writing a poem is better then an orgasm. This shit makes me come, Eddie. I haven't had so much fun since the Baker twins."

"The Baker twins?"

"Bobbi and Barbi. One gave me a blowjob while the other was stroking my balls. Then Bobbi fucked me while Barbi sat on my face and wiggled around. Then they switched."

I laughed again. When Billy was my work-study I counted on his outrageous stories to keep me entertained from the time he came on until quitting time. "You're more full of shit than anyone else I know."

He shrugged. "You say so, man."

"So why didn't whoever tossed your place find the recordings?" He laughed. "They were still in my pocket. I forgot to take them out of my jacket when I got home. So I'm sitting here at the Townie and those scumballs are going through my drawers and picking through my shit-stained underwear looking for those CDs and they were in my pocket with me. There's some bucks in those recordings, dude. Serious bucks."

"Okay," I said. "That's one reason for getting me down here this morning. What's the second?"

"Elmore Walker and drugs," he said. I raised my eyebrows.

"If Evans Cornell is ten steps above street dealing, Elmore's one and a half at the most, maybe closer to half. He sits in Albie's, has a couple of stringers out making sure the stuff's on the street, getting sold. His brother, John, coordinates the stringers. If he is just his brother."

"Meaning?"

"Walkers are like rats. They'll do anything, eat anything and fuck anything. You heard about when their old man died?"

I didn't say anything. It had been in *The Graham Enterprise*, our local newspaper, when the Donny Parker murder was big news, but I wanted to hear his version, which I was sure would be more accurate.

"Freddie keels over dead, face down in his mashed potatoes at the dinner table one night." He laughed. "Probably the powdered kind, you know. Ten bucks says Shirley isn't smart enough to peel real potatoes. Anyway, Elmore and the others load the old man into a ratty old Barcalounger they stick in the back of their pickup and drive him around town for one last tour. They stop at Albie's, lift him out of the truck and drape his arms over their shoulders, carry him in, talking to him like he's stone assed drunk so nobody in the place knows he's dead, prop him up a table with a beer in front of him and proceed to get their asses fried on vodka and whiskey. When they're done, they drop him off outside the emergency room and take their sicko perverted Walker asses home."

"The bit about Albie's didn't make the papers."

"That'd be too much for Graham." His broad grin widened. "You know what else they say? They say that Elmore is the father of the two younger brothers, John and Jimbo. Talk about too much for quiet old Graham, Massachusetts. That wasn't in the papers either. Man, can't you just picture him and old Shirley getting it on. I mean, it's like something out of that old *X-Files* TV show. There's other perverts around that'd pay big money for a video of them doing that. Be a show stopper on You Tube."

"You have pictures?"

He laughed. "Shit no. But them Walkers are such twisted sickos, it wouldn't surprise me to hear they had one." He made a fake shudder. "Jesus, I'd rather eat a live rat than fuck Shirley Walker. You ever look at her close up?"

"Don't think I've ever seen her."

"Double ugly. Ugly as blue mud, my mother used to say. Face looks like somebody stuck her head in the garbage disposal. She's got one leg shorter than the other, maybe five or six teeth, skaggy gray hair that's more nicotine yellow than anything. And Elmore's as ugly or uglier and a shit-load meaner. Just thinking of them making the beast's enough to gag a maggot."

"If I want to find out more about the local drug scene, Elmore's the one to talk to, right, and I can find him at Albie's?"

He nodded. "Just remember, he's a dangerous dude. Ugly, crooked, mean, nasty and bad enough to use it all."

"Thanks, Billy." I left a ten on the table and slipped out of the booth. "Dude," Billy says, beckoning to me. "You forgot your bag." I grabbed bag with the CDs and left. Outside, the weather had turned cool, the sky flat, gray, a strong wind from the west stirring dust, cigarette butts, bits of paper and dried street refuse into the air. The grit blew against my face, into my eyes. I felt it on my teeth. Shoving the bag into my pocket, I started down the street toward the Graham Coop, a local health food cooperative and the only grocery store left in the center of town. It's just around the corner from the entrance to Barton Rooms. My eating habits have improved since it opened. I planned to pick up a jar of peanut butter, a loaf of fresh bread and another cup of coffee and go to my room and figure out my next move.

"Dude." I heard Billy's voice from half a block away. I stopped, waited for him to catch up with me, his grin wide enough to split his cheeks. "Want the capper on this?"

"Could I say no and walk away without you following and telling me?" He laughed. It was a pure and genuinely amused sound. "Hell, no. The capper is, Sandy Grover's mother and Shirley Walker's father were brother and sister."

"The police chief and the mother of all Walkers are cousins?"

"Didn't you ever wonder why nothing was done about Donny Parker's disappearing act until he turned up dead over in the plains and the Ashmont cops and the Staties got involved? Maybe Grover didn't know a thing. Maybe he didn't want to know anything. Maybe he's as good a cop as any cop can be. Thing is, I sure as hell wouldn't trust him."

Chapter Seven

You can live in a town for years and never see the people you don't want to see. They move around you like a faint breeze, ragged coats upon sticks. You feel their wake from time to time, but they aren't notable. Someone says to you, "Who was that guy on the bench by the stationery store," you say, "What guy?" You saw the bench. You noticed the two-tone turquoise and white Fifty-two Packard Caribbean convertible in the parking spot next to it, fuzzy dice hanging from the rearview mirror, the bumper sticker, *Buddy, The Bopper and Richie Live Forever,* taped to the rear window, dual glass packs purring as it idles beside the new shiny bright yellow Nissan pickup with the extended cab. But you can't recall the guy on the bench. It's not that he's beneath your notice. If somebody pressed you on it, you'd say that no one is beneath notice. You just didn't notice him. For you, he wasn't there. And more people like him hang out in places you're barely aware of, places you've never been, living their lives on the gray fringes of the reality you've built to contain your life.

The Prince Albert Bar defines the phrase, hole in the wall. A banner, SMOKING IS A CIVIL LIBERTY, hangs over the door where smokers cluster to suck down their cigarettes. One door down from the Riverside, it's in the same building and is one of the centers of activity for Graham's desperate and addicted.

I rubbed my eyes, trying to see in the relative darkness as I walked into the Prince Albert. The bar to my right was lined with thin, gray men and women. All had glasses of hard booze in front of them; several also had bottles of beer. There were neon lights on the walls and over the mirror behind the bar. An ancient pinball machine whirred and rattled at the hands of a bent and wounded looking drunk. The lights, the heat, the country music pumping from a CD player behind the bar, made the place feel almost comfortable. The music was real country, Merle Haggard's latest album. The barflies turned in unison as I entered, didn't recognize me and returned their attention to their glasses and bottles. I saw their faces reflected in the mirror behind the bar, their eyes empty, their expressionless mouths a silent chorus of despair. Except for the neon and the electric guitars on the CD, I might have been walking into a bar in a Fifties cowboy movie. It was nine-thirty in the morning.

"Elmore Walker?" I asked the bartender who looked past me as she dried a half clean glass. Without speaking, she nodded toward a man sitting alone at a table on the far side of the room, his back to the wall. I crossed the room, took a chair opposite him and sat down.

"Who the fuck are you?" He looked up, his hands around a glass of whiskey, his mouth curled in a sneer.

Between thirty-five and forty, he was shorter than I expected, maybe five-seven, five eight, and fat, soft fat, pudge. His face was puffy and white, eyes red rimmed, black hair scraggy, greasy, hanging to his shoulders, streaked with yellowish white. His beard was scruffy, his untrimmed mustache hanging over his upper lip. He stank of whiskey, stale marijuana, tobacco from the cigarette dangling from his thick purple lips in defiance of the nonsmoking law. There was also about him the faint but unmistakable odor of human feces. He had no teeth. Yet there was something coiled within him, something menacing, lethal. Despite his soft pudgy body, he radiated an agile cruelty, ready to strike quickly, dangerously. Ashes fell from the cigarette onto the front of a filthy fleece vest over a tee shirt already gray from previous droppings. He ignored them.

He took a drink, contempt in his voice and eyes. "I said who the fuck are you? You deaf or some kind of retard or asshole?"

"I'm a guy who's going to ask you some questions and wants good answers."

He looked at his glass and raised a finger to the bartender. "You're not deaf, so you're a retard or an asshole. I put my money on asshole." Pulling a switchblade from his vest pocket, he began to clean his fingernails. Thick with fungus, they were yellowed from nicotine and caked with black dirt, which he dug out with the knife and left lying on the tabletop. I thought of Randolph sitting outside my office, cleaning his nails with the Gerber Applegate-Fairborn RX-350.

"Is there a handbook on how to look tough, with a chapter on cleaning fingernails with knives?" I asked.

"Like I said, fuck you," he muttered, not looking up from his task.

I grabbed the hand holding the knife. Its point gouged the quick of the fingernail he was cleaning, drawing blood. He winced, but stayed quiet. His eyes met mine. They were black, almost all iris, rat-like. There was no humanity in them. Elmore Walker was a predator. Billy was right. At least about this Walker. He was a creature who would do anything, eat anything, have sex with anything.

I tightened my grip on his hand. It was streaked with filth. With my free hand, I took his knife, closed it and stuck it in the same pocket that held the Bukowski recordings.

"Take your hands off me you piece of shit and give me my goddamn knife back." His voice was deep, rumbling, quiet. The barflies drank on, oblivious to what was happening at the table. The bartender saw and ignored us. Elmore would not get his drink freshened until I left.

"Elmore, you listen." I held my eyes to his, trying not to gag at the mélange of odors coming from him. "A young woman died Tuesday night. My guess it was from some bad shit she got on the street."

"So? Lots of kids die. You read about it all the time."

"You read? Don't kid me."

He shrugged. "You see that shit on the television all the time. Kid found dead here, another one there. There's goddamn dead kids all over the place, down to Springfield, Holyoke. Who gives a shit? Most of them nothing more than niggers and spics." He paused, something between a sneer and a smile twisting his mouth. "This is a white kid, hunh? Some rich white kid, too. You wouldn't be raising no shit if it was a nigger or spic got iced. Nigger and spic kids die all the time, just like white kids from places like Elkins Street where they ain't got a pot to piss in." His grin was toothless and smug. "You telling me you give a shit about them? You don't give a shit. Niggers, spics, Elkins Street white trash, whatever, you don't give a rat's ass. Know what else? I don't either. Only thing I care about is you in here bothering me. That pisses me off. I don't care shit about no rich white kid dying no more than I do about anybody dying."

I flashed on Henrietta Lane's skimmed milk skin. She was about as white as you can get. Elmore was a wasted stoner drug dealing useless pile of rat scum, but he was right about me. Andy Lane was a white kid whose rich white mother had put a white guy into motion to find out what happened to her.

"Who's the kid?"

"Her name was Andrea Lane."

He laughed. "Sounds like one of them ritzy streets down in the Meadows." He was referring to a section of rich bottomland, the best farmland in town, that had begun giving way to housing developments more than fifty years ago.

I dug my fingernails into his hand. He didn't react.

"I don't know shit about her," he said.

"Maybe not, but you know who's dealing on the streets and what kind of stuff they've got."

"If I knew anybody that was dealing, if I did, they wouldn't be dealing no bad shit, not if they was connected up with me. If I was to have anything to do with dope and shit like that, it'd be top stuff. That's good business. Sell good stuff and people come back for more. Sell bad stuff they don't come back. Sell bad stuff that kills them and they don't come neither. That's bad business." He tried wrenching his hand from my grip. I held tight. "Sell bad stuff that kills the wrong little shit and somebody's gonna send some asshole after whoever sold it to them. That's stupid business. Kind of stupid business that ends up getting the cops involved. I might look stupid, asswipe, but I ain't that stupid."

I released his hand. Tiger had been right about him. He was smarter than he looked and he made sense. "If somebody was selling bad dope it would hurt the business of anybody who had good stuff to sell, that right?"

"Fucking A. Give me my goddamn knife back."

"Later. Maybe. So, Elmore, tell me, who else is selling drugs around here?"

"You crazy? I never said I was selling drugs. If I was selling drugs, was what I said. If. You some kind of undercover cop, some shit like that?"

"I'm just a guy trying to figure out how a kid died."

"And I'm a guy who doesn't give a shit."

"You will if it gets out on the street that the stuff came from your pipeline. Sales'll go flat and people you won't like will come looking for you. And I'm not talking about cops."

"I ain't got no pipeline and no bad shit came from it."

"Where did it come from?"

He shook his head. "Niggers're moving into town. Whyn't you check them out?"

"Black people I know who are moving to town are coming to get away from places where their kids get into trouble. They're looking for a safety zone."

"Bullshit. They're just niggers, and dope and niggers go together like dick and pussy." He laughed at his wit. I grabbed his hand again, twisting his wrist. This time he reacted. "Cut the shit. You're hurting me."

The barflies turned, looked for a moment, then went back to their drinks. "Then tell me something about how Andy Lane scored bad dope."

"Why do you care?"

"Her mother cares."

"Fuck her mother. Fuck you. Fuck everybody. I don't give a shit about the kid and I don't know shit about how she died."

"Find out. Pretend you're trying to protect your product line and find out whose hurting business by dealing bad stuff."

"I got no product line, whatever the hell that is. I sit here and drink and I get money by finding deposit bottles, helping guys deliver cordwood, shit like that."

"Pretend. I'll come by and talk to you tonight to see how good your imagination is. Be here at ten-thirty. You don't want me to come looking for you. Maybe I'll give your knife back if you've got something to say."

I left him there. Out on the street the sun was shining, the air still warm for the end of October. People wandered around, going into stores, chatting with one another. Graham still has a busy, healthy Main Street, anchored by a local department store, the courthouse, a YMCA and a score of small stores and businesses. Several benches were scattered along the sidewalks. They were often filled with the unemployed, the homeless, with kids hanging out. With its population of a little over eighteen thousand and its small business section, the town doesn't look like a city, but it has many urban problems in miniature.

It was a few minutes before ten when I went back to my Barton room to take another shower, washing the stench and touch of Elmore Walker from my body, but try as I did, I couldn't wash away the fact that I had just enlisted his help in finding Andy Lane's dealer. We were partners.

§§§

The phone rang as I was listening to the first of the Bukowski recordings. I am not the enthusiast Billy is, nor do I have any leanings toward literary scholarship, my academic interests were more complex and the quality of the recordings was poor, Bukowski at times drowned out by background noise, but there were at least three poems that knocked my socks off. They were brief, not much longer than a sonnet, one maybe shorter, but they were lyrical, moving, not a one of them touched by the posturing that too frequently obscures Bukowski's generousness of vision. The shortest, *Walking in the Fog with a Crippled Cat Winding about My Legs*, left me breathless, and I resented the intrusion of the phone as I grabbed the receiver.

"Got your message." It was Shelley.

"You okay?" I asked, relieved to hear her voice. I reached over and switched off the CD player. The crippled cat could wait.

She sighed. "Mostly. I haven't slept the last few nights. I keep seeing Andy on the floor, thinking how frightened she must have been."

"I'd've stayed with you, kept you company, if you'd've asked."

"Hey, you kissed off our dinner date." There was a brief note of joviality in her voice. It didn't last. "Besides, I needed to be alone, even though it sucked. I can't get her out of my mind, how gray she was, so damned small. I'd never seen anybody dead like that before. At viewings and funerals, they're all fixed up so they don't look real. They don't look dead like she looked dead. Jesus, she must have been so terrified."

"Not for long. Dying's the only thing we do that once it's over, it's over. You don't have regrets, you don't have residual fears, you're not wounded by it."

"You're a comforting bastard, Sanders."

"You didn't teach last night."

"I didn't want to stand there, pretending to be intelligent, saying insightful things about Flannery O'Connor and the nature of faith when all I'd really be doing would be looking at the spot on the floor where Andy died, knowing that's all the students were doing as well. Faith and fiction seemed irrelevant."

"They're one and the same," I said.

"May be." Her voice was tired, the tone resigned. "You weren't home."

"After you canceled our dinner date, I decided to go to the Buddhist meditation center in Dublin. Stayed there all day and last night. It's overrated. All it did was heighten my awareness of how shitty I felt."

I didn't say the obvious.

She sighed again. When she resumed speaking, it was with a forced change of tone. "So, how was the open mike? Is Tiger any good?"

"Tiger's one of the best. She rivals anyone I've ever heard."

"Why doesn't she do it professionally?" I let her change the subject. "The music industry wants its women performers to look like they just slunk off the pages of a Victoria's Secret catalog. They're supposed to give men erections and make women buy baubles and rags they think will stiffen men's dicks. All Tiger can do is write good songs, sing like there's no tomorrow and play guitar like Doc Watson."

"There must be some kind of venue for her."

"Forget it," I said, ignoring her using the word *venue*. She was an academic, after all. They can say words other people only read. "I've been over this with her for years. She'd rather play around at local open mikes for the fun of it, go to bars where we can get in fights and be Dawn's partner and Chad's other mother. Besides, the Townie signed her on for a once a month gig, running the open mike."

"I want to see you," she said.

I looked at the clock. It was eleven-thirty. "I don't have to be at work for two and a half hours. Want me to come over or do you want to meet somewhere for lunch?"

"I'm at the pay phone in front of the GCC Downtown Campus. I can be at your place in two minutes."

"Room 305. Ring and I'll buzz you up."

I pulled the covers over the single bed, straightened the tops of my dresser and desk, put the recordings in my pocket and tuned the stereo to WFCR, the local public radio station. They were playing Bartok. It was too jarring for what I hoped would be a romantic few hours. I switched to WAMC, public radio in Albany. They had a Mozart violin concerto going.

I left my door ajar and she walked in without knocking.

"Cute about buzzing me up. That door downstairs looks like it hasn't been locked in years."

"It hasn't." I gave her a quick hug and an impersonal peck on the cheek. The kiss I got back was far more personal.

She wore a green sweatshirt emblazoned with the prow of a rowboat, the words *Long Beach Island, New Jersey* underneath it. Her dungarees were baggy, neither new nor faded. A light tan jacket was slung over her shoulders. She tossed her handbag on the desk and flopped in my only chair, arms hanging down, her mouth a straight line.

"You don't look as though you're here for a morning of wild passion," I said.

She didn't smile. "Did I tell you I have a daughter?"

"I don't know much about you at all."

"Marion...Andy's age...lives with her father in upstate New York. She's studying to be a chiropractor."

"You don't see much of her?"

"We don't speak. She believes I sexually abused her."

"Did you?" She stood. "You bastard."

I stepped back, keeping my arms down, my posture and expression neutral. There was a long silence. Outside I heard several trucks pass by. The fire siren blew five times. Shelley didn't move. Then her eyes filled with tears and she relaxed. Wiping her tears on her sleeve she gave me something that was almost a smile.

"You had to ask that, didn't you?"

"You wanted me to." A fire engine roared by, its sirens blaring. She nodded. "I needed to be pissed off at someone."

"I'm good at that, pissing people off."

"I needed company too." I took her hand, giving it a squeeze and she held on, squeezing back. "I'm good at that too, and I'm flattered you came to me, but what about your friends?"

"You're not my friend?"

"I don't know what we are. We aren't lovers. We've had sex, but under pretty unusual circumstances. We haven't exchanged confidences. We don't know much about each other."

"I like what I've seen, so far."

Letting her hand drop, she smiled but said nothing. "Me too."

"Want to go to a Halloween Party?" I blurted the invitation without forethought. "Tiger's having one. It could be a date."

"Sure," she said and frowned. "Costumes?"

"*De rigueur,*" I said. "You've got to come as somebody you aren't." She smiled. For a moment she seemed a lifetime away, reaching back into a half forgotten past. "I can be pretty good at being somebody I'm not."

"Me too. Let's surprise each other." A light laugh that in anyone else might be described as a near giggle rippled from her. "We already have. You know, I do have some good friends. There are a few ex-lovers around, but there's nobody right now and hasn't been for a long time. I came to you because you were there when Andy died. And because what happened afterwards meant something to me."

I sat on the edge of the bed, my back to her, and looked out the window. Main Street was busy. Shoppers went about on foot, got in and out of their cars, stopped and chatted with one another in front of stores and along the sidewalks. Across the way, between a gas station and a law office, I could see the offices of Willey and McClannan, the plate glass windows filled with photographs of properties for sale.

"Loneliness is a funny thing." I didn't know if I was talking to her or to myself. "It creates itself. You don't know you're lonely. You go about what you do and then, boom, realize you've been doing it by yourself. For a long time."

She didn't say anything.

"When something, someone, comes along and makes a dent in your loneliness, it's like anything else that intrudes upon what you've come to think of as normal."

"Why are you talking in the second person?" Her voice was soft, her face sad.

"That's a pretty complex question to be asking a janitor."

"You told me you were a Maintainer II."

"Words," I said. "Words in a contract written by bureaucrats to appease janitors."

"Whatever you are, you're complex."

"Most people are."

"And your verbal fencing is pretty good at parrying any thrusts that threaten to get too close."

"Nice metaphor."

Her response was quick, heated. "Up yours, Eddie Sanders. You've been watching me as long as I've been watching you. What are you going to do about it?"

"I thought we did something the other night." I regretted saying it as the words came out.

She made an exclamation of disgusted impatience.

I swiveled to face her. "Sorry. I'm glad you're here. What's the scoop with your daughter?"

She opened her mouth, as if about to answer, then shut it. Crossing to the window, she looked out at the Main Street scene for a long moment and turned back to me. "I don't know. There was no sexual abuse."

"Her father?"

"No way. I was pregnant at sixteen. He was seventeen. We were from a little town just north of Philadelphia. We got married, because we were expected to. We got divorced because we didn't have anything in common beyond a fertile quickie in the back seat of his father's car. But Ray isn't a bad guy. He's a good father, loves Marion and wouldn't do anything to hurt her."

"Something happened."

She moved from the chair to sit beside me on the bed. "She felt neglected. I left when she was seven. Her father was in graduate school and she needed something to grab his attention."

"He believes her?"

She shrugged. "I don't know. We don't have any contact. I hear about Marion from my sister who talks to his brother. They both live back in the old hometown."

"And this thing with Andy freaks you because you think Marion could be in trouble too."

"It's not rational. Andy flunked out of Wellesley. Marion graduated from Skidmore and is in Chiropractic school. You can't get much further from the drug culture than Chiropractic. It's more that I don't know her. I don't know my daughter, beyond what my sister tells me second hand."

"You don't see her?"

She sucked in her lips and popped them, making the sound of a cork coming out of a wine bottle. "Shit, Ed, I haven't seen Marion since she was eight."

I put my arm around her. She sank against me. A few minutes later we were making love. Afterwards, I held her and she cried until I had to leave for work.

Chapter Eight

"You do manage to get yourself in deep loads of shit." Tiger said when I told her about my conversation with Shelley. "Henrietta Lane's got herself into you. You're mixed up with the Walkers. Shelley Randall's laying her life's problems on you just because you screwed her. Then you go and do her again. I was you I'd take some vacation time and go down to some nice quiet tropical island where they got beaches and cheap rum."

"I used up the last of my vacation time on that fishing trip we took in August. Besides, I don't want to run out on this."

"You didn't tell Shelley about the Lane business?"

"No reason to. It'll be over soon and I can forget it."

It was ten-fifteen. Another week of cleaning toilets, floors and blackboards was over. Tiger, her license restored, had driven to work for the first time. We were in the college parking lot, leaning against the side of my pickup. The weather had turned cold and our breath rose in orange and gray clouds under the amber lights lining the lot.

"We going to see Elmore?" she asked. "I am, at ten-thirty."

"We are."

"I'll drive," I told her.

Ten minutes later we were in the Prince Albert. The place reeked of smoke, stale beer and unwashed bodies. Elmore sat at his table with two other men. Both had the same pudgy stoner look, the greasy hair and thick purple lips and malevolent eyes.

"Get lost," he told them as Tiger and I walked over. They bumped into each other as they headed for stools at the bar.

"Cathy Kelly," Elmore said, looking at Tiger with the facsimile of a smile. You're butt uglier than you were in fourth grade."

She tensed, took a step toward him. "You were still there when I went to junior high, dickhead."

"What've you got for me?" I asked him, my hand on Tiger's arm. "Tommy Finneran, an asshole from Eagle Falls. My brothers say he's been dealing at the college."

"I know him," Tiger said. "He's work-study in the financial aid office."

"You owe me," Elmore said to me. "We'll see," I told him.

"How about my knife?" he asked as I started out.

I turned back, laying it on the table in front of him. "We're even," I said.

§§§

I looked Finneran up in the phone book. He lived on H Street in the Patch section of Eagle Falls, an area of small frame houses by the Connecticut River. It was after eleven when I knocked on his door. From inside I heard the loud deep rumble of music, the heavy bass punctuated by the high-pitched sound of a barking dog. There was no answer and I knocked again.

"No way he'll hear you over that music," Tiger said.

I tried the door. It was unlocked. Opening it, I stuck my head in, calling Finneran's name. There was no answer. We had entered into a narrow hall, the floor scuffed, paint peeling from the walls. There was a living room on one side, a bedroom on the other, the kitchen and a bathroom at the far end. The place was filthy. Newspapers and magazines were scattered on all the floors. A box of cat litter stinking of ammonia had cat turds mounded in it and lying on the floor surrounding it. .

"Something's not right," I said.

"People in Eagle Falls don't leave their doors unlocked," Tiger said. "It's more than that. There's no response to my call, the music's playing and there's no one listening to it. Don't touch anything."

I wiped the doorknob with my shirttail and called Finneran's name again. When there was no answer I moved through the rooms, Tiger following, commenting on the filth and stench. We found Tommy Finneran on a chair in the kitchen, his upper body slumped over the table, the needle that killed him still in his arm. A plastic sandwich bag with white powder lay open by his elbow, spilling over the table.

"We're out of here," I said to Tiger. "You didn't touch anything?" Her voice was weak, uneven. "Not even my crucifix. Looks like Finneran took a dose of the stuff he sold Andy Lane."

"Maybe." I leaned over to get a closer look at Finneran's body. There were small red splotches on his arm, as if someone had squeezed it hard. I backed up against an open drawer next to the sink. There were at least half a dozen more plastic bags of what appeared to be dope in it. I stuck a finger in open bag and tasted it.

"Heroin."

"Pretty neat," Tiger said. "Elmore fingers the guy and when we get to him he's dead with a pile of dope in plain sight."

"You got it," I said. "And we are out of here. Be careful you haven't even shed a hair." I pulled a handful of sheets from a paper town rack on the wall.

I was in the hall, headed for the front door, when I heard a stifled sneeze in the bedroom. I put my finger to my lips, shaking my head at Tiger.

"Let's go," I said, keeping my tone casual. I grasped the doorknob with a paper towel, opened the door and shut it, leaving Tiger and me still inside the hall. We stood in silence by the door, waiting. After a minute or two I heard shuffling footsteps from the bedroom. A girl came out. She was about to scream when she saw us but Tiger grabbed her, muffling her mouth with her hand.

She wasn't more than sixteen, a thin frightened kid with shoulder length hair, colorless, dried and split. Her face was pale, with red acne sores and dark circles under her eyes. She wore a black Brittany Spears tee shirt and a pair of ripped, faded jeans. She was shaking, silent tears rolling down her cheeks, her chin trembling.

"It's okay." Tiger's voice was soft, reassuring, her hand still over the girl's mouth. "You're safe. Understand? We're not going to hurt you. If I let you go, you'll be quiet, right?"

The girl nodded and Tiger released her.

"Tommy." She sank to the floor, her wide eyes looking toward the kitchen. "He's dead." Tiger's voice was still soft. She almost sang the words. "Yeah. They was arguing," the girl said. "Who?" I asked, helping her stand.

She shook her head. "Tommy and somebody. I didn't see who it was. We was in here and I was giving Tommy a blow job so's he get me high, and some guy comes to the door and yells for him. He says for me to wait and went to who it was."

"Did you see?"

She shook her head. "Whoever it was, him and Tommy went into the kitchen and was yelling at each other."

"What about?" I tried to keep my voice as soothing as Tiger's.

The girl shook her head. "I didn't hear nothing but yelling, you know, and Tommy telling whoever it was to go fuck himself. I heard them start in to fighting, you know, throwing things around and hitting each other. I was scared and got down on the floor, between the bed and the wall. Then things got realquiet and aftera while the guy left and I went and saw Tommy in the kitchen and then you come and I hid again. I figured whoever it was that killed Tommy was back and they'd kill me too if they was to find me, you know. I was so scared." She was shivering, her lower lip bleeding from where she was biting it. Tiger got a blanket from the bedroom and wrapped it around her shoulders.

I asked, "You sure you didn't see who was here?"

Her eyes were wide with terror and she shook her head. "That needle, you know, Tommy never did nothing like that. Just smoke and maybe some X. That's what we was going to do after I got him off. Smoke a couple doobies, that's all."

"Tommy wasn't dealing?" I asked.

"Shit no. He was going to college and studying to be an accountant. He just liked to get his cock sucked and do a little smoke. You cops?"

"No," Tiger said. "What's your name?"

"Molly Patnaude. What're you going to do?" Her head was bobbing, eyes wild, darting around the room like a sheep's in a slaughterhouse.

"Get us all out of here," I said. "You don't want anybody to know you were here when Tommy was killed. They know that and they'll come after you." She started to cry. "But I didn't see nothing, you know. I didn't see who it was that Tommy was arguing with, that killed him."

Tiger put her arms around her. "Where do you live, Molly?"

"I crash with friends over on Avenue A. If it's warm, I got a tent in the woods off Route 2."

"What about your parents?" She was smoothing the kid's terrible hair. "My old man's in jail for rape and my mom don't even know who she is no more. The last time I seen her she was downtown dancing under the traffic light across from the library, tossing toilet paper around her head like it was a scarf or something. But Tommy was good to me, you know. I'd suck his cock and he'd get me high and we'd have pizza and sometimes look at a DVD. Sometimes he'd screw me and then I'd get off too, but I could tell he didn't like to do that unless I begged him."

"A real wonderful guy," I said.

"He was okay," she said. "He was as nice to me as anybody's been since my mom went mental, and he was smart ,going to college and all that shit. It was fun making him come, you know. He'd get all stiff all over and moan and say nice things to me and I was the one making it happen, you know? He'd just go out of his head when I did certain things to him. It was cool."

"You do understand that you can't let anybody know you were here tonight?" I said. "Whoever did Tommy will come after you if he finds out you were here."

She ran her fingers through her hair. "With people like me, what's it matter? What've we got, you know? Life's no big deal. Besides, the cops'll find about that Tommy's dead and they'll know I was here."

"They won't know if you don't tell them. So, don't say anything to anybody. You don't say anything and nobody will know you were here."

"I don't tell nobody much. My friends don't give a shit about what I do or where I am. I know how to keep my mouth shut, how to take care of myself. How come you don't want nobody to know you was here?"

"I want to find out who did this to Tommy and I can do that best if no one knows what I already know. You want me to find out who did it too, don't you?"

She nodded. "I guess. I mean, what the hell, there's not many guys who'll get you high and let you watch a movie and give you some pizza for a little blowjob. Tommy was all right as far as guys go."

Tiger laughed, slapping me on the back. "There's hope for this kid, Eddie." Molly looked at her without comprehension. I think Molly didn't ever comprehend much.

We dropped her off on Avenue A in front of the Chinese restaurant. I got out with her and called the police from a pay phone, telling them where they could find a dead Tommy Finneran.

"You sure I can't take you anywhere?" I asked her.

"I'll be all right. Maybe I'll go to a friend's place, maybe I'll go home. "To the woods?"

"I can take care of myself." There was pride in her voice.

I looked at her in the rearview mirror as I pulled out, a skinny kid standing under the streetlight, hands in her pockets.

"There's a lot of kids like her around here," Tiger said. "Strung out parents, strung out kids, they either kill somebody, somebody kills them or else they end up killing themselves one way or another."

I turned my eyes to the road. "So much for the quaint New England with bright autumn leaves and white church spires you see on all the calendars."

"I've heard that heroin's back in style. It's cheaper than ever and stronger, so they say. There was an article in *The Enterprise* about it just the other day." We drove in silence over the deep fast water of the canal running next to the river. It had been built to provide hydropower to the mills and the town. The mills were still there, empty and dark looming buildings between the canal and the river. In spite of those working to create a brighter future, the village designed to be a model factory town was still a model of poverty and despair, encapsulating in miniature the history of the region's industrial past and decaying present.

"I'm going to pay Henrietta Lane a visit," I told Tiger as we crossed the bridge into Graham.

"I thought you were supposed to phone her tomorrow."

"Things are getting complicated. I'm going to tell her what I know right now and go back to being a simple Maintainer II. I'll get a good night's sleep, enjoy the weekend, and maybe she'll think Finneran gave her daughter the dope that killed them both. Maybe she'll think Elmore did it and killed Finneran for cover. I don't give a rat's ass, Tige. She'll get information and she can do whatever she wants to with it."

"You give a big rat's ass, Eddie."

"That's academic. I've walked away from bigger things. I'm walking away from this."

§§§

"This is between myself and you." Henrietta Lane said to me and looked at Tiger who had insisted on coming with me. I had called Henrietta from the car, waking her up. She met us at the door, wearing a flowered robe, which she held at the neck, clutching it around her bony form. She had no intention of inviting us into her house.

"And your goon here." I cocked my head at Randolph who stood off to the side, arms folded over his chest, trying to appear menacing. He looked like a *Mad Magazine* gangster. His wrist was in a fresh white cast.

"I'm his goon," Tiger said, inclining her head at me.

"And my goon can beat the shit out of your goon," I said.

Henrietta shrugged. She lit a cigarette, blowing the smoke through her nostrils, making a faint whistling sound. "Like I care."

Randolph snorted. "Try it, you fat freaking lezzie shit-for-brains piece of crap."

Henrietta glanced at him with contempt. He reddened and looked away. I told her about my meetings with Elmore Walker, his lead to Tommy Finneran and how we found Finneran dead with a needle in his arm. I didn't go into any details, I didn't mention Molly Patnaude and I didn't give her a hint that someone trying to cover ass might have killed Finneran.

"Where did Finneran get the shit?" she asked.

"Who knows? You wanted me to let you know what I could find out. I found all this out and I'm telling you. We're done, Mrs. Lane."

She stared at me, her thin nostrils moving in and out, the sound of her breathing a constant sniffle. "Myself, I think you've just scratched the surface, Sanders, and we're not done by a long shot. If this Finneran sold my Andy the stuff that killed her, he got it from somebody somewhere."

"Everything comes from somebody somewhere else," I said.

She tapped her cigarette ashes on the floor and rubbed them into the carpet with the toe of her slipper. I shivered in the increasing cool of the October air.

"Myself, I don't give two shits if you've got to go to Afghanistan to get to the source. You want to keep on being a breathing janitor, you'll find out." Just before she slammed the door in our faces, I saw Randolph grinning at me, the middle finger of his left hand extended and twitching.

"This is fun," Tiger said as we headed back to my truck. "A ball."

She clapped me on the back. "No, this is fun. This beats the shit out of decking kids in the parking lots of bars."

"This is why I'm a janitor," I said. "Maintainer II," she said.

"Janitor. We're janitors, Tiger. We sweep floors, swab out toilets and urinals, clean blackboards, do scut work like that. It's a quiet job. Things look better and smell better when we've done a day's work. I'm a janitor because I like it when things look better and smell better. I like it even more when things are quiet. I need quiet and I came here to build my life around quiet, and I've had quiet since I came to GCC. I had a nice run of quiet, years of quiet until that kid died in Shelley's classroom Tuesday night. Now, just like a snap of some nasty god's fingers, it's like I never had that quiet. This sucks, Tiger. It sucks in the biggest and worst way."

She didn't say anything until I pulled next to her car in the college parking lot. "I'm sorry, Eddie. I didn't understand. I don't understand."

I took a deep breath and let it out slowly, my head resting against the seat back. "Yeah, I know you didn't. How could you? And you don't have to." I reached over and touched her arm. "It'll be okay. But this is not fun."

§§§

My answering machine was blinking when I got back to the room. I punched the button. It was Shelley.

"Call me as soon as you get this message." There was nothing playful or suggestive in her tone.

She answered on the second ring. "It's me," I said. "I went to Andy Lane's wake this evening."

I didn't say anything. I hadn't known there was a wake and Henrietta hadn't said anything about it when I saw her. After an awkward silence, Shelley continued.

"Everybody who is anybody in Graham was there. The mayor, business people, the college president and deans, most of Town Council, state rep. Tim Ellis and state Senator Jensen. Mrs. Lane was standing next to the coffin, her hand resting on Andy's arm, wearing a sheer black dress that was just on the south side of being appropriate. I went up and told her how sorry I was and she filled her eyes with crocodile tears and began shouting at me, said if I had moved faster Andy would still be alive. It was my fault, she said. Called me a bitch and said I wasn't fit to teach young people. All that in front of President Lewis and Dean Eisner. Talk about who's a bitch."

"You want company? I can come over, or you could come here."

"I'd be lousy company. I just had to vent and you were the only person who'd understand."

"You feel better?"

"Not yet. I'll sleep now, though."

"Call me in the morning. We'll get breakfast somewhere."

"I'd like that." She rang off.

I put on a CD of Doc Watson and his grandson, Richard, playing blues and stretched out on the bed, my shoes still on. It left me empty, listening to Richard trying to play like his father, Merle, who was killed years ago in a tractor accident. He should be playing like Richard. Too often we try to compensate for loss by making others fill holes they can't fill. We should let them dig their own.

Sleep didn't come. After an hour or so of staring at light patterns on the ceiling, I threw on my coat and thumped downstairs and out on Main Street. A police car crept by, the cop looking me over as I stood by the glass door leading up to Barton Rooms. Nothing was open. Walking up to the closed café on the corner, I turned left on Mercer Street and looked through the window into the Prince Albert. It was full, people sitting at the bar drinking, listening to music. Elmore Walker was alone at his table. I walked in, ordered a bottle of Rolling Rock and pouring it into my glass, sat down with him.

"Tommy still alive when you got there?" he asked suppressing a smile.

I looked at him for a long time before replying. He looked back, either impassive or stoned and drunk. "You know," I said.

He nodded. "Got a cousin that's a cop over in Eagle."

"Why did you send me to see him?"

"I thought he'd be able to help you. Tommy knew lots of shit."

"Who killed him?"

"You sound like a cop. Way I hear it, he killed himself. OD'd. Maybe on some of the same bad shit that killed that kid you're so worked up over. Why you asking me?"

"You know." I let the comment hang in the air, hoping it sounded cryptic enough to rattle him into thinking I knew more than I did. He didn't respond. I chugged the beer and left. There was no point in talking to him and I didn't want to sit there smelling him.

I stood on the corner of Main and Mercer, hands jammed into my pockets. The wind had come up. It blew cold dust devils on the street and sidewalks. Small pieces of paper and debris rose in them, swirling up six to ten feet before falling back to the pavement, skittering along the surface like things alive. Across the way St. Andrews church sat next to the Sunoco gas station that abutted Henrietta Lane's real estate office, the church's lawn the only expanse of grass left on Main Street. A mutt was pissing on one of the shrubs planted on either side of the steps leading up to the locked door of the sanctuary. A banner over the door flapping in the wind promised,

CATHOLICS CAN ALWAYS COME HOME!

I headed back to my Barton Room, my footsteps echoing in the empty stairwell. With luck, I'd fall asleep before dawn.

Chapter Nine

Saturday morning things went whacko.

I crawled out of bed at seven-thirty, my head aching like the peak of a three-day hangover. Standing at the single window in my room, I looked down on Main Street, lit with streaks of pale sunlight broken by high fast moving clouds. I picked up my shirt, reaching in the pocket for a pack of cigarettes, tossing it back on the chair with a bemused realization that I hadn't had a ciggie since New Year's Eve in Paris, 1999, when I leaned on the stone sides of the Pont Neuf and looked toward Ile de Cité, Notre Dame huge and dark nearby. I had lit one and took a slow deep drag, knowing it was the last I'd ever smoke. My lungs burned, reinforcing my doctor's admonition to quit, that I was showing all the signs of developing emphysema.

I had resolved to change everything. I'd quit smoking, leave the job and world that seemed to demand the cynicism and danger that went with the work. I took a second deep drag, held the cigarette up, its burning core bright red in the Parisian night. I tossed it, watching the arc of smoldering core against the dark water of the Seine below, and then threw what remained of my last pack. I watched as they hit the water, life swirling around me like the water swirling in the river below. It had taken nearly two more years before I had the courage to walk away from a life that had become intolerable.

I drank several glasses of water, washing down my blood pressure medication and anti-oxidant vitamins, took a quick shower and got dressed. At eight o'clock I was standing at the front door of the Graham Coop. A middle-aged couple sat on the brick and flagstone bench beneath the window, smoking cigarettes and sipping from a bottle of brandy they passed back and forth. As soon as the store opened, I filled my coffee mug and went to the bakery counter where I picked up a fresh baked croissant, a cranberry scone and a bag of ginger cookies. At the checkout counter, I grabbed a copy of the morning's *Enterprise*, rolled it up and stuck it under my arm without looking at it. I paid and walked around the corner to the Barton doorway. My cell phone sat on the dresser, ringing as I walked into my room.

"Dude," Billy Melnick's voice was soft, almost tenuous. "You see the paper this morning?"

"Not yet. I just picked it up and I have to drink my coffee first. No news before coffee."

"You'll want this news. Take a look." He was quiet, waiting for me. I opened the paper, spreading it over the bed. The lead article took up half of the front page.

Bloody Murder Stuns Graham

Ralston College Professor and Wife Brutally Beaten and Slain. Drugs Involved.
By Richard Deane
Enterprise Staff

GRAHAM, Oct. 26. Evans Cornell, Hopkins Professor of English at Ralston College, and his wife, Ariel Winslow Cornell were found murdered early last night at their home on Chancellor Street. The bodies were discovered by a neighbor, Dr. Ira Bradley, who had come to the house to get the Cornells to sign a petition calling for the resignation of Town Councilor Andrew Kosloski who, with his father, local real estate developer Joseph Kosloski, owns many deteriorating buildings in Graham's business district.

"The door was ajar and it opened all the way when I knocked," Bradley explained. "So I walked in, calling Evans' and Ariel's names. There was no answer, but I heard a crackling noise from the kitchen. I went in and found a frying pan of grease about ready to burst into flames. The kitchen was full of smoke. I turned the stove off and opened the windows."

Alarmed, Bradley said he looked around the house and found the Cornell's bodies in the den. He called the police immediately.

"It's the worst thing I've ever seen in Graham," said Police Chief Charles "Sandy" Grover. Their throats were slit. Mr. Cornell was sexually mutilated and Mrs. Cornell had been raped after she was killed. There was blood all over the place, like it had been splattered with a paint sprayer." Chief Grover refused to elaborate further, saying details were being withheld pending investigation by the State Police C-PAC unit.

Chief Grover did confirm Bradley's statement to The Graham Enterprise that large quantities of illegal drugs were found in the room with the bodies.

"There was a pile of marijuana on the desk and envelopes of white powder scattered all over the floor," Bradley told The Graham Enterprise. "I'm a dentist, so I know something about drugs. I tasted a couple of the bags of powder. One of them I didn't recognize, but one was cocaine. I've used dental quality cocaine in my practice," he explained.

According to Bradley, Evans and Ariel Cornell moved to the Chancellor Street address five years ago. "They were good neighbors," he said. "Kept to themselves, yet were friendly if you passed them on the street. I'm sure whoever killed them planted the drugs to distract any investigation. Chancellor Street is not the kind of neighborhood where people sell drugs or get killed because of them."

Chief Grover, when informed by The

Graham Enterprise of Bradley's statement, again declined to comment, repeating that any appropriate reactions from the police would come after the C-PAC investigation was complete.

A spokesperson for Ralston College refused to comment. Several of Cornell's colleagues in the English Department at Ralston expressed shock. "He had great promise," said Professor R. Stanley Higgenbothem. "He was working on a paper discussing imagery of light and darkness in several of Shakepeare's tragedies. This is, clearly, a dark tragedy for Ralston College. Professor Cornell was a rising star here."

"Evans was very quiet about himself," said Sidney Yates, Associate Professor of English. Yates collaborated with Cornell in the writing of a reader for college composition courses. "We had lively discussions about the nature of our work, but Evans always changed the subject when it came around to him. I thought it strange. He never talked about his childhood, his family, or anything of that sort."

Evans Cornell, who earned his Ph.D. at Yale, and Mrs. Cornell, moved to Graham five years ago. Mrs. Cornell is the daughter of Cabot Winslow and Melissa Adams Winslow of Guilford, Vermont, and the granddaughter of Bradford Lord Winslow, a senior partner in the Boston law firm of Cabot, Winslow, Adams and Warren. According to authorities at Ralston College, Evans Cornell's parents died several years ago and their records indicate there are no other immediate family members.

Below, to the left was a five-line article on the death of Thomas J. Finneran of Eagle Falls, due to a drug overdose. Ashmont police, it said, were investigating.

Billy said, "You see that about not being able to contact Evans' family? They'd all shit their pants if they find out who his family is. I tell you man, they must be dancing in the aisles down at *The Enterprise* office. A bloody murder like this is going to sell more newspapers than the debate about letting Wal-Mart come to town, or the new courthouse, or the local elections. It's the best thing for them since the Walker brothers."

"Why were they killed?" I asked.

"Shit, I don't know. Maybe some punks did it, like those kids up in New Hampshire that iced those Dartmouth Profs a few years ago. Shit, maybe some Ralston student was pissed about a grade. Maybe some rival of the Corellis found out about him and decided to send a message." He was quiet for a moment, the hollow sound of electronic space between us on the line. When he spoke again his voice was urgent, excited. "The recordings? Jesus, Eddie, you think somebody wanted the Bukowski recordings?"

"Could be," I said.

"You got them safe, right?"

"They're safe. Don't worry."

He laughed. "It's just poetry, man. Nobody kills over poetry. Hardly nobody reads it, for crissakes. You think somebody'd kill them for it?"

"It bears checking out."

"You're not going to tell the cops?"

"No. We tell the cops and then we'll have to tell them about the recordings and where they are. If the recordings are important, if they're why Evans and his wife were killed, I sure as hell don't want anybody to know I have them. Where did you say the guy was from who Cornell told about the recordings?"

"Trenton State, wherever that is."

"New Jersey," I said. "Trenton's the capitol of New Jersey."

"I knew that, dude. It was a joke. Just because I've never been out of New England, except to train and then go fight for the dear old USA in Middle East, doesn't mean I'm some kind of ignorant shit. So what do we do?"

"You sit tight. I'll check around." "Dude," he said and hung up.

The Cornells could have been killed as a result of any of the scenarios Billy had laid out. The Dartmouth murders by a couple of deranged privileged kids could have inspired some local idiots, even if it was almost ten years later. Students have been known to go whacko over grades, and mob rivals are notorious for their propensity to murder, at least in cheap novels, movies and television shows. Then there was Elmore Walker and his remaining brothers, although I couldn't see any way that Elmore would know Cornell's family was the source of his drugs supply. There were too many layers between them.

Perhaps Henrietta Lane had discovered the Cornell/Corelli connection and taken action to settle accounts over Andy's death. I felt sure Randolph would delight in the opportunity to commit the kind of murder the paper described. There were the same problems about the layers between Cornell and the drugs, but Lane was more sophisticated and would have connections of her own. The hints she had been dropping about me had convinced me of that. And, it could have been the recordings. In today's tight academic marketplace where any full-time teaching jobs, let alone tenure track positions, are scarce, people might resort to all kinds of desperate measures in order to snag a professorship.

I was reading the article in *The Enterprise* for the third time when the phone rang. "That breakfast offer still good?" Shelley sounded tense.

"You all right?"

She hesitated, breathing into the phone. "I want company, that's all. Let's have breakfast."

"Meet me at Michael's Coffee Shop on Main Street."

"Give me half an hour," she said.

While I waited for her, I went to the Graham Savings Bank, rented a safe deposit box and put the recordings in it. I wandered around the farmers market in the town square in front of Town Hall. It was the end of the season, local farmers selling apples, cider and apple products, pies, tarts, sauce. One stand still had tomatoes. Several had colorful bunches of Indian corn and bouquets of dried flowers and weeds. I bought half a gallon of cider, sipping it from the plastic container as I looked at the various wares on sale, schmoozing with farmers and townsfolk. I miss the market when it closes for the season at the end of October. The produce is good, the prices reasonable and shopping there is a social experience, people from all over the area gathering, visiting in the street and filling up with the last fresh fruits and vegetables of the season. Winter in New England is isolating. People cocoon inside their homes. Street life dries up, except for kids and the homeless. The last weeks of the farmers market with its colorful displays and the occasional street musicians who enliven it are like the fall itself, a sweet and sad goodbye to summer.

Thirty minutes later I crossed the street to Michael's. Shelley was sitting at a table, sipping a cup of coffee and reading *The Enterprise*. She looked exhausted.

"I understand there's an opening in the English department at Ralston," I said, pointing at the article in the paper.

She slammed it on the table and flashed me an angry look. "That was a shitty thing to say." She wasn't joking. Her voice was flat, her face grim as she picked the paper up, folded it and set it back on the table. Taking a deep breath, she relaxed her mouth into something resembling a smile. "Besides, if you've ever taught at a community college, places like Ralston won't even interview you. You won't bring the proper class perspective to their golden children."

I sat down with her, sipping from my cider jug. "You look beautiful," I said.

She touched her hair. "After last night, I had to do something, so I washed my hair and put on some make-up. I don't wear it often since I moved to New England."

"It's not the make-up. You're just flat out beautiful."

She gave me a weak smile with her lips. Her eyes looked as though they'd never smile again. "You look pretty good yourself."

Outside, a police car went by, sirens screeching. A moment later, a second and third tore down the street, followed by an ambulance.

"Graham's finest are busier than usual," she said.

"It's good for them. It's easy to get stale in a town like this."

"Tell me about it. I was positively moldy until Tuesday night. I guess in some weird way, I'm grateful to Andy Lane." Her voice broke and she looked stricken. "I didn't mean that the way it sounded. I'm not a horrible person, you know."

"Do you have a computer with an internet connection? " I asked her. She looked startled. "That wasn't the kind of reaction I expected."

"Sorry. My mind's a thousand places at once. Do you have one?"

"Of course. Doesn't almost everyone?"

"I don't. I need to use yours."

§§§

I typed *Trenton State* into the Google search line. It came up on the list as the College of New Jersey at Trenton. With a few more clicks I was at the faculty/staff directory. It was arranged alphabetically with no filters for position or work area. I went to the S section on the off chance there might be someone in the English department with the same last name as mine and I could play the name game as a way in. There was one Sanders, but he taught art. There was a Ramon Sanchez in security, but my experience is that campus security people are a suspicious and officious lot. Frustrated with their lack of police authority, they carry holsters loaded with Mace, swagger around campuses wearing phony cop suits and are not prone to helping strangers wend their ways about the buildings and institutions they are charged with keeping secure.

Two people in the S section taught English, a Melanie Stevens and an Edmund Sutton. I called Sutton's office and was surprised when he answered. I told him I was from Graham Community College in Massachusetts. Did his department have a literary magazine, I asked. I lucked out. He assumed I was a faculty member at GCC and started commiserating with me about the lack of preparedness on the part of writing students these days.

"They don't read, they don't write and they can't think in a linear fashion." He had a deep voice, and spoke in a stiffly cultured manner, the style that says *eyether* instead of *eeether*, *neyether* for *neether*.

I affected a sympathetic tone and led him on. "Or if they do read, it isn't Yeats and Eliot, or even Shakespeare and the classics. They go for the moronic. The poetry of Jim Morrison. Dylan. Tom Waits. Or worse. Charles Bukowski."

"Oh god," he moaned into the phone. "We have an adjunct here who's trying to get the department to sponsor a Bukowski festival, replete with readings from his work, and a contest for young poets. As soon as he made the suggestion I went down to Barnes and Noble and looked at the man's poetry. I was disgusted. It's a nightmare, Professor Sanders. People don't take us seriously as it is. Too many of them remember when we were Trenton State Teachers College and thought we were getting uppity to change our name to Trenton State College. Now that we're called the College of New Jersey at Trenton, we have to prove ourselves worthy of such rhetoric. I've been here thirty-seven years and it has been a thirty-seven year struggle to convince people that we are a respectable academic institution. But you would understand that, teaching at a community college. We used to call them academic Siberia. A Bukowski festival would play right into the hands of those who say we're a third rate institution."

"You think the department will sponsor the festival?"

"God knows." He sighed the words. "There is no literary judgment anymore. The idea of a standard literary canon is obsolete. They'll study anybody today, these young professors with their earrings and tattoos. A woman in the department wants to offer a course in Madonna as a cultural icon. How do you make a literature course out of that? I doubt that she's ever read Hemingway or Faulkner." His voice was filled with pompous indignation. "Next thing you know somebody will want to be studying the poetics of rap music. There just aren't any standards left. It's tragic."

"Is the Madonna scholar the person who wants to do the Bukowski thing?" There was an impatient insuck of breath on his end of the line. "Gracious no. That's Gideon Moss. Gid, as he tells his students to call him. Were he not related to a state senator, he'd be out of here in a moment, I assure you."

I jotted down the name. "Moss," I said, leading him on. "Sounds familiar. Would he have been at the MLA convention last spring?"

Sutton laughed. "We're under funded, you know. The state doesn't see the importance of public colleges."

"I understand," I said, but he talked over me.

"We're strapped to the bone and still the department chair spends professional development money to send these adjuncts off to conferences. And, of course, they all want to go, network, and try to find full time jobs. Moss takes every possible advantage of the school's largess."

"I suppose that means you don't have a literary magazine," I said, bringing the conversation to an end with my cover for calling.

"Not even a literary brochure," he said.

§§§

"What in the hell is going on?" Shelley asked as I hung up.

I told her about Henrietta's blackmail, what Billy Melnick had told me about Evans Cornell's background, the Bukowski recordings, the suspicious nature of Tommy Finneran's death. I concluded by telling her about Gideon

Moss. I expected her to be overwhelmed or outraged that I hadn't confided in her earlier.

She blanched, turned ashen, then red, as though processing a thousand different pieces of information and emotions. In seconds it passed.

"Interesting." Her voice was composed and calm. I had underestimated her. I thought she would be horrified and surprised. Instead, she seemed intrigued and energized. "You think this Moss might be involved in the Cornell murders?"

"I don't know. Could be. Then it could be Henrietta, or it could be unrelated. And there's Tommy Finneran. I'm sure he didn't overdose on his own."

"What about you?" she asked. "What about me?"

"Why do you care? You've told Henrietta everything you know. She's got a big mouth, but I don't think she's a real threat to you. The college isn't going to fire you, even if they wanted to, just to please her. You've got union support."

"Habit. I thought I'd broken it years ago, but habits have a way of surprising you. Just when you've forgotten you ever had one, it can sneak up and your pulse is thumping like a herd of kangaroos." I told her about feeling around for the pack of cigarettes.

She gave me a wry smile. "Getting involved in something like this and wanting to see it through is a strange habit for a Maintainer II."

My reply was quick and dismissive. "I wasn't always a janitor. I've enough of academic training to see the need of getting to the bottom of things. It was a flaccid response. Before she could say anything I typed *Evans Cornell* into the search window.

Three entries popped up. Cornell had written an article discussing reasons for rejecting the theory that Edward Devere wrote the plays attributed to Shakespeare. There was a second article on late Nineteenth Century influences on Ferlinghetti. The third was on sex and death in the late work of Charles Bukowski. It had been published the month before. I typed in *Edward Corelli*. Nothing specific came up but there were a number of hits on the last name.

Traffic on Main Street in Graham was jammed up all the way to the Post Office, three blocks from my room. A huge plume of thick black smoke twisted and rose from the far end. I turned left on Harris Street, which runs between the courthouse and a Unitarian church, and parked in the courthouse lot. As we walked down Main the air thickened with smoke. Shelley was coughing, my eyes tearing, as we made our way through down the street. A block from Barton rooms, fire trucks were everywhere, their hoses snaking over curbs and around trees.

I felt an old rush. I was needed there. If I had been home when the call came, I'd be working now, running hoses, operating the pumps, perhaps going into a burning building, using reflexes too long dormant. We passed the World Bookshop and I could see flames leaping from the roof and upper windows of Willey and McClannan. A crowd stood on the far side the street, gawking at the fire.

"What happened?" I asked Lefty McCort, who lived a floor above me at Barton.

"Bomb," he said. "Had to be. I was coming down the stairs when I heard it. BaBOOM." He threw his arms up and apart in imitation of an explosion. "One big BaBOOM, and there was glass and bricks and all kinds of crap blowing all over the place. Wrecked up a few cars. Blew the door off our place, you know. Anybody could go up there and steal whatever they want from us. Jesus Christ, Eddie. This is something else. Who'da thought in Graham? Arab terrorists, that's what it's got to be. The towel headed bastards are everywhere, you know. Nine-Eleven was just the beginning."

Henrietta's building was totaled. The firefighters were concentrating on saving St. Andrews Church and keeping the Sunoco station from blowing.

"Any injuries?" I asked Randy Leblanc, one of the firefighters, as he ran by. "Don't know," he said, out of breath. He was too heavy to be rushing around the way he was. "Somebody said Mrs. Lane and several other people were inside, one of the insurance guys it was, I think. If she was in there it doesn't look good, Eddie. We haven't been able to bring anybody out."

I felt a hand on my shoulder.

"Dude," Billy Melnick said. "Graham is jumping, hunh? First Evans and his wife, then Elmore, now this."

"What about Elmore?" I said.

"Shot, man. Someone shot him. I heard it on my scanner about an hour, hour and a half ago. A guy in a ski mask walked into Albie's, came up to his table and shot him five or six times. I saw Jimbo a few minutes ago, watching the fire, you know, and he said the dude just walked out and ran down the street, calm as you could be."

"Elmore dead?"

"You shoot into a bucket of shit and it doesn't kill it, right? Elmore's lucky he stinks so bad."

Before I could respond, a fuel tank exploded, flames, smoke and debris spewing everywhere. People ran up and down the street, screaming. A chunk of concrete and bricks flew overhead and crashed through the window into my room.

"That does it," I said. "Now I'm pissed off."

Book Two

Chapter Ten

Using a pay phone outside the College's downtown campus, I reached a 900 number voice mail promising the greatest orgasm since Cleopatra did Caesar. To enter this sexual paradise, all I had to do was key in a credit card number and press the pound sign. I entered a dummy number I hadn't used it in the nearly ten years since leaving the agency, but still had fixed in my mind. A live operator came on the line. I gave her another long unused number. After several more calls and dummy phone drops, the pay phone rang.

The still familiar voice, both authoritative and taunting, sounded the same, assured, in control, as commanding and resonant as ever.

"It's been a long time. If I remember our last conversation, I told you not to call me, that I'd call you."

"I got tired of waiting," I said. "Tell me, if I'd given the operator a real credit card number, what would I have gotten?"

"I doubt you're simply tired of waiting for me. I believe it goes deeper than that, my boy." He laughed. "And, a valid credit card would have gotten you some spectacular phone sex."

"I have an unusual situation," I told him. "You're tired of cleaning toilets?"

"Hardly. I like that better than I liked cleaning up the messes I mucked around in when I worked with your people."

"Things have progressed mightily since you left us shortly after September 11th. Our mission has become increasingly clear."

"Maybe. From what I read in the press, there seem to be a lot of ambiguities."

"Your problem has always been trying to see all sides of an issue. It's not a constructive way to go about our work. It's why you're a janitor."

"I've done far worse acting on your instructions."

"You didn't call me to insult the agency." The voice was impatient, annoyed.

"I need information."

"We've been good to you, Eddie." He spoke with a soft chuckle. "Interesting, isn't it? Even I have come to think of you as Edward Sanders. We've ignored you. We've let you live your janitor's life in the boonies, have your little room above Main Street. We've been very good to you. Not all our former employees live so well." The voice paused just long enough to give emphasis to what followed. "You lived. Why should we do anything more?"

"Out of gratitude for what a fine employee I was."

"Go on." The voice was neutral, uncommitted. There was no trace of threat, no trace of condescension, no trace of interest. Just a flat, *go on*. His face would be as unreadable. In my few direct dealings with him over my years with the agency, I found him expert at conveying nothing, as if his mind was free of judgment, a void where information was processed, policy absorbed and put into action. People were never terminated, either them or us, with animosity. Everything he did, everything he authorized, was the result of a logical process based on the premise of what was best for the agency. Of course, what was best for the agency was always what was best for the country. People like him have to think that way to survive their consciences.

"There were a couple of murders here last night," I told him. A Ralston College professor and his wife, Evans Cornell."

"You mean Edward Corelli." The voice was smug. "We've been watching him. And Eddie, thank you for calling on a pay phone. They are much more secure than home phones and cells. I'm glad you haven't forgotten what we taught you."

I took an involuntary insuck of breath. I had forgotten how much they knew, how deep and far their tentacles went and how fast they went there.

"Why were you watching Corelli?"

"I don't owe you that information, Eddie. I don't owe you any information at all. I didn't even owe you this phone call."

I felt like a kid being put down by a parent. That's how they kept us in line. They recruited intelligent, resourceful, insecure people and played on all those qualities. Intelligence and resourcefulness were essential to doing the work they needed done. Insecurity was necessary to keep us in line, to ensure our loyalty. From time to time one or another of us would grow up and try to walk away. On rare occasions we were left alone, left alive.

"Who killed Corelli?"

"We haven't been watching him that closely. Our priorities have shifted since Nine-Eleven, Eddie. The mob and its drugs and murders kept us funded and occupied after the Soviets collapsed, but they're pretty small stuff compared to international terrorism, wouldn't you agree?"

"The clash of civilizations," I said. "That was the last thing you spoke of in Baku."

"I'm flattered you remember. However, we are, I am, very busy, Eddie. What do you want?"

"No ideas on the Corelli murders?"

He exhaled, rattling his lips as he did. "Operations believe it was mob related, that the blacks and the Hispanics, probably the Russians too, are looking at the territory the Corelli's control. The trade from New Haven to Burlington and on up to Montreal is increasingly lucrative. Things have changed in Norman Rockwell country. It's not all about town meetings, country schools county fairs and Labor Day parades. It's not even about boffing sheep and cows anymore. Those bucolic folk you live and work among are looking for other sweets and the drug traders are ready to supply them."

"There's more to life here than that."

"Rural New England is in the midst of its own clash of civilizations, Eddie.' It's long on landscape and short on the things that keep young people interested in life. They see violence and drugs and glamour all mixed up together in the movies and on television, next thing you know, they feel that they're missing something. The Corellis gave them something to fill the void. With Eddie Corelli gone other players will be trying to move in on part of the market, maybe the whole market."

"The Evans Cornell identity was pretty deep cover for a Corelli. He bought into it so much that he believed in the academic world."

"That didn't stop him from being daddy's little boy and doing daddy's work along with his own. Some people understand the virtues of loyalty to their own kind." His tone was pointed, injured. I ignored it.

"You told me what the people at Operations think. What do you think?"

He sighed into the receiver. There was a squeaking sound and I pictured him reclining in a desk chair, a telephone tucked between his cheek and shoulder, his white hair and chiseled face set off against mahogany paneling in an the office somewhere in the world, although I'd never seen his office, only imagined it. For all I knew he could be in the field somewhere, the Arabian Desert, an African savannah, anyplace his kind worked to advance capitalism's interests.

He cleared his throat. "I'm not sure what to think. Operations could be right. It could also be something else. Something we don't have a clue about."

"Why?"

"You're right about Corelli's deep cover. It goes back to toney New England private schools, Eaglebrook, the Bement School, prep school at Deerfield Academy, then on to university studies at Amherst, graduate school at Yale and his job at Ralston right next door to Amherst and Smith. He had impeccable academic credentials and relationships. His wife comes from a wealthy WASP background, although her parents live in the boonies in

Vermont, part of the old hippie establishment up there. Trenton is a long way from all of that. A long way and a lifetime different. I don't see how the blacks and Hispanics, the Russians could have cracked that cover. A rival Italian gang, maybe. But that kind of information doesn't cross ethnic lines easily."

Trenton was a red flag, waving wildly at me. "The Corellis are from Trenton?"

"It's home base and they exemplify the old American success story. Small city thugs make good, you know. The old man put the New York and north Jersey folks to shame. Put a lot of them in the ground, too. His grandchildren, if he has any, will be governors, Senators, maybe a President. It's happened before."

"The name Gideon Moss mean anything you?"

"Nada. Does it to you?"

"I'm not sure."

"If it does, let me know. The mob may be low priority, but it's still on our list, Eddie."

"That's it? After all these years I call you for help, you tell me nothing and end up asking me to give you any information I dig up."

"Doesn't seem fair, does it?" I could hear the ironic smile in his voice. "Were you ever fair?"

"Often. You are alive and well up there in Graham, right?" He sighed again, prelude to another of his trademark charged pauses. "There's a Corelli sister, Angela, also goes by the name of Cornell, Sylvia Cornell. She lives across the river from Trenton, in a little town called Newtown. She's a stock analyst for the Bucks County Bank and Trust Company there. We believe she's a sleeper. Cornell's good cover for her there. It's an old Bucks County name, with particular resonance in Newtown."

"What don't you know?" I asked.

"How things will turn out without the agency making them happen. I worry about that, Eddie. The agency's a major player, an important one to the Nation's security, and I'm getting old."

"You'll live forever." The old cliché was easy and glib. I regretted it immediately, knowing better than to belittle anyone's sense of mortality, and knowing well never to challenge the Director.

"Don't be an idiot. I'm an old man and not very well. You were my hope for the agency's future."

"That's a future you never mentioned to me and one I never considered; one I do not want, and one I would never accept."

"Remember Sean Connery's final James Bond film?" 'No."

"Never Say Never. Trite, but often accurate." I cut him off. "Thanks for telling me about the Corelli sister."

"Why are you looking in to such dark corners, Eddie?"

"Because I have to." He chuckled. When he spoke again there was hesitation in his voice. "One other thing. There's another sister. Gina. We don't know where she is or what sort of cover she's working under. We don't even know if she is working under cover. She may just have wanted out and disappeared on her own terms."

"You can't find her? I thought you guys were infallible."

"We're superb, but not perfect. She's forty-two and she disappeared from our radar years ago. It's a bit of an embarrassment."

"So she went missing about the same time Evans turned up at Ralston?" He mumbled agreement. "She went to the Caribbean, Tortola, in the British Virgin Islands. We know she sailed out on a charter boat, *Jolly Mon*, as a cook. She disappeared when they tied up on Nevis. It's easy to disappear down there. She could have signed on with another boat, screwed her way on to a yacht or flown off in somebody's private jet, done any of a thousand things we can't trace. People in the islands don't care about names, or where somebody came from. All that matters is what you can do for them and with them at the moment you happen to be sharing earth space with them. It's as easy to launder your identity in the islands as it is to launder your money, and it requires a lot less effort than doing it through exclusive prep schools, Princeton and Yale."

I thanked him again.

"It's always a pleasure to talk to you my boy. You were one of our most useful employees. If the agency needs anything, or I have any information that might be beneficial for both of us if you had it, I'll contact you. Be careful Nathan."

He hung up before I could reply, the name hanging in the air like an icy knife poised over my heart.

§§§

Elmore Walker's room at County Medical Center was under twenty-four hour guard. Two cops stood in the hallway on either side of the door, one paging through a *People* magazine, the other looking toward the vacant nursing station with an absent stare. A third sat on a chair inside the room eating French fries from a Wendy's bag. They recognized me, knew I was an on-call firefighter and didn't even try to stop me as I walked past them. Elmore was watching a U-Mass football game on television. His head was covered with bandages, his face bruised and covered with dried blood. An IV line ran into his right arm. A tray of food sat on the table beside the bed.

"Great fucking town." He grinned as I pulled up a chair to the side of the bed and sat down. Pointing at the cop on the chair, he said, "Last year these guys busted my brothers and cousins, hell they busted my mother, and today they're guarding my life. I mean, is this a fine democracy, or what?"

"Who did it, Elmore?"

"I don't know," he said. "Bastard comes in, blasts me, kicks me a couple times and runs out. Didn't even stay to see if I was dead. Shit, I oughta thank him. I got food, TV, bodyguards, good looking cooze checking in on me, changing my bandages, wiping my ass, all that kind of good stuff. Hell, they even give me dynamite dope for the pain. Beats the hell out of the shitbox I live in." He grinned again. "Man, I ought to pay people to shoot me from now on."

"And you don't know who did it, or why anybody would?"

"You shitting me, man? There's tons of assholes who'd like to see me dead. The family of that retard my brothers did has about a dozen of them and they can't be any smarter than he was. I mean, shit, look at me. I took a bullet, maybe two, got the shit kicked out of me, and here I am, living high. Them fucking Parkers don't believe I had nothing to do with that Donny crap. They're sure I pissed on the little fuck, backhanded him a couple of times, maybe even cornholed him when he was chained over that radiator. They don't know nothing but that don't stop them from believing that kind of shit."

"That's the nature of faith," I said. "The source of the world's problems." He wrinkled his face at me. "What you talking about?"

"Nothing, just trying to piece things together."

"Piece them together somewhere else, okay. I don't want you here unless you know who did this to me."

"What about Tommy Finneran's people? They pissed at you?" He sneered at me and glanced at the cop by the door. He was too busy stuffing fries into his mouth and watching the football game to pay any attention to our conversation. "Why would they be?"

"I'm just throwing out possibilities."

"Yeah, well just throw your ass out of here." He pointed the remote at the television, raised the volume and stared at the screen. I stood by his bed for a bit, then left. The cops outside the door had gotten chairs and were sitting. The one who had been staring at the nursing station was tilted back against the wall, his eyes closed.

§§§

It was late Saturday afternoon when I crossed the iron truss bridge that spans the Elkins River separating Yardley side with the Buckingham side of

Yardley Falls. I drove up the hill past the old railroad station and turned down Oak Street. Tiger was raking leaves and stuffing them into large paper bags when I pulled up to the curb in front of her house. Behind her, in the backyard, Dawn was dragging a green tarp over the top of their swimming pool. I got out of the truck and picked up an armful of leaves, bright reds and yellows of maple, oak, poplar and ash.

"Any old bag or are you color sorting them?" I asked

"Just stuff them," Tiger said. "Seems like good general advice for you, Eddie. Just stuff it."

"Got any sick time left?"

"More than I'll ever need. Crissakes, I'm so goddamn healthy they should give me an award."

"We're both going to get sick, probably through Wednesday." She made her eyebrows into a question mark. I filled her in on the Corellis and

Gideon Moss and the emerging importance of Trenton.

"I could ask you what any of that has to do with a couple of Maintainer IIs. Why in the hell should we be getting involved in this? You'd probably tell me to trust you."

"I probably would."

"And I'd probably trust you, so why go through all the shit to get there? When do you want to leave?"

A kid on a loud motorcycle roared by.

"Why in the hell don't they make bikes muffle that goddamn sound like they do cars," she said. "Some asshole woke me up in at two a.m. last night roaring his mechanical dick up the street."

Shrugging, I waited for the engine noise to fade. The air was warm, the sky a deep blue. The neighborhood was busy with people raking leaves, mowing lawns for one last time before winter set in. Across the street, an elderly couple struggled to move their porch furniture inside. When it was quiet again, I told her I wanted to leave the next day. "I've got some things to do here before I go."

She laughed. "Like getting laid?"

"With luck. And finding out if Henrietta Lane is still alive." I picked up another load of leaves. She held the mouth of the bag open as I crammed them in. "Dawn's going to be pissed. We have to be back by Wednesday. Thursday's Halloween and we're having the party, remember? As it is, she's going to be stuck with most of the prep work. You're coming, right?"

"I promised Chad I'd be there. I asked Shelley if she wants to come."

"And?"

"She said yes."

"Good." Still stuffing leaves into her bag, I asked, "So how come you're having a party? In all the years we've been hanging out, you've never had one. Why now?"

"Dawn," she said. "She can't deal with Halloween."

"She get nervous about strangers coming around?"

Tiger shook her head. "She hates the begging kids. You believe it? She used to send Chad out with a huge bag and let him eat candy for days afterwards, but she can't stand having kids come to our house. If I left it up to her, she'd lock the doors, turn off lights and blast scary music into the yard. In this town that's a sure way to get your house egged and your shrubbery clotted with toilet paper. This year she wants a party. She thinks that'll keep the kids away. Go figure."

I promised we'd be back by Wednesday evening at the latest. I sat around on the porch steps for a while, watching them trim bushes, prune fruit trees and dead-head long thin lily stalks. After a while, I began feeling guilty for not helping and left.

§§§

Graham's firehouse is a six bay brick building set back from Main Street, sandwiched between the post office and the library. I parked behind it and went in. Lenny Broadhurst was polishing the chrome on the pumper. With a pair of earphones clamped to his head, his iPod clipped to his belt, he was singing along in a loud and tuneless voice. I walked over and waved my hands in front of his face. He grinned and turned the Pod off, pulling the earphones down around his neck.

"Eddie Sanders, my man," he said. "You missed a big one."

"I saw it. Any casualties?" He shook his head. "We thought Mrs. Lane was in there. Her butler said she had an appointment when we called to tell her about the fire. She was supposed to be there. We checked, but the place was empty. It wasn't an ordinary fire, though. We found traces of timers and gasoline. The place was torched. Whoever did it, knew what he was doing. There were several ignition sites. It was a professional job. I sure as hell hope they've got backup records of all their business dealings because there's not a computer that didn't melt, not a piece of paper that didn't burn. The place is a total disaster."

"Henrietta must be ripshit."

"Nobody's found her. All we know is that she didn't die in the fire. We went through what's left of the building with a fine-toothed comb. Nothing."

"Then where is she?" I asked.

He made a gesture of dismissal. "Not our problem. We fight the fires. We rescue people and find the victims. Someone disappears and they haven't been toasted in a fire, that's the cops' job."

"What if she set the fire and bugged out on her own?" His mouth dropped. "Jeez, you think so?"

I didn't think so, but I planted the idea. He'd mention it later that evening to the brothers as they sat in their Laz-E-Boys watching television and whiling away the ninety percent of boring time in a firefighter's life, the time that is punctuated by the ten percent sheer terror.

It would be his idea by then. Hey guys, he'd say. You think Mrs. Lane could have set that fire? Why would she do that? someone would ask. Insurance, another would say. She owns the company, so she sure as hell knows all about insurance. Probably she's already bribed the insurance investigators.

If Henrietta Lane didn't show up soon, the buzz at the fire house would have her sitting on a beach somewhere, counting wads of insurance money. The fire department buzz would migrate to the police department and from there to *The Graham Enterprise*. If Henrietta was hiding out for some reason, bad publicity was the best way of getting to her.

Chapter Eleven

The northeast corridor of Amtrak runs through the backyard of America's wasteland. The rear ends of strip malls, factories and mills are littered with junk cars, broken bicycles, trash strewn over the grease and oil drenched ground, rusted cargo trailers lying on their sides, the beached whales of commerce, discarded hulks of cranes reaching up, as if imploring some unknown, uncaring god to take notice. Abandoned buildings, windows broken, doors hanging on broken hinges line tracks which once brought raw materials to loading docks and took away finished goods. Now they provide bleak, cold and clandestine shelter for the homeless, the despair ridden, the frightened inexperienced runaways, the desperate booze and dope addicts who wander the trash strewn railroad right-of-ways, and the malevolent violent lurkers who prey upon them all.

I watched the scenes slip by as I sipped the beer Tiger brought me from the café car. Living in this bucolic western Massachusetts county, it's easy to ignore the desperation haunting much of America and most of the world. The county has its own quota of it: the Tommy Finnerans and Molly Patnaudes, families like the Walkers, the decaying tenements of Elkins Street and Eagle Falls, the cardboard shack town along the tracks just behind the shops on the east side of Main Street, the scratched and dented mobile homes on the back gravel roads of the surrounding hill towns, the crumbling ancient farm houses with sagging roofs and caved in barns.

Poverty and despair are no strangers to the county, nor is the violence that accompanies them. The rural poor and desperate strike out against one another regularly and predictably, most frequently behind the doors of their homes. Frantz Fanon was right; people don't often attack those responsible for their poverty and hopelessness.

The county also has spectacular beauty. The hills, lush and green in summer, are bathed in dramatic reds, oranges and yellows in the fall, white with snow in winter and swathed in soft pastels in the spring. Beauty is distracting. We gravitate to beauty. We delight in beauty, ignoring the unknown, the neglected and uncared for, whose pale shadows drift through the lovely backdrops of our worlds.

Riding the train we are assaulted by what we do not often see. There are no facades along the tracks, just the butt end of the world and its landscape of dead trees, untrimmed bush and humanity's rusted, broken and forgotten refuse.

The train pulled into Trenton at eleven-twenty Sunday morning, only sixteen minutes late. I called the car rental place where I had made reservations. They picked us up within ten minutes, driving us to a converted gas station on Olden Avenue where a dozen late model compact and mid-size cars were parked, several in various stages of being hosed down by a middle aged man in bib overalls smoking a cigar, wielding his hose with the authority of a symphony conductor, directing the activities of a teenaged black kid with a sponge, the two of them exchanging one liners as they worked. Twenty minutes later we drove off in a gray Ford that reeked of stale cigarette smoke. Tiger held a Trenton area street map on her lap. I had gotten Gideon Moss's address from a phone book at the car rental garage. He lived at 32 Lotchahee Lane in Ewing Township.

According to the directions from MapQuest it was almost a straight shot from Olden Avenue. Within fifteen minutes I came to a stop at the curb in front of the Moss house. At the end of the drive was a mailbox in the form of a log cabin, the names Gideon and Terri Moss painted on the side. It was a late Fifties, early Sixties development of split-level brick homes, many with mid-sized vans or SUVs sitting in their driveways. The houses were distinguished from one another by landscaping, the patterns and amounts of brick set off against board and batten trim, and by the ingenuity of their mailboxes.

The Moss's half-acre lot was taken up by manicured gardens. An old hand plow sat beside a rusted wheelbarrow filled with geraniums, still blooming in the Middle Atlantic States October heat, so different from the chill we often have in New England by this time of year.

A flagstone walk curved from the driveway and ran through a row of brightly painted ceramic trolls to the cement pad that served as a front porch. An American flag hung from a pole rising at an upward angle from a bracket to the left of the porch, sharing the pole with a second flag bearing the motto, *United We Stand*. A late model blue Nissan Pathfinder sat in the drive alongside an ancient silver Dodge van. Both had American flag decals on their side windows and *United We Stand* rear bumper stickers. The Pathfinder also had an American flag hanging from its antenna.

"Looks like they're home," Tiger said, nodding toward the cars.

"Unless they walked to church."

"People from New Jersey don't walk," she said.

"Spoken like a Yankee bigot. You're the kind of person who makes the exit joke."

She looked confused. "Exit jokes? What's an exit joke?"

"The one that when somebody tells you they're from New Jersey, you ask, which exit?"

"I'd never do that," she said. "Although it is kind of funny."

"You'd probably like the tunnel joke too." She sighed with resignation. "What tunnel joke, Eddie?"

"Why are people from New York so depressed?" She shook her head. "I don't have a clue."

"Because the light at the end of the tunnel is New Jersey."

"That might have been funny once. It's not anymore."

"You're right," I said. "We're delaying, you know. Banter is a way of putting off what you've got to do." I got out of the car and started across the lawn. Tiger followed.

Gideon Moss answered the door at my first knock. He must have been looking out the window, watching us talking in the car.

"Are you the Gideon Moss who teaches at Trenton State?" I asked. "You must mean the College of New Jersey at Trenton." There was a light mocking tone as he spoke. He was tall and thin, about fifty, bald with long graying fringe growing mid-length over his ears. He wore jeans and a blue oxford cloth shirt, sleeves rolled several inches above his wrists, docksiders and no socks. "And yes, I labor in the vineyard of higher education, for all it's gotten me."

"My name's Edward Sanders and this is Ms Kelly. We're from Graham Community College in Massachusetts. You were at the MLA meeting last spring."

He squinted through his thick glasses at us. "Did we meet there, Mr. Sanders?"

"Not directly. You met a friend of ours and we found out about you through him." It wasn't a lie, exactly. "Evans Cornell."

He reacted with immediate excitement. "The guy with the Bukowski recordings. Yeah. I've thought a lot about him since the meeting." He shook his head in frustration. "It's so goddamned unfair. I bust my balls at Trenton. I've been there part time for twelve years, teaching four sections of freshman composition and then hauling my ass across the river to Bucks County Community College to teach another couple of courses, just to cob together a living with no benefits. I spend my life reading inane papers written by inane people with the inane assumption that I'm going to teach them how to write, when I don't have time to give their papers an even half way decent reading. And I've got about as much chance of getting hired on full time as Osama bin Laden has of getting a job with the CIA, maybe worse. Hell, you're from a community college. You know what it's like in public colleges."

I nodded, encouraging him to go on.

"And there's that goddamn Evans Cornell at Ralston, pulling down big bucks, teaching maybe two courses a semester and, on top of it, he's got those recordings of Bukowski reading. That's an academic gold mine. If he's right and they really do contain unpublished poems and variants of some of Bukowski's signature poems, they maybe could be a financial gold mine too." Licking his lips he added something Billy Melnick would have said. "Bukowski's going to be big, you know. There's going to be a whole academic industry built on him. HarperCollins bought up all his stuff from Black Sparrow and is publishing it under its Ecco imprint. That's big already." He had spoken quickly. It seemed to be a well-rehearsed complaint. "Not for Cornell," I said. "He's dead. Somebody tried to cut his and his wife's heads off a couple of days ago."

He paled, nearly flinching. "Jesus, that's awful. Horrible. I mean, I didn't know him except for getting wasted with him one night during the conference, but that's gruesome." He rested his arm against the side of the door. After taking a deep breath he looked up, his eyes wily, his attitude one of opportunism, any concern over the deaths of Evans and Ariel Cornell far outweighed by greed and ambition. "What about the recordings? Where are the recordings? You know where the recordings are?"

"Safe," I said, repulsed by the nakedness of his craving. It was a look, a ravenousness I had seen before, in many parts of the world. Whether the object of the desire is power, oil, territory or, now as I saw, poetry, the absence of any moral concern is stark and sickening.

He leaned toward me, eyes eager, bright. "Look, Professor Sanders, I don't know why you're here, unless you've got the recordings and you want me to work with you on them. I'd be the right person to do that, you know. I'm an expert on Bukowski. Evans must have told you that. I'm going to put on a Bukowski festival here at the university."

"I've heard." I watched him, measured his words, his expressions. Gideon Moss was one of those people who see the world as little more than a series of events designed to further their own ends. He was the proprietor and sole inhabitant of Mossworld.

"I'd kill to work with those recordings." He stopped. Shaking his head, he gave me a quick nervous laugh. "I didn't, of course. I don't kill people. You've got no idea what it's like, wanting a full time position and having to bow and scrape to old farts sitting in their offices or pontificating in their classrooms, collecting big salaries, with insurance and pension plans. Adjuncts like me have to fawn obsequiously, hoping that when the full-timers are on a search committee they'll remember me and give me a real job.

They're dinosaurs, prattling on about Melville and Twain, yakking about Hemingway, or Alice Walker, for that matter, as if nothing important is being written now. If my wife wasn't an ER nurse, god knows how we'd be living." He sagged for a moment, shaking his head. "And you know how they're laying off people in the hospitals these days. It's scary."

"What's written now grows out of what was written in the past," I said. He waved his hand in front of his face, as if chasing away a bad stench. "The past is a useless illusion. The past is whatever we imagine it to be, want it to be. You can build any kind of past you want if you can find the right documents."

He motioned us into the house and sat on a straight-backed wooden chair in a corner of the living room. Tiger and I sat on a couch opposite him. "I am sorry about Cornell," he said. "But why are you here? Do you want me to work on the recordings? God, I'd love that. It would be a great opportunity to make a reputation for myself."

"Nothing like that," I said. "I needed to see you face to face, make sure you weren't involved in the Cornells' murders."

He sat bolt upright. "Me?" He stammered for a long moment, shocked at the implications of what I'd said. "Are you police?"

"No. We really are from Graham Community College. I have personal reasons for trying to find out what happened to Evans Cornell and his wife."

"They are?" He made his voice deepen, raising his eyebrows. The pose just reinforced my growing distaste for the man.

"I can't discuss them." I got up to leave. I'm no psychic, but I've interrogated enough people to know when they're lying about something this big. Moss didn't have anything to do with the Cornells' deaths and there was no point asking him any more questions or taking up any more of our time.

Gideon Moss's face was at war. He was furious at us for intruding on him, for suspecting him of being involved in the murders. He also wanted access to the recordings and knew he had to placate us if that were to ever happen.

Greed won. He made a smile and shaped himself into a posture of open warmth. "You will keep me in mind. About the recordings, I mean. Buke's been dead since Ninety-four. The academic world's going to wake up to him soon. It always does once a writer dies, and I really am an expert on his life and work. Those recordings could secure my reputation. Get me a full-time job, tenure. Change my rotten life."

I should have bitten my tongue, but I'm not good at that. Besides, he pissed me off, no matter that he was just another poor schlep driving from college to college, doing the scut work of teaching freshman comp. I was repelled and angered by his glib self-centered opportunism. Recordings or no recordings, at his age, with his attitude, he had about as much chance of his getting a full time teaching job with tenure as I did.

He was living in the shit end of the academic world and I would have had more sympathy for him had he been able to think beyond Mossworld, had he not been obsequious and greedy and so indifferent to the murders I had told him about. Then I might have bitten my tongue, choked back my comments, stifled them. Instead, I didn't even struggle to be articulate. Nothing of the kind for me. I leaned into his face and let my disgust pour over him.

"You're revolting. You sit around, drooling over the recordings and you don't care a whit about anybody other than yourself and your pathetic future. You and your academic reputation don't amount to a fart in a cesspool. You've got as much chance of hearing those recordings as Evans Cornell does of ever diddling another sophomore English major."

He lunged at me. "Who the hell do you think you are, coming into my house and pulling this shit?" Tiger grabbed his arm, twisting it behind his back, almost gently, just enough to check him.

"Forget it, Mr. Moss." She threw me a quick look of disgust and spoke softly, placating him. "Eddie's an asshole sometimes. Like now. He had no business talking to you like that."

Moss sagged. She let him go. "Get out," he said.

Back in the car, I glanced at the house. Moss was still in the doorway, scowling at us. Embarrassed by my outburst, I started the engine and drove to the corner, eager to get out of his sight. "We can scratch him from the list."

"And you came down on me for that comment I made to those kids about the U-Mass football team. Jesus, Eddie, that poor guy's got nothing to look forward to. You were cruel. Really low rotten cruel." She looked at me like something she would have to step around on a sidewalk.

I made a u-turn at the corner and drove back down Lotchahee Lane and pulled into Moss's drive. He was still on the porch. I rolled down my window and leaned toward him. "Sorry," I said. "Tiger's right. I was an asshole." He made a face, shot me the finger and went inside.

Now that we had both acted like seventh graders, I felt justified in leaving. Backing out the driveway I turned up the street toward the corner. "Next stop, Newtown, Pennsylvania. Let's call on Sylvia Corelli/Cornell."

§§§

Newtown was eight miles from Ewing, a hop across the Delaware River on I-95. There was no way we were going back to Massachusetts without an overnight, so when we passed a Hampton Inn just off the Interstate, we checked in. I took a shower. We had a quick lunch and drove toward town on a circular by-pass. After several traffic lights, I turned onto Washington

Avenue. A business park, several gas stations, a large cemetery and several blocks of gracious stone and frame homes later, we turned left on Chancellor Street. The phone book listed Sylvia's address as 112 South Chancellor.

"Weird," Tiger said. "Didn't Evans Cornell live on a Chancellor Street in Graham?"

"Coincidences are just coincidences," I said.

Sylvia's house sat in the middle of the block, a comfortable frame Victorian. It had been restored with care, the gingerbread either well maintained or recently replaced, the trim around the windows and doors was painted to match to the siding but of different tones and values. The front porch was lined with three rocking chairs, a thick wisteria vine growing up the far left post. Under the front window a three-tiered plant stand held a number of potted plants. Painted white with a soft gray-green on the trim, the house sat on the far right side of its lot, the land to the left and to the rear filled with perennial gardens, a small fishpond, shrubbery, and miniature fruit trees. At the rear of the lot was an above ground swimming pool with a red cedar deck surrounded by high ornamental grasses. It was a home somebody loved and spent hours thinking about and tending.

We walked up to the porch and I rang the bell.

I stifled a gasp when the door opened. Sylvia Cornell was gorgeous, at least six feet tall, ebony hair, lustrous, thick with a soft wave, flowing around her shoulders, her skin flawless, her body full and firm, well set off by a tight white tee-shirt and dungaree shorts. Her face was astonishing, the purity and perfection of a Botticelli Madonna. She held a paintbrush in her right hand. Tiger did gasp. Sylvia Cornell smiled and Tiger and I lost our hearts.

"Yes," she said and waited for an explanation of why I rang her doorbell and was standing on her porch, my mouth agape, my eyes felt as though they were protruding at least three inches from my face. I knew at the moment that I looked like a dribbling idiot.

"Ms Cornell?" I asked, forcing the words from a constricting throat. I introduced Tiger and myself.

"If you're selling Girl Scout cookies, I've already gotten some this year." A knowing smile played around her exquisite lips. She was used to men reacting the way I was reacting. We can't help it. Certain kinds of idiocy are genetically and culturally programmed. Within prescribed limits it makes for a harmless game. Outside those parameters it is anything but harmless. Amused, she was mocking me with gentle good humor.

"I suppose you have all the magazine subscriptions you need," I said with forced jocularity. I believe my voice squeaked.

She let a full born smile blossom. "*The Nation, The Atlantic Monthly, The Economist, Playgirl, The Utne Reader, The New Yorker,* I think I have everything I need."

"Ms Cornell, we may have some bad news for you." Tiger had recovered from the assault of her beauty. I appreciated her bailing me out. As a reward, I resolved to get her drunk and let her get us into a fight at Ducky's anytime she wanted.

Sylvia came out on the porch and sat in a rocking chair, gesturing to the others with her paintbrush. We sat.

"You have a brother, Evans Cornell," I said.

She nodded and sat expressionless, staring off into the distance as I told her about the murders in Graham. When I finished, she looked at me, her voice flat, her eye expressionless. "You police?"

"I'm a friend of a friend Evans," I said.

"Why hasn't anybody informed the family?" She seemed more annoyed by the lack of official communication about the murders than she was upset about her brother and sister-in-law's deaths.

"I'd guess it's because the cops and all his colleagues at Ralston College think he's Evans Cornell. If the Newtown cops found your body, would they think to notify Angelo Corelli or anyone else in the Corelli family?"

If that caught her off guard, she covered it. She still wasn't showing shock or dismay, or even overt concern at the news. "I doubt it. Isn't he a mob boss in New Jersey? Unless you're saying Evans was somehow mixed up with the mob, which is absolutely insane. Except for women, he is, was, a bit of a goody-two-shoes. In college Evans was more the fraternity type. Since he started teaching at Ralston he's been addicted to academic organizations. Who killed him, angry parents? A jealous boy friend? A husband? An instructor or assistant professor looking for advancement?"

"You don't seem very upset," I said.

She made a non-committal gesture. "If he and I are Corellis, we'd be used to murder, don't you think? We'd have our own ways of dealing with it and with whoever did it. We wouldn't go to the police. We wouldn't talk about it with strangers. We wouldn't even let strangers know how we felt. And you two are strangers. On the other hand, if Evans Cornell was just Evans Cornell and I'm just Sylvia Cornell, and we are," she paused. I thought I saw a trace of wetness in her eyes before she continued. "I am a Cornell, he was."

A school bus filled with football players went up the street. The sound of the engine drowned her words and she waited until it passed. "Council Rock plays Neshaminy today," she said when it had passed through the stop sign at the end of the block. She rocked back in the chair and took several deep breaths. "I'm not upset in the way you expected me to be because we didn't like each other very much. He was an arrogant womanizing intellectual snob who was always putting me down for grubbing in the pits of capitalism instead of being fascinated by whether or not some Elizabethan poet spelled *quaint* as *queynte* to make a pun on an archaic spelling of cunt." She laughed, but it was not a sound of amusement. "In fact, that was a discussion at our Thanksgiving dinner table one year when he was in graduate school. As the Queen of England says, we were not amused. My father does not like discussions of a sexual nature."

Tiger was sitting next to her. She leaned over, placing her hand on Sylvia's arm. "He was your brother. You must have some feelings about his death." She bristled. "My feelings are private. They're not something I wish to discuss with strangers." She drew her arm away, resting her elbows on her knees, her face in her hands. When she looked up, it was with an unreadable expression. She smiled at Tiger, her voice soft. "Sorry. You were trying to be understanding. Trust me, there's nothing here for you to understand. Our family matters are...complex."

I spoke. "A large amount of drugs was found at his house." Her response was quick and terse. "I wouldn't know about his drug problems."

"You weren't just talking hypothetically about not caring for your brother, were you Ms Cornell?"

She looked at me the way people look at a skunk squashed on the highway. "I loved my brother, Mr. Standish."

"Sanders," I said. She shrugged.

"I loved my brother but I did not like him. We were not close. We haven't spoken in over three years. Not because of any fight or animosity. We had no reason to talk. He cared about poetry and language. I'm fascinated by market fluctuations. They have as little in common as Evans and I had. It is possible, you know, to love someone and still not like him very much." She stood to dismiss us.

In as off-handed manner as possible I asked her if had ever mentioned Bukowski to her.

She sat. "The recordings. The ones he made in San Francisco years ago. He talked about them the last time we got together. I'd never heard of Bukowski before, or since, but I'm an economist, not a literary scholar. Evans was ecstatic about those recordings. Do you think they have anything to do with the murders?"

"Why would they?" I asked

"Evans thought the recordings would be valuable some day. He said it was like finding recordings of Robert Frost reading unpublished later versions of *Snowy Woods*, or *Fixing the Wall*."

"*Stopping by Woods on a Snowy Evening* and *Mending Wall*," I said.

She rolled her eyes. "Whatever. I don't much care for snow, walls or poetry. I don't much care for this conversation. It's over."

She stood again, gesturing for us to leave. I started down the steps to the front walk, Tiger behind me. I heard Sylvia speaking to Tiger behind my back.

"You in the area for any length of time?"

"I imagine we'll be going back tomorrow, Tuesday at the latest. Tomorrow probably."

"Where are you staying?"

"The Hampton Inn," Tiger said.

"I'd like to see you again, before you leave," Sylvia said. "Room 211," Tiger told her.

"I'll call before I come." She mumbled something I couldn't hear and shut the door behind her.

We walked to the car. Inside, the windows rolled up, Tiger whooped. "Holy shit, Sanders. You hear that? She wants to see me. And what a major babe."

"What else did she say?"

"Nothing. Nothing for your ears."

"And you're going to see her?"

"Bet your ass. Pussy like that doesn't grow on trees."

"What about Dawn?" I said, as much shocked at the fact that I was shocked by Tiger's willingness to cheat on Dawn as I was by the fact she was willing to cheat on her.

"What would you have told her if she asked where you were staying and said she wanted to see you again?"

"Room 213," I said. "See."

"I'm not in a long term relationship, living in a jointly owned house and raising a kid."

"And if you were, what would you say then?" I had to grin. "Probably room 213."

"Besides," she said. "Who knows what I can find out? Tongues get pretty loose after a night of sex."

"I'm not going to touch that one," I said.

Chapter Twelve

Sylvia called as Tiger and I sat in her room at the Hampton Inn, drinking beer and watching an Eagles game on television. The Eagles were winning, no pleasure for a Patriots fan, so I didn't mind the interruption. I put the TV on mute and paged through a local real estate guide. Newtown was as pricey as anything in the Boston area. I've been spoiled by the depressed prices in Graham, where even I could afford a nice home, if I wanted one. Barton Rooms suited my philosophical and emotional needs just fine. Tiger and Sylvia spoke for a few minutes, Tiger cupping her hand around the phone and her mouth to keep me from hearing her side of the conversation. After hanging up, she gave me half the remaining beers and told me to get lost.

"I can't understand why she didn't want me," I said, half joking. "It's your dick." She was laughing at me.

"She likes it better that you don't have one?"

"No. She likes what I do have. There's a big difference between those two positions, Eddie my boy."

"I suppose," I said.

"There's no supposin' why she's chosen. I've just got the cunt that some girls want." She tousled my hair. "Although there's a hell of a lot more to it than that."

I laughed back. She was right. There was no arguing over the convolutions of human sexuality. We were lucky that Sylvia wanted to be with one of us. We were both willing to pump her for information. Tiger happened to draw the long straw.

I was glad the walls in the Hampton Inn were almost soundproof. With the TV turned to a healthy volume, I was able to ignore any noises that might come from room 211. I called Shelley, hoping for some phone sex, getting nothing but her answering machine. I breathed into the receiver for a few moments, then said, "Just joking, but I sure wouldn't mind jumping your bones when we get back."

I switched the TV to CNN only to find they were rerunning a five year old Tammy Faye Bakker interview on "Larry King Live." Not caring for either King or Bakker, I surfed the channels, settling on an ancient "Have Gun Will Travel." It was background noise and I had trouble following the plot. Nothing would have entertained me. I was pissed at Billy Melnick for foisting the Bukowski recordings off on me. I was furious with Henrietta Lane for dragging me into her investigation, awakening latent patterns and ways of thinking I had long ago buried and consigned to what I had hoped was an irretrievable past. I was even irked at Shelley for teaching a class in which a student had died, as if she had any control over it. I cursed Andy Lane for getting herself involved with drugs. I self flagellated over my inability to turn my back on any of them, on the situation, and go back to my Maintainer II closet where I could be as happy as a clam. For a moment I imagined clams sitting in a circle on the floor of the bay, laughing, hanging out, singing old clam folk songs, having a fine bivalve hootenanny.

Despite the image, there was nothing funny about my situation. I had been drawn in after years of avoiding engagement and entanglement. I was fearful something precious had been irreparably broken. I had constructed a contained, safe, comfortable life. Now I was looking down an unmapped path, winding through deep woods, dark woods, where things long kept in check could be unleashed. My Barton room and my Maintainer II closet would be meager shelter against them.

I channel surfed for a while, marveling over the abundance of programs available on cable television as well as the dearth of anything worth watching, settling on a channel running an evening of John Wayne movies. They soothed my male ego while indulging a need for simple, mindless justice, as he rode horseback over the plains, shooting guns, killing bad guys and beating the crap out of the bad guys he didn't kill. I ignored the wooden acting and suppressed the rumors I'd heard about Wayne and Rock Hudson. I fell asleep in the middle of *Rio Bravo*, awoke for a moment to a torrid scene with Rhonda Fleming in *The Wake of the Red Witch* and dropped back off to sleep, awakening to a knock on the door.

I rolled over. Muted morning sunlight shone through the blinds. The knocking persisted. The red numerals on the clock by the bed said six fifty-three. Forcing myself to get up, I flicked off the TV, put on a white terry cloth robe I found hanging in the bathroom and opened the door. Tiger stood there with an insulated black pitcher of coffee and a box of doughnuts.

"Sleep well"? she asked. "Like a log. You?"

"Not a wink." Her grin was wild and malevolent. She came in and set the coffee on the desk by the window, the box of doughnuts next to it. "Sylvia left about twenty minutes ago. I had her drive me down to the Seven/Eleven first to pick up these. The doughnuts aren't real, like Crewitt's, but they're made with sugar and grease." She plopped herself into a chair and sighed with pleasure.

"You look pleased with things."

"Sylvia is something else."

"I don't want to hear about it."

"You don't want to hear about how she screams in Italian when she comes?"

I poured a cup of coffee, picked up a juicy looking jelly doughnut and took a huge bite of it. "I'd prefer you'd told me about her linguistic abilities in a different way."

"She's got all kinds of linguistic abilities."

"Enough," I said. The coffee was hot. I blew on it, taking small sips, washing them around my mouth with the doughnut. "You find anything out?"

"Aside from the way she screams in Italian at the height of passion, not much, but neither did she."

"What was she trying to find out?"

"She wants to know where the recordings are."

"She didn't say anything about the Corellis, about the drugs in Evans' house, about the murders?"

"Not a word. She brought the recordings up three or four times, very subtly each time, but the only Italian connection came when she..."

"Stop," I cut her off. "My envy can only take so much. Did she talk about anything other than the recordings?"

"Not anything you'll want to hear about. She wants them, Eddie. She agrees with her brother that they're valuable."

"And she told us she didn't care for poetry."

"She doesn't. The only thing she cares about is money and she thinks of the recordings as a commodity. I think she believes she can make a pretty good profit on them, given how hard she tried last night to find out where they are."

"You didn't tell her? Blurt it out in English at the height of passion?"

"For crissakes, Sanders, what kind of an asshole do you think I am?" I apologized. She waved it away.

"No big deal. What is a big deal is that she's hot for those recordings. If things were complicated before, they're sure as shit a lot more complicated now. She's going to be looking for them, and I'd guess she's got the resources to look hard and deep."

§§§

Late Monday afternoon Amtrak dropped us at the railroad station in Springfield and we drove back to Graham. Through Pennsylvania, New York and the lower part of Connecticut, the fall colors had been at their peak, their splendor in stark contrast to the trackside scenery. With each station stop they became more muted, the trees more barren, the land more brown.

It was like riding a train into winter. By the time we got home the trees were cold bare ruined choirs where late the sweet birds sang.

Tiger had left her car in the college parking lot. We sat next to it in my truck, the motor idling, "All Things Considered" on the radio.

"At least we're back before Wednesday," I said.

She nodded. She had been quiet since Hartford, muttering single syllable replies to everything I said.

"I'm not sure it was too valuable a trip. Moss and Sylvia Cornell didn't seem to know anything helpful."

She grunted.

"Maybe all we did was create problems. They both want the recordings. I hope they don't show up here looking for them. Things are messy enough as it is."

"That would be a nightmare, but don't be surprised when Sylvia shows up with some members of her extended family." She exhaled a deep and trembling sigh. "I don't know what I'm going to say to Dawn. If Sylvia's in town...Jesus, Eddie, what will I do?"

"Don't tell her. Sylvia was a job. Ignore her if she shows up here."

"You don't ignore sex like that, no matter why it happened."

"I thought you and Dawn were solid. Like Ozzie and Harriet, Ward and June Cleaver, all that kind of Fifties TV stuff, only with a bit of gender difference thrown into the balance."

"Nothing's ever solid, Eddie. Things shift. Solidity is something we convince ourselves exists so we're not always frightened. I've got a cousin out in San Francisco, scared all the time. Can't even trust the ground under his feet. One minute it's hard as can be, he says, next minute it turns to liquid. Hell, you can't trust the ground, how can you trust emotions?"

"You're making too much of this," I said, but she was right. Anybody who thinks about the nature of our lives knows how tenuous our holds are on anything. There's no point dwelling on it. We have to act as though each moment is real and solid, connected to those preceding and following. It's like pushing a broom. You keep going straight ahead, down hallways and into rooms you've gone into a hundred times. You know the hallway. You know the rooms. You just have to keep them free of clutter and dust. Tiger didn't wax philosophical often, but she was as tuned in as anybody I know.

I said, "Go home, give her a hug. Take some flowers. Go out to dinner."

"And you're making light of it, Eddie. I did a terrible thing to Dawn, and even if she never knows about it, I do." She rolled down the window and lit a cigarette. I didn't stop her. Sometimes you can't worry about second hand smoke and a few ashes in a pickup. "It gets worse. If Sylvia shows up in Graham, I'd do her again, if I had the chance. Now, does that suck or what?"

"If Sylvia does show up here, we're going to have heavier shit to deal with than whether or not you should boff her. Besides, I hate to break it to you, but she won't be here for sex, she'll be here either for the Bukowski recordings or to find out who killed her brother, or both. I'll bet you're right about what you said back in the hotel, too. She won't be alone."

"You believe that Corelli shit?"

"Absolutely. Beyond a doubt. One thousand percent. Don't you?" She rubbed her hands over her face, sighing. "I do. I believed it before she came. I was sure of it afterwards when she came in Italian." Outside, the campus cruiser went by, Security checking the lot. Its windows were darkened and I couldn't see who was driving. It slowed down as it passed us, then sped up heading toward the lot's exit. "Still, she seemed so into it...with me. It's hard to believe she wasn't."

"Nothing says she wasn't, Tige. That doesn't mean she wasn't looking for information, or that she won't come here up with all barrels loaded. Good sex is good sex. You can be into it, involved to the core and it still doesn't change who you are or what you're looking for. She wanted the recordings before you two went at it. She had a good time, got off, practiced her Italian, and she still wants the recordings."

She snorted a quick laugh. "I know that. Shit, I sound like a teenager with a crush. You're right. Flowers. A hug. Dinner in Northampton. It sounds like a plan. I do love her, you know. Dawn. She's the love of my life."

"I know," I said. "Everybody should be so lucky to have that kind of love." She patted me on the shoulder and got out of the truck. Before shutting the door, she leaned in the cab. "Maybe you should do something with Shelley tonight."

"Maybe I should."

§§§

My room was cold. The landlord wouldn't turn the heat on until we'd had several days of below freezing weather. At least he'd repaired the window. Chunks of concrete and bricks were still there, some on my bed, some on the floor. I put a pan of water for tea on the hotplate. I turned on my electric space heater, cleaned the debris from my bed, and lay down waiting for the water to boil. I'd called Shelley as soon as I got home but she either wasn't in or wasn't picking up. Her answering machine was turned off. There was a knock on my door as the teakettle began to whistle. I turned it off, pouring the boiling water into my cup.

The knock was repeated. "Dude, you in there?"

I opened the door and Billy Melnick came in. Throwing his coat and baseball hat on the floor, he flopped in the bed, leaning back against my pillow, his shoes on the blanket.

"Saw your lights on, so I came up. Got the recordings, man?"

"I do."

"I'll take them now." I was about to reply when the phone rang.

"You're back on the payroll," the familiar voice said. "I don't think so," I said.

"You've been busy," he said, ignoring my remark. "Ewing Township, Newtown. Sylvia is a lovely woman, eh?"

I felt a cold shiver. Whatever had been unleashed in those deep woods, dark woods, was rushing toward me, its eyes red, saliva drooling from its gaping maw. How long had they been keeping such close tabs on me? I looked at Billy, sitting on the bed, watching me.

"I can't talk now."

"Sure you can. Look at this as a bonus. You'll keep your mindless swabbing job at the community college and you'll collect a sizeable salary from us too. It's quite a practical solution, Nathan. Edward."

"Call me back in half an hour." Hanging up before he could reply, I turned back to Billy. "What are you going to do with the recordings?"

"Sell them, dude. Put them up on eBay and let people bid on them."

"I thought you wanted them for their poetic value, for what they meant."

"Yeah, that too, you know. But that poetic value man, it translates into money. Just think about it, me, Billy Melnick, having Charles Bukowski for sale and all those academic dudes begging to buy the recordings from me. Pretty soon they'd start calling them the Melnick Bukowski recordings. In the same breath, dude, Melnick and Bukowski. Mega cool, right?"

"They're not yours to sell." He whirled, eyes flashing anger. "Then whose are they, dude? Evans sure as hell doesn't need them. You've got them because I gave them to you for safekeeping. I figure they're mine as much as anybody's."

"He had a sister. She knows about them."

"So what? Why should I care about some chick wanting them?"

"Think about her family," I said.

He nodded. "They are awesome, but I don't see them as poetry people."

"They're not. They're money people." I told him about Tiger's remark that Sylvia viewed the recordings as a valuable commodity. He persisted.

"Shit, man, the Corellis got bigger fish to fry than some recordings of a dead poet."

"People like them never have enough," I said. "Anything that'll bring in bucks is what they're interested in, and the recordings are worth bucks."

"Mucho bucks, dude. Get them on eBay and people'll be bidding like crazy for them. Once the price gets high enough I'll offer them to his publisher." He leaned forward. "So, where are they?"

"Safe," I said. I wasn't sure why I was being evasive. There was something about his eagerness, his tone, perhaps his posture, which sounded an alert in a primitive portion of my brain, a reptilian ancestor's contribution to the complexity of my being, a warning so successful that I existed and survived eons later.

"Safe where?"

"Safe, Billy."

His face twisted in anger, revealing a Billy Melnick I had never imagined, tense, ready to spring, malicious. "You trying to rip me off, dude?" He rasped the words from thin, twitching lips.

"That's horseshit and you know it," I said. "They're safe. Right now, the fewer people who can put their hands on them, the better. If I don't tell you where they are, then you've got what politicians call deniability. If anybody comes after them you can say you don't have a clue where they are. All I'll tell you is that they're nowhere around my place or me."

His eyes were cold. He never voiced it, but there was a threat in the tone of what he said. His hands were curled, his body tensing even further. "I want the recordings, dude. They're mine. I've earned them."

"Earned? How?"

He shrugged. "Leave it. I'm entitled to them."

"Maybe you are, but then maybe Sylvia Cornell is entitled. Maybe I'm entitled, since you gave them to me."

"Dude," he said, his voice ringing with icy fury. "I trusted you to keep them safe for me."

"They're safe."

"You're trying to rip me off." His response was sharp, his anger rising.

Mine was just as sharp and angry. "I'm protecting you. What if those recordings got Cornell and his wife killed?"

"Now that really is horseshit."

"Or not. What if I'm right?"

His hands turned upward on his knees, his body relaxed. There were no signs of concession in his words, but his voice sounded the resignation his body showed.

"You're not giving them to me?"

"Trust me, Billy. They're safe. I'm not trying to rip you off. I'm not denying that they should be yours. I don't want them and I haven't even listened to them. I don't give a rat's ass if the version of *Love Is a Dog from Hell* in them is a paean to romantic love that will change the minds of everybody who does care about Bukowski's outlook on love."

He started to speak. I held up my hand and continued. "What I care about is you. You'll have to trust me on this, too. There's more going on here than either of us knows. We've got to play it cool, Billy. The recordings are safe. If the recordings did get the Cornell's killed, nobody's going to do to you what they did to them if they think you don't know where they are."

"What if they don't believe me?"

"That's your job. Make them believe. Tell them you gave them to me."

"Then they'll come after you." I heard Nathan Hunt's frigid steel in my voice. "Let them."

§§§

I crossed the room and stood at the window looking down at the street. Billy walked from the Barton Rooms doorway to his car, his jacket collar up, his baseball hat brim low over his brow, hunched against the cold wind blowing up Main Street, raising the usual dust and litter. The phone rang as he backed out of his parking place.

"He's gone. Now let's talk about you and the agency," the voice said. The son-of-a-bitch, I thought. "You're watching pretty closely."

"Not me, but we are keeping tabs on you, Eddie. That's what we do. Observe, analyze and act."

"And me, what do you want from me?"

"Observation, analysis and action."

"I thought you had different priorities since September 11th."

"We do. That doesn't mean the old priorities have become obsolete. They're just no longer paramount. You've got an interesting scene up there in the Massachusetts boonies. If it leads to us getting something on the Corellis, dandy. If not, your salary is still money well spent. We'll know something we don't know now. Above and beyond that, we need contacts in the academic world in order to keep our eyes on potential terrorists. They can go to ground for years at a time in places like colleges and universities. Your schools are great academic institutions. They're also safe haven for all kinds of people, from founders of NAMBLA to militia members to wild-eyed neo-Marxists."

"NAMBLA?" I asked

"The North American Man-Boy Love Association, a pacifist pederast society with a major base at a community college in the Boston area. Wonderful group of men."

"I hope you're giving me a major raise in salary to come back in," I said.

"Of course. Two of the best things about government work are the cost of living increases and the pensions. The Feds are a hell of a lot more generous in both respects than the Commonwealth of Massachusetts. There've been quite a few COLAs since you went on leave. I'll also put you up for a reclassification to a higher grade, as a measure of how much the agency values your work in the past and what you can do for us now." He made his voice low, broken and harsh in a poor imitation of Brando's Vito Corleone. "It's an offer you can't refuse."

He was right. If I didn't sign back on, the results would not be as poetic as finding a horse's head in my bedroom. Besides, Massachusetts state workers have seen their salaries frozen for years at a time, several times over. We've been forced to take unpaid furloughs and asked to take voluntary ones to save money. Our contracts have been allowed to expire before negotiations for new ones begin and there has been no retroactive pay for the months and years gone by before the negotiations are complete. That has not happened at the Federal level. It was certain to happen in the state next year. Already politicians and their fellow travelers were talking budget doom and gloom.

"I don't want this," I told him. "You're forcing me. I'll do the job, I'll take the money, but I do not want to. I don't want this."

"Too bad. You've got it. You do understand the alternative." I understood. Dark corners in places like the New Jersey Pine Barrens can easily hide the remains of a former agent who didn't get it. I had come to fancy my final resting place as being on a sunny hillside, my ashes mixed in with the top soil, a dignified stone providing a place where people could come, on the off chance they'd choose to mourn a man who never managed to make long term connections, often driving the few women he had relationships with away in frustration and anger.

"You'll take care of my pay by direct deposit?"

"Of course," he made his voice sound pleased and relieved. "You are proving a point I made to you that day in Baku when we were discussing the importance of the agency."

I can only imagine how confused my face must have looked judging from how confused I felt.

"Come now," he said. "You are the individual embodiment of the need for conservative action to preserve a liberal condition."

"That's a hell of a stretch."

"Not at all. You've been living in your pleasant quiet little world with nothing more challenging to do than sweeping up after people, untroubled by what you have to do day by day. Suddenly evil intrudes on that illusory existence and you're ready to swing into action. Just as in the old days when you worked for me, you'll do whatever it takes to preserve the dull life you've come to regard as your right. Tell me I'm wrong."

"I don't believe in evil and you're dead wrong."

I could hear him take a deep breath. "No, Eddie, I'm right. You may not believe in evil, but you're ready to act against it as you have so many times before."

"I'm just doing what I have to do."

"Exactly."

"You don't understand."

He took another deep breath. "I'm sorry, Eddie."

"You should be. You don't understand what I'm doing."

"I do. That's why I'm sorry. For you, not for me, not for the agency."

"Forget that I ever contacted you."

"Too late for that." For a moment neither of us spoke. Then he said, "One more thing."

I sighed into the phone, making it as loud and obvious as possible. He was right on one account. I was who I was and I would act in accordance with my training and my experience. And that experience had taught me that with him there was always one more thing. "All right," I said. "What is it?"

"Get a cell phone. We need to be able to contact you at a minute's notice, so do it right away."

"You'll pay for that too, right?" It was a question that expressed everything. I was on the payroll again. My leave of absence was over. He might not ever contact me, but the direct line was open, no longer the vague indication that I might be tapped again that he had given me in Baku. This time there was a line and it was literally open.

"Yes, Eddie, we'll pay for that too." His tone was exasperated and patronizing. I didn't care as long as the agency paid for the phone. "Get a smart phone, an i-Phone, a Blackberry, and charge it every night so you can keep it constantly on standby."

"I thought cell phones weren't secure."

"Of course they're not, but they're fine for initial contact."

"I'll call you with the number as soon as I have one."

"That won't be necessary," he said.

Ignoring his condescending tone, I agreed. "That it? Anything else?"

"Nothing else at the moment but you know how fast things can change. Keep in touch now. Ta-ta." He disconnected.

It was that fast. That simple. I was back in. All those years later and I was back in. That's why they keep some of us alive. There's no telling when they'll need our experience, our facilities for duplicity and stealth, our willingness to kill to survive.

When I went out I had known this could happen, but I had done my best to forget it. My broom closet was remote from life in the agency. I had come close to believing I was just another Maintainer II, my life in Graham the only reality I dealt with. I liked that. I treasured it. My years here had been healing years. I had gotten out and found safety, all I had to do to earn it was keep things neat and clean, keep blackboards clear and shadows at bay. I worked, I read, I slept well. In Tiger I had the best friend I'd ever had. She, Dawn and Chad had become my family, sweet compensation for the families I had lost, the ones I never had. And, Tiger was a great bar hopping buddy. Sure, from time to time she might get us into a good old knock-down drag-out brawl, at least for us. The poor saps on the other side of her fists might not see it as a good time.

Now I had been pulled back in. I was furious and intended to play things carefully. I wasn't about to let any of the bastards who had intruded themselves upon my life in the last few days destroy the bit of equanimity I had managed to achieve.

The Apple store at the strip mall on the edge of town was still open. I bought the latest model i-Phone and loaded it with the most expensive options and apps. Hell, the agency was paying for it. Let them get the best. After all, they were getting the best when they put me back in the field.

Chapter Thirteen

Henrietta Lane was alive. It was a foggy raw day, the weather stuck between fog and drizzle, not unusual for the Connecticut River valley in late fall and early spring. Randolph braced me in the parking lot behind Barton as I unlocked the door to my truck, ready to drive to work. Before I could react, his good arm was around my neck, cutting off my breath. He had a strong hold on me, a professional hold, tightening with every attempt I made to free myself. I almost admired his skill.

"Ease up or I'll take you to Mrs. Lane unconscious. You don't want that. She might start gnawing your balls off so as to wake you up."

I relaxed, planning to deck him as soon as he loosened his hold. Plans changed when I felt his gun press hard into my ribs. He prodded me along the brick wall at the rear of my building, toward a creamy white Mercedes with tinted windows. He opened the back door and with his free hand gave me a hard shoved. My head went forward, hitting the top of the opening.

"Get in," he said.

Henrietta sat there, her face expressionless, wheezing through her slits of nostrils. She was pointing a snub-nosed pocketbook gun at me. It was accurate only at very close ranges. I was close. Randolph pushed me onto the seat and shut the door. Henrietta stared at me, her lips a thin uneven line across her jaw. Randolph walked around the car and got into the driver's seat. She held the gun unwaveringly at my crotch as he started the car and pulled out of the parking lot, just missing a car headed in. He rolled down his window and shot the driver a bird.

"Fuck you asshole," he yelled.

"Enough, Randolph," Henrietta said, in the same kind of tone she might use on an unruly dog. "We don't need to attract attention."

"Road rage is a terrible thing," I said. "A prime example of arrested emotional development."

"And you shut up too." She poked my nuts with the gun barrel just hard enough to be painful.

"You're back," I said.

"I've never been away, janitor. I have been keeping a low profile since they blew my office up. In case you haven't noticed, somebody tried to take myself out. I've been very careful that myself should not be an easy target if they try again."

Randolph drove us to the entrance of Poet's Seat Tower and Park, which overlooks Graham. A winding narrow road leads to the high rocky ridge where the tower rises above the red stone ledge. A sign at the entrance warns people that the park is closed after dark. A gate made of heavy pipes runs between two stone pillars. It's locked every night at dusk and opened every morning at first light. Randolph drove into the park, got out of the car and pulled the gate shut behind us. Taking a padlock from his pocket, he snapped it shut on the chain that holds the gate to a hasp cemented into a pillar. Henrietta had planned well.

He crept up the steep road through the park, stopping the Mercedes next to the tower, the grille inches from a low stone wall built to keep cars from plummeting off the ledge and flying down through the woods onto the playing grounds of Tuckerman Field below. It failed to deter the occasional suicidal jumper or daredevil teen who ended up splattered at the base of the ledge.

He switched off the engine and got out. Walking to the rear door on the side where I sat, he lit a cigarette and leaned against the car, cradling his cast with his good hand. The cigarette dangled from his lower lip, making him look like something out of a B *noir* movie, an effect underscored by fog, thick, dark and gray, turning the October afternoon into twilight. I could not see beyond the second story of the tower. Graham, below us, was invisible.

"Somebody tried to kill me, janitor," Henrietta said. "I guess my luck was good and theirs was bad."

"It will be worse. Hope that I don't come to think it was you." "It wasn't," I said, knowing my denials were worthless. If she wanted to believe it was me, she would believe. That's the nature of faith. We believe what we want to believe, evidence, reason, truth be damned. Faith is the source of most of the world's problems. It is also one of our graces. Janus, the two-faced god, is the lord of faith. Coincidentally, his name is also the root of the word, janitor. He is the one god I am partial to.

She didn't say anything, just stared at me, keeping the gun close to and pointed at my balls.

"My contacts at the fire station say there's no doubt that the fire at your office was arson."

She snorted. "It doesn't take an Einstein to figure that out, just a good nose. Arson, by the way, is a skill my sources tell me you have some experience with, along with some other proficiencies unusual in a janitor."

I went cold, speechless. There it was again, this time more than just a hint that she knew more about me than my personnel file at the college contained. Was she fishing or had she managed to ferret out details of my past? And if so, how? The agency is as secret as one can get. Congress funds it through a maze of other intelligence organizations, but has no clue as to what it's funding. The parent agencies know little about it, except that from time to time they receive reliable intelligence. They have no knowledge of its activities, of its personnel. They have perfect deniability, yet can be sure things they need done will get done. Information comes their way. Enemies and potential enemies find research labs destroyed, weapons caches blown up, machinery sabotaged. Troublesome people disappear. And the public never knows a thing.

Not even the President knows about it. For very good reasons. Presidents are political creatures who come and go, most of them leaving little real mark of their tenure in the White House beyond the puffs of their press agents and media hype. The agencies and the bureaus go on. The men and women who staff them are the government. They do the real work. They build roads. They make contracts for planes, ships, monuments and buildings. They gather information. They see to it that bad people, or at least people they believe bad, are neutralized, terminated, done away with. Agents and bureaucrats carry out the many and various policies and activities of government. A President may set the tone, and some, when they have the chance to appoint Supreme Court Justices do succeed in affecting the future, but in most cases agents and bureaucrats are instrumental in developing policies and in carrying them out. Presidents sign on to them.

The agency is specialized, efficient and far more invisible than even its creators had hoped. It is so low key, so underplayed, that it is known only as the agency, all in lower case letters. There is no other designation.

It was my knowledge that the agency was so covert that led to the sharp cold snaking through my veins. What did Henrietta Lane know? And how? Who was she?

She was watching my face, smiling as questions flitted through my mind. I was sure she knew exactly what I was thinking.

"Don't ask," she said, confirming it. "I'm the one asking the questions. You're answering. Then she rapped on the window with the pistol. "Randolph," she called. He opened the door. "Help the janitor out, please."

Still holding his gun, he grabbed my arm and dragged me from my seat. Henrietta got out the other side and came around the back of the car, momentarily touching my right temple with her gun. As she pushed he dragged me to the wall, forcing me to lean over, face down, looking into the featureless fog hiding the drop to the field below. My heart was pounding. I had been in worse situations with worse people, but that was when I had been at my peak, a long time ago. In the most literal sense I was staring into the abyss, the void that threatened to overwhelm the existentialists with fear and trembling. In spite of the dire nature of my situation, I managed to be struck by the absurdity of it, being kidnapped, perhaps murdered, by an anorexic real estate dealer and her Texas henchman.

"Hold him over further, Randolph," she said. "The way you've got him now, if you have to let him go, he might not fall much beyond a few feet." Holding my belt with his good hand, Randolph scraped me over the stone wall until nothing but my knees rested on the top.

"Now, janitor," she said. "Who burned my office?"

"I don't know."

"Randolph," she said.

Randolph pushed me further toward the void. The rocks dug into my knees and lower legs. The wet fog swept around my face as I stared into it, seeing nothing but a raw featureless gray.

She repeated, "Who burned my office?"

"Lady, if I knew, I'd tell you. I'm no hero."

"Randolph, give him a little more memory reinforcement." He leaned over the wall, his belly on the rough red stone, pushing me further until only his grip on my belt was keeping me from falling. My heart was pounding harder, my breath coming in gasps. I thought I was having a heart attack. Shutting my eyes, I concentrated on the specks of light floating through the blackness behind the lids, wondering if they would be the last things I saw.

"Who burned my office?"

"I don't know." I heard my reply from a distance. I was already halfway into a chasm far deeper than the fall to the field below.

She made a sound, something between a sigh and a grunt. It voiced both disgust and resignation. "This asshole doesn't know squat." I felt the cold steel of the gun barrel on the bare skin behind my left ear. When she spoke again, her tone was harsh, rasping. "Janitor, you have two jobs now, find out who sold Andy the dope and find out who burned my office." She got back into the car. Just before shutting the door, she said, "Have some fun, Randolph. Give me your gun and let's beat the shit out of him and get out of here."

Hitting my head with his cast, Randolph pulled me back from the edge, Henrietta jabbing me with his gun, as he pushed and pulled me over to the tower. They forced me up against the stone and he jammed his knee into my groin. I gasped and doubled over. He grabbed my head and rammed his rising knee into my jaw. I arched back, hitting my head against the tower, struggling to breathe as he held his cast against my throat and pummeled his fist into my stomach. All the time Henrietta kept the gun jammed against my neck. I lost count at thirteen, each of his jabs landing and higher on my body as I slipped to the ground. The last blow I remember was his cast crashing down on the right side of my head, just above the ear.

§§§

Draw a straight line from Poet's Seat to Barton Rooms and it would be less than a mile. Walking, it's about two and a half. Walking it after a bald ugly thug with a bad east Texas accent has pounded the daylights out of you, then cold cocked you with plaster cast, and it's at least twenty-six miles.

Back in my room, I stood under a hot shower examining my wounds. My knees and legs were scraped, already beginning to scab. My arms and abdomen were purple with bruises. I didn't want to see my face. If it looked half as bad as it felt, I'd be scaring the pants off of children and old women. It hurt to do so, but I smiled at the thought. Maybe it would work on Shelley, touch her with the kind of sympathy that ends up in the sack. I called her instead of going to work. I was two hours late anyway.

"I'm in trouble," I said when she answered the phone. "What's wrong?" I told her how I'd been worked over. "I'll be there in as soon as I can." "I'll leave the door unlocked. Just come in. If I'm asleep, wake me up."

§§§

She rushed toward me as soon as she saw me lying on my bed, gave me a brief hug and backed off when she heard me groan from the pain of her embrace. She took off her jacket and hung it on the back of a kitchen chair. She was wearing a clinging white silk blouse and a light blue skirt.

I lay there, my lower body covered with a towel. The few lights I had were arranged to illuminate my injuries, in hope the dramatic scene would get me laid, give me a few moments of respite from the pain. I turned my face, which was as cut, bruised and swollen as I had feared. "Does this scare the pants off you?"

"I don't have any on." Crossing the room, she looked me over. "I should have worn them. It's cool outside and you don't look as though you're in any shape to take advantage of their absence." She leaned in, examining me. "Somebody did a thorough number on you."

"Oh, I am in shape," I said. "I need to be. It'll help me forget how much I hurt. Henrietta Lane turned Randolph loose on me."

"You didn't fight back?" She sounded surprised.

"They were both armed." I told her what happened, omitting any mention of my fear that Henrietta knew more about me than she should. When I was finished I stuck out my lower lip and tried to look winsome and sad. "Doesn't it make you want to make love to me out of pure pity?"

"That sounds good, although pity's got nothing to do with it." The towel had begun to look like a circus tent.

"Look at that," she said. "I can see I'm going to take care of you, and I expect you to return the favor as soon as you've recovered.

"Consider it a commitment."

She stopped what she was doing and looked up, her eyes wide. "Commitment? Don't say commitment. I don't do commitments."

"I only meant that I'd return the favor. That kind of commitment."

"That I can deal with." She ran her tongue over my lips before lifting her skirt and carefully lowering herself onto me. "Enough of that silly stuff. You be sure to say something if I'm hurting you."

"Right. Like I'm going to put a stop to this."

"They're your cuts and bruises."

"Forget about them," I said. "I have." We were really getting into it when the phone rang. "Ignore it," I said.

"I am. What phone?"

It rang four times before the machine picked up. It was Tiger. "Sanders, where the hell are you? It's five-thirty and you're not here, you haven't called in, and I'm trying to cover your area and mine. Thanks asshole."

"She sounds pissed," Shelley said.

"I'll explain it to her later." I reached up, pulling her lips down to mine. "I hope you'll be selective about what you tell her."

"I'll be discreet," I said.

She laughed and kissed me.

Afterwards, we lay on the bed. I told her about the trip to New Jersey and Pennsylvania, but she seemed almost disinterested other than commenting that no one should poach in another person's relationship when I told her about Tiger and Sylvia. She was curled into my arm, her lips resting against my neck, one hand caressing my chest. I was sore and aching and content.

"Why would Henrietta think you'd know anything about her office fire?"

I shrugged, formulating an answer. Even as I spoke, I saw how lame my response was. "Probably because I've been nosing around among Graham's low-lifes. Maybe I hit home with questions about Andy and the fire was a warning to shut things down."

I felt her head shaking. "That doesn't make any sense."

"You're right. I don't know and I don't want to think about it anymore. I've got to get dressed and go to work. Maybe scrubbing a few toilets, washing a few blackboards and hanging around in the halls of academe will clear my mind."

She rolled over and sat on the edge of the bed. "I've got class tonight and I promised to hand back their papers."

I looked at my watch. "Ain't gonna happen."

"Nope. Think I ought to tell them why?"

"I wouldn't. They'd probably dis you for doing a janitor."

"Maintainer II, right?"

"Not according to Henrietta Lane."

"Screw Henrietta Lane."

"No way in Hell." I buttoned her yellow silk blouse and she zipped my trousers. We held on to each other for long minutes.

"See you after work?" she asked.

"We'll go to the Townie for a burger and beer."

When I managed to show up for work at the college, Tiger began to snarl as I walked down the hall toward her. She got a good look at me and her mouth dropped.

"Don't ask," I said. "I'll tell you."

"We'll kill the dickheads that did this," she said when I finished. "That's one of the nicest things you've ever said to me," I told her.

Chapter Fourteen

Shelley was sitting at a booth in the Townie, a glass of wine in her hand. I walked toward her, nodding to Billy Melnick who sat at the bar talking to a heavy man sitting on the next stool, his butt overflowing the seat. It was almost ten-thirty. Three of the booths were full, two tables were taken and seven or eight people sat at the bar. Miles Davis' *Kind of Blue* came from the speakers.

"Dude, got a minute to talk?" Billy called, waving to me and pointing to the man next to him. "I want you to meet Elsworth Buell."

"Later." I eased into the booth across from Shelley. She smiled and took my hand. "I've got a date."

"Who's the man with Billy?" she asked.

"I would guess he's Elsworth Buell, but I've never seen him before." Buell said something and Billy shrugged, slid off his stool and moved unsteadily toward us holding a glass, the beer spilling over the rim. Buell stood and followed him. In his early to mid forties, he must have weighed 230 and was at least six and a half feet tall. Dressed in khaki pants, a gray sport jacket over a light blue tee shirt, and boat shoes with no socks, he had a heavy black beard and long wavy black hair that reached two or three inches below his ears. The floorboards creaked as he moved toward us, a glass of red wine in his hand. Billy sat next to me. Buell pushed in next to Shelley. She moved toward the wall, trying to make room for him, but he took up most of her side.

Billy raised his hand for the waitress. She came over, standing well away from the man who was now crowding Shelley into the wall. "Cat," he said. "Bring me another pitcher of beer and another Montepulcian of or my friend here."

When she was gone he clapped his hand on my shoulder. I winced. He gave me a close look.

"Dude, what happened to you?"

"It was an accident," I said.

He gave me an unconcerned shrug and gestured across the table. "Eddie, I want you to meet Elsworth Buell. El teaches English at Ralston College. He and Evans Cornell were close. El, this is Eddie Sanders, my good friend."

"I wouldn't exactly call us friends," Buell said. 'We're acquaintances." He didn't offer to shake my hand and he barely looked at Shelly. "I understand you are in possession of the Bukowski recordings." His eyes were dark, heavy lidded, and he spoke with the cultivated accent people acquire when they wish to give the impression of being members of the New England elite. There was a slight curl to his upper lip, as if talking to me was equivalent to eating a plateful of cat shit.

I ignored his words and tone. "This is Shelley Randall," I said, directing my eyes to her. "Shelley teaches English at Graham Community College."

He looked at her briefly, shaking his head as if in sympathy. "I can't imagine doing that. There can't be much going on in a community college to keep one's brain active." Turning back to me, he sniffed his wine before taking a sip. "I want Evans' recordings."

"It's quite challenging," Shelley said, seeming to take no notice of his disregard for her. "I've had classes with students who were sixteen, dual enrollment high school kids, sitting next to seventy and eighty year old men and women still excited about learning and changing their lives. I would assume classes at Ralston are far more homogeneous. Now that would be dull work."

"Screw Ralston students, which I do every chance I get." His laugh was unpleasant as he looked at me for verification of the success of his humor.

Billy grinned. "This dude is too much, Eddie. I'd've stayed in school if I could've had more Profs like him."

"He's a riot," I said, turning to Buell. "Don't worry about the recordings. They're safe."

He took another sip of wine and pointed a finger at me. "From what Melnick tells me, I understand that you're a janitor."

"Maintainer II," I said.

He ignored the comment. "I've got a doctorate from Yale in modern American poetry. I did my dissertation on Ezra Pound, who most people can't even begin to understand. I've published seven books and close to a hundred articles in juried academic journals on Pound and other modern American poets. I've edited and co-edited five introductory literature textbooks for college students, as well as a definitive text on Twentieth Century American fiction for upper level students. I was a tenured full Professor at Ralston College before I was thirty."

He gave me a smile that was mostly a smirk and leaned across the table, hands folded in front of him. "You do sweep halls in a community college, is that not correct?"

"Among other things. I swab out toilets and make sure the classrooms are clean, well-lighted places."

"That's about as low in the academic world as one can get," he said, the editor of a text on Twentieth Century American fiction missing my reference to Hemingway's story.

My mouth struck before my mind could react. It was that old hair trigger that among other things led me to leaving the agency. Under cover means under control, something I felt I was in danger of losing toward the end of my time at the agency. My life in Graham was a struggle for control. "There's much lower, Professor Buell. An elitist motherfucker acting as if he is the king cat who's got to blow or we can't quite make it."

He frowned, confused, maybe a bit frightened by what I hoped was the image I presented of someone capable of unpredictable rage and violence. It frightened me.

"Lawrence Ferlinghetti," I said. "He's a Twentieth Century American poet."

Black impotent rage moved in waves across his face. He pointed at me again. "I must have those recordings."

"They're safe," I repeated. There had been a time when I would have grabbed his finger and bent it backward until it snapped with a loud and satisfying sound.

"What possible use could you have for them?"

Cat brought the drinks and empty glasses for Shelley and me. Buell drained his first glass and took a sip from the fresh one. I poured a glass of beer from Billy's pitcher, passed it to Shelley and poured one for myself. I sipped quietly, my eyes locked on Buell's. He tried to stare me down and lost after less than half a minute. I let a minute of silence pass before asking, "How do you know about the recordings?"

He cleared his throat. "After Cornell died I went to his office, just to make sure his papers and such were in order, you understand. It was only a matter of time before the department head or a dean would clear things out in order for his replacement to move in. It was a nice office and there's already been a great deal of jockeying for it. I wanted to be sure there was nothing there that Evans had left undone, or that he wouldn't want anybody to see." He smiled, as if including me in some conspiracy. "Some of us have friendships with students that others wouldn't understand. I wanted to find out if Evans had left anything around his office, notes, souvenirs, pictures, things that could cast any relationships he might have been having in the wrong light. If Evans had such things, I would have removed them. There is no point in leaving something for administrators to find, misinterpret and use as an excuse for a witch hunt."

He stopped and watched me, looking as though he were hoping for an expression of understanding. I kept my eyes on his face, saying nothing.

He continued. "There was an unfinished letter in his desk to a woman named Sylvia Cornell, his sister, I assumed from the name and tone of it, saying he had given the Bukowski recordings to a Billy Melnick for safe-keeping and that she should be sure to get them from him should anything happen to Evans."

I asked, "Had he ever mentioned them to you?"

He shook his head. "Never. I assumed they must be important if he had to give them to someone to keep them safe. I looked up Melnick in the phone book, called him, and with a little finesse, got him to confirm their importance in some detail."

"This dude scammed me brilliantly," Billy said. "You gotta admire someone who can make you think he's telling you things when he's really getting you to tell him whatever he wants to know."

"Interrogation is a subtle skill," I said.

Buell smiled, his lips red from the wine. "I took a graduate course in unobtrusive techniques when I thought I might do folklore research.' "You didn't contact the sister?" I asked Buell shook his head.

"Judging from the fact he was writing her a letter, didn't you think that Evans Cornell would have wanted his sister to know about the recordings?"

"You listen to me," he said.

I thought of a hundred situations I had been in over the years when anyone who spoke in that tone would have been on the floor before he could inhale again, but I kept silent, never moving my eyes from his.

"I'm the expert on American poetry," he said, looking away. "If those recordings contain variant readings of some of Bukowski's signature poems, they're very important."

"I'm surprised that a main line academic would be interested in an outsider poet like Bukowski," Shelley said.

"Things change," Buell muttered, not looking at her. He was not the type to credit a woman with much importance. He moved his eyes back to the lower part of my face. "Besides, he's a phenomenon. Students read him, quote him. He's become significant in spite of more cultured, more important academic values and tastes. Soon he'll become an established figure, like Frost who, some say was misanthropic, anti-intellectual, cruel and angry. Maybe, maybe not, but literary fame can erase a writer's worst characteristics. It's all marketing. One day a writer is unknown or marginal, the next day there are seminars on his work at every Ivy League university."

"Or hers," Shelley said.

He didn't acknowledge the remark.

She said, "You mean now that he's been dead for more than a decade, it's safe for parasites like you to use his work. There's no chance of him showing up, doing a reading on your campus and beating the shit out of you." She gave him an evil smile. "He liked to do that, you know, beat up on pompous jerks at academic readings."

He looked at her with contempt. "As I said, nobody's going to care about that aspect of him. He'll belong to the world."

"Time to go, Mr. Buell," I said. The conversation had become unproductive and would soon turn further unpleasant unless we ended it.

"I prefer Dr. Buell," he said.

"Mr. Buell, I have a date with this lovely, brilliant woman you're crushing against the wall. Now, leave. You're not getting the recordings, but you are pissing me off."

"Dude," Billy started to say. "Don't," I told him.

Buell started to object. I cut him off. "Shut up. And in case you don't understand that, it's janitor-speak for, get your fat useless butt out of here or I'm going to pound you so hard your dick is going to run up your asshole to hide."

He looked like he was about to argue, but in spite of his size he was not a fighter and probably never had been. He slid out of the booth and left the Townie without another word.

"That was harsh, dude," Billy said.

"Billy, I want to be alone with Shelley."

"He'd've paid us big bucks for those recordings," he said. "He's the man who's got the connections to do something real with them. We can use him, dude."

"We'll talk about it tomorrow," I said. "After the funerals?" he asked. "Funerals?"

"For Evans and Ariel. Tomorrow morning. According to the paper, him at ten, her at eleven, then both of them being buried at noon."

"Sure," I said. "We'll talk tomorrow, but no more now, okay?"

He got up and stood at the end of the table. Resting his hands on its surface, he leaned toward me. "Those recordings can make us serious money. Take care of them."

"Tomorrow," I said. "We'll talk tomorrow."

"They're mine, you know."

"Cornell gave them to you for safe-keeping and you gave them to me for the same reason."

"And Evans is dead."

"Exactly. Tomorrow, okay."

"Okay." He gave me a weak smile and went back to his seat at the bar. He'd tried every play in the book to get the recordings. I felt sorry for him and his desperation. "Cat," I said as she walked by, "Give Billy another pitcher of whatever he's drinking tonight, on me."

Shelley leaned toward me. "Why not give him the recordings? He is right, you know, Cornell entrusted them to him."

"They got the Cornells killed and could do the same for him." She didn't answer and I didn't say anything further. Maybe I was fooling myself. Billy had a claim on the recordings. Shelley was right, Cornell had entrusted them to him. Who was I to decide that to protect him I needed to keep them? The truth was I liked having those recordings. They were a secret and being in on a mystery, even one a small as this, was a connection with my covert past. Not the recordings themselves, but the danger my clandestine possession of them was coming to represent.

Shutting down that line of thought, I reached out and took Shelley's hand. "Lean over a little more and show me your tits."

She pulled her hand away. "This isn't New Orleans." Her voice was laced with mock reproach.

"I don't mean here. Back at your place."

"You have such a smooth line," she said. "Women must fall all over themselves for you. Not my place. It's a mess. How about yours?"

"It is closer."

"Good. I'm in a hurry.

"Spoken like a woman after my own heart."

"Eddie, it's not your heart I'm after. I'm sure you have a very good heart, but my tastes run to something less complex and more carnal. Are you sure you're up to the required physical activity? You look pretty sad and I saw you wince when Billy touched your shoulder."

"Try me."

"Why not?" She did.

Back in my room, she showed me her tits. I gave them a close examination. They were still magnificent, flawless, as was the rest of her.

"You must have had an easy pregnancy with Marion," I said. "Who?" she asked.

"Marion. Your daughter. You've got no stretch marks on that exquisite belly of yours."

After a long minute, she said, "Easy all the way. It was an easy birth too." She pulled my hand to her stomach. God, that horrible man wanted the recordings, didn't he?"

"He won't get them," I said, letting her change the subject.

"Bukowski was quite disgusting, you know. He puts women down and he writes about revolting things, like skid marks and dog turds."

"Skid marks and dog turds are two of the most common elements of life. Not many poets address things that basic. Can you imagine Yeats, or Wordsworth or Shakespeare talking about them?"

"Shakespeare, maybe, Chaucer no doubt. Still, some of his poems are nothing but jerking off in print."

"Chaucer's?"

She laughed, pretending to slap me. "Bukowski's. Some of his stuff is just masturbatory garbage."

"You bet. And some of it's moving and lovely and right on about the tenuousness of life and the truth of loneliness."

She fell silent and there was no more conversation. Later, as we were each about to fall into the separation of sleep, she turned her back and snuggled into me, spoon fashion.

"It's kind of nice," she said.

"It's very nice. Even beat up the way I am, I'm feeling better than I've felt in years."

"Well, that too," she said.

"What were you saying was nice?"

"That there's all this fuss about poetry. Poetry doesn't intrude on the real world very often. It's been relegated to classroom discussions."

"Most poets don't know the real world," I said. "At least the ones who end up in modern poetry journals."

I dropped into a deep and restful sleep. When I woke, sunlight was pouring into the room and Shelley still lay scrunched up against me. It was eight o'clock. I pulled myself up and resting on an elbow stared her awake.

We are odd creatures, so committed to our faith in reason, so quick to ignore or denigrate the vestiges of behavior that allowed the species to survive and develop the skills for rational analysis. What jungle instinct alerts us to some one or some thing staring at us as we sleep? What is the nature of sleep that we can still sense the predator crouched, ready to pounce unless we stir and fight or flee?

"Hey," I said when her eyes were wide open, her expression alert. "Hey, yourself." She reached up, pulling my face down to hers. We kissed and I pulled away.

"What's wrong?" she asked.

"Nothing. The Cornells' funerals are this morning. I'm going."

"Me too," she said.

"Why would you do that? I didn't know them, but I've got a connection through Billy and the Andy Lane thing. I want to watch and see if I can pick anything up. I don't see why you'd want to go, why anyone would want to go to a couple of strangers' funerals."

"I have my reasons," she said. "For one, I get to spend a little more time with you, plus, I'm curious. What kind of people will be there and will there be more talk about the Bukowski recordings? Maybe it's morbid, but I'm going."

I shrugged. She got out of bed. I lay there, hands behind my head, watching as she moved naked around my room, got her clothes and slipped them on.

Putting her shoes on, she said, "I've got to go home and dress properly. I'll meet you at the funeral home. Where is it?"

"I don't know. Hand me yesterday's paper from the table." I turned to the obits. Burial was from the Sturdevandt Funeral Home, a converted Victorian house on High Street, near the corner of High and Riddell. We made plans to meet in front of the building at ten of ten.

Chapter Fifteen

Shelley had just closed the door on her way out when the telephone rang. "Sylvia's in town." Tiger sounded as close to panic as Tiger can get. "She called me last night. Luckily, Dawn was already asleep and I was watching wrestling on television. Said she wants to see me and asked me to come to her brother's funeral this morning."

"You going?"

There was a pause. I could hear her breathing into the phone. She cleared her throat and mumbled. "Yes."

"Think about it, Tige. She's a Corelli. Evans was a Corelli, no matter how laundered he was. He was a Corelli in New Jersey, a Corelli from New Haven to Burlington, a Corelli all over western New England, and a Cornell in Ralston and Graham. She's not here just to mourn. Think about her reaction when we told her Cornell and his wife had been murdered. Next to nothing. I don't trust her. You shouldn't either."

"I know that, Eddie."

"You've got a great life with Dawn and Chad."

"I know that too. I love them both."

"Then why see Sylvia? Why risk it?"

"Three reasons. One, you need someone there to watch your back. She's up to more than just coming to her brother's funeral. Two, I'm curious. Who's going to be there, just the Ralston College types, or will they be elbow to elbow with gangsters from Jersey and New York? And what kind of a scene will that be? Three, I want to see her. Sex with her was fireworks and earth moving."

"Looking for a replay?" I asked, with some level of understanding given my own recent fireworks display.

She took a deep, deep breath and let it out in a blast that sounded like an explosion over the phone. "No. No, I'm not looking for a replay. It's a nice fantasy, but I can't afford it. I won't risk the life I've built here. Maybe I just want to look at her and see if she holds the match that lights the fireworks, even if I can't send them up. But that's just part of it, Eddie; I'm concerned about you. There's too much going on for you to be flying solo."

"You're right, and I appreciate it, but you can't kid me and don't try to kid yourself, you'd go with her again if the chance came up."

"And I was a thousand percent sure Dawn wouldn't find out? Bet your sweet broom chasing ass I would."

§§§

The parking lot at the Sturdevandt Funeral Home was filled with Volvos and Saabs with Massachusetts license plates and Mercedes, Jaguars and BMWs from New Jersey and New York. I pulled my truck next to a black Mercedes with a Jersey vanity plate displaying the initials AXC and a picture of a lighthouse. Several cars away, a tall man, lean and elderly, tan and fit, was locking the driver's door of a Lexus with low number Massachusetts plates.

As I cut my engine, an antique Volkswagen mini-bus with Vermont plates pulled into the lot, parking next to me. It was covered with faded painted flowers, the words Peace and Love beneath them. There were Grateful Dead bumper stickers on each side of the rear, see through decals of rainbows, unicorns and stained glass designs on several of the windows. Another tall man, this one with salt and pepper hair pulled back into a braid got out of the driver's seat and came around to the other side. He wore a denim jacket with intricate needlepoint designs, some abstract, some of flowers and animals, corduroy pants and heavy leather-tooled boots. He opened the passenger door. Thick marijuana smoke wafted out, filling the air around me.

A heavy woman got out and stood by the door, a thin plume of smoke rising from a joint in her hand. The man put his arms around her and held her as she sobbed with a deep violent sound. She wore a navy pea coat over a light cotton dress that was as blue as the jacket and so long that it almost concealed the white cotton socks she wore beneath scuffed, muddy sneakers. Both wore round gold-rimmed glasses. She took a deep breath, controlled her sobbing and eased herself away from the man as she took a hit from the joint and passed it to him. He toked and exhaled. Then wetting his forefinger and thumb, he extinguished the joint, popped it in his mouth, chewed and swallowed it. Arms around each other, they walked toward the funeral home.

The older man from the Lexus crossed the lot in front of them. "Dad," the man said.

He glanced their way, nodded, and walked into the funeral home.

James Sturdevandt, the funeral director, was standing off to the side of the parking lot, smoking a cigarette. He waved as I locked the truck door and walked over to him. We played on the same summer softball team. As a result of his great sense of humor, his generosity in the community, and the fact that he was a worse outfielder than I was, we had become friends, despite his being Graham born and bred and my origins in Long Lake, New York, a minuscule town in the central Adirondacks of New York state. Only those native to Graham are looked on as true townies. The rest of us are okay, but since our diapers weren't bought in the same stores as those who have lived here all their lives we will never be insiders. Good friends, yes. Elected to office, yes. Real Grahamfeldians, never.

"Hey, Corky," I said, using the name everyone in town knew him by. He grinned at me and tossed his cigarette on the pavement, crushing it under his foot. "Eddie, good to see you, even here." He caught himself and slipped into a more solemn, professional manner. He reached out for a handshake. "Sorry. You a friend of the Cornells?"

"Never met them. I've met his sister. That's why I'm here. Who were the ancient hippies?"

"Ariel Cornell's parents. They were here last night too. Wanted to see her. I told them it wasn't a good idea, that the murder had been brutal, but they insisted. I stayed with them, just in case, you know. I do good work, but I can't cover everything up and it wouldn't be good to have someone faint in here and hit their head and get hurt. I can't afford to get sued. They took it pretty hard, but Cornell's sister was here and took them out to get something to eat and got them a room at Howard Johnson's. Then she came back and started in with the flowers."

He grinned again, the funereal look gone as fast as it came. "Some sister that Sylvia, eh? Except for taking the wife's parents out, she was here from yesterday afternoon until after eleven last night, double-checking all the arrangements, making follow up phone calls on everything I'd done. A babe. Tough, a control freak, but a real major babe. The kind that makes you cry just to look at her, knowing she doesn't even see you. Know her well?" He raised his eyebrows.

"Nope. We've met briefly. I figured since she'd come some distance, from the Philadelphia area, it might be nice for her to see a familiar face or two. Judging from the out of state cars in your lot, I guess I didn't have to bother. Did she arrange the funeral?"

He shook his head. "Like I said, I set it all up. She was just double-checking. Although you ask her, she'll probably tell you she did it all, but it was really my work. I did it. Somebody by the name of Leonardo Corelli called, said he was a business associate of Cornell's father and told me to set it up. Gave me a budget of sixty-five grand. Can you believe that? You don't get many sixty-five grand funerals in Graham." He shook his head in amazement. "This is the first one I've had."

"I can believe it," I said.

He gave me an odd look. "He told me to arrange everything, the service, the burial, the reception. Make it first-class, he said, the best of everything and the ace place for the reception. Those were his words, the ace place. Told me not to stint on anything, but whatever was left over was mine, if the family was satisfied. And," he jerked a thumb toward his building, "from the looks of them, it's not a family I want to have dissatisfied with me."

He took a cigarette from a pack in his coat pocket, stuck it between his lips, but didn't light it. "The coffin's top of the line. Bishop White's come up from Springfield to do the service, but here, not in a church. Odd, eh? And there's a reception at the Elkins Inn afterwards. Took over the whole place for the day. Full menu, lunch and dinner, open bar, breakfast tomorrow. Evans and Ariel Cornell are going out in style. A few funerals like this each year and I could start thinking about retirement. A chain with headquarters in New Jersey has been trying to buy me out for a couple of years now. The price is good, but they won't guarantee that I'll stay on as director for more than two years. I can't afford to stop working, even if they pay what I'm asking for the place."

He rubbed his arms against the cool October air and put the cigarette back in the pack. Leaning over, he picked up the one he had stubbed out earlier and put it into a plastic sandwich bag he took from a pocket. We walked toward the front entrance and I saw Shelley standing on the porch dressed in a dark blue suit, the jacket cut straight, the skirt rising to her mid-calf, her blouse white with a ruffled collar. She wasn't wearing makeup and her hair was pulled back into a bun. Corky shook her hand when I introduced them and went inside.

"You look like a Yankee mourner, very austere," I said.

She smiled. "Guess I've lived in New England too long." She took my arm and held it tight as we walked into the home's central hall. The interior light was soft but not dim. People milled around, some looking at a table displaying Evans Cornell's books, monographs and articles from academic journals. Surrounding them were pictures of Ariel and him, separately and together. Her parents were there, the mother touching the photos of her daughter as though she could feel her substance, will her back into being. There were shots of Ariel as a baby, a young girl, at many stages of her life. Summer beach shots, formal school portraits, family scenes, Ariel with her parents, looking separate from them. Even as a child, she had adopted a distinct non-hippie style. Her life was documented on that table. She had been a tall, slender, stately, beautiful woman. The youngest pictures of Evans had been taken when he was in college. They documented the life of Evans Cornell. For the purposes of the funeral, Edward Corelli had never existed.

We passed through the small crowd to a service room marked by a sign with removable white letters stuck into a grooved black background.

Poet's Seat

Evans Cornell, Ph.D.
July 14, 1970

Ariel Cornell
September 3, 1975

"Amid a place of stone
Be secret and exult,
Because of all things known
That is the most difficult."

"Yeats," Shelley said. It's from a poem, *To a Friend Whose Work Has Come to Nothing*. He loved Yeats."

I looked at her. "He did? How would you know?"

"One of the monographs on the table back there was on Yeats as a romantic singer," her response quick. "You didn't notice? So he must have admired his work. Why else would it have been displayed here?"

"I didn't even look. Scholarly writings don't mean much to a guy who sweeps up after people who care about them."

She took my arm again, pressing it against her so I could feel the swell of her breast against my forearm as she led us into the room. Even there, among caskets and mourners, I felt myself quicken. Sex is such an odd thing. I went for years without it; got to a point where I hardly thought about it, and then whammo, a few sexual encounters and it's all I can think about. A hint of breast under a jacket and a bra, next thing I know I'm practically pole vaulting every time I see her.

I eyeballed the room from the doorway. Two caskets, barely visible through the mass of flowers surrounding and cascading over them sat in front of twenty to twenty five rows of folding metal chairs.

Shelley squeezed my hand. "Just a dumb and ignorant janitor? Right. You're full of shit, you know that."

"I know. But I didn't know the Yeats poem. In fact, I don't know much about poetry at all. I'm counting on you teaching me."

Before she could answer, Sylvia Cornell came over, extending her hand to me. A quick look passed between Shelley and her, then both dropped their eyes. She wore a black sheath dress, no jewelry, her makeup just subtle enough that someone might ask, is she wearing any makeup? Men throughout the room were watching her. I introduced her to Shelley. They shook hands, saying nothing. Sylvia turned back to me.

"Thank you for coming, both of you. Will Catherine be here?"

"She told me she would."

"And I always keep my word." Tiger's voice came from behind me. Sylvia walked past us, giving Tiger a quick hug. "Good to see you, Catherine. I appreciate your coming."

"Catherine?" Shelley whispered to me.

"Not a word to anyone at school," I said. "It would ruin her reputation. And what was that look you gave Sylvia?"

"I told you, I don't like people who poach in other people's relationships."

"Me neither," I said, more out of loyalty to her sensibilities than from my own moral stance.

Tiger wore a man's black suit, a white shirt with a dark maroon silk scarf under the collar and tucked in the front. Her shoes were black running sneakers. They looked almost in keeping with the suit. With her broad shoulders and narrow waist accentuated by the cut of the jacket, she looked like a bouncer from an expensive but rowdy club.

Most funeral homes are sterile, cookie cutter places, with anonymous prints of tulips and country hillsides on their walls and expensive unimaginative furniture from upscale chain stores. They all seem to have the same muted lighting and the same piped organ music. It's the furniture you see and the music you hear in hotel lobbies, waiting rooms in doctors' offices and elevators. Nothing's different anymore, unique. We're born in hospitals that are parts of huge corporate chains. We spend our lives in cookie cutter places. We die from eating food products with a high grease and cholesterol count at franchise restaurants and more and more often we're buried from chain funeral homes. Corky and his wife Linda Adams have made sure that the Sturdevandt Funeral Home is different, that it reflects them and the community.

Linda is a painter, with a master of fine arts degree from Rhode Island School of Design. She's one of the more esteemed realists in western Massachusetts art circles. The walls in all the public rooms of the funeral home are hung with her watercolors and oils of local scenes and people. The furnishings are expensive and tasteful antiques purchased over the years by Corky's grandfather and father, J. Reins Sturdevandt, Senior and Junior, who established the business. The music tends to be Bach, Handel, even Mozart, rather than somber organ versions of hymns and sentimental tunes.

The result is a funeral home that almost makes you feel comfortable. Of course, no funeral home can really do that. They are places for the dead and the grieving, after all. Still, Corky and Linda are genuine in their understanding of loss and grief and their place of business reflects that.

This time the music was not piped in. At the rear of the room a string quartet of two men and two women played an arrangement of Vivaldi's *Four*

Seasons. An aisle, leading from the caskets to the string quartet, divided the seating. One side was filling with academic types. The men wore sport coats, pastel shirts and designer ties. Several of them even had patches on their elbows. Their trousers were Dockers and dungarees. Almost all wore running shoes. Most had varying types of beards and mustaches. Few of the women wore makeup and many wore their hair pulled back. A handful wore skirts, mostly gray, brown or dark blue. They had on muted blouses, some with vests, a few with jackets, many with sweaters draped over their shoulders, the arms hanging over their breasts. All seemed to be carrying or holding cloth or canvas bags.

Men and women were chatting among themselves, their side of the room a soft hum of modulated professional voices. If someone were to begin keening or otherwise displaying grief in any way other than wiping a stray tear from a cheek, these people would look on with horror and disdain at the mourner for daring to reveal the pain of sorrow and bereavement. One of the most egregious misuses of the cultured intellect is allowing it to shelter us from the anguish of living.

To the left, the seats were filled with unsmiling men, dressed in black suits with white shirts and dark ties, their hair carefully combed. Except for a few trimmed mustaches, all were clean shaven, most wearing several gold rings, gold cufflinks and gold watches, their black shoes shining like mirrors. They sat, looking straight ahead, not at the coffins, not at the two or three of their number who, at any time, were kneeling on low padded prayer benches before the caskets, staring into the air between the tops of the caskets and the ceiling. Two, in the second row, spoke in inaudible tones, the others sitting silent, as if waiting for some divine presence to manifest itself in the room.

I watched as Sylvia led Tiger to a corner at the front of the room. In the shelter of the masses of flowers, they spoke for several minutes until distracted by a small commotion coming from the hallway. As they turned to look, the people crowding the doorway between the hall and the room parted.

A bent, elderly man entered, moving with the aid of an aluminum walker, flanked by two huge men in black suits with jackets that did little to disguise the obvious guns in shoulder holsters beneath them. The old man's hair was white, his face drawn and bony, cheekbones looking as though they could at any time burst through the taut paper skin stretched over them. Two other black suited men rose from their seats. Each taking one of the old man's arms, they led him to a chair in the front row near where Shelley and I stood. They stepped aside so the bodyguards could sit, one on either side of him. Shelley stared at the old man for a moment and turned away.

"I am so sorry, Don Angelo," one of the men sitting in the row behind him said. He was tall, his body bulging with strength, obvious even under his tailored suit coat.

Don Angelo shot him a murderous look. "Be quiet, you idiot," he said, his voice deep and strong, in dramatic contrast to his frailty.

The man bowed, his face stricken. "I'm sorry. I didn't think."

"Thinking is not why I keep you," the old man said. His eyes burned with strength and power.

Angelo Corelli was a force of nature, physically diminished by age, but someone to be reckoned with. People like him make things happen; make others submit to their will in the pursuit for power. For good, for evil, these men and women shape the world, more men than women still. Their single minded quest for domination, wealth, respect lays some low, raises others up, and in so doing determines who lives, who dies, who mates with who, who is born and who prevails.

Without the Medici, would there have been a Renaissance? Without Moses, would there have been an Israel? Without some long forgotten warrior, would there have been an Aztec Empire? How would the world have changed had there been no Alexander, no Cleopatra, no Hitler, no Stalin, no Cary Nation, no Mohammed, no Elizabeth I, no FDR, Martin Luther King, no Nixon or Mao, no Hillary Clinton or Margaret Thatcher?

Angelo Corelli was such a force. His arena smaller than an empire, a continent, a nation, or the liberation of an oppressed group, it was made up of the mob domains in New Jersey and New York. His goals, his ambitions were matched to his arena. His vision may have been limited, but his vigor in realizing that vision was different in scope, not in kind from other, greater, villains and kings and reformers and saints. I saw it all in his eyes, heard it in his voice. Old, physically weak, sitting near the casket of an only son he could not acknowledge in public, he was no one I would choose to tangle with.

I turned and saw Shelley staring at him. Tiger and Sylvia had returned to their conversation, Sylvia's hand resting on Tiger's arm.

"Cornell's father," I said to Shelley, indicating Angelo Corelli with a sideways tip of my head.

"He looks so old, so frail," she said.

"That's what happens to us, if we're lucky. But look at those eyes. There's nothing frail about them."

"It's sad," she said.

"Sad my ass. That old man has killed plenty of people, and probably had more people killed than he did himself. His underlings sell dope to poor schmucks like Tommy Finneran and Andy Lane. He corrupts politicians, union officials, judges. People like him don't give a shit about anybody except themselves, or anything except piling up the money and accumulating power over other people."

She retorted in an instant. "Is that any different from the Enron executives and their hangers-on, or the financial vampires who caused the great recession?"

"No," I said. "One's as bad as the other."

Ariel's parents brushed past us, breaking up our conversation. They walked to the far side of the room, sitting in a row behind Angelo Corelli, who turned and took the woman's hand, raising it to his lips, then holding on, rubbing it between his own as he spoke to her, his tone sweet and soothing, his words too soft for me to hear.

Shelley said, "They're all human at some level. Look at him. I'd call that compassion."

We sat in the front row on the academic side of the room. The string quartet finished and fell silent. Angelo Corelli, still holding the mother's hand, said something to Ariel's father who nodded and patted him on the shoulder. I could see his lips form the word, *thanks*. It was confusing. Billy had said that Ariel didn't know about the Corelli connection to Evans Cornell, but her parents looked as though they did. It was possible, I suppose, and it said something about marriages between families, although just what wasn't clear to me. I guessed Ariel had known all along and Evans had been protecting her, even in his conversations with Billy.

Tiger gave Sylvia a quick embrace and sat next to me. Sylvia nodded to Angelo and walked to the rear of the family side, sitting on the aisle, just in front of the quartet. Corky and Linda walked across the front of the room. She held a pitcher of iced water and an empty glass. Pulling a curtain aside, he removed a wheeled lectern with a mahogany finish, a microphone attached, and pushed it to a prominent spot beside the caskets. He locked the wheels and plugged the microphone cord into a receptacle on the floor. Linda placed the pitcher and a glass on the lectern. Corky looked at the quartet, nodding. They began playing *Ave Maria*.

Bishop White walked into the room, took his place behind the lectern, poured iced water into the glass and took a sip. As he did, Henrietta Lane and Randolph came in. Henrietta walked across the front of the room. Her skimmed milk skin seemed paler and bluer than ever in the black dress she wore. Looking neither to her right or her left, ignoring the Bishop who was about to speak, she took a seat near Angelo Corelli, who looked at her with sheer loathing. She returned the look. Randolph stood in the doorway until she was seated, then left.

I saw it all and understood nothing. Then the Bishop began to speak of the consolations of eternal life with Christ.

The funeral began.

Sixteen

"She's staying at the Elkins Inn," Tiger whispered to me as the Bishop's voice rose. "She wants me to come back there after work."

"Why?"

"She's lonely, filled with sorrow. Her brother's dead. Her sister disappeared years ago. She needs someone to talk to."

"Someone to get off with, you mean."

"Maybe."

"You're nuts if you do it."

"I know."

"You going to?"

Before she could answer, I felt a tap on my shoulder. I turned. The man behind me put his forefinger to his lips and whispered a brief shhhh. He was about my size, wearing khakis, a pink shirt open at the collar, and an expensive wool sport coat. His hair was thick and blond, and he wore it cut to just above his ears. His beard and mustache were of soft, fine hair, so thick that the only skin visible on his lower face was that of his lips. I gave him a silent snarl and jabbed my forefinger toward his chest, stopping less than an inch from the front of his shirt. His look of astonishment was satisfying. I turned back to Tiger.

"So, you going to?"

"Yes. Maybe. I don't know."

"Don't"

"I'm counting on you to convince me of that at work tonight."

"Deal," I told her.

The article in *The Graham Enterprise* was wrong. There was one service for both Evans and Ariel Cornell, and it started at ten-fifteen.

The Bishop spoke and prayed and chanted and spread incense around and blessed some water and wafers and held a mass right there in Corky Sturdevandt's funeral home. He took an hour. When he was finished, Corky came to the lectern and asked if anyone in the room would like to speak.

Sylvia came forward, moving with beauty and grace to the lectern. She looked over the crowd, grinned at Tiger, gave me a curt smile, took a sheet of paper from her purse, which she unfolded and placed on the top of the lectern, smoothing it out with her hands. Adjusting the microphone, she spoke with seasoned composure, never once looking at the notes before her.

"Evans was my brother. We lost our parents in an automobile accident when we were in grade school." She looked at Angelo who, I was sure, gave her an almost imperceptible wink. "After that, we held each other together, even while going separate ways. He went to Amherst, then on to Yale to take his doctorate in literature before coming back to western Massachusetts to teach at Ralston. I studied at UCLA, and did my MBA at Wharton. He was interested in poetry, in fiction, in the spirit of imagination that drives men and women to create them. My interests were the intricacies of business cycles, the mysteries of economic change, the poetry of profit and loss. Our intellectual worlds could not have been more different, yet we were family and we understood, we embraced the fullness and the majesty of family. Not a week went by without a phone call to discuss the excitement of discoveries in our professional lives. He was my brother, my only sibling, and my life will be inexorably lessened by the loss of his." She glanced again at Angelo Corelli, who wiped a handkerchief over his eyes and stared at the caskets beside her.

Clearing her throat, pinching her cheeks between her thumb and forefinger, she leaned forward, making eye contact with everyone in the room. "Now I am alone in the world. But I tell you all this, I tell you this. Whoever murdered Evans and Ariel, you will be found out. If you are in this room, listen. You will receive punishment for what you have done. I urge you to pray that the police are the ones to find you and the courts are the ones to exact punishment. You do not want me to find you. You certainly do not want me to punish you. Because, God help me, I want to. I want to be the one to find you. I want to be the one to punish you. If there is any justice in this world, I will."

She stood there for a long moment, gazing into the faces before her. Then with an abrupt flourish picked up her notes, refolded them and strode back down the aisle to her seat.

I looked over at Angelo Corelli. He was beaming. The man behind him reached out, clapping him on the shoulder.

"Holy shit," said the man behind me. "That is one tough woman. I'd hate to have her sight in on my balls."

A tall, well-dressed man with a razor cut hair and beard took the lectern, explaining for those from out of town that he was Howard Presnell, Dean of Faculty at Ralston College. He spoke of the tragedy of a promising academic life being cut short in mid career, praising Evans' academic accomplishments, noting his dedication to his students, which gave rise to several spates of coughing from the rows behind me.

"There don't seem to be many student types at this service," Tiger said. I hadn't noticed. I looked around the room. There were mobsters and academics, Bishop White, Corky, Linda, Sylvia, Henrietta, Shelley, Tiger and me. Billy Melnick had not come. Nor had any students. Evans Cornell was no Mr. Chips.

Dean Presnell finished. He was followed by a string of English professors, each struggling to outdo the one before, all sounding rehearsed and stuffy. The last to speak was Elsworth Buell. Jarring several people in their chairs as he moved his bulk from his seat to the aisle, he walked to the front of the room. Standing behind the lectern, he took several deep breaths, pounding his chest for humorous effect. "I think I can say I was Ev's best friend on campus."

The man behind me whispered to someone, "Ev? For Christ's sake, nobody called him Ev. You might as call him Corny. Evans was not the nick name type."

Oblivious to the whispering springing up among the academics, Buell continued. "We were simpatico. Neither of us was satisfied with simple academic categories. Some people specialize in medieval studies and never stray from the past wherein they have transplanted themselves."

"I think I'm going to barf," Shelley said, just loud enough for Buell and the people behind us to hear.

Buell lost his way for a second, and then continued. "Others live in the Faulknerian south, while still others dwell with Shakespeare their entire professional lives. With Ev, as with me, all of literature was our passion, our domain."

"Right. All of literature and freshman boys for you, the girls for Evans," the whisperer behind me said. Several others laughed, trying to be quiet about it. Buell heard them, grimaced, and continued.

"The individual with an eclectic mind threatens those of lesser intellect. With Ev, as with me, it was natural to analyze a passage of Chaucer one day, study the imagery of color in *King Lear* the next, move on to an article on William Burroughs, or Joyce, or Yeats, or Hemingway. Before he...died," Buell paused before saying *died*, make it clear that he was uncomfortable with the circumstances of Cornell's death, but unable to utter the word murder. "He was working on a project involving lost poems of the writer Charles Bukowski. I have no doubt that Ev's work, had it continued, should it be continued by someone else, as we certainly pray it shall be, will serve to establish Bukowski's academic reputation."

"I loved the way you reminded him that Buke really did beat the shit out of guys like him," I said to Shelley.

"That would have been a great service to humanity, even if he'd never written any poems at all," she said.

"Academic reputation," I said. "Sheee-it. I heard a kid eating at the Graham Coop talking to his girl friend the other day, saying that Bukowski was his favorite poet. I wonder if that kid's ever heard of Elsworth Buell?" Shelley said, "I've got a Ph.D. in literature. I've been teaching college level English in this area for seven years. And I never heard of Elsworth Buell before last night when he almost crushed me to death at the Townie."

"I'm nearly finished, if I could be granted the courtesy of your attention." Buell looked directly at us. He couldn't have heard our words, but he could hear our voices and our tones had not been polite. I nodded, smiled and gave him a slight mocking bow from my seat.

"Ev had some irreplaceable recordings of Bukowski reading. They were instrumental in the work he was doing on the poet, and they are missing. If whoever has them could turn them over to me, I could ensure that Ev's work is completed. It would reflect positively on both Evans Cornell and Charles Bukowski."

A voice, trembling with rage came from the back of the room. "Shut up and sit down you fool."

Everyone turned to look. Sylvia stood red-faced and shaking, hands resting on the seat in front of her. The woman sitting in it had turned around and was leaning toward her, watching intently. "This service is about Evans and Ariel, not about you and your pretentious bullshit."

People on both sides of the room applauded. Buell's face twisted and reddened. He bit his lowerlip, staring at her for several long seconds. Taking a deep breath, he started to say something, stopped, exhaled and stomped away from the lectern and out of the room. Seconds later we heard the front door open and close.

We sat in silence, looking at one another, some people shaking their heads in bemused wonder, others looking as furious as Sylvia. She stood there, eyes on her hands, then sank into her seat, sobbing. The woman in front of her reached over the back of her seat and patted her shoulder. Sylvia looked up, tried to smile and shook her head, returning her gaze to the carpet beneath her feet.

Following Sylvia's outburst, there was a long period of silence. It appeared as though no one else was going to speak. Corky stood, about to go to the lectern to announce the end of the ceremony. Before he could, Ariel's father led her mother up the aisle. She moved behind the lectern and he stood inches behind her and to the left, his eyes never leaving her face. Gripping it with her hands, she looked over the crowd. Her head trembled. Her eyes were filled with tears, but her breath was even and spoke with a singer's voice, the words like music flowing from her and wrapping around everyone in the room.

"My name is Bliss, and this is my husband Woodland Green. Ariel was our baby. We lived in a commune in Vermont when she was born. From the moment she popped out...we had a home birth, you understand...we knew she was different. The other babies were so mellow. Ariel was always tense, on edge. Even at two months Woody and I knew she would not be satisfied with easy answers, with doing things in any way but her own.

"At first, we were afraid she would turn to the world we had left. I was born and raised in Newport. My father is a surgeon and mother's a stockbroker. Woody comes from Boston, Beacon Hill, an old family." She glanced at the tall tanned man I had seen leaving the Lexus. "His father is a senior partner in a prominent law firm and manages the family trusts. His mother is a hostess of some renown. I'm telling you all this so you have some idea of where Ariel came from. Of how unique she was. Her father and I both left our worlds and set out to find ourselves. I met Woody at the Old Time Fiddlers' Convention at Galax, in Virginia. He came in fourth that year. I was playing banjo along with some friends on guitar and bass, singing some old timey mountain music. Woody heard us and joined in. We haven't spent a day apart since them."

She started to weep. Woody put his hands on her shoulders and pulled her back toward him. "You don't have to do this," he said.

"I do. I do." She took a deep breath, wiped her eyes with her sleeve, and looked out over the people assembled before her. She reached inside, found a smile, and gave it to all of us. "We came to understand that it would be all right if Ariel grew up wishing to return to the world we'd left. She would find herself, just as we had found ourselves. We left the commune, bought several hundred acres of land north of Brattleboro and built a log cabin. We lived there, just the three of us, until Ariel was ready for school. We sent her to the Putney School, to George School in Pennsylvania, where she would get a good Quaker background, and then to Swarthmore College, another Quaker school. She wanted to go to Yale for her graduate work in history, and we sent her. That's where she met Evans."

She reached back for her husband's hand, holding it as she went on. "Her life after that was very different from ours. We raise llamas and yaks. We play music in small folk clubs around New England. We live in our cabin overlooking the river and fall asleep each night to the music of water rippling around and over rocks. Ariel was gracious, social, every bit a lady."

"A couple of hundred acres of land north of Bratt, Putney School, George School, Swarthmore and Yale cost a hell of a lot more than making music and raising llamas and yaks can provide," Shelley whispered.

Tiger clicked her tongue. "The hippie broad said they turned their backs on their parents' lifestyles, not on their money. I'll bet they're loaded, sitting in their cabin clipping coupons and counting interest."

Bliss continued. "She took her father's birth name when she started college. Ariel was all right, but Ariel Woodland Green, or Ariel Bliss Woodland Green as we had put on her birth certificate, was too much for her. When she went off to Swarthmore she said she liked Winslow because it sounded like money, sounded like class. She was so different from us. But we were different from our parents, and they never turned their backs on us. They were always there to help, and we wanted to do the same thing for Ariel."

"See," Tiger said. "Daddy and Mommy's bucks were always there for good old Bliss and Woodland Green."

"When she and Evans moved to Graham, she was excited. 'I can be close to you and Daddy,' she told me. 'I can live the way I want to and still see you anytime I want to.' And we did see a lot of her. She visited us at least once a month, sometimes more. We didn't come down here. Woody said it wouldn't be fair to her if her neighbors and Evans' colleagues saw what unregenerate hippies we were. They might look down on her, he believed. She never stopped inviting us down, but we never came. I wish now we had. I wish I could have seen her operate in her own element."

She stopped again, overwhelmed by grief. It took her several moments to control herself. No one spoke. No one moved. We sat and watched, waiting for her to finish saying what had to be said. When at last she spoke, there was steel in her voice.

"Ariel was our baby. She was our only baby. We loved her. We respected her. We will never stop missing her. Never for a minute the rest of our lives." She looked toward the back of the room where Sylvia still stood. "I'm with you Sylvia. The bastards that did this better get down on their knees and pray for all they're worth that the cops and courts get them before I do. I'll cut their skin off with a butter knife if I get hold of them. God knows what Woody will do to them."

"It's unspeakable," he said. He put his arm around her waist and led her back to their seats.

After another long silence when no one else got up to speak, Corky went to the mike, inviting all to come to the cemetery for the burial service and then to the Elkins Inn for a self service luncheon, an afternoon of celebrating

Evans' and Ariel's lives, then dinner. The bar, he announced, would be open throughout.

I took Shelley's and my coats from the cloakroom. Standing in the crowded hallway, I helped her on with hers and put mine on. We headed for the door. Angelo Corelli was right in front of us, moving with the aid of his walker, the tall, strong, clean-shaven young men with the bulges under their jackets on either side of him. As he reached the door and walked outside, there was a distant pop. Angelo Corelli fell back against me, blood spurting from his head. I put my hands under his arms, staring in disbelief as his hands loosened their hold on the walker and his body slid to the floor, his shattered head lying in a widening pool of blood. After a brief and stunned silence astonished people began to scream and run.

I knelt for a moment beside the body, my hand on his wrist feeling for a pulse. It was a useless reflex. His head was shattered. I did not need the absence of a heartbeat to confirm his death. I was shoved aside as one of his bodyguards stripped off his jacket and put it over the old man in a gentle, almost loving way, covering his broken, bloodied face. The other was on a cell phone. I looked up and saw Henrietta Lane staring down at the body, her face twitching.

Sylvia was standing against the wall, a look of shock on her face. I watched as she fought the impulse to run over and somehow acknowledge her father's death. Years of preserving her cover won out and she turned away, going back into the room where Corky's attendants and the pall bearers were removing flowers from the caskets in preparation for walking them to the hearse for the ride to the cemetery.

There were several minutes of chaos and terror, then I heard the sirens of police cruisers headed for the scene. There had been no more shots, the target fatally hit by the first shot in a clean, professional way. The hallway was empty of all but the most curious. Angelo Corelli's men had scattered, guns drawn, searching for the shooter. By the time the cops arrived, most of them would be gone, speeding down I-91 homeward. The few who remained would be invisible.

I looked around for Shelley, sure she would be terrified and shocked by such horrific violence. I couldn't find her. I looked for her on the porch. She wasn't there. I went back inside, looking in each room. From down the hall where the rest rooms were, I heard a choking sound. The door to the women's room was ajar. Shelley was leaning over the sink, the water running, puking. I could see her brow in the mirror. Her skin was ashen. Grabbing some paper towels and wetting them in an adjacent sink, I wiped her face, holding her head steady with my other hand.

"Pretty horrible sight," I said.

"I don't want to talk about it."

"It's normal to react this way."

"Eddie," her tone was severe. "I don't want to talk. Get me out of here."

I took her elbow and led her down the hall and out a side door. The front door was filled with EMTs, cops and photographers. Angelo Corelli hadn't been dead for more then ten minutes and the official processing of his remains had begun. I couldn't help but try to imagine Sandy Grover's face when he realized who the corpse had been.

"My car's in the parking lot, right next to your truck," Shelley said. "You're in no shape to drive." She didn't argue. I led her to the truck. She got in and I shut the door. Walking around to the other side, I saw the caskets being carried out through the milling onlookers and a growing number of bustling police, looking important as they talked over their radios and stood in small clusters nodding their heads. Cruisers were everywhere. I got behind the wheel. Shelley watched as the first casket was loaded into the rear of a glimmering black Cadillac hearse.

"Where do you want to go?" I asked "The cemetery," she said. Her voice was flat.

Chapter Seventeen

Attendance at the graveside service was sparse. Sylvia, Tiger, Shelley and I, along with a handful of the academics from the funeral home were there, but no one from the Corelli side of the aisle came. Dean Presnell stood apart from everyone else, his expression the pained one of a man doing a duty he didn't care about, didn't want to do, but knew came with his job. The Bishop said a few hasty words, prayed, and headed for his limousine. The chauffer was closing the door when my cell phone rang. I walked twenty or thirty feet away from the grave.

"The Corelli hit is yours," the voice said. "Find out everything you can. I'll be in touch." He disconnected before I could reply.

There were even fewer people at the Elkins Inn, three or four of the academics, Elsworth Buell conspicuously absent, a few of the Cornell's neighbors and friends, several of them trying to comfort Ariel's parents, who stood in aimless silence beside a table filled with food. No one from the Corelli cortege there either. Sylvia sat by a window drinking straight vodka. Tiger was with her, a bottle of Rolling Rock in her hand. I walked over, rattling the ice in my gin and tonic. Shelley stayed at the bar, sipping on a glass of Chardonnay.

"I'm sorry about your father," I said.

Sylvia looked up, nodded. "I hadn't seen him in person for six or seven years. We had a secure phone line and he'd call me from time to time, I'd call him, but I hadn't kissed him or held him. And for what? My brother's dead. My father's dead and I can't even acknowledge it in public. There's nobody to replace him. Our businesses will be taken over by rivals my father would have had whacked before he'd even consider talking about cooperating with them."

"What about you?" I asked, bemused that I would be offering any consolation to someone grieving over the disintegration of a crime organization. "You're smart. You've got business savvy. You're an MBA from Wharton, for crissakes. With the money you father must have socked away, you could move into legitimate business, if you wanted to."

She took a long drink from the tumbler of vodka and shook her head. "Yeah, right. Can you imagine those goombahs of father's taking orders from a woman? As for taking things legit, it would kill them deader than a hit. They love doing things the way they do. Let the boys sort things out. It's the way life's supposed to be, for them." She shook her head. "I'm better off staying Sylvia Cornell and working with my MBA. The bank's not a bad place for me, and I'll move up the ladder. I don't need my father's business and I'll inherit a lot of money. I was playing Sylvia Cornell to please him, but it's great cover for me as well. Now all I have to do is completely immerse myself in Sylvia Cornell and forget all about my birth name."

She took another long drink of vodka and straightened in her chair. "Besides, Sylvia Cornell has a better chance of finding out who killed my father and brother than Angela Corelli does. I can go places, talk to people she can't."

"You talk as if she's somebody else," Tiger said.

"She is somebody else, and she's got to become more somebody else. From now on she's as dead to me as her brother and father are. Come upstairs with me, Catherine."

Tiger looked at her watch. "I have to be at work by two. Cover for me Eddie?"

"You sure?"

"Absolutely."

"You know a lot about me," Sylvia said to me. "I do."

"The recordings are yours. Good price for your silence. Your silence is a good price for your life."

"Watch it," Tiger said to her.

I flattened my hands in the air between us. If Sylvia wanted to, she could find out more about me. I was sure Henrietta had, although I didn't have an idea as to how. Sylvia would have resources to track me if she chose to. After all, what is the mob but a secret agency? One thing about secret agencies, their operatives end up talking to one another from time to time. They have to. It's the best way to get information on each other and control it at the same time.

"It's okay, Tige. All I want to do is go back to my broom closet. The recordings are a nice benefit of what we've gone through over the last week, although they could end up being a pain in the ass with dickheads like Moss and Buell salivating over them."

Sylvia smiled for the first time. "I have a feeling you handle dickheads well."

Tiger roared with laughter. Shelley gave us a disdainful glance, as though the laughter had violated some unwritten command of solemnity and silence.

"No doubt about it, Syl," Tiger said. "Let's go upstairs and I'll tell you all about Eddie and me at Ducky's not too long ago."

When they were gone, Shelley slipped into the chair where Sylvia had been, her wine glass full. "You ready to go?" she asked.

"Two minutes. Let me finish my drink. You don't want yours?"

"I've had three already and I'm a little woozy. Enough's enough." I chugged my gin and tonic. "Where to?" I asked. It sounded a little too bright, a little too hopeful.

"I want to go home, pull the covers over my head and sleep for the rest of the day. I've got to teach a class at Graham Community College tonight and, the way I feel now, there's no way I can do it. Maybe with a nap, who knows?"

I put my hand on top of hers, but she drew it away. Her eyes were red, her voice tiny, with little inflection. Even her hair looked flat.

"I've got an idea for something that'll perk you up and then put you to sleep," I said.

She almost smiled, and put her hand back, this time on top of mine. "It's a nice idea, Eddie. I'll take a rain check. All I want you to do right now is drive me back to the funeral parlor, let me get my car so I can go home alone."

The police were still working at Sturdevandt's, cruisers on the street, in the lot, across the lawn. Cops and forensics investigators went in and out of the building as Corky stood to one side of the porch, watching. He did not look happy.

Shelley got out of the truck, came around to my side and gave me a quick, friendly kiss through the window. "Don't feel rejected," she said.

"Rejected? Naw. Nothing of the kind," I told her, making an exaggerated downcast face. "I'll just go back to my room, page through a Victoria's Secret catalog and whack off for a while. I'll be fine."

She laughed. "Which hand do you hold the catalog in?"

"The left."

"My brother used to say he could change hands without missing a stroke."

"I didn't know you had a brother, let alone such a talented one."

"He's dead," she said. "I'm sorry." Her smile was sad. "I don't let it bother me. Everybody dies."

"Andy Lane bothered you."

"That was different." She started to say something more, stopped and moved back from the truck. "See you tomorrow night. Let's go to the Townie after my class and you finish work."

"Can't," I said. "We've already got a date. Tiger's Halloween party." She snapped her fingers, a distracted look in her eyes. "I forgot and I haven't come up with a costume yet.

"Me neither," I said. "You got any ideas?" She tousled my hair. "Lots of ideas, cutie."

"I mean for a costume."

"Maybe."

"What? I'm pretty good at costumes and I'm still drawing a blank on mine."

Wagging a finger in my face, she shook her head. "Now, Eddie, I thought we were going to surprise each other."

"And?"

She grinned. "I'll feel a hell of a lot better tomorrow night. I think you're in for several surprises."

I watched as she got in her car and pulled out onto the street. Before I could start the truck, Corky came over.

"Jesus Christ, Eddie," he said. "You know who that guy was that got shot coming out of my place?"

"Who?"

"Angelo Corelli. Christ. That's like having a Kennedy shot at your place."

"A Kennedy?"

"Well, maybe not. Maybe more like a Congressman, but it's big in its own way. I bet it'll be good for business. I mean, local reporters are already all over the place. Channel 22 and Channel 40 from Springfield have been here and Channels 4, 5 and 7 are coming out from Boston. I've had calls from newspapers all over the state. From *The New York Times* even. Holy shit, Eddie, *The Times*. That's big."

"It's big, Cork. You'll handle it."

He looked excited. "Yeah. I know. I just want the cops to get their cruisers off my lawn. I had sod put down last spring and those damned cop cars are ruining it."

"Hear anything on the shooting?" I asked

"The cops think maybe it came from the ridge." He pointed toward Poet's Seat Tower. "Maybe the tower itself."

A cop stepped off the porch into a patch of mums.

"Oh, no," Corky said. "Sorry. I'll be right back." Leaving me, he ran over, berating the cop and pointing to the crushed flowers.

I sat in the truck, watching him pointing, his voice, but not the words, carrying across the lot. Looking at the hill across the way, I remembered Henrietta Lane coming into the funeral home, Randolph standing beside her in the doorway. He had disappeared once she entered and sat next to Angelo Corelli. I wondered about the look of mutual hatred that passed between Angelo and Henrietta. How would they know each other, and why the hate? And where had Randolph gone? To Poet's Seat?

§§§

"What do you know about a woman named Henrietta Lane?" I said into the cell phone.

"Why do you need to know?" the voice asked. "And remember, this is not a secure line. Keep it bland."

"I think she had Corelli taken out. She's got a bozo working for her, a shaven headed ape name Randolph, with a Texas accent, and I believe he did it. Lane was connected with Corelli in some way. At the Cornells' funeral she sat next to him, and if the looks they gave each other could kill both of them would have keeled over right there. She also indicated earlier that she knew things about me."

"This is not bland enough for the cell phone. You'll be at work tonight?"

"As ever, sweeping and swabbing."

"An associate will meet you in the parking lot at ten." Cell phone be damned, I began to ask what he knew about Randolph, but true to his practice, he had disconnected the moment he considered the conversation over.

It was twenty after one. I was starving and had forty minutes to kill before I had to be at work, just enough time for lunch at the Riverside. I parked in the free lot on Mercer Street and walked the half block to the restaurant. The place was almost empty. I grabbed a *Valley Advocate*, the local alternative newspaper, a freebie filled with articles about local politicians, some courageous muckraking, some petty and nasty, arch and cute and negative film reviews, listings of every kind of concert, play or club date worth attending in the Valley, and pages of entertaining sex ads.

I ha a grilled tuna with cheddar and drank water. Eating, I read an article about the dire state of funding for public higher education in Massachusetts. At least the news was getting out that the state was second only to Mississippi in its lack of support for its public colleges. In another year, it would be flat last. It was almost funny. It was shameful. Massachusetts, the state of Harvard University, Boston University, MIT, Northeastern University, of Williams, , Emerson, Amherst, Ralston, Smith, Mt. Holyoke and Hampshire Colleges, Massachusetts, the Education State, with perhaps the most deprived system of public higher education in the country. Their classroom buildings and dormitories were falling apart and the library budgets were so terrible they were discontinuing subscriptions to many of the most basic journals and papers.

I tossed the paper down, unable to read any more, and stuffed the French fries into my mouth. They were excellent.

§§§

It was quiet at work. Tiger didn't come in until nine-thirty. She looked tired and happy.

"Sorry," she said. "I'll work late."

"I've done all the toilets, yours and mine. They may not be as shiny as usual, but they'll do until tomorrow. I've got my blackboards and floors finished and was starting to think about moving over to yours."

"You've been a busy beaver," she said.

"And your beaver's been busy. Too goddamn busy for your own good." She waved me off.

"What'll you tell Dawn?"

"That you and me went to the Townie and drank until closing time. You'll back me up, right? Beside, she'll probably be asleep by the time I get home. Hell, she usually crashes by nine."

"I mean, what'll you tell her about Sylvia," I said, ignoring her request that I back her up.

"Nothing. It's none of her business. It has nothing to do with her and me."

"You've been with Sylvia all afternoon and it has nothing to do with Dawn?"

"It's a short term deal. Dawn's a long term deal. Syl's going back to Pennsylvania in a few days. I doubt I'll ever see her again."

"But you'll see her tomorrow?"

"I'll see her tomorrow, for a little while, but I called Human Resources this afternoon and put in for vacation time on Monday. I'm going to pick her up at nine in the morning and we're going up to a bed and breakfast in Newfane, coming back in time for work on Tuesday."

"A little tryst in Vermont, and how're you explaining that to Dawn?"

"That you and I are still working on that business we went to Jersey and Pennsylvania on last weekend."

"And I'm supposed to confirm that?"

"She won't ask."

"If she does?" After a long, uncomfortable silence, she nodded.

"Shit, Tige. I hate this. Sylvia is not safe. I don't like lying, especially to Dawn. It sucks. She's my friend too, you know."

"It's just this once, this one thing. Have I ever asked you for anything like this before?"

She hadn't. I agreed. "Just this time and only because I don't want anything to happen to you and Dawn. You're my family, Tige. If you guys are in trouble, the whole round world's in trouble."

She guffawed and put on a macho swagger. "Hell, Eddie. Sylvia's a good time, that's all. Dawn's my partner. She's my life. Sylvia's just the greatest sex I've ever had. She's taught me a few things, and Dawn will be the beneficiary of what I've learned."

"You sound like those asshole guys who sit around in barrooms talking about their sexual exploits."

She laughed again. "That's why I'm the butch in the relationship." But there was no humor in her voice, no joy in her eyes.

She was on the edge of an obsession. I knew the signs. I'd been there, once. It was not a happy time. There was no satisfaction in it. I lied to myself, to the woman, reveling in the way she lied to me, the way she manipulated me and let me manipulate her. She tried to get away, I tried to get away and she kept letting me come back to her, all the while both of us knowing that I was debasing her and debasing myself.

Tiger was almost there. I wanted to stop her, grab her shoulders, shake her, and put my knowledge in her head. There was no way. Still, I had to try.

"Don't blow things for yourself," I said.

She looked me straight in the eyes. Her face was composed, her voice calm. "I won't Eddie. I promise."

That's what she said. She promised. I knew she would try to keep the promise. I hoped she would. She had to. I couldn't afford to lose the family Tiger and Dawn and Chad had become.

I hugged her. She hugged me back, harder. "I love you, Tige," I said. "You know that."

"I know. I love you too, asshole." She stood back and from the way she looked at me, I saw she meant it. I was as much a part of her family as she Dawn and Chad were mine. "Now, let me get to work."

She headed for her closet, stopped and turned around. "One other thing, Eddie. Syl mentioned the recordings of that poet you and Billy are so all het up about."

"Charles Bukowski," I said. "And it's Billy who's all het up."

"Whatever. She wants you to know she was serious about them being yours."

"Tell her thanks," I said. She went to her closet. I finished what I had to do and left.

A Ford Escort was parked beside my truck. I had left it near the only lighting fixture in the lot in need of a new bulb. It was dim and flickering. A tall man, in a trench coat and a gray felt fedora got out. His features were hard to make out in the weak lighting, but I could tell he was white, with a long nose and a sharp chin. His hat hid his eyes and hair. He lit a cigarette and blew the smoke out his nose.

"Edward Sanders," he said, a statement, not a question.

"I don't believe that outfit," I said. "Nineteen-fifty-three, late film *noir*, the kind they made to try and recapture the glory of real film *noir*. You have any idea how ridiculous you look?"

Without responding he held a folder out to me. "Read this and burn it. If I get lucky, you'll screw things up and I'll get to terminate your wise ass. It's shitballs like you thinking you can drop out and drop back in again, that're ruining our work."

"I didn't ask to drop back in. Better people than you have tried terminating me in the past. I'm still here. They're not." I grabbed the folder, got in my truck and drove off. I watched him through the rearview mirror standing by the Escort, smoke from his cigarette rising in shifting ribbons into the flickering light from the dying bulb. Cheap film *noir* all the way, his look and my dialogue.

Chapter Eighteen

Madam Butterfly drifted from my stereo as I paged through the folder, struggling to contain my fury. The walls of my room seemed closer, darker than when I sat down, before opening the folder. I had picked the pictures on my walls with great care. I was drawn to color, light, in some cases to simplistic images of New England, even going so far as to have a Norman Rockwell print showing a rural town meeting. Now they seemed full of sinister shadows and shadowy meanings.

For years the agency had been sitting on the information I was reading. They had known Henrietta was in Graham. They had known I was in Graham. I had a long, frightened moment of total paranoia, fighting the idea that they had drugged and programmed me years before to come here in the eventuality they'd need me to counter her. It took me several minutes to trust the accuracy of my memories of having lived in town before Henrietta, Arnold and Andrea showed up. Even then, I wasn't comfortable until I checked through the records I keep in a chaotic pile in a blue plastic eighteen-gallon tote box.

The saving clincher was a photograph of a very young Chad and a much younger me standing up for Tiger and Dawn at the ceremony of commitment they held at the Lovers Lane Inn at the edge of Yardley Falls, back in the years before they had been able to marry here in Massachusetts. The four of us stood before potted palms beneath a gaudy stylized painted paper sun, its rays shooting out at the stations of the clock, a lewd smile on its face. We had our arms around each other. Off to the left, his smile benign, was Jim Pain, the Methodist minister who performed the service, a ritual of music, prayers and promises that resembled a wedding but conferred no legal rights for Dawn and Chad to share in Tiger's medical insurance or pension. The truth and beauty underlying the ceremony, Pain went at lengths to say, was between them and God, not between them and the Commonwealth of Massachusetts. She, Dawn and Chad had signed and dated the picture for me. I breathed a sigh, at once relieved that I had found proof of being in Graham years before the Lanes arrived.

The inability to have faith in the authenticity of experience is a lousy feeling, one I believed I had dumped when I left the agency. Working there, you come to accept as a general truth of life that there is no reality. There is nothing you can hold on to. There is no place you can stand and say, this is where I am; here I am who I am. There are only deceptions, false faces and forged cards of identity that are discarded and replaced by new ones as fraudulent as those preceding them. You know only what someone else decides you need to know. You are who someone else decides you need to be. You come to fear, to believe there is nothing more to life. Of course, we all have names and we have papers to verify those names. We know things, but who is to say what the names and papers and things we know mean, what realities they signify? I came to question everything, even people I had known, experiences I had long before I had ever heard of the agency. Nothing in my life was safe from doubt.

I was, after all, Edward Sanders, holder of a passport, a driver's license, a social security card, a birth certificate, all the papers of identity we carry and trust to confer legitimacy upon us. But Edward Sanders was a fiction, a name over the door in a tree in the Hundred Acre Woods, until he emerged full-born from Baku in Azerbaijan in 2001.

Once out, I fought hard to establish reality in Graham and to re-establish at least a form of intellectual connection with my pre-agency existence. My brooms and scrubbers were real. My closet was real. My private domain at Barton Rooms was real. My life had become one of atonement for sins I revisited in tortured dreams and for sins I could not remember. Nathan Hunt disappeared during a raid into Iran, and his parents had been told that a grateful nation regretted his loss and extended its sympathy to his survivors.

Tiger, Dawn and Chad were real. Graham was real. I had put myself down here years before, into a concrete world where I was comfortable, safe in every way. I knew who I was. Eddie Sanders. I knew the names of the streets and where they led. The sidewalks were familiar. Even the cracks in the pavements seemed like old friends. Now they were playing with me again. Bending truth, twisting my hard won reality. I was not going to be sucked in. I'd do their job. I'd take their money. That was a matter of survival. But I was solid, more solid than I had ever been, and I was not going to let them turn me back into smoke.

I threw the folder across the floor and lay back on the bed letting the music from *Madame Butterfly* float over and around me. Reaching for the phone, I dialed Shelley's number. There was no answer. After four rings the machine picked up. I disconnected without leaving a message.

I took thirteen deep breaths, forcing myself to calm down by picturing pelicans soaring above the ridges of Maho Bay on the island of St. John, the white sand beach lined with sea grapes. I had trained with the SEALS in St. Thomas a lifetime ago. On days off I took the ferry to St. John and lay on the beach, soaking up the sun, the blue/green Caribbean waters breaking around my toes.

It wasn't easy maintaining the images of the island. For the first two minutes I imagined assholes with guns hiding behind the rocks at the far end of the beach and the hands of drowning men reaching from the water. It required sweat and shaking, but after ten minutes I stopped trembling. I lay stretched out on the bed, staring up at the sky that had replaced the ceiling, pelicans and frigate birds and white puffs of cloud moving across it. I could almost feel the wind.

After half an hour I sat up. Rage had faded into irked resignation. The Caribbean faded, my room resuming its normal, comfortable pattern. I saw the folder's contents scattered across the floor. Several pages had landed under the dresser, one almost under the crack at the bottom of the door. I picked them up, rearranged them, and continued to read.

The first few pages were about Henrietta Lane who, it turned out, wasn't a Henrietta, or a Lane. She was Frederica Vlasenko, born in Leningrad. When she was seven years old, the educational authorities, realizing she was brilliant in languages, sent her to a KGB training program in Ukraine run by Leonid Nabokov, a linguist and master spy maker. There she studied American English and American culture in such thoroughness and with such success that she would easily pass as an American. She could even identify the pitchers in winning World Series games from 1903, name the members of Bill Haley's Comets, from their earliest incarnation as The Saddlemen until the time of Haley's death. Even the few grammatical peculiarities of her speech, such as her use of the reflexive myself, were all too common among speakers of the language. Once her work at the institute was complete, it was a simple matter to create an American identity for her, placing her in the States with a family already working under deep cover. The Soviets were willing to wait for years, decades if necessary, to cash in on sleepers of the Vlasenko/Lane quality they had living around the country.

In Henrietta's case they waited too long and she settled into an American life. Her identity outlived the USSR, but not the KGB agents who had managed her. In the mid-Eighties it was clear to Nabokov that the Soviet Union's days were numbered. He came to the states, changed his name to Arnold Lane, and recruited Henrietta Chambers into an organization that would become integral to what even during the Soviet era was evolving into the Russian mob. She divorced her husband, a surgeon in Cleveland and married Nabokov/Lane. They found Andrea through an adoption agency and a new American family was born.

The Lanes prospered. As the Soviet world collapsed, more and more Russians came to the United States, most of them looking for educations and jobs that would allow them to become productive citizens. A significant minority did whatever was necessary for them to become dominant players in an already functioning underworld. It only took a small portion of the money the Lanes had made since coming to America to buy the Willey/McClannan Agency, setting themselves up as wealthy and model members of the community waiting for opportunities to expand their extensive and invisible illegal and clandestine holdings.

I sat with the folder in my lap for half an hour, staring at the information, trying to piece it together with what I already knew, wondering what the agency expected me to do with it. I was sure Henrietta's sources had long ago informed her that a former federal agent was working as a janitor at Graham Community College. I understood the loathing between Angelo Corelli and Henrietta. It was a safe guess that the Russians were after the drug trade in the Valley and that Corelli was aware of it and knew the players involved. It was another safe guess that Henrietta was behind the Cornell murders and the hit on Angelo. Still, they were guesses. I was back in the game without a clue as to what the game was, or how to play. My survival as a living man, and the survival of my life in Graham, depended on discovering the rules others were playing by and creating my own rules in order to play the game as a team of one.

It was infuriating and terrifying, threatening to undermine all the hard work of making Edward Sanders real, of becoming him and maintaining the identity, making him me, me him. Identity is a funny thing. I'd dealt with several people in the witness protection program during my years with the agency. Not one was content with the new identity the program had set up for them. They longed for home, for their old patterns and associations. Not me. I was Eddie Sanders. Their identities were products of a bureaucracy designed to provide cover and protection, rather than something they had created. I constructed Eddie Sanders and the agency provided his documentation. I built a life for him and fit into it so well that after a few years I almost never questioned who I was.

Now a past I had walked away from, a past I had stopped thinking about was about to stick its knife into my tent and rip the fabric. Perhaps it would shred it into pieces. Perhaps it would make only a small slit. Either way, things were bound to change in ways I could not control. It more than pissed me off. It infuriated me, blind, hating, raging fury.

My land line phone rang.

"The pay phone outside of your hippie co-op," the voice said and the line went dead.

The phone rang as soon as I reached the front of the Graham Coop. "You've read the folder?" I let loose with a string of invectives measuring the anger I felt. "This is pure dog shit," I said when I had exhausted my vocabulary. "Why in the hell can't you just leave me out of things?"

"Articulate, as ever, Eddie. I see you haven't lost your propensity for bringing in canine excrement when you're excited and angry. You should explore the reasons for that. It could represent some childhood trauma you have yet to deal with."

"Horseshit. That better?"

The voice laughed. "The horse is a nobler animal than the dog. I suppose it represents some evolution on your part."

"Thanks." I took a deep breath to stifle an unwanted chuckle at the quickness of his wit. The bastard could charm Osama bin Laden right out of his beard.

"I assume you have read the folder. Correct?"

"You must have been happier than a pig in shit when I settled in Graham where the Lanes had set up shop."

"Ah, pigs now. You are expanding your vision. Having you in town with the Lanes there was indeed a convenience for us. You were an ace up our sleeves if ever we needed it."

I was silent for a moment. Outside my window, by the street lamps on Main Street, I could see the yellow plastic fire scene tape around Willey and McClannan swaying in the breeze. A cruiser stopped. The driver flashed a search light through the rubble for a brief time, then moved on

"You still there, Eddie?" the voice asked.

I sighed as I replied. "Yeah, but why? What do you want from me? What is the game? And who was the asshole in the fedora and the cigarette you sent with the folder? He looked like something out of *The Rocky and Bullwinkle Show*."

"We want things cleaned up and then maintained clean. It is our understanding that you have become quite adept at cleaning and maintaining."

"What do I get out of it besides a load of grief?"

"The salary I have committed to, which, as I indicated in our earlier conversation, is considerably higher than what you would be earning had you stayed with the agency. You were not exactly on the high road to an upgrade in those days. We will also include a large monthly cash bonus to compensate for the benefits we cannot provide to someone in cover as deep as yours."

"Such as?"

"Health insurance. Life insurance. The Government's contribution to the pension plan. You will have to invest that yourself and I suggest you avoid the stock market and real estate. Our intelligence says those are not going to be good places to invest for some time. Tax free municipals are the most reliable. Avid the Euro. It looks fine now, but our financial intelligence analysts are nervous about what may happen a few years down the line."

"I see you've taken to reading *The Wall Street Journal* and *The Times*." He ignored the jab. "And Eddie, the money and its source must remain anonymous, even to our sister organizations. We will place everything in a bank account on Tortola in the British Virgin Islands. They have developed quite enlightened procedures for protecting certain funds from scrutiny. Neither we, nor you, want anyone to trace it. For us, it's a matter of national security, as well as self-protection. For you it's a matter of personal and financial security."

My nerves were tingling. "The agency has never been so furtive with my pay. What else is going on?"

"There is something," the voice said. "You're on your own from now on. There can be no unsolicited contact between us. The phone numbers you have used in the past will no longer work and you won't get new ones. There will be no way for you to get in touch. No mail drops. No email, certainly. No way, Eddie, for you to contact us."

"And you?"

There was a small laugh on the other end. "Of course we may need to contact you. We are your employers. Keep the cell phone, and keep it on. You do keep it charged as I told you?"

"I do."

"Good. We may need to give you instructions from time to time, but remember you are on your own. And we do expect results."

"What kind of results?"

"The Lane operation shut down. The Corelli operation controlled."

"Why not shut both down?"

"The Corellis have been useful. The old mob is conservative. They've got no interest in changing the status quo. They embody the stability this country needs, operating an underground economy that compliments the legitimate one. In many respects they're a safety valve, siphoning off energy and problems the legitimate economy doesn't deal with. After all, Eddie, legitimacy is a legal fiction. We say such and such is legitimate and such and such isn't for social, economic and political reasons more than for moral ones. Why are coffee, cigarettes and alcohol legal and cocaine, marijuana and heroin illegal?"

It was an old argument, a fruitless one I hadn't expected to hear from a representative of the agency. I didn't follow up.

He continued. "Organizations such as the Corellis' are the flip sides of organizations like the agency. They go to war with each other from time to time, and the less perceptive of the Federal boys think the Feds are at war with organized crime, but the Corellis, the Gambinos, organizations like that, have their uses. We protect them, within limits of course, and we have some level of communications with them."

"And the Russians?"

"Wild cards. Ties to terrorism. No ethics. No loyalty to the American way of life. Angelo Corelli was a registered Republican his entire adult life. Evans Cornell was a Democrat and Sylvia's an independent. Angelo and Evans were generous contributors to their parties. All three of them voted regularly. Of course, we don't know anything about Gina."

"The missing sister?"

"She could be a Trinidadian revolutionary or a Rasta in Jamaica for all we know."

"Or dead."

"We've considered the possibility. It's a real one. She's dead, or she's gone native in the islands, living on a boat and cavorting with the other degenerate expatriates the Caribbean crawls with, or she's working undercover so expertly that she's an embarrassment to any good intelligence organization. Whatever, she doesn't matter. What matters is that you shut down the Russians in western New England. The Corellis, or their successors, will take care of themselves."

"From what you say about Gina, it sounds to me as if Sylvia's the only Corelli left who counts, and she's not interested."

"We'll see, Eddie. Maybe she is, maybe she isn't. It doesn't matter. What's important is that somebody like the Corellis will take over the organization if the Corellis don't. It's a culture, a predictable and useful one. Just remember, you're on your own now, but you're still ours. We'll send you a bankcard and your account number in Tortola."

"I never had any choice in this did I?"

"None. But it is a limited assignment. You're still Eddie Sanders and a janitor at your little community college there. Your identity is secure, and that's no small thing my old friend."

"When this business is settled, it's back to the way things have been for me. Just good old Eddie Sanders with his broom and his beer and his buddies?"

"I'm sure that will largely be the case."

"Guaranteed?"

He paused before answering. "There are no guarantees in life, certainly not in agency life. We will need you to be ready to serve, especially in the area where you are living, but I don't foresee yanking your cover and sending you back into the Middle East."

"That's reassuring."

"Good. Then it's settled." He sounded pleased. Clearing his throat, he added, "And Eddie, don't stint on us. We expect quality work and total loyalty. The chap you referred to as the asshole in the fedora with the cigarette is one of my best men. Every bit as good as you were at your peak. He won't look anything like he did tonight should we need him again. After all, it is the night before Halloween and he was in costume. If we have to use him again, chances are you'll never see him. You wouldn't recognize him if you did catch a glimpse of him. And, Eddie, go easy on Randolph."

"Randolph, Lane's gofer? What do you know about him?"

"Randolph Baines. From Bleakwood, Texas, near the Louisiana border. Wanted in Oklahoma for murder, in Texas, Louisiana and Mississippi for aggravated rape, for bank robbery in Tennessee, Virginia, Delaware, New Jersey, Connecticut, and Massachusetts. As far as we can tell, banks financed his move from Louisiana to Massachusetts."

"You want me to go easy on him? He could have killed me."

"He didn't. He has some value to the agency."

"Murdering, raping and robbing banks?"

"Information on the Lane woman. We know her moves through him."

"What have you got on him?"

"DNA on the murder and rapes, bank videos from Tennessee to Massachusetts."

"You pay him through a British Virgin Islands bank too?"

"His salary consists of being alive and out of prison, as long as he does what we want him to do."

"And if he murders and rapes again?"

"Then we'll have that evidence on him too."

"That's all?"

The voice sounded amused. "We should lose a valuable informant just to lock up a petty criminal?"

"I wouldn't call murder and rape petty." I should have just shut up and let it go. His rationalizations were like those of a religious fundamentalist. There was nothing I could say to break through his closed system of belief. The more I argued, the more sure he became of the correct nature of his position.

"Eddie, Eddie," he said. "How many people have you killed in the course of your work for the agency?"

My heart went flat for a moment. "Too many."

He grunted. "And how many men have you beaten within inches of their lives to further your work with us?"

"Too many."

He grunted again. "And how many women have you seduced to get information, to pass on information, to delay or further an action?"

"Never enough," I said in imitation of the macho sensibility we all affect, the tone covering the seething rage once more coursing through me.

"Aha," he said. "So, Randolph Baines or Edward Sanders, what's the difference? You both have your value to the work the agency is always conducting to protect the American way of life. A conservative military and intelligence community is critical to the preservation of a liberal democracy, ever my credo. Now, Eddie, ta-ta again. And remember, you can't call us, we'll call you."

As always, he disconnected before I could respond.

I walked back to my room thinking that going after Henrietta and Randolph could be a pleasure. The phone was ringing as I walked in.

I picked it up and yelled into the receiver, "Haven't you laid enough of your crap on me."

"Dude, is that any way to talk to a buddy? I'm hurt dude, deeply hurt."

"Sorry, Billy. I thought it was someone else."

"Jeez, Eddie, I'd hate to be that somebody else. But no, it's me, dude, Billy, just like I always am. I'm at the Townie. I thought we were going to talk tonight. About the recordings, you know?"

I had promised him the night before, when he and Elsworth Buell interrupted Shelley and me. "I'll be there. Give me fifteen minutes."

I heard a smile in his voice. "I'll have a pitcher waiting for us, Eddie. Want me to order you any food?"

"Hell yes, I'm starving. Get me a Cajun cheddar cheeseburger, rare."

§§§

He was waiting in the last booth before the kitchen, pouring each of us a glass from a pitcher of amber beer. Cat brought my cheeseburger as I sat down. It was steaming, a pile of red bliss potatoes roasted with rosemary on the plate beside it. I took a bite of the burger. The cheese was warm, fully melted, the meat red and juicy. If my heart is anything like my old man's, I should have stopped eating things like this long ago. Instead I'm still savoring them.

"Glass of Montepulciano?" she asked.

"Sangiovese, as soon as we've finished with the pitcher," I said around a mouthful of cheeseburger. "I've been spending almost as much time here as back in my room," I said, once she was gone.

"It's a good place," Billy said. "I've tried to convince them to let me sleep in a room off the kitchen, but they got no sense of humor, you know."

I leaned forward, resting my forearms on the table, the burger in my hands, chewing as I spoke. My mother would have been horrified.

"You didn't go to the funeral."

He shrugged. "Yeah, I don't do funerals, man. I hate them. The cat was a good dude and all, but I doubt if he'd've gone to my funeral, not that I plan on having one."

"It was something else, definitely not your run of the mill Graham funeral."

He laughed. "I heard. Some old guy got his head blown off."

"I was Angelo Corelli." He shrugged. "I heard that, but hey, guys like you and me, war vets, seeing someone get blown away's not so special, right?"

"It's always horrendous," I said.

His response lacked any emotion. "Whatever, dude."

"I know you want the recordings, Billy."

His head snapped up, eyes burning. "Bet your ass I want them, Eddie. They're mine. Cornell gave them to me."

"And you gave them to me." There was no point in telling him that Sylvia had said I should keep them. He was close enough to the edge as it was, and even though I was sure I didn't want them, I hadn't decided he should have them.

"We've been through this before, dude. I want them for safekeeping. Just for safekeeping."

"That's why Cornell gave them to you and it's why you gave them to me." He shrugged. "And his ass is dead, so they should be mine and I'm ready to take the risk of having them."

"You don't think they should go to his sister?"

"We've talked about that before too."

"What if she wants them, Billy?"

"So?" He adopted a belligerent tone and posture. "She's a Corelli."

"Corellis don't scare me. I learned how to take care of myself years ago, in the Gulf. I've been doing pretty well since."

"I'd describe you as maintaining," I said.

Like a striking snake, he grabbed my wrists, smashing my cheeseburger to the tabletop, scattering lettuce and tomato over the surface. I tried pulling away, but he was strong and more determined to hold me than I would have believed possible. His eyes locked on to mine. There was nothing easy about them. No Billy Melnick, Town Common denizen. No Billy Melnick, good old boy. No Billy Melnick, former work-study student and apprentice poet. This was another Billy Melnick, one I did not know, one I had only seen a glimpse of the other night. This was a Billy Melnick who should have disappeared years before, when the first president Bush's Iraq war fizzled. A Billy Melnick who should have been as lost as the vaunted warrior he often told me about, but had never shown me.

The man holding my wrists, the man who scattered my cheeseburger, was a Billy Melnick who had done whatever it had taken to smuggle heroin into the country. He had concealed it and dealt it with success and profit. He was hard, determined and angry. His grip tightened.

"You're the maintainer, Eddie. I'm the writer. I'm the guy who knows what to do with those recordings." Eyes still locked on mine, his words were slow, almost menacing, delivered in deliberate and measured terms. "They're mine by right."

"And you'll sell them to some asshole like Elsworth Buell."

"If I want to. Or I'll find some other asshole with more money. Or I'll do that eBay thing I was telling you about. Maybe I'll contact Bukowski's publisher. Man, there's shitloads of things I can do with those recordings."

I cracked my foot hard into his shin, breaking his hold on me and grabbed his hands, twisting his wrists until tears came to his eyes. He relaxed and sat back in the booth, forming his face into a neutral mask. Only his eyes revealed the anger boiling behind them.

I kept my voice soft, soothing. "Don't ever try that again. I could have broken your wrists. Clean up the mess you made of my meal, then order me another one." I passed him a napkin to clean the tomato, potatoes, ground beef and grease spread across the table. He held it, his expression seething. Then his faced relaxed. He smiled. The façade the old Billy was had returned. He wiped the table, wrapping the detritus in the napkin and placing it on the table, near the aisle.

"Billy, I told you I don't give a rat's ass about the recordings. If and when the time's right, I'll give them to you. For now, I have them in a safe place. For their protection, for yours, for mine."

He waved his hands in the air, a motion of dismissal of all that had gone before. "Sorry, dude. I get anxious, you know. I'm doing all right for money. Like I'm not starving or living in a cardboard box down by the railroad tracks. Those recordings, though, they're worth bucks. I could really use them. Besides, once I have them, maybe I could use them for leverage to get Ecco to publish some of my stuff. I mean, they are really going to want what's on those recordings."

He was all over the place. The recordings had become an obsession, but he had no clear plan for them. Something else was going on with him, with the recordings, and what to do with them was secondary.

"Think about Evans and Ariel," I said. "Is that how you want to be found? You want your mom and dad to go down to the morgue at County Medical and when they open the hat box in the cooler, say, 'yes, that's our son's head. Gosh, it looked so much better on his shoulders. And where are his shoulders anyway?' 'Over here,' the morgue attendant will say and pull open a drawer and unzip your body bag, so your mother can say, 'oh gosh, his shoulders looked so much better with his head on them. Oh Billy, pull yourself together.'"

His face was flat, expressionless. "Funny. But that's not going to happen, dude. Not to this cat."

"You can't be sure."

He shrugged, grinned. "Okay, Eddie, I'll go it your way for a while." He built an expression of smiling reconciliation. The construction was slow, the final result a little lopsided. "I guess I should thank you for looking out after me."

"It would be nice."

"Okay. Thanks."

"Sure," I said.

"Can we meet here tomorrow night when you get off work and talk about it again? I'll come up with a new angle to convince you it's safe to give them to me."

"Not tomorrow night. I'm off. Tiger's having a Halloween party. We both switched nights off with Jody Lyon and Bob Teschner."

"Shit dude, and I wasn't invited? Halloween's my favorite holiday." He finished the last of the beer from the pitcher and got up from the booth.

"It's really for Chad," I said. Billy would be less interested if he thought it was going to be a party filled with high school kids. I didn't mention Dawn's dislike of the begging Halloweeners going from door to door, bags open for candy. "It's his last year in high school. Dawn and Tiger figured this was the time to throw him one final kid party. You know, dunking for apples, pin the tail on the donkey, guess who's behind the ugly mask or under the fright wig kind of thing. It's going to be full of high school kids and a few adults to keep order and make sure there's no drinking."

"Dude, all those kids drink and smoke dope anyway."

"They do," I said. "But not at this party. This is a throwback Halloween bash, the kind sixth graders have. That's the idea, clean, innocent, old timey fun."

"Then it's a good thing they didn't ask me." He gave me one of his shrugs, rolled his eyes and clicked his tongue. Anyway, thanks for looking out for me, right?"

"Think nothing of it," I said.

He turned away, walking toward his regular perch at the bar, but I heard him mutter as he went, "Don't worry asshole, I won't."

I let it go. Let him save face. I had enough to worry about without pissing off Billy Melnick any further. He was already unpredictable. If he got too angry his unpredictability could become dangerous. Hanging out with him had been one of the better parts of my life in Graham. Now that was all changed. Things had been said, emotions had been raised that could not be forgotten. It would never be easy between us again. Maybe we'd settle our disagreement over the recordings, maybe we wouldn't, but it was too late for anything except a détente.

Book Three

Chapter Nineteen

Halloween day started with an exquisite late October New England morning, the sun a radiant silver white disk in a sky as blue as sky can be, the air still and warm from a front blowing up from the south, carrying deep earthen scents of warmer climes. I awoke to the sounds of heavy machinery on the street, a bulldozer loading rubble from the ruins of the Willey and McClannan building into a dump truck. Looking out the window I saw a charred desk and filing cabinet tumbling into the bed.

The Graham Coop was hopping. I paid for coffee and an *Enterprise* and sat at a table by the window. The paper was filled with articles on the elections coming up the following Tuesday, letters to the editor predicting that one or the other candidate for governor would destroy the Commonwealth. In truth, either one of them was capable of making a mess of things.

An article on page four quoted Chief Sandy Grover as saying the police still had no leads in the deaths of Evans and Ariel Cornell or the assassination of Angelo Corelli. When asked by the reporter why Corelli was present at the Cornell's funerals, Grover was described as shrugging and saying that it didn't appear relevant to the police investigation into the murders. In response to the reporter's question about the fear and tension in town, especially in the Cornell's neighborhood, Grover said leads were forthcoming. What did forthcoming mean, the reporter asked. Grover reminded her that there had not been an unsolved murder in Graham in over fifty years. What about the drugs found in the bedroom where they were murdered, she asked. Grover said there was no evidence they were not planted.

"That was Dr. Bradley's assumption upon finding the bodies and I tend to agree," he said.

The reporter went on to describe the near panic in the Chancellor Street area. People were beefing up their locks. Security systems were selling faster than fried dough at the county fair. The article ended with a comment by Ira Bradley, the dentist who had discovered the bodies. "The bottom line is that five days ago two fine young people were murdered in our neighborhood and the police have done nothing to bring their killers to justice. Chief Grover assures us his people are working full time on the case, but nothing has changed. There are no suspects. There is no evident progress. Meanwhile we close our doors at night praying that we will be alive to open them in the morning."

Grover didn't have a clue. Nor would he, acting alone or with his police force. The Cornell murders were outside his scope. Corelli's death was off his radar. The local cops could find a drunk who stuffed a pack of cigarettes down another drunk's throat, rolled him and left him to choke to death by the Green River a few blocks off Main Street. They had no trouble busting the jail guard who stabbed his pregnant girl friend, left his fingerprints all over the knife, threw her body down the cellar stairs, rolled down after her and claimed they were the victims of a home invasion by a Chinese gang. Neil Connors, an anesthesiologist at the hospital who followed his partner to Springfield and shot him in the head as he was getting a blowjob from a hooker behind the Amtrak station was an easy collar once detective Bobby Strunk discovered the two million dollar life insurance policy Connors had taken out on the partner less than a year earlier, and the Walker brothers' torture of Donny Parker had been done by fools too stupid to cover their tracks and its details too well known among the lowlifes on the street to remain covered up for any length of time.

Even Grover had to have known those murders were different from the Cornell murders and Angelo Corelli's death, but he had no way of knowing how they were different. The drugs found at the Cornell murder scene remained a mystery. Neither of the Cornells had any kind of criminal record. I figured Grover would continue in his choice of believing the drugs were a plant. To accuse either Evans or Ariel of drug involvement would bring him head to head with Bradford Lord Winslow, Ariel's high-powered Boston lawyer grandfather, and that could lead the town into a costly law suit, putting Sandy's head on the railroad track. He would let the investigation limp along and die out of the news, then retire with eighty percent of his highest three years salary before the Cornell murders could turn around and bite his ass.

I folded the paper and turned my attention to the coffee. Come right down to it, I was the one on the tracks. Put your ear on them, I've heard say, and you can hear a train coming miles away. There was a rumbling in my ear, and I was alone beside those tracks, my head on the rail, my ass in the air. I needed someone to pull me off if the train got too close for me to jump away in time.

To do that, I needed someone I could trust with my story.

§§§

Tiger was sitting on her porch steps in the sun, picking the guitar, a bottle of Sam Adams open beside her, a cigarette hanging from her lips. She looked up as I pulled into the driveway, shading her eyes with her right hand, and followed my progress as I got out of the truck and walked across the yard.

"You're early for the party. Where's your costume?" she asked when I sat down beside her and took a sip from the Sammy. Oak Street was quiet, a few kids cruising on bicycles, a neighbor several doors up the street raking leaves, and Tiger sitting on the porch, drinking beer and playing guitar.

"This isn't about the party, Tige."

She picked up on my tone of voice, her eyebrows shooting up. "Sounds serious."

"It is, but before I say anything you'll have to swear you'll never tell anyone a word of what I'm going to tell you."

"Swear, like in taking an oath?"

"Exactly. A solemn oath on our friendship."

"Jesus, Eddie, what've you done?"

"Swear you'll carry this to your grave."

She looked at me as if I were one of those television aliens, suddenly ripping back my skin to reveal the lizard creature I really was. She caught herself after a moment and gave me a smile of recognition. "This is what we were talking about back that day we were canoeing in the cove when I said that you're a man of mystery and you said it sounded like something from a cheap novel. Is that it?"

"Yeah, that's it," I said. I took a deep breath, hesitating for a moment, then told her about my life before Graham, the agency, the skinny on Henrietta Lane and Randolph, what the agency was making me do, weaving it all together with what she already knew about the Corellis and the Cornells. She was silent as I spoke; lightly strumming minor chords, as though giving tonal punctuation to my story. I explained the agency's amoral position regarding the usefulness of the Corellis and the demand that I shut down Henrietta Lane, severing her ties to the Russians.

"Shut down," she said when I came to that. "You're supposed to shut down Henrietta Lane?"

I nodded.

"What does that mean, shut down?"

"Put out of business."

She fell quiet, running her fingers over the guitar strings, finding fragments of tunes, plucking them in a soft collage of sound. When she spoke, her voice was heavy with subdued fury. "They want you to kill her. That's their way of putting someone out of business."

"Probably." The answer was supposed to be vague. She would have none of it.

"Probably, horseshit. Kill her, that's what they're saying."

"You're right. Killing Henrietta Lane, Federica Vlasenko, is the best way to put her out of business."

"That's murder, Eddie."

"Not when you work for the agency."

"You've done this before." It wasn't a question. I looked away.

She laid the guitar on the porch and chugging the remains of the beer, went in the house and came back with two more. She put one down on the step beside me. Noting that she had not opened it or handed it to me, I picked it up, screwed off the cap and took a sip.

She glowered at me. "Why are you laying this on me? And who in the hell are you anyway? I don't want to hear this kind of shit. I'm just a goddamn janitor. I got no interest in spying and killing and torture and intrigue other than what I watch on '24.' What the hell are you up to, Eddie, telling me this crap? I don't want to know it, and now I do and there's no putting that toothpaste back in the tube. Fuck you, Eddie. Fuck you."

"Maintainer II," I said. "You're a Maintainer II."

Her face was red with anger. If I'd told her I just finished screwing Dawn, she couldn't have been more furious. I had told her I was a lie, that our friendship was based on a fiction, a story concocted so someone she never knew could become Eddie Sanders and worm his way into her life and her heart.

"Stuff it." Her voice was a loud rasp from deep in her throat, her expression dripping with contempt. "The joke ain't funny no more. Who the hell are you?"

I took her hand. She pulled away, shaking.

"I'm still Eddie Sanders. We've known each other for a long time Tige. I intend to remain Eddie Sanders, no matter what."

The red in her face deepened, rage pouring from her eyes in tears and in the narrowing slits they had become. "Bullshit. You know me. Clearly, I didn't know diddly shit about you. I still don't. I'm me because I was born me and lived me my whole life. You're you because you chose to become you. Who you going to be next year? Tell me that, Eddie. Who will you be next year?"

My answer was a mumble. "Eddie Sanders."

I turned the beer bottle in shaking hands, afraid I'd made a mistake. Over the years with the agency I became accustomed to inhabiting shadowy selves that drifted along like smoke on a river and had at last settled to the ground and grown solid. I believed I turned Eddie Sanders into a true person, someone of substance, made his story into my life. She had believed the life and now saw only a story. She had always been solid. The move from Catherine Ann Kelly to Tiger had been along a slow and safe continuum, given the relative open mindedness of people in the Valley to other peoples' recreations of themselves. Perhaps she could not absorb what I had told her. I knew she grasped the words and the story, but the implications of the story, its unspoken narrative of violence and deception were outside her experience, a window on a world she would never choose to look through. I had to hold on to her, make her comprehend.

"You know me, Tige. I'm your friend, the guy you've been hanging out with all these years we've worked together. Eddie."

"Right. Eddie. Eddie Sanders. I suppose that's not your real name."

"I've got a birth certificate says I was born to it," I said.

She looked at me, shaking her head. "I read shit, Eddie, crummy novels, stuff like that, with characters whose names are whatever the fake papers they have say they are. So, I ask again, who are you?"

I took a deep breath, looking into a past I had worked to banish from memory. "My mother was Elaine Kowalski. My father was Nathaniel Hunt. Everybody called him Nate. He hated the name, Nathaniel, but wanted a Nate junior, so I got Nathan."

She laughed, a sharp, sudden sound, and her face broke into a wide grin. "You're Polish. All that WASP Sanders shit, and your mom's a Polack? We got that immigrant stuff in common. Polacks and Micks, we've been put down and shoved around, made fun of. Bet there's more bad jokes about the Irish than there are about the Polish."

"Yeah, but we've had a Pope. When was the last time a Mick was Pope?" We laughed together. It was an uneasy truce, but it was a start. She chugged the Sammy and belched. For a long time she sat and stared toward the surrounding hills. She sighed, cursed, snorted, and drank more beer. After a third beer and what seemed like hours, she looked at me.

"Goddamn you Eddie, you fucking son-of-a-bitch. You lump of turd. I thought you were my friend, my buddy, and you hand me this ration of shit. Why couldn't you keep your goddamn mouth shut and just keep on being Eddie?" She turned to me, her face twisted with fury and sorrow. "Why couldn't you do that, asshole? Why couldn't you just stay Eddie?" Asshole was a good sign, almost a term of endearment, given the situation. I focused my attention on the hills she had been staring at. Sunlight shone through the bare trees, the shadow of their limbs sharp on the thick cover of fallen leaves beneath them. I sat in silence, waiting. She would either come through, or she wouldn't. I was betting on her loyalty overcoming her anger at my years of deception.

It felt like my old game. I would make people like me, get them to trust me so I could use them, and ask them to risk their lives to help me fulfill a mission the agency had schemed up. No, not me. Not Eddie. Nathan would do that. And Nathan had walked away, into Eddie Sander's skin. And goddamn it all to hell, here I was, Eddie Sanders, asking the same thing from my best friend, the one person I respected, the one person I cared for, in all honesty, the one person I loved more than anyone else in the world. I was about to get up and leave when she put a hand on my leg, patting it twice.

"So, like I said, Eddie, why are you telling me all this shit?" My eyes filled with tears and I turned to hide them from her. "I need help, Tige. The agency swooped down, picked me up after all these years and left me hanging on a high limb, no net, no support, no direction. Just shut down Lane and control the Corellis."

"And me? What do you want from me?" She looked confused. Her voice was small, almost like a young girl's. "I might get in a fight here and there, just for fun, kick the shit out of somebody, like those assholes in Ducky's that night, but I don't kill people. I don't care about agencies and governments and mobs. I live. I do my job. I got my family. I got Dawn and I got Chad, and I thought I had you." She paused, looking at me pointedly. "What the fuck do you want from me?"

"I want what I've always gotten from you, Tige. That's all I want. This is something like those kids at Ducky's last week. You got us into that one. I got us into this one."

"You got yourself into this one. Now you want me in." She shook her head. "This is different, Eddie, nothing like those idiots at Ducky's. Somehow, I don't think I can scare Henrietta Lane or whoever she is, into saying she's an asshole, and that'd be the end of it."

"No doubt. It'll be a lot more complicated."

"And dangerous," she said. "That too."

Then she laughed. It was like the sun after a terrible northeaster. "Jesus, Eddie, you're a piece of work, a piece of work. So who are you coming to the party as? James Bond?"

"You'll see." I lowered my voice.

She laughed again. "I can't wait. Maybe it'll be Dr. Jekyll, or Mr. Hyde. You Mr. Hyde, Eddie?"

And that was it. She was in. Now all I had to do was figure out what to do.

§§§

"*Edward, this is Dr. Loblolly. Please call my office as soon as you hear this.*" The message on my answering machine was as cool as it was terse. I called back and got Becky Cohen, the Dean's executive assistant, a euphemism for secretary, useful when the college wants to keep someone out of the bargaining unit and require confidentiality of them. She was friendly, but reserved, refusing any comment when I asked her why the Dean was calling me.

Loblolly came on the line. "Edward, good of you to call back. We need to talk about your work."

"It isn't good enough?"

"It is excellent, when you're here. You were gone Monday and you're taking today off. Is everything all right?"

"Everything's fine, ma'am."

"I am glad to hear so, Edward. You know, college policy asks for classified employees to give more adequate notice before taking time off than you've done this week."

Her voice was stiff and she was wheezing between words. I imagined her, that huge globular body, a pale skin filled with fat and water, dressed in a designer tent, sitting behind her desk, a box of chocolates open in front of her, drug store reading glasses at the end of her nose, fiddling with a pencil as she spoke into the phone, testing how much it would bend before breaking. It was a scene anyone who had been called on the carpet in her office would describe.

I tried to sound contrite. "Sorry," I said. "I'll be more careful."

"Do," she said. "Your contract requires an informal, oral warning before anything is written and placed in your personnel file. Consider this conversation that warning. Give Human Resources at least a five day notice, whenever possible, before taking vacation time. Do you understand, Edward?"

"I do, Dr. Loblolly."

"Of course, there are always emergencies. It is President Lewis' position that we remain flexible about the rules as long as possible here."

I thanked her, shot the receiver the finger, and once I heard the disconnecting click from her end, slammed the phone down as hard as I could. "Asshole, fat lard-assed piece of shit."

She was lucky. It was an Eddie Sanders reaction. She would not want to face the anger of a Nathan Hunt, and he was rising dangerously close to the surface.

§§§

At ten after two I pulled into the parking in front of County Medical Center, planning to speak with Elmore Walker. The sky, so clear and blue a few hours before, was now streaked with high thin clouds, precursors of the rain predicted for that night. Inside, a woman wearing a blue smock who appeared to be in her late eighties sat at the information desk paging through the cartoons in a *New Yorker*. She laughed and looked up at me.

"They used to be better," she said. "The cartoons. Thurber, Charles Addams, Peter Arno, Helen Hopkinson. They were funny cartoonists."

"We need to believe that everything used to be better," I said. "As if it were a rule of life. Actually, it isn't true, you know. I can say with great authority that things were a lot worse before."

She smiled, waiting for me to ask a question she could answer, something that would justify giving up her free time to sit behind the information desk in the hospital lobby, wearing a blue smock with her name in red stitching on the left breast pocket.

"Is Elmore Walker still here?"

Her smile didn't fade. It dropped from her face like a late fall apple. She made a show of clicking the computer keys. "Yes. Room 231."

Without another word, she handed me a visitor's pass and turned her attention back to *The New Yorker*.

All but one of the cops were gone, and he was outside the room schmoozing with a young attractive nursing student who wore a plastic badge bearing the name, Amy Ledger. I'd seen her around the college a few times. I smiled and nodded to her. She gave me a brief smile, the kind that says *who the hell are you*, and turned her attention back to the cop. Janitors, no matter what contrived title you give them, are invisible. That's just fine with me, except when attractive nursing students act as though they've never seen me. The worst part of it is, in a very basic way, they never have.

Elmore was still in his bed, his head swathed in gauze, the IV in his arm. His bruises had faded a bit and he was cleaner than he'd been last time, perhaps cleaner than he'd ever been. He looked away from the television as I entered the room.

"What you want coming back here?" He snarled the words.

I stood at the foot of his bed, resting my hands on the metal rail. "Tell me about getting shot."

He looked at me like I was an idiot. "I been down that road a hundred times with the cops, and I already told you once. I ain't telling you again. You got anything to drink?"

The cop leaned around the door, checking me out. He'd been distracted when I went in and was trying to cover for his lapse and impress Amy Ledger at the same time.

"You all right, Walker?" he asked.

"I got pain, man. Make them give me some more painkillers. I hurt awful badly."

"Not my job," the cop said. "All I got to do is make sure someone doesn't shoot you again, and that's a waste of my time, watching out for slime like you."

"Fuck you," Elmore said.

The cop grinned at me and went back into the hallway. "Hurt pretty badly?"

Elmore grimaced. "Ever been shot, man? It feels like your insides are on fire. It feels pretty shitty where the son-of-a-bitch kicked me, too."

"I could talk to the nurses about getting you some medications."

"Demerol would be good. Think you can get me a shot of Demerol?" He looked expectant, hopeful. "Man, they give me some of that shit when they brought me in here and I thought I was in fucking heaven. Got a few more shots of it too, but they ain't given me none since yesterday, maybe the day before. Demerol's really good shit. If I could get my hands on some, I could sell that stuff real good. You get the nurse to bring me a shot."

"Maybe. I could get you something to drink, too."

"If I had a bottle of vodka under my pillow here I'd feel a shitload better."

"Then talk to me about who shot you."

"You take care of me first. You do that and I'll talk to you." I told him I'd do what I could and left the room. Amy was leaning against the wall, the cop supporting himself against the wall by one arm, hanging over her. The nursing station was empty. I walked down the hall looking for someone in charge. There wasn't any point in trying to get Demerol for Elmore, but it wouldn't hurt to remind them that he was in pain and ask if he was due for any meds.

I found two nurses standing in the sunroom at the end of the hall. I asked about Elmore's drugs.

"He should just die," one of them said as the other nodded in agreement and walked off.

"Doesn't look as though he's going to," I said to the first one. She was in her late thirties, dark brown hair cut short, a soft, pretty face and no wedding ring. Her name badge read, Linda Dryer.

"Fine, let him suffer. I've got real people who are sick in here, like the little boy in the room next to him. Seven years old and he's got a brain tumor and I've got to go in there as soon as you leave me alone and give him his meds. There's an elderly woman in 233 recovering from a kidney transplant. She gave one to her forty-eight year old daughter. Elmore Walker should be in jail with his brothers and cousins, not here where decent people have to take care of him."

"But he is and you do."

She gave me a smile of philosophical resignation. "Sucks, doesn't it?"

"Sure does. He scheduled for any pain medications?"

"Tylenol with codeine." She looked at her watch. "Two of them in ten minutes."

"He's asking for Demerol," I said, smiling.

"Yeah, right. And I'm going to hold his hand and sing lullabies to him." She looked at me as if she knew me from somewhere. She may have been a nursing student at the college, like Amy Ledger, where I drifted in the background, creating order and cleanliness. "You don't look like you'd be a friend of his."

"I'm not. I'm just trying to find out if a friend of mine shot him." She laughed. "If your friend did it, I've got two things for you to tell him. Tell him he did a public service, and tell him I hate him for not finishing the job and saddling us with the scum. Putting him on and taking he off the bedpan is the worst thing I've ever had to do. Your friend needs to do more target practice and then come back for the slimeball."

"I'll tell him," I said.

"Every time I put him on and take him off, he moves around so I have to look at his penis. It's the ugliest penis I ever saw, little, pasty, and covered with sores. Can you believe he's even got a name for it? Little El." She folded her arms over her chest, shaking her head in disgust. "He told me that Little El liked me, that he wanted to get to know me better, and that he'd be my best friend." She uttered a sound of disgust.

"That's a lot more than I wanted to know," I said.

She smiled, her eyes tired, her reply coming with a sigh. "Yeah, well that's life in the healthcare profession, just full of glamour and romance."

"I apologize for the shooter," I said, and left her in the sunroom as she tried composing a cheery expression to face a little boy dying of a brain tumor.

I went to a nearby liquor store and bought a bottle of the cheapest vodka they had.

"Stuff's more like rubbing alcohol," the clerk said.

"Guy I'm getting it for should be drinking wood alcohol distilled in a diesel truck's radiator," I told him.

When I got back Amy was gone and the cop stood more or less at attention outside the door. I had hidden the bottle in my back pocket. I smiled, nodded at him, and went into the room. Taking the bottle out, I extended it toward Elmore. He snatched it from my hand, unscrewed the cap and took a long drink.

"Want to know what that bitch nurse brought me? Two aspirins with some shit she says is Cody in them. That Cody ain't worth dog piss, man. "

"Tylenol," I said. "With codeine. That'll give you some relief."

"Shit, they look like aspirin to me. And fuck Cody. I want some Demerol. You get me some Demerol and we talk, you know what I mean."

I grabbed the vodka from his hand. "Tylenol with codeine is what they'll give you. You have as much chance of getting Demerol as you do of spending a weekend on The Riviera with Madonna."

He snarled. "Give me that back, you shithead. And what's Geraldo got to do with any of this shit?"

"You get the bottle back after we talk."

He put his head back on the pillow and shut his eyes. "So talk."

"Who shot you?"

"I told everybody, shit, I don't know. Guy was wearing a ski mask. He come in like Batman and shot me."

"You don't remember anything about him?"

"He had a ski mask and a gun. I remember that pretty goddamn good."

"Did he say anything to you?" His face knotted up. Elmore wasn't used to reflecting on things. He wiped the back of his hand over his lips, picked his nose and let loose with a long, loud fart. He laughed. "He didn't say that."

I backed away from the bedside. "What did he say?"

He fell back into what passed for thought in a Walker mind. I stepped over to the door, away from the stench of his gas. When he saw what I was doing, he made a sly smile and crooked his forefinger, beckoning me over. "I remember. He said something."

"What?" I asked

He sat up and pointed to the door, then moved the finger to his lips. I walked into the full range of his lingering fart trying not to gag at the odor. He smiled, watching me.

"I always liked the way my farts smell. When I get laid, I like to fart and pull the sheets up over the bitch that I'm with. If they like it, I'll let them cum. They don't like it, I just go at them as fast as I can, get my rocks off, and the hell with them."

I pushed him back down, flat on the bed; being careful to hurt him just enough to scare him, then waved the bottle of vodka in front of his face. "You're a useless piece of shit, Elmore, but I'm going to be nice to you. I'm going to leave you this bottle and I won't hurt you if you tell me what I want to know."

He looked toward the door, a rat-like panic in his eyes.

"Don't," I said. "You bring the cop in and you get no vodka." He licked his lips. "All right. The shooter comes up to me and says 'this is for you shitball and when I leave here you are going to be dead.' Then he shot me."

"That's it?" I asked "That's all he said?"

"That's it. But it ain't the way he said it."

"Meaning?"

"He sounded like a reb, you know?"

"A reb? What in the hell is a reb, Elmore?"

"A rebel, you know a redneck, a cracker."

"You mean he had a southern accent?"

He nodded, still looking at the vodka bottle. "And he used it real mean, nasty. There he was, trying to kill me, and he wanted me to know it, to think about it before I died. That's about as nasty as you can get."

"It is," I agreed. Elmore may have said the most reflective analytical thing he had ever uttered. I handed him the bottle. He took a drink and looked at me.

"I know who shot you," I said.

He gulped the vodka down. "Tell the cops."

"I can't prove it, but I know him. You're lucky you lived."

He took another long drink. The bottle was half gone. He gave me another sly look. "Yeah, ain't I the lucky one?"

"Yeah, you're lucky," I said. "There's a kid in the next room dying of brain cancer and an old lady short one kidney in another because she gave one to her daughter. A year from now you'll have forgotten you were shot, but the kid'll be dead and the old lady and her daughter both will be worrying about their kidneys."

"Who gives a shit? At least they got somebody to love them. My life is a real pleasure, a garden of earthly delights."

Surprised by the unexpected elegance of his words, I looked at him, but all his attention was on the bottle. I turned to go.

"Is this all I get, Get me another bottle." He looked at me with a sad, imploring expression. "Please, man. I really need it."

I studied him. He was mean, ugly and foul smelling. He'd probably been mean ugly and foul smelling since he was a kid, and his parents had undoubtedly been mean, ugly and foul smelling. It didn't excuse him and I didn't feel sorry for him, but getting him another bottle of vodka wasn't going to change my life one iota, and it might make a few minutes of him more bearable.

"What the hell. Sure," I said. "I'll bring you another bottle."

I went back to the liquor store and bought him more vodka. The clerk gave me a suspicious look. I would swear he sniffed the air to see if I had polished off the bottle, but he sold it to me and I took it back to Elmore, who was woozy from the codeine and the vodka he already had. He didn't say anything, just took the bottle, uncapped it and had a swig. Then he recapped it, stuck it under his pillow, turned up the sound on the television and closed his eyes.

Chapter Twenty

Henrietta Lane's Llanarch was decorated for Halloween, the driveway lined with huge plastic jack-o-lanterns, their electric bulbs already lit. Artificial cobwebs hung from porch pillars, the porch itself bedecked with grinning plastic skeletons, witches with long noses and warts on their faces wearing pointed hats, and black cats, their backs arched, their eyes yellow/green. Although it was only four o'clock, the sky was gray, the air damp and raw. A panel truck, green with gold lettering, *Green River Caterers*, was parked in front of the house, its doors open. Several people carried large covered trays and urns of coffee and punch from the truck to the house. I watched as a second panel truck pulled up behind it. Two women and two men got out and opened the rear doors, taking out a cello, a viola and two violins.

I knew the cello player.

"Want some help lugging that thing?" I asked

"Eddie." She gave me a big grin and spoke in mock reproach. "It's been over four years. You never did call."

"Sorry, Beth. You know how time gets away."

She laughed. It was a happy sound. "Tell me about it. I'm married with two kids."

I looked at her, blonde, small, compact, and was surprised by a brief pang of loss. We'd been mucking around together for about a year when she told me she loved me. We were on the lawn at Tanglewood, the final concert of the summer, listening to Beethoven's Ninth. I was sitting on a blanket, her head in my lap, and two empty bottles of Malbec lying beside us.

I told her she was pretty special too.

"Pretty special, eh?" she said. "And what does pretty special mean?"

"Pretty special is pretty special. "Pretty special isn't love." I told her I thought it was damned close. She sat up and opened our third bottle of Malbec. Later that night, driving down the Mass Pike headed for Graham, she suggested we move in together. I said my Barton room was too small for more than one person and she had an apartment with three other roommates. She said we could rent our own apartment, perhaps even buy a house.

I watched the taillights of the cars ahead of us as I tried to frame a response. After a long silence I said something about how Seiji Osawa had breathed life into the Boston Symphony Orchestra and wouldn't it be a shame when he retired. She replied that there were more than enough talented conductors and yes, while he was special, whoever replaced him would be special in a different way. I took her home, said I'd call her about dinner the next night. I didn't.

Now Seiji Osawa has gone to Europe and Beth's married with two children and I still live in Barton Rooms.

"You take the cello," she said. "I'll grab the sheet music and the music stand."

I carried it in, following her into the living room. The windows were hung with black velvet, the normal light bulbs replaced by purples, reds, greens and blues, with a scattering of black lights. A full sized skeleton stood by the fireplace, wearing a long blonde wig and a white dress.

"Thanks," Beth said when I set the cello down. "Good to see you, Eddie. Things all right?"

"Dandy. I'm glad you got the life you wanted."

"Me too. You have the life you want?" I gave her a Gallic shrug. "The life I deserve."

"Sorry." She didn't sound it.

"That's not all bad, you know."

"I guess that depends on what you think you deserve." Her tone was not sympathetic. She and I had different concepts of my just desserts.

"I have to go," I said.

"Sure. Let's do lunch. I'll bring pictures of the kids."

Henrietta was standing in the hallway glaring at me when I came back out. She was nursing a martini

"Why are you here?" she asked. I could hear her breath whistling through those narrow nostrils.

"I need ten minutes of your time," I said.

"Impossible. Even you can see I'm getting ready for a party." Her fingers gripping the glass were whiter that the rest of her skin.

"Ten minutes," I said, leaning close to her, my voice little more than a whisper. "Madame Vlasenko, or is it Madame Nabokov?"

She stiffened, eyes dark, surprise quickly covered with contempt. "My study. Ten minutes. No more."

I followed her down the hall. She unlocked a door, motioning me to follow her into a library furnished in antique Chippendale, the walls lined with mahogany shelves filled with books. A large desk was cluttered with files and loose papers. A computer and a printer took up a corner of the room where she had moved her business as a result of the fire. A gas log burned in the fireplace, drying and warming the room. She stood by it, her right arm resting on the mantle, the martini still in her hand.

"Talk," she said.

"I'd rather listen, Madame Vlasenko/Nabokov."

"Lane," she said. "Ms. Henrietta Lane. Mrs. Arnold Lane." I stared at her. She stared back. At least three minutes passed. She sipped her drink, never taking her eyes from mine. I had to admire her self possession. She didn't appear rattled. Neither did I.

"So, we know each other," she said at last.

"No. We have scant information about each other. You have no idea what I've done and what I'm capable of."

"You're a dead man, janitor."

"Like the Cornells? Like Angelo Corelli? Like Tommy Finneran?"

"Tommy who?"

"Finneran. An o.d. in Eagle Falls."

"Never heard of him. I had nothing to do with the Cornell's deaths."

"And Corelli's?"

"I was in the funeral home when it happened, remember?"

"Randolph wasn't."

"He was waiting for me in the car."

"Did he shoot Elmore Walker too? You trying to kill off the competition at all levels?"

She snorted through those narrow nostrils. "Randolph doesn't shoot people."

"Right. He just beats them for you, drops them from cliffs, things like that."

"I might have him shoot you."

"Let's cut to the chase. You wanted me to look into your daughter's death because you knew something about me. You thought that by using me you might get a handle on what I knew about you. Funny thing is I didn't know shit about you, beyond your cover. Bad for you, good for me, and your idea backfired and now I know a great deal about you. You're connected and you're trying to horn in on the Corelli's markets. That gives you a perfect motive for knocking off the Cornells and Angelo Corelli. Randolph wasn't in the funeral home when the old man was killed, and I'd be willing to bet no one saw him waiting in the car for you."

"I'm sure no one saw him shoot the old dago either." She finished the martini, set the glass on the mantle and walked toward me. I think she was trying to be seductive, in an underbelly of a mackerel kind of way. "What do you want, janitor?"

"You out of business."

"You and whoever bombed my building. I'd already be out of business if I didn't take home backups of everything on the office computers every day."

"That's not the business I want you out of. You can rebuild your office, sell real estate and insurance and enjoy your status in the town. You can go right on being Henrietta Lane with all the rights and privileges that go with being her. I'm sure it's a pretty good life. It's the other business I want you out of."

"You assume much, janitor. You come here, call me odd names, talk about some business you want me out of and I don't know what you mean, or what standing you have to be making such statements."

I leaned in toward her. She stepped back a pace. "Let me be blunt, Comrade Lane. Leave the Corelli's alone and pass that along to your comrades."

"Or?"

"Else," I said.

"You won't go to the police. I've got perfect documentation of who I am, of Henrietta Lane." She sneered at me. "And how *passé* you are. Comrades are a thing of the past. Surely you must know that."

"And I'm Eddie Sanders, also well documented."

She laughed, froth in the corners of her mouth dribbling on her chin. "A janitor in a boondocks community college. You could have picked a better life."

"Not for me, Henrietta. I like my life and I'm going to hang on to it. It's an approach I recommend."

She looked contemplative for a moment, then nodded, sucking in her lips as she did. "I'll think about it."

"Do." I turned, leaving her standing in the middle of the room, the gas log burning behind her.

I heard gravel crunch behind me as I unlocked the truck door. I crouched, swiveled, ready to fight. Randolph stood there, dressed in a pearl button shirt, tight denims and high leather boots, six shooters strapped to his hips.

"Gonna try that Kung Fu shit on me, asshole? I seen a movie once where a guy did that, got all ready to do that martial arts crap, rip a guy's heart out and the guy pulled out a gun and shot him, just as cool as can be. You try that shit on me I'll shoot you before you get your first jump off the ground." He flexed his fingers above the handles of the pistols, *Gunsmoke* style.

I relaxed. "Funny thing about that. Henrietta just tried to tell me you don't shoot people."

He made a guttural sound in an attempt at laughing. "Yeah, right, and the pope don't shit in the woods."

"Why did you kill the Cornells?" He looked surprised, confused. "I didn't."

"Angelo Corelli?" He smiled at that. "I don't kill people."

"Then the bear isn't Catholic?"

He frowned, shaking his head from side to side, unable to figure it out. "I heard the old bastard's head exploded like a melon. That would have been a sight, hunh?"

"That's a bit of an overstatement. I saw what happened. It wasn't quite so dramatic, but it wasn't pretty."

"You know, I could kill you." He smiled with pleasure at the thought. "That would be fun."

"I wouldn't try it, Randy." I got in the truck and rolled down the window. "You didn't kill the Cornells?"

He frowned with confusion again. "Shoot Elmore Walker?"

He grinned again. "A piece of shit that should be dead. I got no doubt but what it was dope from him that got Andy dead."

It wasn't an answer, but it told me a lot. I cranked the engine and drove off. Randolph stood in the driveway, the orange glow from the jack-olanterns lighting his face. He shot Elmore and killed Corelli, I was sure. The murders of Evans and Ariel Cornell were a different matter. There was no gloating denial when I asked him about it, just that look of confusion. I believed he hadn't killed them, but I didn't have a clue as to who did.

§§§

Both sides of Oak Street in Yardley Falls were lined with cars, a quarter of a mile each way from Tiger and Dawn's house. I parked at the end of the line and checked myself out in the rearview mirror. The mustache was perfect, as was the tweedy hat. The trenchcoat's collar was up.

"How do I look?" I asked Shelley. She was dressed as Natasha, Rocky and Bullwinkle's nemesis.

"Poorfect, comrade Clousseau," she answered, rolling her *r*'s in a cheesy Russian accent.

"Excellent. It's about time something went right." We got out of the truck and walked up a street peopled with ghosts, goblins, Richard Nixon, witches, Barack Obama, Sarah Palin, Bill Clinton, both the Bushes, Jedi knights, Klingons and Vulcans, fairy princesses, ghouls and other assorted creatures. Some were small children, going door to door with bags; others were headed for Tiger and Dawn's place.

With the rain it had turned colder. The air was sharp, the tang of winter already in my nostrils. I shivered in the trench coat as we walked up the street. Their lawn had three of the same plastic jack-o-lanterns I had seen earlier at Henrietta Lane's. The porch was decorated with similar artificial cobwebs, skeletons, witches and black cats. Halloween, like all our holidays, has become manufactured and stereotyped, an illustration of Thomas Pynchon's lament at the end of *The Crying of Lot 49*, mourning the loss of diversity in an America where everything looks the same, tastes the same and reflects the same values. I believe Pyncheon was wrong in decrying the loss of diversity, but it unquestionably has been buried beneath mass marketed sentiments, decorations and practices. Unquestionably endangered.

Tiger and Dawn stood on the porch, greeting people. Strains of spooky music, non-melodic pieces played on a Theremin wafted from the stereo in the living room. Tiger wore lipstick and eye shadow. She had on a light blue dress. Her shaved legs packed into a pair of nylon stockings looked like gigantic sausages. Dawn was dressed in a tight black body suit, a black mask covering her eyes, and a skullcap with pointed ears.

"Hi," Tiger said in a high voice, extending her hand to be kissed. "I'm a soccer mom. Be nice to me and I'll vote for you."

I bowed, taking the hand and pressing it to my lips. "Enchanteé, Mademoiselle. I am Inspector Clousseau. Please allow me to present my companion, the lovely Natasha."

"Police," scoffed Dawn. "Cat Woman should scratch your eyes out."

"I am hardly zee poleese," Shelley said, adding as she pointed to me. "Allzo zis man is trouble."

Tiger put an arm around my shoulder. "I think there's something wrong with my furnace. I turned it on yesterday and it reeked of fuel oil. Give me a consult." She eased me away from Shelley and Dawn, toward the cellar stairs.

"Hey," I said in a loud voice. "That's maintenance and that's what we do. Let's take a look."

In the basement, she turned on the workbench lights. The furnace was humming in the corner. There was no odor of fuel oil. She leaned back against the workbench, her fingers splayed across the top.

"I want you to know I'm not going to Vermont with Sylvia."

"Good."

"Good? That all you got to say, just well?"

"Good decision, Tige." She laughed. "It was easy. You see Dawn in the Cat Woman outfit?"

"It was hard not to." I didn't tell her it was always hard for me to stop looking at Dawn. I often look at her wishing I were a lesbian.

She gave me an evil smile. "Hard, you say?"

"Very."

"Shelley looks pretty sexy in that Natasha outfit."

"Very sexy."

"You're pretty stingy with the words tonight."

"You're right. I'm sorry. I'm relieved you're not running off for a couple days of wild sexual bliss with Sylvia Cornell. You tell her?"

She grunted affirmatively. "How did she react?"

"Fine."

"Fine?"

"Fine."

"Now who's being miserly with words?"

"You didn't like that, right Eddie?"

"Nope."

She cuffed me on the shoulder. "I've thought a lot about your advice and I've realized that I have to take it. I've got too much at stake to risk it. I told Sylvia as much and she said nothing was worth risking a good life for, that if she had a good life she'd do anything to protect it, and that she admired me for coming right out and telling her."

"I'm glad, Tige. If anything happened to you and Dawn, I'd be lost. You're anchors for me. You do know that?"

"I know. So doesn't Dawn."She hugged me, using an odd local phrase that never made any sense to me. It meant, so does Dawn, while sounding like the opposite.

"Your furnace is jim dandy," I said.

"Good. I won't worry about it. You'll tell Dawn?"

"About the furnace?"

"Of course, about the furnace, asshole."

"Yep. All it needed was a simple imaginary adjustment, which I made with an imaginary screw driver and now it's as good as new."

She hugged me again. "Thanks, Eddie."

"Sure," I said.

We went back upstairs, bobbed for apples, pinned tails on donkeys, voted on the best costume. I won, no doubt less for the cleverness of my costume, than because of my willingness to bumble around, saying pardonez-moi, each time I bumped into someone. We drank cider, danced to rock and roll, nothing later than The Beatles' *Rubber Soul*, and found dark corners to grab a quick kiss or grope. There was no alcohol, but several times I caught the sweet smell of marijuana wafting through an open window. It was, as Tiger had promised, a masquerade of innocence, the kind of party our parents would have liked us to have when we were between sixteen and eighteen. No one did, of course, so the nostalgia we felt was for something that never existed, at least outside of *Archie Comics* and the imaginations of political conservatives.

Shelley was the only faculty member present, a fact that most of the party goers made sure to point out, always in good humor tinged with an edge of resentment. There are social barriers between faculty and classified workers at the college, even though many of the classified people have bachelor's degrees and some have masters. Others have licensures in complicated and technical fields. We're not a hell of a lot less educated than the faculty. People seemed pleased she was there, and that was tempered, I'm sure, by the fact that she was an adjunct and they could see her as even more exploited as they were. At the same time, her presence made clear how unusual social mingling was between faculty and staff.

We started to leave just after midnight. We were standing on the porch, shivering, saying good night to Tiger, when Chad came out.

"You guys seen Mom anywhere?"

Shelley and I shook our heads. "She probably went to bed," Tiger said. "She said she had a headache an hour or so ago."

"I checked," he said. "She's not there."

"Look on the couch in the TV room," she said. "No way. Gary and Linda are boffing in there." Tiger made a face. "Uh-oh. Where are Joanne and Ted?" Chad made a funny sound. "I think they're in the guest room."

"This is going to make some lawyer happy," she said. "My guess is that she took a walk, you know, to get some fresh air for her headache."

"Yeah, probably. When you see her, tell her I borrowed her car to take Patty home." Chad went back inside.

"Good kid," Tiger said. "I couldn't love him more if he was mine."

"He is yours. Yours and Dawn's." I turned to Shelley to explain. "His louse of a father hasn't seen him in seven years and he hasn't paid child support for over twelve. Tiger and Dawn have been together since he was three."

"Anyway, I'd say he was yours," Shelley said to her.

"Thanks," I said to Tiger. "It was a great party. You make a great soccer mom in that outfit. Thank Dawn for me."

Shelley gave her a hug, told her what a wonderful time she'd had. "I don't get to many parties. Full time and part time people don't mix much" Back on the Mohawk Trail headed toward Graham, Shelley said, "Let's go to your place. It's closer and I'm horny."

I answered by speeding up.

Chapter Twenty-One

The phone rang at three twenty-seven. Jarred awake, I disentangled myself from Shelley. She whined and grumbled, turned over on her side and was back asleep before my feet hit the cold floor. Racing across the room to grab the receiver before it rang a second time, I sat on a chair by the kitchen window. It was Tiger

"What's up?" I kept my voice soft so as not to wake Shelley. "Dawn's missing." Tiger's voice sounded small, frightened.

"Missing? You sure?" In contrast my voice was suddenly loud, large. "She's not here. She's always here. Now she's not. That's missing, Eddie. I woke up and she wasn't in bed. I waited a couple of minutes and didn't hear anything or anyone stirring in the house, so I got up to look for her. She's not here."

"Was she in bed when you went to bed?"

"No. I was bagged and laid down around one. I figured she was still partying. There were about a dozen people left, both from Chad's crew and ours. She's not here, Eddie. Not anywhere. I looked."

"Call the cops?"

"They said they gotta wait twenty-four hours. I don't get it, Eddie. She's not here. Chad and I don't have the slightest idea where she is, but the cops say she isn't missing until she's been missing for twenty-four hours."

"They're reasons for that, Tige." She exploded. "Reasons? For crissakes, Eddie, she's missing now, not twenty hours from now. I'm scared shitless those twenty hours from now she'll be just as missing as she is now. What am I going to do?"

I sat on a wooden chair by the kitchen window. Outside, a patrol car cruised up Main Street, flashing a spotlight into the doorways of stores and the alleys between them. The cops were not going to be much help. The Yardley force consisted of a full time chief and a handful of part time patrol officers, dependent on the state police for truly complex work. They wouldn't be useless in trying to find Dawn, but they were already stretched to their limit. Like most police and fire departments this far west of Boston, their budgets were being cut and if people weren't being laid off, no new people were hired when someone retired. Traffic stops on Route 2, the occasional drunk raising hell, chasing kids away from the glacial potholes on the Elkins River at night, those were the problems occupying most of their time. The Staties out in the west county area were equally overtaxed.

But then I don't have much confidence in the police. Not long before, the Staties had shot an unarmed man, and a few years ago, twenty miles to the north, in Brattleboro, Vermont, two local cops had shot a man in a church who was holding a penknife to his throat, threatening to kill himself. The state attorney general backed them up, I suppose on the theory that a dead man is a threat to himself and killing him is the best way to keep him from committing suicide, perhaps to save him from eternity in Hell for committing a mortal sin.

In Graham Sandy Grover ran the show. Months away from his pension, Grover wasn't aggressive enough to deal with the growing nature of Graham's urban problems, some of which were due to his relatives, if Billy Melnick was right that Grover was Shirley Walker's cousin. The town has had stable population numbers for close to a hundred years, never varying much over or below eighteen or nineteen thousand. However, there has been a dramatic shift in the demographics of that population.

Once an important industrial center, the home of major tap and die mills, in the Seventies and Eighties Graham saw the mills close, move south, leave the country, sold off as tax losses by multi-national conglomerates, putting a skilled workforce on the unemployment lines or working at non-skilled service jobs.

Now we have high unemployment, anomic kids, homeless men and women living in the woods across the railroad tracks behind the Cumberland Farms store on Main Street. There is also a growing number of African Americans and Hispanics, most seeking refuge from the crime and poverty of cities to the south. The town doesn't know how to deal with their needs and has been slow to develop resources to service them. Chief Sandy Grover, with dreams of a doublewide by a man-made lake in a Florida trailer park, wasn't going to go out of his way for anything or anybody with needs and demands very different from those of the town's traditional white working class residents.

Tiger was asking me what to do and I couldn't think of anyone who could help. Except me, and I wasn't what anyone would call a superhero.

"I've got an idea, Tige. Let me call you back in a few minutes."

"Okay, but I'm going nuts, Eddie. I'm freaked. We gotta do something." Her voice was as small as I'd ever heard it.

I hung up and called the agency number I had used earlier. An operator told me the number had been disconnected and there was no further information. He'd done just what he said he'd do. I was on my own. I called Tiger back, told her I'd be right over.

Shelley was sitting up, resting against the pillow when I gathered my clothes from the floor where I'd thrown them in my haste to get her into the bed earlier.

"What's wrong with Tiger?"

"Dawn's missing. I'm headed over there."

"What're you going to do?" In the half-light from the street, her eyes looked tired. She yawned and stretched, ran her fingers through her hair and yawned again.

I sighed, pulled on my pants and tightened the belt buckle. "Shit, I don't know. Go over there and figure out what to do next."

"Police?"

I explained the twenty-four hour policy. If kids go missing, they're considered missing as soon as someone notices. Adults can be anywhere, doing anything with their free will and independence. It's only when they don't return to their normal patterns that the police get alarmed. It makes sense, but it can play havoc with the nerves of anyone caught on the other side of it. She lay back down, pulling the covers up to her chin.

"Wake me up when you get back." Her voice was rich with suggestion. "I don't know when that'll be, and I've got to work this afternoon."

"Want to get together after work?"

"Get together?"

"You know. Get together."

"Carnally or socially?"

"Your choice."

"Both?"

"Sure. A little boffing, a little late dinner. Sounds good." She made a kissing sound. "If I'm not here, call my place."

I reached down, pinched her butt. She squirmed a little, pretending it hurt. "Don't worry, I'm sure Dawn's all right," she said.

People always say that when things look bad. *Don't worry. They do wonderful things with prostate cancer nowadays.* Right. They take it out. You're in agony from major surgery, your dick wilts and the cancer metastasizes and then you die. *Don't worry; it was just a minor heart attack.* Of course you can't ever eat a steak again, have ice cream, and you're going to be on drugs forever, which as you know isn't anywhere near forever, as you wait for the big one, convinced that every belch, every upset stomach is prelude to it. *Don't worry, hell, you'll be like new as soon as you get your new knee.* . Sure. As long as you don't carry anything over twenty pounds, don't swivel on the leg with the new knee, and are careful that you take antibiotics every time the dentist fills a tooth. With luck the knee might last anywhere from eight to eighteen years and you may not get an infection in it that spreads throughout your body so that you die screaming from the pain.

§§§

Tiger and Chad were frantic. Both rushed from the house as I drove up. "What can we do?" Chad asked. In the light from the streetlamp I could see his cheeks were stained with tears. Tiger was shaking. I couldn't tell if it was from rage or fear. Probably both.

We went inside. Tiger sat on the couch. Chad hovered over her. I sat on the arm of the couch, a hand on her shoulder. There were two possibilities. Either Dawn left on her own or she'd been kidnapped. I suggested both.

"Make us some coffee, will you Chad," Tiger said. "Please."

"Mom wouldn't leave us," he said. "Not if she had any choice."

"Coffee," Tiger said.

He leaned over, kissed her cheek and headed for the kitchen.

"She might leave if she'd heard about Sylvia," Tiger said once he was gone, shaking her head. "Christ, I'm such an idiot, a goddamn insensitive idiot. Shit."

"How would she find out?"

She shook her head and breathed a long, quavering sigh. "Not from me. I did Sylvia, decided not to do her again and it was like it never happened, you know. You put things like that in some kind of never never box and they don't exist anymore."

"But they happen anyway. It happened with Sylvia and you."

"Yeah, but the meaning is lost. It's like a wreck you pass on the highway. It's there, but you go by it and it doesn't mean anything to you and pretty soon you can't see it anymore."

Her metaphor was stretched, but I kept my mouth shut, for once. It occurred to me that I might be reaching some new level of maturity, not jumping in to prove someone had said something just short of stupid. "She didn't find out from me," I said, hoping my tone didn't sound defensive.

"I know." She patted my hand. "Sylvia?"

"She wouldn't do that."

"She could be pissed that you decided not to see her again."

"No. It was a fling. For both of us. She's got her own life. We were both indulging a little not so innocent lust and that was it."

"So, she didn't hear it from you, from me, or from Sylvia. No one else knows about it, so how can your peccadillo be a reason for her leaving?"

"She didn't leave, Eddie, she's been taken." Chad came back with two cups of coffee. He handed one to each of us. "That was fast," I said.

"Instant," he said, shrugging in apology. "Who'd take her and why?" I asked

She exploded. "Who in the hell knows? There's a world of creeps out there, cruising streets in vans looking for someone to snatch, rape and kill. Christ, girls and women disappear all the time."

"Boys too," I said.

"Yeah, boys too, but it's mostly men who take them."

"Not always."

"Most always."

She was right, but women can be sick and vicious too. It wasn't the proper time to pursue the topic. It rarely is.

Tiger said, "She could've been taking a walk, getting some fresh air after the party and some creep saw her in that costume and snatched her. Jeez Eddie, just think of that van we saw last week."

She was right. Even in bucolic western Massachusetts there have been at least half a dozen such disappearances in the years I've lived here. Just the week before we had been walking up Main Street toward the Y after having had coffee and pastries at the Graham Coop. At the main intersection, waiting for the light to change, two men sat in a ten year old blue van with Jersey plates, the pain flaking, rust along its edges and blue tarps covering the all the windows except those by the front seats and the windshield. Both had cigarettes hanging from their lips.

"That looks like something out of a movie, 'Silence of the Lambs,' maybe." She had hugged herself, gesturing toward it with her head.

"Scary," I had said.

As if he had heard her, the man in the passenger's seat turned and looked at us, took a drag on his cigarette and tossed it out the window. It landed by the curb a few feet away from us. Then the light turned green and the van went on up the street, passing the Courthouse, the Y and the Post Office and bearing right into a residential area at the yellow blinking light at where Main Street ends.

Once it was out of sight we had both taken deep breaths and continued walking toward the Y. It was Tiger's work out day and I was going with her as a guest.

"Dawn wouldn't just go off and leave Chad if she was leaving me. Hell, she'd kick me out," she continued, trying to convince us all that Dawn didn't leave on her own. It wasn't necessary, except to convince herself. I picked it up.

"She wouldn't leave you, for any reason."

Her eyes flicked up at Chad when I said that, but I wasn't going any further along that line. "Dawn's solid, Tige, one of the most solid people I know."

Tiger nodded. "If she was going to leave me, she'd sure as hell tell me why, throw whatever it was in my face so I'd know how I'd loused things up. For chrissakes, she'd draw me diagrams to make sure I knew exactly where I'd screwed up. This is bad shit, Eddie. She's in trouble."

She was right. I couldn't argue, even to ease her fears. I also knew that the longer someone was missing the less chance there was that they'd be found alive.

"We'll find her," I said. *Don't worry; it's just a brain tumor. They can do all kinds of wonderful things for people with brain tumors.*

"See," Chad said. "Eddie knows what to do." She grasped at the straw. "So, let's do it."

"When was the last time you saw her?" I asked

She was quiet for a long moment. "Not long after midnight. You and Shelley had left. Remember earlier, when I was looking for her? She had been out in the back yard getting some fresh air for her headache. I was listening to Cloyce Peck and a few of the other guys doing barber shop harmony in the living room. Dawn came in and hit him up for a cigarette. I told her to take it outside. She almost never smokes, maybe a pack a year, always other people's, and she raises holy hell when I do it in the house, always telling me to take it outside, so I was hosing her a little, you know." She stopped, her face stricken. "Shit, Ed, it's my fault. If I hadn't made her take the ciggie outside, she'd still be here. Someone saw her out there by herself and took her. Some creep in a van, or something, cruising for someone to torture and kill. Maybe even those guys we saw the other week."

"No way," Chad said. "I went out with her and smoked a little weed while she had the cigarette. We came back in together."

"That the last time you saw her?" I asked him as Tiger fidgeted with her fingers, curling and uncurling a fist.

He thought and shook his head. "There was a phone call. She answered it." He frowned. "Funny, there were a couple of other phone calls I answered and whoever it was hung up. Maybe three, four times."

"That's it," I said. "It wasn't spur of the moment. Somebody she knew was trying to get her on the phone. Whoever it was had a plan and was working it methodically."

"The phone's in my name," Tiger said.

"So it's someone who knows you, or at least knows about you and Dawn being together."

"I'll check the caller ID," Chad said, picking up the receiver and surfing through the numbers on its LCD screen. "Unavailable, it says. You called last. The call before that and three before it, all unavailable."

"Try star 69, I said."

He did. "They just give you the last call, and that was from you." I suggested we look around outside. I didn't think it would do any good, but Tiger and Chad needed to do something, and there was little to do except wait. Come morning, I would try to pressure the cops, tell them about the phone calls.

It had turned bitter cold for the end of October. I pulled my jacket collar up and scrunched my shoulders. In the light of the waning moon and the streetlamp, we poked around the yard and along the street. Twenty feet up from the driveway I saw a small dark shape lying at the edge of the pavement. From the distance, it looked like a cat or possum that had been hit by a car. It turned out to be a black skullcap with pointed cardboard ears attached by straight pins.

§§§

The Yardley cop listened carefully. He was a slight man in his early forties, head shaven, with an intelligent looking face and sympathetic expression. A name badge identifying him as Officer J.L. Danielson was pinned to the flap of the left pocket on his shirt.

"Sounds like a kidnapping to me," he said when Tiger, Chad and I finished our three way account of Dawn's disappearance. "I'll put out an APB and report it to the Staties. Then let's go up to your place and nose around some more. Maybe you guys missed something. Tire tracks, something that fell out of the car or whatever she was taken in. Maybe the neighbors saw something and didn't think it was important."

"No more of that twenty-four hour wait and see shit," Tiger said. Danielson gave her a nervous glance. "Not when things look this bad. We need to get on it right away."

I liked his style. More cops like Danielson would make me reassess my prejudice against the police brotherhood. He went to get his jacket and the keys to the cruiser, leaving the three of us standing by his desk.

We looked at one another. Chad was on the edge of tears again. Tiger's mouth was a thin tight line across the bottom of her face. I could feel the pain on my face. They were as close to family as I'd ever have again. Not only would losing Dawn be unbearable to me, it would be far more than unbearable to them, and their pain would be my pain. I would do anything to spare them suffering.

Back at Oak Street, we scoured the sides of the road, concentrating on the area where I'd found the skullcap. There were tire tracks in the soft dirt. Danielson put orange cones in a square on each side of them, wrapping yellow plastic Crime Scene Do Not Enter tape around the cones. He'd have the states cops C-PAC unit come make a cast of the tracks in the morning, he told us. It didn't have to be done immediately since the sky was clear and the weather prediction was for a clear dry and cold night.

We went back into the house while he woke up neighbors, explaining what had happened and asking if anyone had seen anything that might help. He looked discouraged when he came back.

"Nada. Nobody saw a damn thing." He smiled at Tiger. "We'll find her, Ms. Kelly." He paused for a moment. "You don't remember me do you?" Tiger shook her head.

"Jared Danielson. I was a student at the college a few years ago."

"Students don't tend to remember janitors," I said.

"I remember both of you. A lot of students do. You both had reputations for being good to students who worked for you."

"You didn't work for me." Tiger's voice had the flat, drained sound of someone forcing conversation in an attempt at making an abnormal situation take on a semblance of normality.

"No ma'am," he said. "My girl friend, Kendra Donalson did. Six years ago."

"I remember Kendra," Tiger said. "She was a good kid."

"You saved her life," Danielson said. "The guy she was with before me got her pregnant and you helped her through the abortion. She couldn't tell her parents, but she told you and you held her hand all the way."

"She's okay now?"

"We're getting married next summer. November's my last month here. Been a cop since I was eighteen, so I'll get a pension. I just finished my master's degree in Sociology at U-Mass and got a job teaching at the community college, starting in January. I begin work on my doctorate next fall. Kendra and I are taking December off, going on a cruise for part of it, doing Christmas up big, things like that."

"Full time teaching job's a pretty good thing. Rare as hell these days," I said. "You're a lucky guy."

He grinned. "Yep, full time. It's a one man department and the guy who's taught it for over thirty-five years is retiring and they need someone full time." Turning back to Tiger, he put a hand on her arm. "I know you're worried, Ms. Kelly. I'll make sure everything that can be done, will be done to find her."

"Thanks," Tiger said.

"I'm going back to the office so I can write up a report for the chief and the day guys." He headed toward the door. "I'm going to ride herd on this, Ms. Kelly. If your partner...if your partner's anywhere around here."

"You started to say if your partner's still alive," Tiger said." His face reddened.

"It's all right," she said and collapsed on the couch. "It's something we've gotta face, that possibility."

In early middle age, he was more like the young cops I've known. Most go into the work hoping they can help people, determined to help people. Too often, as they get older they become cynical or corrupt or burned out, or all three, facing the reality of low pay, public hostility and the futility of the criminal justice system. Officer Danielson was changing jobs with his hope and integrity in tact.

He took a notebook from his pocket and after explaining that the questions he had to ask were part of investigating any missing person, and apologizing if they were offensive, assuring Tiger they weren't meant to be, he began. Did Dawn have any enemies? Was she in any kind of trouble? Was there another lover? He went through about twenty such questions and Tiger answered calmly. After fifteen minutes, he closed the notebook.

"Ms. Kelly," he said. She looked up and he continued. "I'll ride herd on this, and not just during working hours. It's a priority for me, during and after work hours."

He left, pulling the door shut behind him.

Tiger buried her face in her hands. "The son-of-bitch piece of walking dog turd that took her is cold dead meat if I get my hands on him."

In spite of his fear, Chad laughed. "That, Tigermom, is eloquence." She looked up then smiled. "It felt good to say, kiddo. I'm so goddamn mad and scared."

"We all are," I said.

She leaned back against the cushions. Across the room was a fireplace, above it a painting of Tiger and Dawn done by another work-study student who had been an art major. Dawn was sitting in a chair, Tiger standing next to her, a hand resting on the back of the chair. They were gazing at each other. It looked like the classic New England portraits done in the Nineteenth Century by itinerant painters who would go from town to town, farm to farm, painting for room, board and pocket change. The artist had emphasized Tiger's masculine features and exaggerated Dawn's feminine delicacy, but in that gaze had caught their love and devotion.

Resting her head against the back of the couch, she closed her eyes. In a minute, she was asleep, her breathing slow and deep. Chad covered her with an afghan and yawned.

"Me too," I said, looking at my watch. It was six-thirty. "Stretch out in the guest room," Chad said.

I did. I had to sleep. With Laura L. Loblolly, Jr.,Ph.D. riding my ass, I had to be at work later that afternoon, on time and well rested.

Chapter Twenty-Two

I awoke at nine, the house filled with the smells of coffee, bacon and onions. I followed them to the kitchen where Tiger was slicing potatoes, the air warm with the odor of sautéing garlic, onion and jalapenos. Bacon, crisp and brown, lay on several layers of paper towels. A television hung from a bracket mounted on the ceiling, tuned to Encore Westerns. *Shane* was playing, the sound turned off. Alan Ladd had just shot Jack Palance who lay dead in the dust.

I asked, "You sleep much?" I sat on a chair next to the table. She plunked a cup in front of me and filled it with coffee.

"No. I woke up on the couch about seven-thirty, and went back outside to see if I could find anything else that might help find Dawn."

"Did you?"

"Nothing. I called the cops a little while ago, talked to Andy Shedd, the chief. He said Danielson had filled him in and they were putting all their resources into the case. He called it a case. Makes it seem normal, Eddie, you know, calling it a case. Call it something and it's not so bad. Shit, Eddie, Dawn's just another case to them and the truth is, she's out there, god knows where, and there's probably some creep pawing over her like a piece of meat." She finished slicing the potatoes and dumped them in the pan with the garlic, onions and peppers.

There wasn't anything I could say. Of course she was upset. To the cops Dawn was a case. Had to be. That's what cops do; they get cases and try to solve them. It's a job and a process, a routine, like keeping a college clean and neat, like anything people do that starts at one point and runs to another. To somebody, Osama bin Laden was a case. Lee Harvey Oswald and Jack Ruby had been cases. The Lindbergh kid. Hell, I'd had a number of cases in my day. They were processed and I was the processor. Somebody else worried. Somebody else cried. Somebody else mourned, celebrated, buried a loved one or embraced one who came home. The rest of us try to breathe order into the situations by calling them cases, naming them and using manila folders to alphabetically file relevant information about them.

She changed the subject. "The cop was nice."

"Danielson." I was relieved. It would have been fruitless to talk about Dawn, to raise our fears any higher than they already were.

"Paper's on the table," she said. "I'll make some more coffee if you want."

"I'll die without it." She banged her fist on the table. "Not even jokes about death, hear me?"

"Sorry," I said. She measured the coffee into a paper filter, put water in the coffee maker and turned it on.

I sat and opened *The Enterprise*. There was a color picture and lead article about a timber framed barn raising taking place at the New Hope School, a toney prep school for the wealthy young. It was an interesting piece. I find it encouraging that people still do timber framing and build hand hewn log homes. Along with the organic gardeners, traditional musicians and storytellers, they might someday be responsible for passing on skills and culture to a technologically imploding world. There was more trouble in the Middle East. I couldn't bring myself to read about it.

When I left Azerbaijan, I told Nathan's control that the best thing we could do with the Middle East would be to nuke it back into the sand age, sparing only the oil fields, give the survivors a tent and a camel and use them for target practice. It was a bad joke intended to poke fun at the neo-conservatives who prattle on about the need for a barbaric American policy, but he didn't laugh, just said he'd pass it along. It's probably sitting in a tactical file somewhere as a contingency plan.

We occupied the kitchen in separate silences. The only sounds were the rattling of the newspaper, the soft hiss and spit of the frying pan and Tiger's clattering of dishes and cooking utensils. The coffee maker sputtered and steamed. A few minutes later, Tiger set a mug of hot coffee in front of me.

"Thanks," I mumbled, picking it up and breathing on the coffee to cool it at the same time I sipped.

She nodded. Taking a spatula, she heaped fried potatoes on a plate, put several slices of bacon next to it and set it on the table in front of me. She poured a second cup of coffee, filled a plate for herself, put them on the table and sat across from me.

"I made Chad go to school. He argued, but he went. We'd drive each other nuts if he stayed home. Christ, we'd end up bumping into each other with both of us pacing around the house and going nuts."

"You're right," I said. The potatoes smelled good, cooked in olive oil and sprinkled with rosemary. They tasted even better. I ignored the bacon. I love to smell it cooking, but never eat it. Just the odor satisfies me. It mingles with the food I'm eating and I can almost convince myself I'm eating it as well.

"Think it'll rain?" Her voice was tense and angry.

I looked out the window. The sky was clear, blue, the sun streaking across the lawn. "Nope."

She yelled, "Jesus Christ, Eddie. We're talking about the weather? Chad going to school? Nice cops? You reading the paper, me cooking breakfast? What in the hell are we doing talking like the weather's important? That any of this shit's important? God knows what's happening to Dawn right this minute. Some creep could be peeling off her skin to make a coat he can wear while he's whacking his noodle and looking at videos he made of himself slitting her throat at the same time as he's sticking his sick pervert dick up her ass, and we're talking about rain and normal shit and nothing's normal, nothing's normal."

She swept both our plates and cups off the table. They crashed and broke, scattering food and shards of china across the floor, dark coffee spreading across the linoleum like blood.

I leaned over and held her as she cried, shaking. Great wailing sobs of fear, loss and rage broke from her like something alive being released from captivity. Holding her was the most I could do. It was a waiting game. Whoever had taken Dawn would either contact us, or wouldn't. Contact would mean the kidnapper wanted something from us, from Tiger. No contact would mean that Dawn herself was the target. Contact would be good. It would mean we had something to bargain with. That Dawn could be saved.

After several minutes, Tiger's storm of tears eased. I fetched a damp face cloth from the bathroom and handed it to her. She wiped her face and blew her nose. Putting her fists upright on the table, she rested her forehead on them.

"Sorry." She sighed.

"Nothing to be sorry about. People shouldn't feel they have to apologize for letting others see their hearts."

"I blew." She looked up at me. Biting down on her lower lip and shaking her head, she said it again.

"I would've blown too. Shit, I wanted to blow. You blew for both of us." That got a hard won grin. "What're we going to do, Eddie?" I puffed my cheeks and blew the air out, rattling my lips. "There's not much we can do. I vote we call the cops again, just to remind them we're here and we're scared. You take a shower and I'll clean up the kitchen. Then we go out for something to eat. I don't think those potatoes are going to be much good."

She gave me a kiss on the cheek and stood up. "We also need to go to work," I told her.

Her face stiffened, eyes filled with tears, her voice cracking as she spoke. "I can't do that. For crissakes, Eddie, we don't know where Dawn is or what's happening to her, and you say we go to work? I can't."

I kept my voice level, my manner calm. "Sure you can. What're you going to do, sit around the house freaking out? The best thing is to go to work and focus on getting things clean and orderly. Trust me on this. There's nothing we can do for Dawn sitting around here with our dicks in our hands." "Your dick. I don't have or need one, remember?" The jocularity in her voice was real, in spite of her terror. She could be at once vulnerable and irrepressible. It was a quality that defined her and it has bailed us both out of bad situations a number of times.

"It's a figure of speech."

"A sexist one, asshole. How would you feel if I said there's nothing we can do for her except sit around here with our fingers up our twats?" She stopped, turned her back to me and looked out the window, shaking her head and weeping.

"Like I was missing something essential to be successful?" She wiped her eyes. "Not bad, Sanders. You're catching on."

"That's me, slow but not dumb. Besides, that was a question, not an answer. We should go to work, Tige."

Going to work made sense. It was logical. It was healthy. For me it was essential, given Loblolly's warning. The job was too important to my stability to risk losing. It was also hard to imagine going in and cleaning as though nothing had happened.

"What about Chad," she argued. "He'll come home from school and there won't be anybody here."

"We'll go over to the high school, leave him your car. He can drive into Graham after football practice and meet us at the college. He can follow us around at work, or study in the library, but you'll be close by. He won't be as alone as he would if he came home after school."

§§§

There was an envelope taped to the door of my work closet. I knew what it was before I saw my last name spelled out in bright mismatched glossy letters cut from a glossy magazine. My fingers trembled as I opened it. The note, also in mismatched letter cut from a glossy magazine was simple and stark: *Mail Bukowski recordings to 353 pleasant Street, Northampton, Mass 01060, Box 34, or the dike dies. Don't tell anybody.*

I read it several times, ripped the envelope open to see if there was anything else inside. Nothing. I took it to Tiger.

"Son-of-a-bitch doesn't even know how to spell dyke," she said.

"The note's good news," I told her. "Whoever took Dawn has a reason, a purpose. It's no serial rapist killer cannibal skinning her in a black van, just someone who wants the recordings of Bukowski reading his poems."

"He's still going to die," Tiger said.
"Not a bad idea, but it's still something we can deal with." "So what do we do?" she asked.
"First, we mail the recordings," I said.
"Who'd do this, Eddie? Who'd do this to Dawn?" she asked.
"My money'd be on a toad by the name of Gideon Moss, if it weren't for that Northampton address."

She smiled, nodding her head. "I'll back that bet. Bet you something else, too. Bet you that the address is a mail drop, with a forwarding address in New Jersey."

She was partially right. We looked through the yellow pages and found Connections of Northampton, mail, fax and Internet services, at 353 Pleasant Street. I called the number. A flat voiced young man answered the phone. He spoke in the current generational dialect, pronouncing his words in the front of his mouth. I asked who held box thirty-four.

"I'm very sorry sir," he said in an officious tone that didn't sound sorry and was definitely not *very* sorry. The sir almost like an expletive. "That information is confidential."

"This is an emergency," I said.
"Everyone has an emergency, sir," he said.
I spoke in a growl. "Listen, kid. Someone I love very much has been kidnapped and the kidnapper is using your business as a conduit for ransom."
"Are you the police, sir?"
"No. I'm a guy who's going to come down there and rip your nuts out through your nose if you don't cooperate with me."

He hung up.
I called back.
When he answered I said, "Don't hang up. I'm a friend of the victim and I'm very upset."

"You've been watching too much *Law and Order*, sir," he said. "I'll have the police call for the information," I said.

"They'll have to get a court order, sir. Even then, there's no guarantee that the name we have on record is the party's true name."

"I suppose we'll just have to camp out down there and wait to see who comes to open the box."

"That might not be practical, sir. You would be trespassing. This is private property, you know. Besides, many people have their mail forwarded from here. A lot of married folks like to carry on correspondences with people they don't want their spouses to know about. Sometimes they'll even send their mail through two or more forwarding address to make them more difficult to trace."

"I don't suppose you could tell me if box thirty-four's stuff is being forwarded."

"Sorry, sir. I've told you everything I'm able to."

I was about to let go with another verbal blast, when I realized he had told me a great deal. He had told me everything he was able to and a tad more. He didn't have to volunteer the information that many box holders have their mail forwarded. It was code for *box thirty-four was being forwarded.*

"I understand," I said with as much emphasis on the words as possible, hoping he heard my appreciativeness. "Thanks."

"Hope I helped, sir." The sir was softer, friendlier.

"You did." It was scant help. The best he could do without getting fired, perhaps without breaking the law. It didn't tell me what the forwarding address was. He was right, that would take a court order.

I hung up and looked through the notebook I keep in my bag. I still had a scrap of paper with Gideon Moss' phone number. Using my phone credit card, I dialed. It rang three times before a woman's voice answered.

"I'd like to speak with Professor Moss," I said.

"He's not here. He went to a conference. I don't expect him back before Monday."

I feigned interest. "Oh, where? I've been editing that paper he wrote on Charles Bukowski for him."

"Tulane," she said. "A conference on contemporary southern poetry. How do you like the Bukowski paper?"

"It's not very good." I heard a loud insuck of breath at the other end of the line. "The writing's awkward, the analysis is trite and the research is shoddy."

"He works so hard on his writing," she said.

"Too bad. Some people have it, others don't."

I don't know why I do things like that. I had no reason to trash Gideon Moss to his wife, or whoever the woman was. A distant part of me thought it reprehensible. There was no evidence that he'd snatched Dawn. It was just that I hadn't liked him at first glance. Perhaps I knew intuitively that he was a scumbag. Maybe I knew at some gut level that he had taken Dawn and was holding her against the recordings. Maybe it was because he had finished his degrees and was teaching, even if only as an adjunct, riding the Interstates between schools, while I was a Maintainer II at Graham Community College, an insignificant laborer in the kind of institution that academic elitists describe as the vineyards of academic Siberia. I don't even get to stomp the grapes. Perhaps it was something baser, an irrational need to foul things up for somebody else, a drive that had served me well during my days at the agency and had been lying fallow for far too long.

I heard her mutter, "Oh dear," just before I hung up. I called Tulane, got a switchboard and asked to be connected to the offices for the conference on contemporary southern poetry, only to be told there was no such conference at the university that week.

I called his house again. When the woman answered, I explained there was no conference at Tulane. Was there another number where I might reach him?

"That bastard." Her voice was so loud I had to hold the phone several inches from my ear. "He's running around with her again. I'll have his balls for this."

"Who's her?"

"Annie Davis. She's a counselor in the learning center at the college. He thinks I don't know about it. He's got a surprise coming. I'm going over to her place right now."

"Wait," I said, trying to keep her on the line for another minute. "You have a phone number for her?"

"So you can call and warn him? Forget it." She hung up.

I dialed information. Two A. Davises were listed in the Trenton area. The second was listed as A. Davis, Ed.D. That sounded like it could be guidance counselor. I called the number and got an answering machine, with a singsong groovy voice asking callers to leave a message after the beep, assuring them she would return the call as soon as possible. Not really expecting to hear from her, I left my cell phone number. I took the phone from my bag, turned it on and stuck it in my pocket.

"I don't think it's Moss," I told Tiger as I hung up. "He's off running around with a guidance counselor and his wife is pissed."

"Maybe he and the babe are in it together," she said. "Doesn't sound that way to me."

I found Cloyce Peck and explained to him there was a serious problem and it was necessary for Tiger and me to leave campus for an hour or so. Could he please cover for us?

"No sweat," he said. "The layout of this building is like a rabbit warren. Faculty members who have worked in it since it opened in Seventy-four are still sometimes finding rooms they never knew were there. I'll just tell anybody looking for you that I saw you a couple of minutes ago and direct them to another area of the labyrinth. Then I'll go somewhere else, so they have trouble finding me when they can't find you."

"Thanks," I said.

"Chances are," he said, "by the time they find me again you'll be back. Least it usually works that way around here."

§§§

I got the recordings from my safety deposit box and mailed them according to instructions. Then we took the note to the Yardley state police barracks out on Route 2, a mile or so east of the Falls. Perhaps the Staties could lift prints from it. They could also start putting pressure on Connections of Northampton to reveal the forwarding address for box thirty-four.

We were sent in to talk with Detective Jack Wysocki, who'd been put in charge of the case. He was a large man in his early fifties, six four, twenty to thirty pounds overweight for his height, his face pock-marked from childhood acne. A shock of white hair hung over his forehead. He had a distracting habit of combing it out of the way with his fingers as he spoke. There was a picture of Charlton Heston on the wall of his office, the NRA logo in the background. Next to it hung the official portrait of the governor and beside that a photo of Wysocki shaking hands with George W. Bush. I didn't have much confidence that he'd be a lot of help.

I gave him the note, told him we had mailed the recordings. Tiger gave him the details of Dawn's disappearance.

"I'd like to sit on this for another day or so," he said after listening to her story. Tiger gasped with alarm and anger. He raised his hands defensively and explained.

"That doesn't mean we aren't investigating. We'll be doing everything we can, and we'll go over that note for prints, DNA, the works. The guy that did it had to leave something, all that glue, cutting all them letters out, you know. I just don't want to do anything officially yet so that the papers can get hold of it. *The Enterprise* will make a big deal out of it, headlines, pictures, interviews, and all that kind of shit. Could scare the perp into doing something we don't want done."

"It is a big deal," Tiger said.

He clucked his tongue. "I'll treat it like a big deal. Newspapers have a different definition of big deal. We try to save lives, solve crimes. The paper tries to sell papers, you know. They got to so as not to go under. They're in big trouble these days. The way I'm going to go about it just isn't the same big deal for me as it is for the papers. See what I mean?"

He was right and Tiger got it. Her face relaxed. "Thanks," she said. "I'm just wiped out and freaked out and rip shit."

"Anybody would be," Wysocki said. "I can't promise you anything, Ms. Kelly, except that I'll do anything I can to find your friend."

"My partner," Tiger told him. "Dawn's my partner."

Great, I thought. Shove that in the face of a homophobic state cop who idolizes Charlton Heston and George W. and has posters and pictures to prove it. That'll sure as hell encourage him to go all out for you.

Wysocki surprised me. "You married?" Tiger shook her head. "Not yet."

"Massachusetts started it all," he said. "Letting people get married that love each other no matter what. That civil union thing they got up in Vermont is okay too, and New Hampshire's coming along. My son and his boyfriend got hitched by the town clerk right here in Yardley. It was terrific. The boyfriend's parents were there, me and the wife, all our other kids and a couple of grandchildren, my parents, maybe a hundred other guests. I was his best man and his partner's father was his best man." He laughed. "They each had their mothers as maids of honor too. We had the reception at the Newfane Inn up in Vermont. A hell of a good time. You decide to get married you ought to check that out too."

"Newfane Inn." I grinned at Tiger. "Now that's an interesting idea. A very romantic place, I hear say. You could have a wedding that would make your old commitment service look like children playing."

Glaring at me, she turned to Wysocki and held out her hand. "Get her back for me, Detective and I'll convince her to marry me. I'll make you and Eddie here joint best men."

He took the hand in both of his. "I'll do everything I can." I gave him my cell phone number and we headed back to GCC.

§§§

There was a note from Cloyce Peck on my cleaning cart asking me to buzz him as soon as I got back.

I found him on break in the café. "Loblolly was checking on you," he said. "I told her you was around, that I'd seen you not five minutes earlier."

"How long ago was that?" He took a bite from a ham sandwich, answering around the food he was chewing. "Half an hour ago, maybe twenty minutes. Not long. She riding your ass?"

"Some," I said. "She'd like to see me gone."

He took a swig from a cardboard coffee cup, swirling it around in his mouth. "She gets off in making people uptight. We got the cleanest college in the system and she's sneaking around like we're a bunch of slackers. And they lie, man they lie. Remember how Graydon Eggers, Dean of Administration before her, swore up and down there wasn't no asbestos in this building. Guaranteed it was an asbestos free place. So why are they shutting down the place part by part for? To remove asbestos, that's why. Shit, god save me from administrators. Most of them, only thing they can say is, no. They're great at giving you reasons something can't be done, but there ain't many of them can figure out ways to do something."He finished his coffee and sandwich. Standing up, he slapped me on the shoulder. "Watch out for her, Eddie. She likes being mean. If she asks where you was, tell her you was cleaning up a bunch of puke from one of the men's rooms. Guaran goddamn-tee you she won't check that out."

As he was leaving, Tiger beeped me. She was in the library.

"We got a problem," she said when I got there. "Chad's talking to a reporter from *The Enterprise*."

Over her shoulder I saw through the glass door leading into the library. Chad was standing next to the card catalog talking with a young man who was writing in a notebook.

"How'd this happen?" I asked

She shook her head and sighed in exasperation. "He told some of the kids at school about Dawn. I can't blame him. Christ, he's freaked about his mother. Anyway, word got around, somebody called the paper and they tracked him down here. Can you handle it, Eddie? I'm no good for anything at this point."

I walked over. The reporter had just finished asking Chad a question.

"What's going on here?" I asked, holding a hand out to the reporter. "I'm Ed Sanders, a friend of Chad's"

"Brent Bouchard," the reporter said, shaking my hand. "I work for *The Enterprise*. Do you have any more information on his mother's kidnapping?" He was thin, with black hair and fine features, dressed in a burgundy turtle neck and faded dungarees, a small leather bag hanging from a shoulder strap. He couldn't have been more than twenty-two, one of the journalism school graduates *The Graham Enterprise* hires and trains, and then loses to larger papers when they realize the big stories and the big salaries aren't in Graham, Massachusetts. The lucky ones will go on to bigger things, like Andrea Caputo, who went to *The Boston Herald*, broke a major murder in Boston with her reporting, and covered the O.J. Simpson trial for *The New York Daily News*, doing short clips for CNN at the same time. Most end up at medium sized papers in medium sized cities covering medium sized stories for medium sized salaries.

I gave him my most practiced winning smile. "Mr. Bouchard, Brent, this is very delicate. We're trying to negotiate her release. Printing a story in the paper about the kidnapping and how the cops are trying to take care of it could undermine our attempts at saving her."

His face was bright with excitement. "This is big news, Mr. Sanders. Usually big news in Graham consists of a fire, or a dog that needs to be put down."

"You had the Walker story," I said. "That sold a lot of newspapers."

"I wasn't here for that. Danny Perkins covered the Walkers and he's writing for *The Hartford Courant* now, making a hell of a lot more than what *The Enterprise* was paying him. Working here is reporters' grade school, Mr. Sanders. We have to make our way up."

"Give us two days," I said. "Two days and we'll give you an exclusive interview with the whole family. Early publicity could put Dawn's life in jeopardy. Chad called you because he's worried, but he didn't consider the implications of a newspaper story on his mother's safety. You don't want to print something that could queer the deal to release her and maybe get her killed, right?"

He blanched. "No, no way, not at all."

He left, agreeing to back off in the interest of saving a human life and in exchange for the exclusive once Dawn was safe. He clearly was more interested in the exclusive than in Dawn's safety. I had a talk with Chad about the importance of keeping the lid on things. Tiger told him about the note, that we had mailed the recordings as instructed, and that the police were working to find his mother.

"I thought you didn't trust the cops," he said.

I said, "I don't, but I trust them more than I trust a kidnapper. Besides, Wysocki, the Statie detective, seems okay."

"More than okay," Tiger said. "For a cop."

Chapter Twenty-Three

The rest of my evening was routine. Dean Laura L. Loblolly, Jr., Ed.D. never did show up to check on me. Bathrooms got cleaned. Hallways got swept. Classroom carpets got vacuumed. Chairs and desks got lined up in neat, straight rows. Blackboards got washed. I made sure the spaces where I worked were well lit as I cleaned, creating order where there seemed to be none, restoring order where it had been disrupted. There was no darkness at the end of the halls; there were no shadowy corners in the classrooms.

Chad stuck to Tiger like glue, following her from room to room, emptying trash cans for her, sweeping when she'd let him. Driving out to the Yardley barracks had thrown us off schedule and we finished later than usual. At eleven-fifteen we were walking down the pathway toward the parking lot. My truck and Tiger's car sat alone. A cat scooted from the surrounding bushes, pouncing on a chipmunk that had scampered, screeching across the pavement. It squeaked one last time as the cat tossed its head several times and broke its animal's back. The cat slunk back into the bushes, the chipmunk's body hanging limp in its mouth.

"Hungry?" I asked. We hadn't eaten since breakfast. "Starved," Tiger said. "Me too," Chad said.

I suggested the Townie. "Food and drink," I said.

Tiger heaved a deep sigh. "Why not? It won't make any difference to Dawn if I'm freaking out at the Townie or freaking out at home." She stopped, staring at the bushes where the cat had disappeared. "There really isn't anything we can do, is there?"

"Nothing," I said. "It's a waiting game."

"Pray," Chad said. We looked at him, then at each other, shrugging. There's no accounting where the young get their ideas, no matter how clear an example you set for them. He noted our reactions.

"What's wrong with prayer?" He snapped the words at us. "Nothing," Tiger said, her voice flat.

"Everybody who believes in gods prays," I said. "The sons-of-bitches who rammed their airplanes into the World Trade Center prayed. The people they killed prayed. The President prayed for victory over the godless terrorists. The terrorists prayed for victory over the godless west. All to the same god. I want a bumper sticker, God Save Us from Religion."

"Yeah, well I'm praying for Ma."

"I hope it works," I said, hugging him. He hugged me back. We both wanted the same thing.

Driving uptown, I called Shelley on my cell phone, filled her in and told her where we were headed.

"I'll meet you there," she said.

It was Friday night and the place was packed, even at that late hour. A boy with bright red dreadlocks was playing guitar and singing Celtic songs, backed up by an older man with hand drums. The only empty table was set up for two. We took it, scouted around and found a couple of extra chairs, one for Chad, another for Shelley when she showed up. Billy Melnick sat alone at the bar. He looked toward us and waved as we entered. We sat and Cat came over to take our orders. I opted for my usual blackened turkey burger platter and Tiger asked for a chef's salad.

"And a glass of Montepulciano, right?" Cat asked.

I had become too predictable and grinned at her. "Nope. Tiger and I will split a pitcher of beer, and change the sandwich to a tuna melt."

"You're really living on the edge tonight," she laughed.

"You don't know how right you are." I said in a joking tone to cover the chill I felt with the words.

As soon as Cat brought the pitcher, Billy came over to the table, a wide beery and forced smile breaking across his face, a half empty mug in his hand. He sat down in the chair we'd gotten for Shelley, filled his mug from our pitcher and started hassling me about the recordings.

"Dude," he said, low-fiving me, drawing the word out into three syllables, filling his mug from our pitcher. "You really ought to give me those recordings. They're all that's left."

"There are the tapes and Cornell's copies."

"They're gone, might as well be destroyed. You can't get into a safety deposit box unless you know where it is and have a key and Cornell's dead. The copies you've got are all there is. For crissakes, Eddie, you got to give me them."

"This isn't a good time to talk about it," I said.

"So what's a good time, man? After you've sold them and stashed the bread away somewhere?" He was trying to make it sound like a joke, but his face was hostile, his body tense. I tried to placate him.

"I'm not going to sell them, Billy. Trust me."

He ran his fingers through his hair and shook his head, his voice disconsolate. "Shit man, I need those recordings."

"You or Elsworth Buell?"

He waved a hand. "I don't need that fat dipshit. I did a little checking on my own, you know. I called a dude I know who knows a guy in publishing and the dude said he'd get the guy to check around with the people that publish Buke. Dude gets back to me, says the guy says the publishers never heard of the recordings. My dude said that when the guy told them about the shit that was on them, how it was different from anything they had, said they went ape shit when they heard about them. He told me they said the recordings were historic and worth bucks, *beaucoup* bucks." His voice was hoarse. He took a long swig of beer, swishing it around in his mouth before swallowing. Then he whined, "Ah, come on, Eddie, you've got to give them to me, man. Give them to me and I'll go to the publisher's web site and let them know what we have." He emphasized the *we*."

Cat brought the pitcher as I rested my hand on his shoulder, giving it what I hoped was a gentle reassuring squeeze. "Later. We'll talk later."

"Fuck you," he mumbled. Pushing my hand away, he refilled his mug from our pitcher and headed back to his roost at the bar.

Tiger said, "You're gonna have to tell him they're gone, Eddie."

"Not in here and not with him drunk," I said. "He's going to go ballistic."

"He'll go ballistic no matter when you tell him and how drunk he is," she said.

"Maybe not when he realizes I did it to save Dawn. He's been acting like an asshole over them, but at heart, Billy's all right. Hell, maybe I'll have them back before I have to tell him."

Shelley came in, raising her eyebrows at Tiger as she sat down. "Dawn?" Tiger shook her head.

Tuning out, I let Tiger fill Shelley in. I was tired, depressed and worried. For each hour we didn't find Dawn, there was an increased chance that she was dead.

Sending the recordings to the Connections address, then having them forwarded could take several days. To complicate things, the next day was Saturday, a half day at the post office. Sunday, nothing would be open. The kidnapper would get the recordings on Monday at the earliest.

§§§

Tiger took Chad home. Shelley and I went to her apartment. We collapsed on the couch and made half-hearted attempts at seducing each other, but we were both tired and I was stressed out. Shortly before one-thirty I stretched and getting up, walked to the window. Dark, heavy clouds were blanking out the stars.

"I should get home," I said.

She came over, resting against me, her head on my shoulder.

"You could stay. You don't have to screw me to get a good night's sleep in my bed."

"I'd love to screw you. I just don't have it in me tonight." She pinched my arm. "No, you don't have it in me, yet." We stood in the living room, holding one another and she led me toward the bed. We lay down and she put her head on my chest. "You have much vacation time?"

"A lot. I don't vacate well. It's up to the max, twelve point eight weeks."

"Point eight?"

"According to our contract, we can't have more than five hundred and twelve hours built up, ergo the point eight. Why do you want to know?"

"I know about a villa on St. John we could rent for a week or two between Christmas and New Years, or longer. It sits on a ridge overlooking the Caribbean to the south and the Atlantic to the north, swimming pool, lots of decks and incredibly private. Nude sunbathing is *de rigueur*."

"Sounds good to me," I said, feeling myself stirring. "Speaking of *rigueur*," she said.

I rolled over, wrapping her in my arms. She was beautiful, warm and sweet. We made slow, easy love. It was comfort sex that came to little for either of us. We fell asleep in the middle of a conversation about the sinful pleasures of nude sunbathing in the privacy of a Caribbean villa.

I awoke with a jolt, heart pounding, from a dream in which I had been walking hand in hand along a tropical beach with Shelley. The sea was a crystal turquoise sheet of glass beside us, free of ripples even as we splashed our feet, pattering through the spots where it rose and fell upon the powdery sand. On the horizon, bright red, blue and green sails skittered across the water. In the manner of the expanding and contracting time of dreams, we may have been walking for hours or seconds or both. The beach was speckled with leaves and small twigs from the sea-grapes bordering the beach, dried seaweed and a small pile of beer cans and crumpled paper bags. Unlike the water, its surface was irregular. Small mounds of sand alternated with depressions and holes, as if scores of children, now vanished, had been digging there. A dead fish lay in our path, flies darting around its eyes.

As I was thinking how cleaning and raking could improve the beach, a man emerged from the sea grapes and coconut palms a few feet from the water's edge. Riding bareback on a donkey, his toes scraping the sand, he wore a flat black felt Mennonite preacher's hat and a black overcoat, hanging open, nothing under it except for two ammunition belts slung over his chest in an X. A rifle, equipped with a scope, was resting in his arm, muzzle pointed at the sand. He looked at us, then up at three frigate birds circling high in the blue sky. He pointed his index finger at them, tracing their movements through the air. Then he stopped, turned back to us and put his closed fist in the air, raised three fingers. Raising the rifle, he took aim and fired. One of the frigate birds stopped in mid-flight, feathers exploding outward as it spiraled downward and splashed into the ocean twenty feet out from where we stood.

That's one, he said, pointing to the carcass floating atop the waves. Two to go.

I looked at the bedside clock. Twenty after three. Shelley lay curled on her side. I leaned over and kissed her shoulder. She stirred, pulled the sheet over her and lay still.

For fifteen minutes I tried going back to sleep. When it was clear I was awake for the day, I arose, slipped into my clothes and left the bedroom. I turned on the living room and kitchen lights, put water and coffee grounds in the coffee maker, and while waiting for it to brew returned to the living room where I idly began looking through the books and magazines Shelley had left lying around. There were freshman English readers and handbooks, introduction to literature texts, novels, issues of *The Nation, College English, Newsweek*, and *Elle*, and several collections of poetry. One, a paperback entitled, *Cold Mountain: 100 poems by the T'ang poet, Han-shan*, lay folded open on the arm of a chair. She had circled number five in red ink:

"Han-tan is my home," she said, "And the lilt of the place is in my songs. Living here so long I know all the old tunes handed down.

You're drunk? Don't say you're going home! Stay! The sun hasn't reached its height. In my bedroom is an embroidered quilt So big it covers all my silver bed!"

Beneath it she had written: "Through Han-shan's words his knowledge of this woman's desire comes to us down the long and twisting corridors of the centuries."

I paged through the volume. She had not put notations on any other poems. I set it down. Across the room an unpainted rough-cut pine bookcase covered an entire wall. It looked as though she had built it herself. The bottom shelf was lined with half a dozen photograph albums. I picked the one closest to the near end. It was filled with pictures of people at parties, some of whom I recognized other faculty, students and local folk. Some were taken at parties, others had scenes from the surrounding landscape as background. A few were taken at ocean beaches, people lounging in the sun, reading, playing in the water. Shelley was in about half of them.

Closing it, I put it back and took out the second one. I opened it to a picture of three children; a boy in his early teens sat on a lifeguard stand on a wide beach, gray ocean waves breaking behind him. He was smiling, posing with the confident air that only an adolescent boy can muster. Two girls were in the picture, one on either side of the stand, the taller about twelve, the other nine or ten. I stared at the boy, recognizing him from the photographs on the table at the funeral home. It was a young Evans Cornell/Eddie Corelli. In spite of the years that had passed since the picture was taken, I could tell the taller of the two girls was Sylvia Cornell/Angela Corelli. The youthful face and angular child's body did not conceal her beauty and the camera had caught the flash of her eyes, arresting even in that prepubescent image.

Most startling was the third and youngest child. It was Shelley Randall, younger, but unmistakable. I studied the three faces. All had the same dark, clear eyes and self-mocking smiles. I had never met Evans/Eddie and Sylvia as Angela had affected a styleso completely different from Shelley's that their resemblance never dawned on me. I touched the photographs, the paper cool and glossy beneath my fingers. I paged through the rest of the album. There were many pictures of her, with Angela, with Eddie, a number with Angelo, much younger and vital looking than he had been the day I saw him at the funeral home. I looked at them over and over trying to dispel what I knew; Shelley Randall was the long missing Gina Corelli.

My hands shaking, I put the album back on the shelf.

Filling a coffee mug, I returned to the bedroom and sat on a bedside chair, staring at Shelley. Light from the streetlamps shone through the window, highlighting her hair, her face half hidden in soft shadows. I drank in her beauty as she slept, her body rising and falling with each breath she took. The evidence in the photograph album was indisputable and yet at one and the same time, while certain of the truth, I fought my rational self in a struggle to refuse the fact that she was Gina Corelli.

Trust is a complex, many-sided thing. I had trusted Shelley with my company and with my body, but not with my secrets. There had been several times when I had been on the verge of confiding in her, but had held back. Doing so had not been a conscious decision but, sitting in that chair, watching her sleep in shadow and light, I came to understand it had been an intuited one. Human beings pick up on a number of signals, spoken and unspoken, as we decide about our relationships with others. With that natural ability augmented by my training and experiences over the years, there must have been countless cues and miscues leading to my discretion. I thought of the man on the donkey in my dream, pointing at the dead frigate bird floating on the unnaturally still sea. *That's one.*

I watched her sleep, my brain buzzing with questions. Why the elaborate cover? Why would Gina Corellibe in Graham? Was she working with Evans? Was she there because he was her older brother, there for family reasons but not involved in the family business? Was her picking up with me when she did coincidence or was it planned? Why had she been so careless, keeping Corelli era photograph albums in her Shelley Randall apartment?

She lived under deep cover, but no one with even halfway adequate training for life under cover would make such a mistake. Her cover had to be self-created, a clever, well-thought out plan by a brilliant amateur. It was not the product of a professional. Her brother must have known she was here. I recalled the glance between Shelley and Sylvia at the funeral home and later at the Elkins Inn, the disinterested cordiality they had treated one another with when they were physically close, the sort we reserve for strangers in such situations. Nor had Angelo Corelli reacted when he saw her at the funeral. Whatever her motives, whatever their motives, her family knew and concealed her secret.

I freshened my coffee cup and went back to the living room. I called Tiger. She answered on the first ring.

"You're awake," I said.

"Couldn't sleep. Couldn't even lie down."

"Hear anything?"

"No. Where are you?"

"At Shelley's."

She laughed. It was half-hearted. "No wonder you're awake. You've probably been mucking around with her all night."

"Not quite. I have been getting screwed, though. Big time." I told her about the photograph albums.

She was quiet for a long time before breathing into the phone. "You're sure?"

"One thousand percent, as George McGovern said all those years ago about Thomas Eagleton. Shelley Randall is Gina Corelli."

"The long lost sister?"

"The long lost sister," I said.

"Not lost if you knew where to look," a voice from behind me said. I turned. Shelley stood in the doorway, naked and beautiful.

"Tige," I said. "Talk to you later." I hung up before I could hear her objections.

Grabbing a throw from her couch, I crossed the room, draped it around Shelley's shoulders and stood back several feet. I needed distance from her and I sure as hell did not need to see her naked while I was striving to get that distance.

"You look too distracting for the conversation we have to have," I said. She clutched it around herself and crossed to the kitchen. Pouring a cup of coffee, she turned and stood outlined against the window.

"I hope this doesn't mean you won't go to the Caribbean with me," her lower lip jutting out in an exaggerated pout.

I made myself smile at her. "Depends on what you tell me." She came over to me, placed her hands on my shoulders and pushed herself tight against me. It felt good. Hating the thought of losing the opportunity she represented for reconnection to sexuality and the possibilities of love, I was prepared to listen to whatever she had to say, hoping that I could bring myself to believe whatever she wanted me to believe.

"You like me, right?" There was no coyness, no gaminess in her tone or the way she pressed her body to mine. She was there, I was there and we both felt it.

Without thinking, I pulled her even closer. "I liked Shelley Randall. Who was she?"

"She's me. She is me. The me I want to be. The me I have become." Her voice was soft and hesitant; her eyes never wavering as they looked into mine. "I am Shelley Randall, Eddie. Didn't you ever want to be somebody else, somebody other than who you were made to be by other people?"

"Everyone does," I said in an inane mutter, stunned by her question, my mind roiling with contradictions. I was sure she could not know anything about my life before GCC. My cover was deep, well constructed and professional. Yet a pin prick of doubt stabbed through my certainty. Henrietta Lane had known a little too much about me. Could Shelley be working with her? I shook the idea off as absurd. The Corellis knew Shelley was here. There was no way she could be working with Lane. Beyond that, everything about her tone and expression when she asked whether or not I ever wanted to be somebody else was guileless, a kind of innocent question designed to justify her position, not say something about mine. Things about her did not add up, but in that brief frantic moment I convinced myself that my cover was intact.

Shelley was still speaking. "That's what I did. I became somebody else, somebody other than who I was made to be by other people, and I did it better than my brother did. I am Shelley Randall. Gina Corelli is just a girl in some old photographs."

I held her tight, rubbing her hair with my chin, yearning for what she said to be the truth.

"I left the family early," she said. "I had known my father was a man of some controversy, but I didn't know just how much until my first year at prep school in Connecticut. I was in history class when FBI agents came to the door and asked to see me. They took me into an empty classroom and told me Daddy had been indicted for loan sharking and that they were placing me under protective custody. I could stay at school, go to classes, carry on as before, but there was going to be an agent with me at all times. I told them I wanted to go home. They took me there and left me with my mother."

"What happened?"

"Daddy beat the charges and I ran away to New York. He found me and had me brought back. They hired tutors and educated me at home. Eddie and Angela were already gone. They knew all about Daddy and position with the mob. They were raised to be part of it. I don't know how Daddy pulled it off, but both of them had been sent away to school with new identities so they could help take his money and businesses legitimate at some point."

I breathed deeply, smelling her hair. I liked the smell. I liked the way she felt in my arms. "If you've got the right connections, the right kind of money and determination, it isn't difficult. America makes it easy to become whoever you want to become. That's why there's so much resistance to a national identity card. The right to go out for a pack of cigarettes and never come back is an essential part of the national psyche."

She nibbled at my neck. "I was the innocent one, the one Daddy and Mama wanted to protect from the family secrets. They wanted me to stay a Corelli, go to college, go to medical school and launder the family name. Eddie and Angela were supposed to launder the family money."

"So, you ran off to the Caribbean and laundered yourself. Where did you go after you jumped ship in Nevis?"

She gasped. It turned into a chagrined laugh. "My god, Eddie, how do you know about that?"

"If I get the right answers from you and things check out, perhaps I'll tell you someday, but that's a very different conversation from the one we're having. The story I want to hear now is about you, about how you fit into everything that's been happening around here."

"How do you feel about me?"

The troubled tone of her question matched that of my answer. "Torn."

"Did you feel torn earlier, when we were making love?"

"No." She pulled herself away from me and sat on the couch. She looked at her hands, resting palms up on her legs. "The doctorate's real. So is my academic career. I went to Trinidad after Nevis. Mama and Daddy knew I was there, just like they knew I was here. In spite of their plans for me, they ended up respecting my decision to become who I am. They were proud of me. I did my Ph.D. at the University of the West Indies. I came here for a couple of reasons. One, because my brother was here. I thought because he was an academic and I was too, we might be able to establish a relationship based on who we had become, not on who we had been." She stopped, looked at her hands for a moment before continuing. "I didn't realize the extent to which he was still who he had been, still Eddie Corelli."

"Meaning?"

She stared into the air for a moment. Her brow wrinkled and she played with her hands. She took a deep breath. "He was schizy. He loved being a professor, although I don't think he liked teaching very much. He was into his academics, the papers, the conferences, the show of it all, but that's what it was, a show. He was Eddie Corelli starring as Evans Cornell in a movie about the life of a college professor." She stopped for a moment and laughed. "He wanted to teach at Williams or Amherst. He thought they were the quintessential New England colleges, but they didn't have any openings when he started looking and he was happy to get the job at Ralston."

"A lot of people would be happy to get a teaching job one of the little Ivy Leagues. How was he schizy?"

"Because he was always Eddie, playing Evans, and he didn't really understand that. He never made it real."

"His doctorate was real," I said. "And he did teach at one of the country's most elite and prestigious schools. Sylvia's MBA from Wharton is authentic, I assume."

"*Touché.*" She sighed, making a small smile of resignation.

"Okay, so your brother's the first reason you came to the Valley. Did you make the connection with him you wanted to?"

She shook her head. "No. I tried but he wasn't interested. We were too different. He was what was and I was what I had become. Besides, he looked down on me for teaching in a community college."

"I'm sorry," I said.

She shook her head again and shrugged. "I'm just fine with it. I like GCC and I believe in what we do there and in the opportunities community colleges provide."

"What's the second reason for coming here?" I asked

She laughed. "It should be obvious. This is one of the great places in America to live. It's beautiful, the hills, the river, the country towns, the farms. It's got colleges and universities, fine music and food, a strong progressive political climate. It's an hour and a half from Boston, less than three hours from New York. People here are tolerant. It has everything I was looking for." She reached for my hand. We touched fingers for an instant before I pulled mine back. "Even more, since I met you."

I drained my coffee mug. "So you came to Graham both to be close to family and because of lure of the Valley. What did you have to do with Evans and the New Haven to Burlington to Montreal drug trade?"

She breathed with exasperation. "No more love making or sleep tonight, I guess."

"Nope. Just talking."

"I need some more coffee."

"Good thing I made a big pot."

She took my mug to the kitchen, poured herself another cup, refilled mine, then sat back down on the couch, her feet tucked under her. I had to restrain myself from sitting next to her and putting an arm around her.

Her voice was tense, angry, as she continued. "I have squat to do with the family business. Actually, Evans wasn't glad to see me here, and we had almost no relationship. He saw my presence as a threat to his jobs, both of them."

"Ralston professor and crime executive."

Sighing, she nodded and took a long and thoughtful sip from her coffee. "He took them both very seriously, even if the professor was just a part he played."

I plopped myself in a chair opposite her. "But you stayed."

"As I said, despite the abominable winters and the short summers, the Valley is a wonderful place to live. You know, a lousy climate given the weather but a great social and political climate. I don't care that I have to cob together a career working as an adjunct instructor at several places. People are more open, more tolerant here than anyplace else I've been. Besides, there's always a chance that GCC will eventually hire me full time." "Not in this economic climate." I had to smile. "So, you've got a career, but not a living, right? I assume money must not be a concern for you."

She inhaled and spoke with the exhale. "There's a sizeable monthly deposit made to my bank account from a family trust. I invest most of it, but keep enough to live comfortably." She paused, once more looking into the space between us. "Most adjuncts don't have that luxury."

"And that's it?"

"I'm Shelley Randall, Eddie."

"Shelley Randall with financial benefits."

"Guilty. But I am Shelley Randall. That's who I became and that's who I am and that's who I will always be. I used to be Gina Corelli. Sometimes at night I dream I still am her, but when I wake up she's a shadow, someone who comes in images while I sleep. Her past intrudes into my present, but I am not her, not anymore, not in any way that counts."

"I'd say having family trust money in the bank counts."

Her smile was almost apologetic. "I suppose there are a couple of ways the past counts."

"What's another?"

"Just between us?" There was a plea in her gaze, intimacy in her expression. I didn't answer immediately. The only sounds I heard came from the refrigerator motor, the clicking of the quartz clock atop the television, my breathing and the beating of my heart. I knew I would agree. Anything she said in confidence would stay confidential. I had fantasized about her for years, since the first day I saw her on campus, and the past week and a half had exceeded anything in my fantasies. The sex was fine, but I knew what was happening between us promised something far more important, the possibility of a rebirth for me, a return to a world I had long thought lost. I would not abort it without a fight.

"Between us. Shel." I heard the softness in my voice, the significance of the pause before I spoke her name, the intimacy of calling her by a nickname.

She rose from the couch. Moving to the window, she looked into the night, standing with her back to me. Her hair was backlit, sensuous shadows curving around her neck. "I trust you, Eddie. You know more about me than I ever thought I'd let anyone know."

"And there's more to tell," I said. "Yes." She fell silent.

I wanted to touch her, see my hand caressing her hair, moving through its lights and shadows. I didn't. It would be distract me from the questions I had. "What about Marion?" I asked.

"She's the daughter of a high school friend. The story was about them. I used it as part of my cover. If people thought I was hiding something, I'd bring the Marion story out. It worked well enough that they were afraid they'd hurt my feelings if they pursued it any further, but that's not what I was going to tell you, Eddie."

"Something worse?" Even as I asked I was relieved to learn there was no lost child. If there had been and if Shelley and I became seriously involved, something I wanted more that I had ever wanted anything, I would have had to do something to set right the situation.

From behind, I saw her nod, her hair bouncing with the motion. "Between us," she said again. This time it was a statement spoken in a relieved tone.

The room seemed suddenly far larger than its physical dimensions. The space between objects inflated, the way it does when a fever alters perception. She turned, came over to my chair and sat on the arm. I felt warmth radiating from her body, heard her breath soft and rapid. I could have touched her, reached across that immeasurable space and felt her skin, warm, soft and smooth beneath my fingers. I did not move.

It would not have been appropriate. The space was hers to bridge, to eradicate. I watched and waited. She radiated and breathed. I looked away for an instant. When I looked back, she had folded her hands and rested them on her thigh, her silence immense. Her face was a battleground. She bit her lips, sucked them in and closed her eyes. When she spoke it was in tones so soft I had to strain to hear her words.

"Eddie, I had Henrietta Lane's building torched. I tried to kill her."

Chapter Twenty-Four

I was silent. For a moment I didn't breathe. I don't remember hearing the refrigerator, the clock or the beating of my heart.

"The bitch killed my brother and Ariel." There was no softness, no hesitancy in the words or their tone.

"Do you know that for a fact?" I asked

"I know it like you know when it's raining. It touches you. It runs down you. You walk through it and in it."

"Why would she kill Evans and Ariel? Was it the upstart Russians moving in on the established Italians?"

She was startled. I had caught her off guard again, and it showed. She looked at me for a long minute, her face betraying her emotions as she thought it through. It was fine for her to have secrets. It had never occurred to her that I did. Her response, when it came, was minimalist, few words with many implications.

"You know a hell of a lot for a Maintainer II, about Nevis, about the Russians, about the Corellis."

"Janitor," I said. "Janitors always know where the dirt is, what's written on the walls. We're a treasure trove of information."

That broke the mood. She giggled and tapped my shoulder playfully. "You're full of shit, Sanders, and you've got to level with me too."

"Not until you're finished leveling with me."

"If you're asking do I have proof that she killed them, I don't. Even if I did, I'd still have to deal with it myself. It's not the kind of thing I could go to the police with."

"You did it by yourself? You don't strike me as an accomplished arsonist." She giggled again. The sound was girlish and out of context, nervous. "Hardly. I called a guy I grew up with in Trenton. We were close friends once. He learned the trade from his father and grandfather. They'd buy buildings, insure them and burn them down. He's a major real estate developer now. I've heard he owns half of Trenton and a good bit of the South Jersey Shore, including a property or two on the Atlantic City boardwalk."

"And he endangered it all to come up here and help a childhood friend?"

"He couldn't to that, but he did send a couple of his people."

"Lucky for you they didn't kill her. Sandy Grover's not going to expend a lot of energy on an arson investigation, given the sorry condition of town and state budgets this year, especially since there's no been no great financial loss to Henrietta. She'll have had it insured to the hilt. The death of one of the town's leading citizens would have been another thing. He would have had to move on it, fast and hard."

"It wasn't lucky for my father. I think she killed him too." She was calm and dispassionate, as though her father's death was remote from her life, not touching her in any significant way.

"That's something I don't understand. Why did your father take the risk of coming up here for Evans' funeral?"

"It wasn't much of a risk. According to Sylvia, Daddy had prostrate cancer. The stubborn guinea bastard never had a physical. He used to say wasn't about to let someone stick a finger up his ass, so the cancer wasn't discovered until it had metastasized. He didn't have much longer and he wanted to show the Russians that he wasn't backing down, even if they had killed his son. She said it never occurred to him that they'd go after him up here in the boonies."

"The Russian mobsters aren't rational."

"They're crazier than shit house rats and killing daddy was a stupid thing to do," she said.

"I'd be willing to bet that you're right about Henrietta being behind killing your father," I said. "She was in the funeral home when he was shot, but her Texas goon left before the service started. He's number one on my list for the shooter."

"That's what I told the family. I don't think Henrietta or her cowboy will be doing business much longer."

"How will that be handled?" I asked

"Quietly and professionally. One of Daddy's businesses owns several thousand acres in the Pine Barrens near Waretown."

"That's a good disposal place."

She squinted at me. "You're too cool about this for a Maintainer II or a janitor. What aren't you telling me about yourself? You're less who you are than I am."

I cupped her face in my hands. "I have my own interests."

"Which are?"

"My interests."

"In other words, butt out Shelley."

"Those are your words," I said.

She smiled. "I can do that. I was taught to butt out as a kid. I'm well practiced. Later, if we get married, you can tell me everything."

"Married?"

"You like me. A lot." I nodded, surprised that I wasn't shivering.

"So maybe you'll ask me to marry you. Or I'll ask you. Or maybe I just did."

"Making me an offer I can't refuse?"

She clucked her tongue at me. "Now that was a cheap shot. Besides, the Corellis aren't horse people."

I leaned toward her, raising my eyebrows. "You still haven't answered my question. How will Henrietta and Randolph be handled?"

She toyed with her coffee mug, running her forefinger around the rim several times. She smiled at me. It was a sweet smile, genuine, affectionate. I smiled back. She was an exquisite woman, talented, intelligent, beautiful, sexual without being tritely sexy.

Her reply was soft. "I answered as much as I could, as much as I know, or guess. It'll be handled with great discretion and not around here. Henrietta and her assistant will simply be gone from Graham one day soon. You haven't given me an answer to my marriage proposal."

"Your people work very much like some other people I know. They'd be pleased to have Henrietta gone. I tried marriage. It didn't work. I did a terrible job of it."

"Do you mean my people work like your people? You're not married now, are you?"

I wagged my forefinger under her nose. "Tsk tsk. You're fishing with two lines. Strictly speaking, I don't have any people. And whoever takes over the Corelli family businesses will restructure things and keep them going. There are some very influential people who find comfort in that. I'm single."

"Better the devil you know," she said. I shrugged.

She got up from the chair's arm and walked back to the window. "My God, it's snowing."

"It's November. It's allowed to snow in November."

"It's not just snowing; it's snowing hard, Eddie. Look. It's beautiful." I stood behind her, letting our bodies touch. It felt fine and I kissed the side of her neck. She backed up closer. Outside, small snowflakes fell in thick swirls, the wind sweeping them along the street and sidewalks.

She spoke as though explaining something to a dense student. "The Corellis sell things people want to buy and can't get anywhere else. It's a service industry, like groceries, cigarettes, liquor beer and wine, like insurance."

"Your family may be more honest than the insurance people."

"No doubt. They'll protect their markets just like the others do. Their methods might be different from those the Fortune 500 use, but it's business. Business is business, you know. The Rockefellers and the Kennedys, the

Carnegies and the Mellons, the Bushes, they all understand that. Eddie, Angela and I are just second generation. Our kids, if we have any, I guess it's now down to if I have any, will be doctors and senators. They'll have a larger social perspective than Daddy's generation, but they'll know how to protect their own interests just as well, and with a hell of a lot more legitimacy. Hell, they'll create legitimacy, legislate it and enforce it." She stopped and sighed. "Now Angela and me are the second generation. Eddie's out of the picture. Damn it."

"I don't think Angela's the reproducing kind," I said.

"No. She's probably not." She turned, her face looking up at mine. She slipped into my arms. We kissed, her tongue darting feather-like on my lips. "Let's go back to bed, Eddie."

§§§

I awoke at ten, Shelley asleep beside me. I brushed my lips over her hair, breathing in the odor of her shampoo. Rolling off the bed, I walked to the window and stood staring at the falling snow. Several inches were already piled on the ground. The day was gun gray. Still warm from Shelley's bed, steam radiators clanking in every room, I looked out at the early winter weather and shivered. I got dressed and headed for the kitchen.

Neither of us had thought to turn off the coffeemaker and the contents smelled like old athletic socks. I dumped it out, washed the pot and basket and started a fresh batch brewing. There was nothing in the refrigerator except a four ounce bottle of maple syrup, a can of tomato juice, several packages of moldy cheese, a small tub of margarine, its lid proclaiming it deadly to cholesterol, and a carton of milk dated October 3rd. I shook the carton. Something inside thudded against the sides and I decided not to open it. In the freezer I found a package of frozen waffles and several tofu sausages in a frost covered plastic baggie.

I threw on my coat and hat, planning to walk to a nearby convenience store and pick up some frozen bagels. My hand was on the doorknob when someone knocked on it from the other side. I yanked it open. Tiger stood there, snow lining the shoulders of her red and black wool jacket and the top of the navy blue wool hat pulled down over her ears. She held a plastic grocery bag in her hand. Pushing into the room, she set the bag on the coffee table, pulled off the coat and hat, scattering snow across the floor. She grabbed the bag, taking an ancient telephone answering machine from it.

"Thought you'd still be here, day like this. You have to hear what I got. Goddamn." She spoke in quick bursts. She plugged the machine in and pressed the play button. "Listen, Eddie, just listen to this tape. I drove Chad to work this morning, stopped for coffee and a couple of muffins and this was on the machine when I got home."

It was a cheap machine. It probably hadn't cost more than forty bucks at Wal-Mart. The voices were scratchy, and wavered in pitch as we listened to several messages, girls calling Chad and leaving suggestive remarks.

After the fourth one, Tiger held up her hand. "Now, Eddie, listen." Dawn's voice came from the speaker. I could tell from its strained sound she was trying not to cry. *Tiger, you've got to help me. He says he's going...* Here the words were hard to discern because of background noise and the poor quality of the recording...*unless you get the recordings to him like his note said, the ones Eddie...reading. Please Tige...blindfolded all the time...I'm so scared.* Her pitch and volume rose with the last three words. It was chilling.

Tiger pushed the stop button. "That's all there is Eddie. The bastard has her scared shitless. I find him; I'm going to kill him."

"That means I'd better find him first. I want that pleasure."

"Maybe we can do it cooperatively," she said.

I played the tape again. It wasn't any clearer a second time. "I can't understand it all," Tiger said.

"What's going on?" It was Shelley. She came into the room wearing a blue terry cloth bathrobe.

"It's Dawn," Tiger said. "Listen." She played the tape a third time. "We can't get it all because this cheesy machine of mine sucks and there's too much goddamn background noise."

I leaned into the machine. "It's music. The noise is music, but the machine's distorting it too much and it was playing too far away from the phone she was calling from for me to make it out."

"Play it again," Shelley said. Tiger rewound the tape and we listened to the three other messages, before Dawn's.

Shelley sat close to the answering machine her eyes shut, concentrating on the sounds behind Dawn's voice, her head bobbing as she listened to the tape two more times.

"Got it." She snapped her fingers. "It's Louis Armstrong, *Do You Know What It Means to Miss New Orleans.*

"You sure?" Tiger asked.

"Positive. I grew up with that stuff. My brother was a huge Louis Armstrong fan. He played that stuff all the time."

I went cold. It was a cold I hadn't felt since I left, since Nathan Hunt left, the agency. The last time it happened I had arranged to meet an Azeri informant at the Kobustan reserve, about fifty miles south of Baku, where a number of caves with prehistoric paintings would give us the privacy we needed for a long and detailed discussion of dissent in Iran, south of Azerbaijan. I had cultivated the man for three years and his information on the state of policy and dissent in the area had always been accurate. I had planned many successful operations based on what he had given me.

When I arrived at the caves his car was in the parking lot. There was no other sign of him. I waited, pacing, annoyed, checking my watch every few minutes. After half an hour, afraid he might have been discovered and taken out, I went looking for him, first in the largest cave, then poking through others, looking behind rocks, both in the caves and surrounding them. He wasn't anywhere. There was no one else around. The wind was strong off the Caspian, a few yards away on the other side of the highway. That far south there were no oil derricks in the water. It was clear, the sea deep blue, lapping at the rocks and sand along the shore. The air was fresh, the sky cloudless, except for contrails from the jet fighters streaking overhead, patrolling the Iranian border.

I returned to the car park, passing a privy off to the side of the lot. I don't know if I heard a sound, saw a shadow, smelled him or noticed something in the flight of birds, but that was when I went cold. I turned. He was standing beside the privy, the nine-millimeter pistol in his hand pointing at my heart.

Had he been a professional, he would have shot me before I saw him, and he should have. Instead, he was a true believer, eager to let me know my death would help punch his ticket to Paradise, where a bevy of virgins were waiting to pleasure him for eternity, their virginity renewed each night for his pleasure. He explained he had come to understand that the West I represented was every bit as much an enemy of Allah as the Soviet oppressors had been ages before. Azerbaijan's salvation, he told me, lay in the Iranian revolution to the south, in submission to the true Islamic faith as found in the teachings of the Ayatollah Khomeini.

He talked, preached of his confidence in reaching Paradise, of all true Azeris reaching Paradise once an Islamic republic replaced the current godless state. I watched his eyes, noticed the slight tremble of his gun hand. A cloud briefly obscured the sun. When it passed and full light returned suddenly and brilliantly, he blinked. Fast as a serpent, my right hand struck his throat, breaking the cartilage. He crumpled, unable to breathe. I took the gun and watched him die, his eyes tearing as they stared into mine. As he faced the void where no naked virgins would ever dance, the fear on his face belied the confidence he had expressed in attaining Paradise.

I looked at Shelley and barked the words, "It's Billy, Tiger. Billy Melnick has Dawn."

"No," she said. "He wouldn't."

"It's the music," I said. "When he told me about Evans Cornell, he told me about some cabins Cornell owned in the Parsons District of Yardley, how they would go up there, work on the buildings, get stoned and listen to jazz. He said Cornell had a great collection, including a massive Armstrong one."

"That's right," Shelley said. "Eddie was into Louis Armstrong since he was a kid. Daddy was always trying to get him into Sinatra, Tony Bennet, guys like that, but Eddie thought they were corny. I actually dig Sinatra," she added. It was an inappropriate aside, but it contributed an aura of normality to the situation.

"He's holding Dawn in one of Cornell's cabins. He was playing music when she called and never thought about it," I said.

"Let's go," Tiger said.

"We need to call the police," I said.

"No way." Tiger's voice was hard with fury. "I want to do this myself." Shelley and I exchanged glances and nodded. We both understood.

§§§

We crammed into my pickup. Tiger was in the passenger's seat. Shelley sat in the jump seat in the rear of the extended cab, her knees close to her chin. I slammed it into four-wheel drive and headed across the river to Graham. Before driving the hilly back country roads up to the Parsons district, I was going to stop at my room to pick up several well-hidden, long unused guns.

For the first time I was glad I had kept them. It wasn't the result of careful planning. When I came to Graham, I was going to dump them in the river, bury them somewhere, get rid of them somehow, sure the part they played my life was over. I never got around to it. They were oiled, wrapped in old bed sheets and stashed in a trunk under my bed. I had nearly forgotten about them. Not completely, of course. Every time I clean the room, vacuum under the bed, there they are. Not that I clean under the bed very often. Dusting and vacuuming the open areas of the room are satisfactory.

Spaces I can't see don't bother me. Under the bed, the trunk with the guns became invisible. On those rare occasions when I do a thorough cleaning, or drop something, get down on my knees to fetch it and see the trunk surrounded by dust balls, I think: *right, there it is, got to get rid those damned things one of these days.* Then I'm up off my knees, back to reading, or eating, or doing whatever the hell I do by myself in that little room over Main Street, and the guns disappear again. Like Nathan, they become memories of shadows, almost dreams, substance without form.

I suspect most peoples' pasts are similar, in a lower key, of course. All they have to disremember are botched attempts at getting laid in the back of a car after a junior prom, a stupid remark made at a party under the influence of too much booze, getting stopped by a cop for speeding past a school or, at most, ex-husbands and ex-wives. Repression, suppression and denial are wonderful psychic survival tools.

I had Nathan to forget. At times, I am so successful that when I meet someone named Nathan, I have to ask myself how to spell the name, Nathen or Nathan. I believe I trained myself to fail to remember the spelling.

I drove from Eagle Falls to Graham over slippery roads. It was the first snow of the season. New Englanders seem to forget how to drive on snowy roads over the summer. When they go out on the roads after an autumn snowfall, their cars end up in ditches, crunched against trees, resting against one another at intersections, drivers standing alongside them talking and shaking their fists and yelling at one another. It's as though each summer we convince ourselves that winter will never come again and when it does we're startled, and inept on the roads. We passed four or five fender benders and an accident where EMTs were loading someone into an ambulance, the car lying on its caved in top.

"The driving'll be rotten up in the hills," Tiger said. "You got enough weight in the back of this thing to get up Parsons Hill?"

"I will if you sit on the tailgate," I said. She didn't laugh.

"We'll pick up some bags of sand at Home Depot on the way out of town," I said.

I parked in front of Barton Rooms. Leaving the truck running, Tiger and Shelley sitting in it, I leapt up the steps to my floor two at a time. Pulling the trunk from under the bed, I took the key from my wallet and opened it. The guns lay wrapped in two rows, each with a paper tag indicating what lay under the wrapping. I took three, a CZ 75 B nine millimeter Luger, a Bill Wilson modified Remington 870 short barreled twelve-gauge combat shotgun, and a Smith and Wesson twenty-two pistol on a thirty-eight Police Special frame. I grabbed two hunting knives and ammunition for the guns, including hollow points for the twenty-two.

Glancing out the window as I moved across the room, I saw a car door open. Randolph got out and ran toward the Barton entrance. He must have been sitting there waiting for me to show up. The snowfall was heavier. The few cars on the street crawled along, their drivers sitting straight up, looking ahead, their hands taut on the steering wheels.

Unsheathing a knife, I opened the door, but heard nothing. No footsteps on the stairs, no shuffling in the hall. I knew Randolph would be in the building by then. The hallway was cold, the air rushing past me into the room. My back against the wall, I sidled toward the staircase, holding my breath as I moved. At the edge of the opening, I stopped and peered around the corner. A gun barrel crashed against the side of my head. The blow glanced off my temple and the silencer slashed against my cheek.

"Got you, shit for brains," Randolph gloated.

Gloating was a mistake. It gave me time to snake out my foot and trip him. He arched backward and fell down the stairs, his body thudding on the treads as he tumbled. The gun clattered and stopped a few steps beyond where he came to rest. I pounced and was on top of him. I dropped the knife as he snarled, squirmed, batting at my face with the cast on his arm, trying to bite my arms, my neck, gnashing anything he could get his teeth near.

"You piece of shit," he growled, spittle spraying from his mouth.

That was his second mistake, wasting energy and focus on words. I brought my knee into his groin, fast and hard. Gasping, he collapsed inward for a moment. Collecting himself quicker than I would have thought possible he lashed out again in a red fury, spitting, biting, kicking, slamming at me with the cast. Protecting myself from his blows as best I could, I felt around for the knife. He saw what I was doing and kicked it, sending it several steps down. It came to rest by his gun.

I rolled off him and down the steps, using my elbows to stop on the stair where the knife and gun rested. I grabbed the knife. Randolph leapt toward me and I swung it upward. He saw it too late. His eyes wide, his face taut with horror, his mouth open in a scream that never came, he fell upon the open blade. As it sank into his abdomen I pulled it upward, slicing him from his lower belly to his sternum. Blood and fluids, warm, dark and foul smelling, poured over my face and chest, his dead weight crushing the breath from me.

I pushed him upward, rolling out from beneath his body. Pulling him to the side of the staircase, I slipped out of my shoes and carried them back to my room. Nobody had come to see what the thumping and snarling was about. The drunks living in most of the other rooms were already at the bars or sleeping off the previous night's benders. My remaining marginal neighbors were probably watching television, reading cheap novels, whacking off, or any of several combinations of all three. The few who were functional were busy, some at work, some perhaps visiting children living under the custody of their ex-spouses, an exceptional few in classes at GCC, others reading in the town library or in other ways engaged in the small activities that occupied and defined their lives.

I rinsed the knife and stuffed it, the other one, and the three guns into the trunk. I took a quick shower, changed clothes and stuffed the towels and blood soaked shirt and pants into the trunk with everything else. I checked the hallway, relieved that I hadn't tracked through the pooled blood, leaving footprints leading to my room. Locking my door, I dragged the trunk to the top of the stairs, hefted it onto my shoulder and carried it to the truck, tossing it into the back.

I didn't have time to do anything but leave Randolph lying where he had died. Somebody would find him and call the cops. He wasn't going to tell them who killed him. I had cleared my room of the knives and guns, along with anything that had blood on it. There was nothing to connect me to his death. Nathan had taken out enough people like him for me to know how it was done, how hard it was for local police to trace the actions of a professional. Not that it mattered a hell of a lot. I was in a hurry and couldn't be sidetracked by anything else. If worse came to worse and the body caused complications, the agency would help. I hoped. Since the Director had cautioned me about Randolph's value to them, I couldn't be sure.

I looked around before getting into the truck. There was no sign of Henrietta. It didn't matter. If I didn't deal with her soon, the Corellis would take care of her later.

I got behind the wheel.

"You took long enough, for crissakes," Tiger said.

"It takes time to prepare for this kind of action," I said. "What was that in the trunk?"

"Guns, knives, support for when we get to Parsons Hill." My voice was flat. I wasn't feeling a thing. It was a state I was familiar with, one that had played a large part in my leaving the agency. I had killed before and each time a little of my human feelings died with the victim. It had taken me years to reclaim my humanity. Now Randolph had taken another piece of it. I was glad the son-of-a-bitch was dead. Glad I had killed him. In that pleasure lay some of my lost humanity.

Chapter Twenty-Five

At Home Depot we loaded a dozen forty pound bags of sand in the rear of the pickup bed and set off on Route 2, west. The snow was wet and heavy, falling with increasing thickness. The road up the hill out of town was steep and buried under a thick gray slushy cover. Just beyond the last strip mall in Graham the road becomes steeper. A Volvo had spun into the breakdown lane, skidded into a ditch and come to rest with its left wheels off the ground, its track still fresh in the slush. The driver stood next to it, kicking the fenders, his furious yelling carrying through the closed windows of the truck.

"You'd think the Swedes could build a car that can handle snow and ice," I said. Neither Tiger nor Shelley responded.

I slowed down, and dropping into four-wheel drive headed up the hill and out of Graham. The snow seemed deeper with every mile. At the top of Parsons Hill it could already be nearly impassable. The road there is built on a geologic dome of three hundred foot thick granite. It skirts along the side of the dome at close to fifteen hundred feet above sea level. Even though it's less than ten miles from the center of Graham, there's often snow piled inches deep on the hill when we're having rain in town.

About four miles out of Graham, we came to Dublin Road, which turns off to the right just after Ducky's. I looked over at the bar, the parking lot filled with pickup trucks outfitted with snowplows, lights on, engines idling, their drivers inside, preparing themselves to tackle the driveways they had contracted to keep clear all winter. Across the highway, in the Yardley Coffee Roasters café's parking lot, two or three late model cars were pulled in. They probably belonged to people waiting for their driveways at home to be plowed.

I glanced at Tiger. She was slumped down in her seat, hands over her eyes, breathing in short quick gasps. I'd seen people in that state before. They're overwhelmed, tuning out on the moment, threatening to escape into lethargy. In a crisis, they're useless. I gave her a soft jab with my right fist.

"I don't suppose you want to stop in and pound the shit out of a few snow pushers," I said.

"Not funny, Eddie." Tiger's voice was weary, depressed.

"We could go across the street and have an easier time with the commuting crowd."

"Stop it, Eddie, just stop it." The weariness and tension evaporated. Not being amused had morphed into anger. She was sitting straight up, her hands balled into tight fists.

"Sorry. Just trying to ease the tension."

"I think you added to it," Shelley said from the jump seat.

"Maybe," I said. I looked over at Tiger, pleased that she had re-engaged, looking at me with a mixture of anger and awareness of what I had done.

I turned onto Dublin Road. A few hundred yards down I made a left turn onto Skinner Road, one of a series of back roads leading to Parsons Road and the Parsons Hill area of Yardley, where Evans Cornell's cabins abutted the Audubon preserve at Dutchman's Ridge. With the sandbags in the bed and the three of us sitting in the cab there was enough weight in the truck to keep it plodding upward through the snow, but the wipers weren't strong enough to keep the windshield clear of the wet, heavy stuff falling on the glass. I drove with my side window down, the heater and defroster on full blast, hanging out every minute or so to sweep the windshield with a long handled brush. Snow caked in my hair and beard and my eyes stung from the cold.

We crept through the snow, shivering. The heater was useless, unable to keep up with the cold air pouring in the window. A mile or two further I turned on to Frank Robbins Road and followed it until we came to Little Robbins Road, which led us on to Parsons Road. The driving got worse with each turn, the snow heavier, the visibility more impossible. Just before the point where Parsons Road meets Tower Road, Parsons Road veers sharply uphill and to the right. Half a dozen cars were parked there, residents who could not make it past that point. All were pulled off to the side, except for a blue Toyota Corolla, which was blocking half the road.

I swung out to pass it, pulled too far to the left and drove into the ditch, my muffler dragging against the snow covered ground as the engine stalled and we stopped.

I howled in rage, pounding my fists against the steering wheel.

We sat in silence for a moment, listening to the hiss of melting snow on the hood.

"That some kind of primitive invocation?" Shelley asked.

"We're going to have to walk the rest of the way up there," I said. "In this shit, no boots, no heavy jackets, just us and this goddamn snow."

Recovered from her funk, Tiger took charge. She patted my leg. "Chill, Sanders. Take a deep breath, start the truck up, and let's try it." She pointed at the shift lever for the four-wheel drive. "You're only in four high. Drop it into four low and try easing it on out of here."

I did as she said. We had to rock back and forth five or six times, the engine whining, but at last the truck began to inch forward. I wrenched the steering wheel to the right and gave it a little gas. It stalled. My breath exploded from my chest.

"Again, Eddie," Tiger said, her voice calm.

I turned the key. The truck whined, coughed and fell silent. I pounded the wheel, sighing in exasperation.

"Once more," she said.

I tried it once more, then once more again. On the sixth try the engine caught, sputtered and kept on sputtering.

"It's wet," I said.

"That's good," Tiger said. "Wet things get dry. Give it the slightest bit of gas and keep your foot on it at that level and let it idle for a few minutes. It'll run."

I did and it worked. Soon the engine was humming. In four wheel low, I dropped the shift handle into low drive and eased forward, keeping the wheel turning right, but not as sharply as I had before. The truck lurched twice. I heard the muffler scrape, the rip of metal as it was torn off, then the sound of the motor rumbling in our ears, echoing in the cab, the odor of exhaust coming through the open window, immediate and nauseating.

"Goddamn it." I slammed my fists on the wheel again but the truck crept on. Then we were out of the ditch, back on the road moving forward. "We sound like a herd of Harleys on the Fourth of July," Shelley said.

"We're going to have to walk anyway," I said. "Billy'll hear us coming from all the way down here."

"Everybody on Parsons Hill will," Shelley said. "And not one of them is going to know what in the hell it is. I've been to Evans' cabins and they're far enough into the woods that Billy's not going to notice the noise, if he's there and we're not chasing wild geese."

"He's there," I said.

"Park at the end of the drive if you're worried about him hearing us. The cabins aren't so far in that it's going to kill us to walk, even in this weather."

I made the final sharp turn. The truck kept moving forward, through the turn and uphill. A tenth of a mile further on, the pavement ended. The gravel roadway provided better traction. In another two or three tenths of a mile, we came to a lane leading into the woods on the left, a green sign with gold lettering announcing that it led to the Cornell Cross-Country Cabins. Snow was beginning to drift into a single set of tracks on the lane, evidence that someone had just come, or gone.

"He's just come," Tiger said when I raised the question. "They're real fresh and we haven't passed anyone. He's in there, Eddie. He's there and I'm going in and I'm going to kill him." Her voice had become a low snarl, a lethal growl. She was fully back, ready for action.

I parked a few hundred yards further on, in a pullover beneath a grove of maples and pines. The truck bed was thick with snow, as was the trunk I had tossed in there after Randolph had leapt onto my knife. Brushing it off, I opened the lid. Tiger looked over my shoulder. She saw the blood drenched clothes and made a grunt of horror. I told them what had happened on the staircase at Barton Rooms.

"You weren't going to tell us that," Shelley said with so little inflection, I couldn't tell if it was a statement or a question.

"I was," I said. "When the time was right."

"And when was that going to be?"

"Once we weren't so focused on Dawn."

I gave Tiger the nine millimeter, took the twelve gauge combat shotgun for myself and passed Shelley the Smith and Wesson twenty-two pistol. She looked at the weapons, then at me, but said nothing.

I doled out ammunition. We loaded the guns. I put the knife that had killed Randolph into a holster and clipped it to my belt. The other one I put into a pocket. Latching the trunk, I clicked the padlock and we started down the lane toward the cabins. Shelley explained they were hidden behind a sharp bend, about a tenth of a mile into the property.

Just before reaching the bend we stepped into the woods. Under cover of the thick stand of trees and bushes we moved parallel to the lane. Soon we stood inside the tree line across from a cabin, its roof covered by at least five inches of snow. The tracks on the lane continued into the property. Staying behind the trees, we followed. The tracks ended at the fifth and final cabin. Like the others it was a log cabin built from a kit, the logs rounded tongue and grooved affairs, an abomination to true log home builders who pride themselves on squared, hand-hewn logs artfully notched and with chinking, not tongue and groove plastic between the logs.

Smoke curled from the chimney. Billy's rusty yellow Subaru was parked in front, the snow still melting as it landed on the hood.

"Damn," Tiger said. "He hasn't been here very long. If we'd gotten there an hour earlier, we could have walked out with Dawn and dealt with Billy later."

I caught Tiger's arm and stopped her as she moved toward the open ground.

"He'll see you," I whispered. "If he's watching," she said.

"He's watching. Don't forget, he's combat trained and experienced. He's watching, no doubt. He may not be peering out the windows, but he's got ways of knowing if someone's coming at him. I'd bet there's a video camera, and he's capable of setting up booby traps, trip wires and god knows what else."

"Billy," she said in wonderment. "It's hard to believe Billy did this."

"This isn't good old Billy Melnick, our favorite work-study poet and barfly. This is former Sergeant Willard Melnick, twisted by rage, twisted by booze, twisted by years of failure, twisted by greed and just flat out twisted. In a very real way he's fighting for his soul. That makes him dangerous as hell, Tige."

It was the soul thing that made Billy dangerous. He had become snaky. What had snaked through him, the deadly serpentine evil possessing him, was a desperate need for his soul to connect to something larger than himself. In a lesser, but equally perilous way, it was the same thing that makes fundamentalist radicals dangerous, that drives and makes all fanatics dangerous. Billy believed he was in pursuit of something beyond himself.

Like all people who justify their murderous excesses by seeing them as furthering a cause that promises some form of transcendence from their sorry lives, Billy had taken Dawn and was threatening to kill her to ensure his connection to something greater than himself, by possessing something of a dead poet that no one else had, the recordings and the singular versions of a few of his poems. A dead poet who, if he lived, would have shat on Billy rather than praise his poetry or stroke his soul.

Billy's immortal yearnings might seem petty, but immortality of any kind is petty, a denial of the importance of living, a desperate hand hold to being for those for whom life is in one way or another unbearable, those who have not found a way to reconcile the tragedy we call the human condition with their own situations. The Bukowski recordings had become Billy's link to greatness, to art, to the cosmic doodely-shit that drives all true believers into madness.

Tiger's voice, iced ferocity, jarred me from my thoughts. "So Billy's dangerous, big deal, because I'm dangerous too, Eddie. Red raging furious and ready to dismember that fucking bastard dangerous."

"We both are," I said. "Only I'm trained to be dangerous and survive danger."

"I can be pretty tough, too," Shelley said from behind us. "I wasn't raised by a bunch of wusses."

I reached around and hugged her, long and hard. She found my lips and kissed me, our cold noses touching, melting snow running from our hair into our eyes as we stood shivering outside the cabin where Billy Melnick was holding Dawn hostage. It was a long, tender, unforgettable kiss.

"Cut the mush and let's get cracking," Tiger said. "Dawn's in there." The best way to approach the cabin was to stay within the tree line, following the lane deeper into the property, out of sight from the cabin. There we could cross the lane, go back into the woods on the other side and approach the cabin from the rear, at the point where it backed up to the woods.

It was growing dusky, the temperature dropping quickly. Snow piled into my shoes as we slogged along. My socks were wet. My beard was icing. My hands were cold. Tucking the shotgun under my arm, I blew on my fingers. I needed them warm, limber, sensitive for triggering. Walking was difficult. The deepening snow hid roots, deadfall and rocks. I tripped several times, catching myself on trees to keep from falling. Tiger did fall. I heard a thump, whispered curses, and saw her face down in the snow, still gripping the pistol.

"We can make snow angels later," I said. "Not funny, Eddie."

"You've been saying that a lot."

"You've been too cute for any other words a lot, asswipe, and this shit sucks."

Shelley and I grabbed her arms, holding them as she got her knees under her and grunted her way into a standing position. "Worse than swabbing toilets?"

"No comparison."

I hugged her. "It'll be all right."

Her eyes filled with tears. "I hope so, Eddie. I'm scared. I'm scared for Dawn. I'm scared for us. I'm not like you. I didn't do this kind of shit for a living."

Shelley pounced on her words, "What does that mean?"

I put my finger to my lips. "I told you we had things to talk about later, okay?"

She nodded, but her lips were a thin line. I knew her secrets. She knew I had secrets. It wasn't the same. If things worked out with us, I would figure out a way to tell her enough of mine to make it seem even.

The cabin, the largest of the five, was small. It was the one Evans reserved for his personal use, Shelley said, explaining that there were four rooms consisting of a common area, including the kitchen and dining area, a small bathroom and two bedrooms. We made our way to the rear. There were three windows, a door and an enclosure holding two one hundred pound propane tanks. Several cords of firewood were stacked beside the door. A piece of corrugated roofing lay atop the stack. Dim light shone from one of the windows.

"Let's go for it," Tiger said, ready to move in.

I put my arm out, staying her. "Charge in and there's a good chance you'll get Dawn or one of us killed, maybe both."

She snorted in frustration. "So what do we do?"

"Move slowly. Check everything out. Go in when the time's right."

"When's that?"

"When I say it is. Trust me." I told them to wait inside the tree line and left them there. Brushing snow aside with the tips of my shoes, looking for trips and traps, I edged toward the cabin. In spite of my concerns about Billy's training and wiliness, there didn't seem to be booby traps, trip wires, any of the tricks I expected. Perhaps Billy never thought we'd know he'd taken Dawn, never thought we'd find him here. That's when I saw the video camera mounted on a small, crude platform above the door.

I slipped back into the woods. Tiger raised her eyebrows. "What's up?"

"Camera," I whispered, pointing to the spot over the door. "Let's hope he wasn't watching the monitor closely. I wasn't out there very long, so let's hope he didn't see me. He'd've probably done something if he had. I think we're okay, for now."

She craned her neck and saw the camera. "Think he's got more cameras?"

"We've got to assume he does."

"And?"

"And we wait until dark."

"That's a long wait," she said. "We could freeze to death out here."

"I don't think it's that bad, but it ain't going to be fun."

Shelley said, "We could wait in one of the other cabins. They've all got rear doors. If we go in that way we won't leave any tracks he can see if he tries driving out, then, if he does, we can go in and bring Dawn out."

I waved my hand through the snow. "I don't think he's going to try driving out in this storm. There wouldn't be much point in it."

The next cabin was tucked further back into the woods but still within a clear line of vision from the main one. The door was locked, but the window next to it was unlatched. Inside, the air was cold and dank, heavy with the odors of unused cabin, stale ashes, mouse droppings and urine and moldy fabric. There was a galley kitchen, a tiny bathroom, and a combination living room, sleeping area. A fireplace took up most of one wall. The other walls were hung with Navajo rugs and watercolors of southwestern scenes.

"Each cabin has a different theme," Shelley said. "The one next door's got a French motif, Provençal. There's one decorated to look like a rural English pub, another's filled with African art and furnishings. The main cabin's done up in cute Yankee country style. The pub, the Navajo, Provençal and African things are real and valuable. He even went so far as to buy a bar from a pub in Wiltshire and have it sent over here for the cabin. The Yankee country stuff came from antique shops and cutesy touristy stores in Vermont. Evans might have had Elkins and Yale pedigrees, but he could still be tacky, and the Yankee cabin's very expensive tacky."

We couldn't turn on the lights or build a fire without revealing our presence, but I found three small cube shaped electric heaters. We plugged them in and cranked them to high. Soon the main room was toasty. I filled several cooking pots with snow and set them in front of the heaters to melt for drinking water. We waited for nightfall. Outside, the wind came up, howling around the corners of the cabin. Snow devils swirled in rising eddies that skimmed across the surface.

"An early blizzard. Damn." Tiger's frustration and rage filled the cabin. "That could be good," I said. "He won't be expecting anything in weather like this. My guess, he's in there listening to music, sitting by the fire and talking Dawn's ears off about how cool he is." As soon as the words were out, I knew I had blown it.

Tiger jumped. "Oh my Jesus, Mary and Joseph. If she knows where she is and who's got her, she's dead. He can't afford to let her get away."

"We'll get her out, Tige. Trust me. I've dealt with worse situations." She put her head down shaking it. "Dealt, or prevailed, Eddie?"

"Prevailed. They paid me for results, not attempts."

She looked up and gave me a quick, uncertain smile. I high fived her, glancing at Shelley, who was watching me with a curious, almost suspicious look, as though she didn't know who I was.

She didn't. That gave me some satisfaction, knowing we were somehow almost even.

Chapter Twenty-Six

I sat by the window, watching the air darken from the storm and the coming night. I assured Tiger that Dawn would be all right, doing everything I could to convince her that I was more confident than I was, that I have been more successful in the past than I had been. In truth, success depended more on Billy Melnick than it did on me. It depended on his realizing the game was over when it was over and finding a reserve of decency and drawing on it once we reached the endgame.

We went back out at full dark, guided through the woods by the pale light coming from the cabin where Billy was holding Dawn. The unlatched window in the cabin where we had waited gave me hope. I told Shelley and Tiger to wait inside the tree line as I made my way to the rear of the building.

"You're my backup," I explained. "You hear me call, you hear shots, you hear Dawn, you hear anything that sounds like trouble, you come fast, ready to shoot. Not shooting, just ready, and ready to be careful with your shooting."

Nearing the cabin, I heard music coming from within. No jazz this time, it was The Stones, *Sympathy for the Devil*, blaring from a stereo. I was pleased. It should mask any sound I made opening a window.

I went to the furthest one, on the corner diagonal from the room the light came from. It was latched. I moved to the next one. Not only was it unlatched, it was cracked open several inches. I piled firewood beneath it, enough to boost me so I wouldn't have to kick and scrape noisily against the side of the cabin to get in. I pushed it all the way open. There was risk. The open window could cause a draft, alerting Billy. It could open into a room he was using. I could knock something over, break something, clatter something.

Once it was open far enough for me to fit through, I climbed in. My foot settled on a hard surface a foot or more above the floor. It was the edge of a toilet. I was in the bathroom and assumed the window had been slightly opened to provide ventilation. I hoped Billy didn't get the sudden urge to take a crap. The floor creaked as I stepped on it. I was depending on the sounds from Mick and the boys to cover for me. I pulled the window back down to a slit and looked around.

The door leading to the rest of the cabin was closed. I turned the knob and opened it inward just far enough to see I was between two other doors, one closed, the second ajar. In front of me was a half wall, perhaps six and a half feet high and eight feet wide, a partition separating the living area of the cabin from the bedrooms and bath. Light seeped from either side of the wall. The air was sweet with wood smoke, apple, judging by the odor, and marijuana. It was a good sign that Billy had made himself cozy and was probably stoned.

I took off my shoes and eased out of the bathroom. I went to the room with the open door. It was a bedroom. Dawn was there, gagged and tied to the bed. As soon as she saw me, her eyes widened and she struggled against the clothesline holding her down. I smiled, made a circle with my thumb and forefinger, giving her the okay sign. If she noticed, it didn't do any good. She didn't relax, but struggled harder against her bonds.

I moved to her and leaning over the bed I almost retched. She had been lying in her excrement for a long time. I turned away, took a deep breath and leaned in again, whispering in her ear.

"I'm going to untie you. When I do, you have to be quiet. Do you understand?"

Eyes even wider, she nodded.

I held my nose with one hand, waving the other beneath it. "Whatever you do when you're loose, don't hug me, okay?"

For the briefest moment her eyes smiled and she nodded again.

I turned away for another breath, then took the knife from my belt and slit the lines across her chest, the ones on her arms and legs. She tried to sit up, but she had been tied down too long and her muscles were weak. She fell back against the bed.

"Try again," I whispered. "We have to get out of here. The bathroom window's open and Tiger and Shelley are waiting outside. I'll take care of Billy once you're out of here and safe."

I took her hands and pulled her upright. I untied the gag, signaling her to be silent. She crooked her finger, motioning me closer. I bent my ear to her mouth, trying not to gag at the stench from her bed, the foulness of her breath.

"He's crazy," she said in a whisper so hoarse it barely sounded like speech. "He thinks those recordings are going to make him famous, that people will realize he has them because he's a great poet, or that he's a great poet because he has them. He says all kinds of stuff like that. None of it makes much sense. I think he killed someone in there." She pointed toward the living area.

I put my hand on her cheek. "We'll talk about this later. We've got to get you out of here. Try to stand."

She stood, and fell back. I pulled her up again, holding her upright as circulation returned to her legs. After several minutes she said she thought she could make it and we sidled to the bathroom. Once inside, I pulled the door shut behind us and opened the window. The fresh air was a relief. I was about to give her a boost when the door flew open, the light flashing on.

"Dude. Good to see you. Did you bring me the recordings?" Billy was framed in the doorway pointing a sawed off double-barreled lever action shotgun at us with one hand, smoke curling from a joint he held in the other. He raised the joint to his lips and took a deep toke. He was wearing camouflage clothing, a green beret sitting on his head at a jaunty angle. Pointing at two hair thin wires stretched across the threshold, he shook his head at me. I had taken scrupulous care moving about outside and had failed to consider wires and booby traps inside the cabin.

"Pretty careless, dude. I've got them over every door in the place, wired to a warning light in the living room."

"And nothing outside?"

"I got cameras, one on each side of the house. They don't work at night. There's a couple more wires out there, but you didn't trip any. I'll be more careful next time. I thought I was pretty safe out here, you know dude."

"You're not going to ask how I found you?" Exhaling smoke, he grinned in a relaxed, almost cheerful way. "I don't give a shit, dude. You found me. That's cool. I just want the recordings. They're my ticket, you know. They'll change everything."

"Just what will they change, Billy?" I asked

He took another hit from the joint. "Everything, dude. Everything, you know?" He wrinkled his face in an expression of disgust. "Jesus, the lezzie smells awful. Let's go into the living room where we can be more comfortable and there's a little more air circulation."

He spoke it like a host trying to shift a party out of the kitchen into a space prepared for his guests. Gesticulating with the gun, he stepped aside, ushering us out of the bathroom.

"Excuse the mess," he said as we walked ahead of him into the cabin's living area.

Newspapers were strewn over the floor, along with pizza boxes, beer cans, empty potato chip bags, other trash and garbage. But the biggest mess was Elsworth Buell. His huge body half lay, half sat against the far wall. Billy had blasted him in the chest with both charges from the shotgun. Drying blood pooled around him. His eyes were open, blood caked at his nostrils and the corners of his mouth. He held a twenty-two pistol in his death grip.

"Dude was convinced I got the recordings, came to my place and demanded them, said he'd kill me if I didn't give them to him. I said, sure dude, I got them and I'll give them to you. Brought him out here, him holding that little diddlywhacker twenty-two at me all the way. Fat fuck didn't know shit about how to deal with a hostage, you know. We get out here and I say I got the recordings in a drawer. I got this lying on top of a cabinet," he indicated the shotgun with a tilting of his head. "I pick it up, pull both triggers and the gun goes boom, boom. I had to shoot him, you know. Just like I had to kill Cornell and his wife. I got to have those recordings, dude. I got to."

It was one of the few times in my adult life when I was shocked by another person's actions. "You killed the Cornells?" I heard the disbelief in my voice.

He smiled the super pleased Billy Melnick smile. "Cool, hunh, dude? Who'd've thought it was me?"

"You surprise me, Billy."

"Now you surprise me, dude." The smile was gone, in its place a predatory, glowering menace. Eyes red from the smoke, lids at half-mast, he was stoned, his judgment clouded and unpredictable, as dangerous as a person can get. The shotgun never wavered from us. "Give me the recordings. Everything's different, Eddie. I've got to have those recordings."

"Different isn't the word for what you've done, Billy. Murder, kidnapping."

"Shit, that's nothing, dude. What's different is that the Buke is *bona fide* big time, you know. Blackbird Press doesn't carry his work anymore."

"Sparrow, Black Sparrow Press," I corrected him.

"Sparrow, then. It doesn't mean shit, Bird, Sparrow. Buke's broken through. One of the majors is carrying his stuff now. HarperCollins. I looked at Big Bird Press's web site and they said you got to go to HarperCollins for all work by Charles Bukowski."

"You told me that before, Billy, about the press change." He toked and waved his hands. "Right, Dude. I forgot. But it's huge, man. That's like going from some backwater team in South Humpback to playing for the Yankees. So I got to have those recordings, Eddie."

"I don't have them."

"The hell you don't. You're keeping them for yourself." His voice was harsh, rasping deep in his throat.

"Your note said to mail them. I mailed them."

"No shit, dude?"

"No shit."

"Cool." He smiled again.

"Now what?" I said, knowing full well he knew he had to kill us, hoping to keep him engaged in conversation as long as possible.

He looked sad, sounded sad. I believe he thought he was sad. "I got to do you, dude. I hate this shit, you know. You've been my man for a long time,

Eddie. Not like the Buke, you know, but my local man. It's not right that I got to do this, but I've got to, you know."

I moved in front of Dawn. "I don't know, Billy. I don't understand. You don't understand. You kill me and who'll be left read to your poetry the way I do and to get it the way I do?"

He scowled, confusion flitting across his face. It cleared and he smiled. "They all will, dude. The people at HarperCollins will get it. I'll give them a copy of the recordings along with my manuscripts and they'll understand that I'm the Buke now." He laughed. "The Buke is dead, long live the Buke."

"It's not a title, Billy. The Buke was a man, just a man. Charles Bukowski. He wrote some pretty good poems and some pretty bad poems, just like every other poet."

"I told you he was crazy," Dawn said from behind me.

Billy edged around me, swinging the gun toward her. "Crazy is calling me crazy, bitch. I don't give a shit about offing you. Eddie's the one I'm conflicted over."

I heard the shot at the same time I saw Billy's arm jerk upward, his gun fly into the air, soar across the room and clatter against the stone face of the fireplace. His shoulder shattered and blew apart. Blood, bone and skin sprayed all over. His eyes were wide, wild, his mouth open in a scream that came out as little more than a rush of air before he fell forward and landed at my feet, groaning. I looked up and saw Shelley standing outside, looking in through a shattered window, holding the nine millimeter I had given Tiger. It was still pointing into the room.

The front door crashed open and Tiger rushed to Dawn and took her in her arms.

"I smell terrible, hon," Dawn said.

"Like I give a shit." Tiger held her, stroked her matted hair, kissed her cheeks, tears running down her own.

Billy lay on the floor, still groaning, his breathing heavy, labored. I looked around, saw a blanket on the couch and tossed it over him. He was going into shock. I didn't want to let him die. We were going to have enough trouble explaining how he'd been shot from behind. He looked up at me as the blanket settled around him.

"Thanks, dude." Too weak to talk, he mouthed the words. He face twisted in pain, tears streaming down his cheeks, it was with great effort that he crooked a finger at me, beckoning me to bend down. "Sorry dude." He whispered the words. "I'm a stupid asshole."

"Yeah," I said, gently running my fingers over his head. His green beret lay on the floor several feet away. "You are that."

His attempt at a smile turned into a grimace.

Shelley came through the door, shut it behind her and leaned against the wall, smiling at me and with film noir sensuousness, blew across the nine's muzzle.

"I traded guns with Tiger," she said.

"Faye Dunaway in Bonnie and Clyde," I said. "I don't think she did this," she said.

"She should have. It's sexy. Bonnie was sexy."

"For all the good it did her with Clyde."

"Thanks," I said. "He was close to killing us both. He killed your brother and his wife."

She kicked away from the wall, tossed the gun on the couch, stepped over Billy and put her arms around my neck. She was shaking, her breath shallow, her skin clammy. "Then I ran true to form and did the Corelli family thing, blood for blood. I should have killed him."

"You did just fine." I rubbed her shoulders and arms.

Tiger led Dawn to the couch, sat her down and began searching through closets. She found a shirt and a pair of pants.

"Time for a shower, babe," she said, laying them on a chair. She pulled Dawn from the couch and led her into the bathroom. "You can't ride back to town with us smelling like you do."

While Dawn stood under the hot water, Tiger called Chad to let him know. I heard his yelp of joy and relief from across the room.

§§§

I had called Wysocki on my cell phone while Tiger was ministering to Dawn, told him to send an ambulance and filled him in. We waited a while, given the storm. The ambulance came first. The EMTs bandaged Billy's wounds, set up an IV and gave him a shot for pain before taking him to County Medical Center. As they were wheeling him toward the door, he held up his hand.

"Give me a second, dudes, to talk to my main man, Eddie." His voice was still below a whisper.

They stopped and he looked at me, his eyes already dull from the pain medication.

"You don't understand, Eddie. I had to do it all."

"Don't try to explain. You were right the first time."

"Stupid asshole, eh?" I nodded.

"There's more, Eddie. You got to understand, there's more." I shook my head. "I don't, Billy. I try, and I have some ideas, but deep down, I don't understand. Ideas are one thing, understanding your twists and turns is another."

With his good arm he pointed to a coffee table. His notebook sat on it. "Read the last thing," he said. "It explains it all." I opened it, paging through until I found his final entry. The poem was printed in neat block letters.

Loaves and Fishes
I bought the old guy a drink.
I met him walking down the street
fishing pole over his shoulder
worms
in a plastic bag
stuffed
into his right side pocket,
licking his nicotine
stained mustache
and looking
thirsty. I took
him into a bar.

It was 8:10 am.
The bar was full,
Dwight Yokum's "I Sang
Dixie As He Died," coming
from the juke box.
I raised my eyebrows.
"Scotch," he said.
"Any kind."
The bartender heard,
put a shot glass before him,
filled it. He looked
at me. "You?"
I shook my head.
My eyes
went over the room.
These were serious
drinkers, quiet,
busy with their glasses.

"Losers," the bartender
said, sipping a beer.

"Can't get the bucks together for any more than a few drinks. Most've em'll spend the rest of the morning scrounging for deposit bottles, then turn up at a redemption center to get a few bucks for their afternoon swigs." He took another sip. "Hey, it pays my mortgage and I got a BMW. Not bad for selling booze to a bunch of losers. Whatayou do?"

"What I can," I said. "Buy a round for them all on me." I dropped three twenties on the bar. The old fisherman raised his glass to me and I walked out feeling like Jesus.

"Bukelike?" He asked.
"Pure Melnick," I said, waves of sadness rushing over me. "See," he said. "It's the old fisherman. You get it?"

"I get it, Billy, but it doesn't account for what you did." He moved his mouth, as though about to reply, then stopped and turned away from me, staring at the wall. "No, dude. I guess it doesn't. Not to anybody else. It does to me." He laughed. The effort made him choke and wince in pain. He looked back at me, forcing a smile as he did a bad Brando imitation. "I could have been a contender, Eddie. I could have been a contender."

"Yeah," I said. "Sure, Billy."

He looked away, his face taut with pain and slowly turning back to me, he raised his eyes to mine. "Dude, keep my seat for me. At the Townie. It's my seat."

I didn't answer. I patted the top of his head and watched as the EMTs took him from the cabin. The western Massachusetts hills are filled with artists, poets, painters, musicians, novelists, storytellers, photographers and filmmakers. With direction and luck many of them could be contenders. Billy included.

The local Yardley police, the Staties and an attendant from the funeral home went to work. The cops set up lights, yellow crime scene tape, took pictures, statements and examined my gun permit. When they were finished, the assistant Corky had sent tagged and bagged Elsworth Buell.

I gave a statement, telling them I'd been the one to shoot through the window to save Dawn, emphasizing that Billy was about to kill her and I didn't have any other choice. Tiger and Shelley were by-standers, I said. It was what the cops wanted to hear and they didn't question it. I was the only one licensed to carry, and I had a permitted gun. Shelley, Tiger and Dawn backed the story. I filled them in on Billy, who he was and what he'd done, and that was the end of it for then. Billy might contradict my version later, but it would be his word against the three of us.

"You can go," Wysocki said after we had told him all we knew. "You got to know there's going to be a formal investigation into all this, including how Billy got shot and an inquest into Buell's death."

We left the cabin and started out the driveway to the car. Wysocki followed us out mumbling,

"You should have contacted me, instead of going after Dawn by yourselves. Goddamn civilians got no business trying something like this."

I tried to give him a hangdog look. "Sorry. It just sort of happened. We weren't thinking."

"Yeah right, you're sorry," he growled.

"What'll happen to Billy?" Dawn asked.

Wysocki rolled his eyes. "My guess, he'll pull some Gulf War vet post-traumatic stress bullshit and convince everybody that he's nuts. Hell he is nuts. If they don't send him to the state hospital over to Bridgewater with the rest of the criminal loonies, he'll probably end up doing a few years in a local jail, to spare him further trauma at Cedar Junction, do a few more years in a half-way house and, bingo, you'll see him back in Graham with a haircut and a shave and a social worker hovering over him. We don't handle these things very well."

He sighed, shaking his head. "Fifteen years ago I had a case, woman killed her husband. They'd been married over thirty years and he beat the shit out of her every Saturday night. Told her Saturday was Judgment Day and he was beating her just in case she did something or thought about doing something.

Finally she cut his throat while he was asleep. She's still in jail. Now what kind of justice is that?"

Dawn nodded. "Billy is crazy, you know."

"Crazy, but I don't give a shit," Tiger said. "He almost killed you."

"But he didn't."

"He would have," Wysocki said, looking at Dawn. "He killed the Cornells and Buell, and Eddie here says he was about to kill you."

We let the subject drop. After a brief awkward silence Wysocki shook our hands, coming to Dawn last. He held hers, looking into those incredible eyes, the ones that make men silly.

Indicating Tiger with a jerk of his head, he said, "Marry the broad and make her take you up to Vermont."

Dawn wrinkled her brow. "Vermont?"

"Newfane Inn, remember?" Wysocki said. "For a honeymoon. For the wedding I got a friend that's a justice of the peace who'll do the job for nothing if I ask him to." He looked at Tiger. "I know a good Catholic girl will probably want to get married in a church, but the way things are going these days, I'm not sure I'd want a priest involved with my personal life."

None of us mentioned that a Catholic priest would rather have sex with a sheep than marry two lesbians. Wysocki was a good guy, but he sure as hell wasn't a theologian.

§§§

Back at Shelley's apartment Dawn took another shower, borrowed some clothing and Tiger loaded her into her car and they headed home. Just before they drove off she rolled down the window.

"Thanks, Eddie."

I waved the appreciation off. "Thank Shelley, not me. I'm just the highly trained professional who nearly got us both killed. If Shelley hadn't bagged Billy from the window when she did..." I didn't finish the thought.

"You figured it out, Eddie, that Billy had Dawn and where they were. So, thanks for that." She wasn't going to let me off the hook of gratitude, so I reached through the open window and squeezed her shoulder. She patted my hand and threw me a kiss.

"You too, Shelley," she said. "We owe you."

Dawn put her arm around Tiger's shoulder and leaned over toward the window. "Big time."

"You can throw me an engagement shower," Shelley said. I felt the cold rush over me again.

Tiger grinned. "No shit? You pop the question, Sanders?"

"No."

"He didn't have to," Shelley said. "I've got enough on him to blackmail him into marriage."

"You wouldn't, though," I said.

"I wouldn't. But I can still have an engagement party. It'll be a good excuse for me to blow it out with a group of women and not have to hassle with men."

"You're on." Tiger laughed, shifted into gear and pulled away from the curb, Dawn snuggled up to her like a high school date.

"Just as long as there's no ceremony afterwards," I said. Tiger and Dawn booed me. Shelley laughed.

Once in her apartment, I made another pot of coffee and called Brent Bouchard at *The Graham Enterprise*. He was delighted with his exclusive. Then we turned the heat high and took off our cold wet clothes and shoes. She tossed our shirts and pants in the dryer. Walking naked across the room, she flopped in a chair, legs out straight, hands behind her head.

"You look great," I told her.

"Nice tits, right?"

"Beautiful tits."

"Want to fool around with them, and the rest of me?" I shook my head. "Rain check?"

"I was hoping you'd say something like that. I just thought you might need it."

"Charity sex?"

"Sure. That a problem?"

"No. Like most guys, I'd normally accept it, maybe feel a little guilty afterwards, but deal with the guilt pretty easily. Tonight, I'm just too wiped for anything."

She made a laughing sound. "Men are so predictable."

"Spell predictable." She did, just as I would have predicted.

Our repartee was played in a minor key. Both of us were weary and emotionally flat, saying the words to create a sense of normality we did not and could not feel.

"You okay?" I asked

"No. I will be. I never killed anyone. It'll take me a while to work it through."

"I know some good therapists. The Valley's crawling with therapists." She shook her head. "I don't need therapy. Don't believe in it actually."

"You and Flannery O'Connor," I said.

She looked surprised. "You really are well read for a janitor."

"Maintainer II."

"Ooops. I forgot." She was silent for a long time. I lay down on the couch and closed my eyes. Sleep was rushing toward me like a charging bull when she said, "Flannery O'Connor had something I don't have. Won't ever have."

"Lupus?"

She threw a pillow at me. "Faith. It was weird and grotesque, but it was faith that kept her going. She said one of her characters would have been a good woman if there had been someone there to shoot her every minute of her life. I guess with the lupus she thought God was there to shoot her every minute."

"You listen to Osama bin Laden, Pat Robertson or Franklin Graham, read *The Book of Mormon* or the *Old Testament* and you'll think God does some pretty weird and grotesque things, demands them too." I heard my voice, as from a great distance, weariness overwhelming me.

She replied in a small voice, "Billy had faith, of a kind."

I was having trouble keeping my eyes open. "Look what it got him. Look at what it did to Evans and Ariel. To Elsworth Buell. Almost to Dawn. Faith can be a dangerous thing."

"Faith didn't get Billy shot. I did that."

"Don't go there," I said, hating the cliché as I said it. "You saved Dawn and you saved me. Besides, if Billy hadn't been a raving fanatic about what he believed those recordings could do for him, none of it would have happened and he'd be falling off a stool at the Townie about now."

"What about the recordings?" she asked. "What'll happen to them?" I chuckled. "It's ironic. Billy will be locked up, unable to get them and they'll end up in a dead letter file somewhere. Connections has probably already forwarded them to another post office box. If Billy was as careful as I think he was that post office has another forwarding address. There may be more. It doesn't matter. There won't be anybody to pick them up at the final drop. They'll end up sitting in a dead letter file, and nobody will ever hear them. A man named Gideon Moss will have wet dreams about them, convinced they would have been his guarantee of a tenure track position, and nobody will ever know if the poems on the recordings were any good, if they did represent shifts in Bukowski's ideas. Someday those recordings everybody was so exercised about, that people died for, will sit in a dead letter file until CDs are just another dead a technology that nobody cares about."

"What about Billy? He could have someone pick them up."

"He won't. He'd have to find someone he trusts enough to let them know where the recordings are and how to get them. He won't be able to do that. He may not even be able to remember their final address."

"What about when he gets out?"

"If he gets out. Wysocki's more cynical than I am. There's a good chance Billy's never going to see the outside of a wall. Who knows, the isolation and blues of prison life might give him inspiration to write. Maybe he'll put out a pretty good book of jailbird poetry."

"But there's a chance he will get out someday."

I nodded. "And if he does, he may go after the recordings, if he remembers where he had them forwarded and how he was going to identify himself there. Chances are once the box rental expires they'll be gone, sent on to that dead letter file where they'll sit until someone cleans it out and throws them away.

"That's beautiful," she said. "Bukowski wrote some poems about working in a post office for a while, sorting letters."

"I know," I said. "He hated it." I shut my eyes again, too tired to move from the couch. "I've got to sleep."

She got up, threw a light blanket over me and crossed to her bedroom.

§§§

The phone rang in the middle of the night. I woke up, heard Shelley answer, heard her talking in a quiet voice into the receiver and fell asleep again before she was finished. When I awoke again it was daylight, sun streaking through the window, the sounds of melting snow dripping from the eaves. The room was rich with the odor of coffee. Shelley was rattling pots and pans in the kitchen. I got up, wrapped the blanket around me and stood in the kitchen doorway, leaning on the casement.

She was wearing a soft aqua silk dressing gown that clung to her body like something from a comic book artist's dream. Slicing onions, she dropped them into a frying pan sizzling with olive oil.

"Who called last night?" I asked

She put the knife down and swept the unused portion of the onion into her hands and dropped them into the garbage disposal.

"Angela. Yesterday, some of Daddy's people came up to…," she paused, searching for words, "…to finish business with Henrietta. They went to her place and she was gone, her papers were gone, her clothes were gone. Everything gone without a trace."

"She's another professional." I smiled. It was what the agency had wanted. The Corellis, or whoever ran the Corelli businesses now, would remain in charge until they no longer were.

"Daddy's people came looking for you, to see if you could tell them anything, and found Randolph on the stairs at Barton Rooms. They cleaned things up there."

"Nobody stopped them?" I walked past her, letting my cupped hand brush over her butt, and poured myself a cup of coffee.

"I don't think anybody saw them, or at least nobody wanted to see them. Besides, it was snowing and people weren't around. Angie said they left him, his gun and his car out in the boonies, the Ashmont Plains, from the way she described it."

The coffee was strong and hot. I blew on the surface as I sipped. "This is good. The cops'll find him. There won't be any connection to me, to any of us. My guess is that they'll do ballistics on Randolph's gun and find it's the same one Elmore Walker was shot with. If the cops are lucky, they'll find a rifle in his car that'll match up with the slugs taken from the hit on your father at the funeral home."

"What about the o.d. you told me about in Eagle Falls?" Shelley asked. "What do you think happened to him?"

"Tommy Finneran?" I shrugged. "Don't know. Maybe Elmore killed him, or he had one of his brothers kill him to deflect attention. It doesn't much matter."

"They killed the poor guy and it doesn't matter?" There was a trace of indignation in her tone. She made a lousy Corelli.

"He's dead. There's no way of proving it was anything but accidental. Maybe it was, who knows? Some people live below the radar. The cops aren't going to investigate Finneran's death. Just like nobody's going to miss Billy Melnick after a week or so. If he'd've been hit by a truck out on I-91 there would've been a couple of days of people saying what a shame it was and poor Billy, we're going to miss him. Then somebody else would sit on that stool at the Townie and next thing you know, nobody's talking about Billy Melnick anymore."

"But he didn't get hit by a truck on 91. He kidnapped Dawn and got shot and he'll end up somewhere, jail, a state hospital."

"So they'll talk about him a little longer than they would have otherwise. Somebody will sit on that stool a little later. But Billy will drop away to the point that someone's going to bring his name up and somebody else will say, oh yeah, Billy Melnick, wasn't he the guy that kidnapped somebody, some woman?"

"Right, until the state turns him loose on the theory that he's cured."

"If they turn him loose."

"They will." She sounded sure.

I was less confident about Billy's future than I had been the night before. There were too many variables. "Something could happen to him in prison, if that's where he goes."

She looked off into space, considering possibilities. "Something could. The family has long arms."

"If they're not too busy defending their turf from the competition. Angelo's death leaves a pretty big hole."

She was quiet for a moment. "And you don't think it matters that the Walkers killed Tommy Finneran and nobody's going to hold them accountable for it?"

"There's no way to prove it. Besides, guys like the Walkers are among the living dead. It doesn't matter if they're breathing and eating at burger joints or not. Places like Albie's are filled with them. Their lives come to less than nothing and they die of cirrhosis, an overdose, AIDS, somebody shoots them, stabs them, they get busted for something else and rot in jail. Elmore won't get it for killing Tommy Finneran, but he'll get it. In the meantime, his life sucks and he knows it sucks, and you know what else, he doesn't give a good rat's ass that his life sucks. He just goes along being miserable and bringing misery to others. There's no joy in Elmore's life. Never has been, never will be."

She thought about that for several long moments. The onions were caramelizing, their smell wonderful in the room. At last she snorted something between a smile and a laugh and spoke in a campy narrative voice.

"And so we say farewell to Angelo Corelli, Tommy Finneran, Randolph Baines, Billy Melnick and the Walker brothers, three of them dead, the others among the living dead. Only the fate of Henrietta Lane remains unknown."

"Henrietta's gone," I said. "She'll turn up somewhere else, as someone else. She'll have money. She'll set herself up in another town, with new ex-Soviet sleepers and begin again. The Russian mob will move in a different direction, leaving the New Haven to Burlington corridor to the Corellis and their successors, at least for the time being. They don't give a rat's ass, as long as they're on the move, growing, making money, wiping out the competition somewhere else."

She didn't say anything as she grated cheese, diced tomatoes and peppers, dropping the peppers in the frying pan with the brown, sweet smelling onions. We had omelets and coffee and hash brown potatoes from a box, along with fresh squeezed orange juice. We ate and listened to the news on the local radio station. The reporter, who usually has nothing bigger than a selectmen's meeting to cover, kept an excited tone each time he re-read his story on Dawn's kidnapping and Billy Melnick's guilt every half hour. But there was nothing new. The radio report was just a rehash of Brent Bouchard's front-page story in *The Graham Enterprise*.

When we finished eating, I did the dishes and drank two more cups of coffee. The radio reporter was into his third reading of the story. Shelley turned it off, opened her silk dressing gown and pulled the blanket from me.

"And where are we?" She asked.

I put my arm around her, pulling her close, her body warm, smooth against my own. Passion, lust, desire would stir soon enough. I needed this moment of calm, of undemanding intimacy.

"I don't know," I said. "We have a lot of stories to tell one another." She tightened against me, her breath soft against my cheek. "I've always enjoyed storytelling."

Epilogue

Boston, Massachuset – Six Months Later

Stepping from the skyway leading from the Marriott Copley into the shopping mall at the Prudential Center, he almost bumped into a turbaned Sikh wearing an expensive suit and a red power tie. He was talking with a tall blonde man, also wearing a suit, a nearly identical tie and carrying an attaché case. He heard them start laughing as the blonde said, "Ayuh, a good goat will that."

"Excuse me," he said.

"Sure." The Sikh nodded and turned back to the other man. "Did you hear about the rope that went into a bar?"

The Walkway was thick with people rushing about. Most were young and affluent looking. There was no dominant race. As many women as men hurried by, dressed for business and leisure. There was a hum of voices, languages, laughter and animated conversation.

Comfortable in the western hills of the state, he had not been to a city in years, and he was overwhelmed by optimism at the mixture of people and the intensity of activity surrounding him. If anything will save us, he thought, this is it, this dynamic mix of ethnicity and energy, of gender and age. He moved through crowded walks, looked in shop windows and at wares on the carts in the center of the walkways.

He glanced at his watch. Half an hour to kill. He stopped at a cart selling baseball hats, with a computerized sewing machine capable of putting any logo or combination of words on the brim.

"I'll take two," he said. "Put *Maintainer II* on each."

While the hats were being done he grabbed a sandwich at the nearby food court and window shopped for things he didn't need and didn't want.

Twenty-five minutes later, carrying a bag with the hats, he walked down the wide, empty hallway of the Hynes Auditorium, his footsteps echoing against the walls. At the far end of the building he took an escalator to the third floor. There were signs leaning against the walls, advertising candidates for the presidency of the Massachusetts Teachers Association. Twenty or thirty peopled milled about, but most were in a large meeting hall listening to the new black Senator from Massachusetts making a play for the union's endorsement of his Presidential candidacy.

He walked to the far end of the hallway, a bank of windows on his right, small meeting rooms to his left, *Western Mass Caucus* hand lettered on a sign hanging from an easel in front of one. The door was shut. He opened it.

"You're right on time," the Director said. He sat in a motorized wheelchair in the far corner, a blanket over his legs. His voice wavered and cracked. "An appropriate room for our meeting, eh Nathan?"

"You said eleven-forty-five. I'd rather you called me Eddie." The Director shrugged. He looked old. A pink skull showed through the once thick white hair and his hand trembled as he pointed to a chair at the table beside him.

"Whatever you prefer. Names don't matter."

"Mine matters a great deal to me."

"Fine, Eddie." The old man waved his right hand in the air and started to laugh. It turned into a coughing spasm, doubling him over. He took an inhaler from his breast pocket and sprayed into his mouth, took a deep, long breath and held it for thirty seconds.

"You didn't take good care of Randolph," he said on the exhale. "I understand they found his body in his car out in the country." The Director nodded. "It appears as if the mob took him out for the Corelli hit. They found the gun with him."

"I heard that."

"He was pretty low on our list of players. Men like Randolph are a dime a dozen. Still, he was useful for a while."

"You didn't ask me here to talk about Randolph." The old man nodded. "We shan't meet again," he said. "The last few years haven't been kind to you."

The Director shrugged. "Time isn't kind or unkind. You were never much of a realist."

"Why are we meeting now?"

The Director looked down at his hands. They were pale, covered with liver spots and wrinkled, his fingers bony, nails thick and yellow but well trimmed. He took another deep breath, coughed again, and looked back up. His eyes were faded and rheumy. Pulling the blanket down, he pointed at an ancient leather briefcase resting on his lap. It was scratched and torn, the brass plating on the latch worn and rusted.

"Take it," he said. "What is it?"

"Nathan Hunt's official file. You can be sure it's the only one. It was my personal file on you. The agency keeps no official files. Deniability, you know." He coughed again, his eyes watering, his frail body shaking and pointed at the case. "Take it."

He reached for it, surprised by its weight. "Why?"

The Director spread his hands, indicating his body. "Look at me. What do you see?"

"An old man in a wheelchair." Nathan thought the words sounded flat in his ears, brutal and frank in their dispassionate descriptiveness.

The Director smiled. "A very old man in a wheelchair. That's what I am now. It's all that I am. The game's over for me, Eddie."

"I don't believe that."

"Thank you. You're finally being nice to me, polite, maybe even thoughtful, but it is over for me, Eddie, even if I weren't in this damned contraption." He sighed and ran his hands over the thin hair. "Things have changed."

"They always do."

"True, but this change is different. Dangerous. People don't understand the kind of work the agency does, why it must exist."

"They never did understand. And precious few even know the agency exists."

The Director leaned forward, his whole being tense, his face angry. "It's far more than that. The people at the top, the ones who make the decisions, they think without analysis. They analyze without thinking."

"Sounds like horseshit to me."

"Perhaps I'm not being clear. Sometimes it's hard for an old man like me to be clear. There is so much in my mind, so much history, so many facts, so many concepts, so many successes and so many failures that it becomes difficult to sort through them for the truth."

"Your truth was always expediency."

He sat up straight, his response sharp, his voice almost normal. "My truth was simple. We do whatever is necessary to preserve liberty. Only with liberty can we live our individual lives with moral dignity."

"Or total depravity."

"True." He smiled sadly. "That's why we have schools, why we try to educate our young, to provide the foundations for moral dignity and enlightened citizenship."

"A lot of good it does. How many murders, rapes and robberies were there in Boston last year?"

The old man made a shushing sound, waving a trembling hand. "Hush up, Eddie. If you will, I will. You're right. It's all horseshit. All that fine talk I gave you years ago in Baku, about the conservative military and intelligence communities making the liberal state possible. It's either total horseshit or totally irrelevant today."

"And that's because these people who matter, who make the decisions, think without analyzing and analyze without thinking, whatever that means. Is that it?"

"That is it exactly. They think in absolutes. In terms of good and evil." He coughed. Small flecks of blood lined his lower lip. He wiped them away with a tissue. "No, that's wrong. They don't think in terms of good and evil, Eddie, they think in terms of God and the Devil. Those are the people making decisions today. They'll forsake liberty to impose their visions of good, their conception of

God on us, and in doing that they're no better than any other fundamentalist absolutist. Forget what I said all those years ago about a clash of civilizations. I'm afraid we're looking at an uncivilized clash of literal minded religious fanatics. It's all over, Eddie, everything I've worked for, everything I had you work for."

"You don't really believe that."

The Director gave him a broad shrug, tilting his head from side to side. "I would hate to."

"So, you hold out some hope."

With another shrug and blood-flecked cough, the Director looked down at the blanket resting on his feet and stretching halfway up his calf. His fingers found the satiny edge and played with it for a moment before he looked back up. "If I had a successor, someone I trusted to fill my shoes."

"Shoes covered in horseshit?" The Director laughed, coughing again. "Guilty."

"And what does all this melodrama have to do with my file?"

"Everything." He pulled the blanket back over his knees. "Well, a great deal. We're shutting down. There's no more funding. The powers-that-be don't want analysis, and they don't want our kind of action. They're on a moral crusade and intellect and analysis is their enemy. I'm cleaning out my files before they realize that files exist."

He reached over and patted the briefcase. "Nathan Hunt is in there, Eddie. Burn, shred or flush and Nathan no longer exists."

"He's already gone."

"Perhaps. There are dinosaur footprints embedded in rocks in western Massachusetts, are there not?"

"I've seen them."

He smiled. "This briefcase is the rocks. Nathan's footprints are what makes it so heavy." He turned the wheelchair toward the door and inched away. "With it gone, you never worked for the agency. Soon there will be no agency. There will be no record of the agency. Indeed, soon the agency will have never existed."

"My salary?"

"Always right to the point, Eddie. That's what made you so valuable." He spun the wheelchair back around. "There is no salary, Eddie. According to government records, there never was. How could there be when you never worked for an agency that never existed?"

"Great. So that's it? Goodbye? Farewell? So long, sucker?" He tossed the briefcase toward the old man in the wheelchair who pulled a lever and backed it away. The case landed on the floor.

The wheelchair stopped and the Director turned, looking at him. "You were a good boy, Eddie. You did good work. There was a sizable final deposit made to your account in Tortola this morning."

"Sizable?"

"You'll never have to clean a hallway, wash a blackboard or scour a toilet again."

"But I will. I have to."

The Director looked at him with surprise. "Why would you do that? Penance? You have nothing to atone for."

"You wouldn't understand." He picked up the briefcase and walked toward the door. The old man followed him into the hallway. A young woman with a blouse covered with campaign buttons approached them, holding a button advertising *Cathy for MTA President* out to them.

"No thanks," he said, brushing past her.

The old man took one. "I collect all kinds of campaign buttons. Thank you," he said to her. "Are you sure your candidate's the best one for the job?"

"The best," she said, walking toward a group of people without buttons. "I do understand, Eddie. More than you will ever know." They moved together toward the escalator. When they reached it, the Director pointed toward the corner of the hall. "There's an elevator over there. Take it with me, Eddie."

They got in the elevator. The door shut. They rode past the second floor in silence before the old man spoke.

"You did fine work, Eddie. I respect the way you walked away from it and the life you set up for yourself. I understand why you do what you do. I wished more for you, but I understand."

The elevator stopped at the first floor. They emerged into the hallway and began moving toward the doorway out into the Prudential walkway.

Eddie stopped and turned toward the old man, softening his tone. "More is possible. I have some clarity, finally. I'm building on that. More is definitely possible."

They resumed moving toward the door.

"I hope the life you're building will have more meaning than my life has had."

"You believed in what you did, in what the agency stood for."

"I still do. It just doesn't matter. We're on the verge of a new dark age, Eddie. Better stock up on candles and learn to illustrate manuscripts." His voice was low, cracking again, his shoulders hunched.

"We may be on the verge of one, but that doesn't mean we're going to cross over into it."

"Has what you've seen, what you've done over the past weeks changed the way you see things, Nathan?"

Without reacting to the name, he met the old man's eyes. They were still strong, belying his seeming illness, still able to penetrate his pose. The feeling rattled him. Dropping his gaze he studied his hands. Bending his fingers, he picked at the nails of his right hand with his thumbnail, loosening the grime under them. It fell at his feet. "I wasn't prepared for the common evil I found."

"Evil is a terribly judgmental word for a philosopher like you. You found things out of balance."

Nathan shrugged. "I found that there's no away and I found things worth struggling for, and I found things that have given me hope."

"I have always believed that," the Director said.

"And the new dark age you say we're on the verge of?"

"There are infinite possibilities and dangerous forces are abroad in the land."

"I believe that," Nathan Hunt said.

Gripping the briefcase he nodded goodbye and walked into the mall, crowded with human life, varied, beautiful and filled with promise, and he disappeared into the rush of people. He did not see the Director rise from the wheelchair, stretch and smile after him as he removed a small plastic tube leaking red dye from under his lip. A man in a Patriots jersey wearing a Red Sox hat came over to him.

"Well," he said. "Did he buy it? Does he believe the agency is shutting down?"

The Director sighed in relief. "He seemed thoughtful."

"And that's good?"

"That's very good. It will take him some time to fully understand how we have had to slip further into shadows in order for the agency to survive." He smiled, pushing his wheelchair back toward the elevator. "Ultimately it will be in very good hands."